THE FALL OF VIVALDI

A SUSPENSE NOVEL BY

Reed Bunzel

coffeetownpress

Kenmore, WA

coffeetownpress

A Coffee Town Press book published by Epicenter Press

Epicenter Press
6524 NE 181st St.
Suite 2
Kenmore, WA 98028

For more information go to:
www.Camelpress.com
www.Coffeetownpress.com
www.Epicenterpress.com
Author's website: www.reedbunzel.com

The Fall of Vivaldi
2024 © Reed Bunzel

ISBN: 9781684921836 (trade paper)
ISBN: 9781684921843 (ebook)

LOC: 2023951890

This one is for Tom Hamil, who instilled in me the love of writing when I was still too young to know better.

Part I

Allegro

Chapter 1

Nighttime in the City of Light, the soft glow of a streetlamp five floors below shimmered through glistening raindrops that trickled down the windowpane.

The floor-to-ceiling draperies were pulled open as far as they could go, dancing on a gentle breeze that seeped through a crack in the ancient wood frame. The scent of jasmine or gardenias, or something aromatic and flowery, tangled with the aroma of sweat and champagne and leftover sex. A Baroque concerto drifted through the ancient plaster walls from the attic flat next door, the muffled refrain of a string quartet yielding the gentle trill of a meadow full of songbirds. Quick ritornello signatures that Gabrielle Lamoines recognized as Vivaldi's Concerto No. 1 in E major, Op. 8.

Spring.

It was her favorite season, both in life and in the concert hall. Her father had played the cello, although not as well as he liked to think, and her mother had dabbled from time to time with the tenor flute. As proper parents they had introduced their only child to classical music at an early age with the obligatory piano lessons, which she had abandoned around the time puberty arrived and introduced her to the erratic nature of hormones. Now that she was in her mid-thirties, however, she had circled back to music, and made a habit of visiting Le Bataclan whenever her busy scheduled permitted—or, more preferably, le Philharmonie de Paris, if she found herself in the mood for a particularly inventive interpretation of the masters.

Now her father was dead—an inexplicable and spectacular fall a decade ago from the first level of the Eiffel Tower—and her mother had been spiraling around the drain of booze and benzos ever since. They had been the ideal French couple: well-heeled financier of European construction projects married to a senior curator at the Pompidou Centre, with a lovely daughter who was just two years out of *université* and already making a name for herself in television news. Gabrielle's life had crumpled in an instant when she'd received the news of her father's accident, and she'd had to pick up the pieces as best she could.

The words of the French poet Anatol Franc seemed to help her through her darkest hours: "If we don't change, we don't grow. If we don't grow, we aren't really living."

She lay naked on the bed and listened to the muted violins, the Egyptian cotton sheets having been scattered to the saxony carpet in a lustful frenzy. She watched as her lover pulled on his trousers and shirt, then his socks, shaking them out before tackling the left foot, then the right. Once again, she studied his strong chin and dark eyes, thick black hair she'd thought might be fake, until she had gripped it as she was nearing climax. His name was Archie Hunter—at least that's what he had told her—and she had known him for all of three hours. That was more than enough time for their cleverly nuanced repartee to engage each other's prurience, share a glass of the bar's best sparkling wine, and subtly agree to mutually acceptable terms.

They then had dodged the raindrops as they hurried back here to her place, a small one-bedroom apartment in St. Germain, just a block off Rue Bonaparte. Weathered limestone set close to the cobbled sidewalk, with decorative iron grates over the ground-floor windows. A blue plaque with white lettering next to the door announced its historical significance for housing resistance fighters during the Nazi occupation in Vichy Paris.

For the briefest of moments Gabrielle wondered what time it was. She couldn't see the digital clock on her dresser, couldn't reach her cellphone on her nightstand. But she had a good internal timer that told her she still had an hour before she needed to think about getting dressed. Her line of work didn't allow for extended personal dalliances, and she had a half dozen calls to return before she finished packing for her early flight to Rome at the crack of dawn. Plus, there was the pending visit from a man who had reached out to her just that morning, insisting they meet at her earliest possible convenience—something to do with the untimely death of her late father, news that he'd promised she would find of critical importance. Secrecy and intrigue were part of the life of an investigative reporter, so she had agreed to meet him here at her flat at ten.

Just as important was the scheduled hand-off of a highly valuable object at midnight, across the Seine at the Jardin du Carrousel. Despite her continued assurances that she would be there, the young man she was meeting was nervous and jittery about the matter.

All of which left her more than enough time to say a fond farewell to the man she was quite certain was not really named Archie Hunter. But then, hers was not really Avril Moreau. Like all valuable commodities, truth is often counterfeited.

He took his time fastening his buttons, then slipped on a pair of shoes that clearly were less upscale than they first appeared. When he finished, he rose to his feet and walked over to the demilune burlwood writing desk to the right of the window. Its surface was bare except for a table lamp they had not bothered to turn on when they'd pushed their way into the room earlier. On a chair in front of it was a leather satchel, which he had set down as they'd tumbled to the bed, lots of groping and kissing and moaning going on in the heat of passion.

He unfastened the clasp and reached inside the case, brought out something that looked—*merde sainte!*—like a semi-automatic pistol with a rubberized grip. It was the sort Gabrielle had seen many times in American gangster flicks, but never with her own eyes.

He glanced over at her with a tight smile, then reached back inside the case and brought out another object—long and cylindrical. He methodically attached the thing to the modified barrel, and she found herself identifying it as a sound suppressor. She marveled at her own lack of panic or alarm as he tightened it, sensing just an odd touch of curiosity as he hefted the assembled weapon in his hand.

He walked over to the bed. His side, after they had finished their lovemaking, and they had laid there in post-coital bliss. He pointed it at her, but all she experienced was a strange perception of spiritual harmony, as if she were chanting *om*, but without the humming sound.

She watched for a moment as if in some sort of dream, then said, "Please put that down—guns are the evil tools of weak minds." They were the only words she could find, in French, the uncertainty of what she was seeing causing her to blink. Her brain was still a little foggy from all the bubbly they'd consumed before falling into bed, and the sex—and maybe something else she had not been aware of until this very moment, when she realized her brain was functioning in a subdued state that was far from efficient, and certainly not normal.

"I promise, my sweet, you won't feel a thing," he said, in the same velvety voice that had seduced her into inviting him back to her flat in the first place.

At that moment the sense of euphoria released its grip on her brain, and she blurted out, "What in God's name do you think you're doing?"

"Simply the fulfillment of a business obligation," he told her in that dreamy tone, almost a whisper—as if he was still making love to her.

"Business?" She tried to shift her position so she could see him better, standing there to her right, but she had momentarily forgotten that her wrists and ankles were still bound to the bedposts. It was her idea, using the silk scarves she'd retrieved from the dresser on a whim—and not a good one, it appeared. "Do you think you're being funny?"

"No, Gabrielle," he said to her, his whisper suddenly turning cold. "There is nothing humorous about this."

"But…a gun?" She nodded at the weapon, the titanium silencer aimed directly above the bridge of her nose. She should have been hysterical at this moment, but it was an emotion she simply couldn't find.

"Arguably the most decisive of all the tools of the trade."

The biting chill in his voice caused her to jerk her head away from the end of the extended barrel. Until now she hadn't even allowed herself to be afraid but, with those words, a wash of fear chilled her blood.

"You can't just tie me up, point a gun at me—"

He cocked his head to get a better look at her, and for a second she caught a touch of sadness in his eyes. Was it remorse for what he was about to do, or perhaps a flicker of conscience? "The tying-up part was your idea, remember?"

"And if you don't untie me right now, I'm going to scream—"

But Archie Hunter—now she was certain that was not his real name, nor was he a fabric wholesaler from London visiting Paris on a buying trip—simply shook his head. The motion was barely noticeable in the thin veil of light glimmering through the rain still trickling down the window. "Actually, you're not," he said with an icy, distant resolve.

It was at that point that Gabrielle realized this man actually intended to shoot her, to take her life, right there and then. Her compromised reflexes—and the damned scarves—prevented her from doing anything more than to wonder: who is this man? Why is he doing this? And after that: who sent him?

"You can't do this—"

His finger gently tightened across the trigger, the pistol steady and familiar in his hand. French gun laws were some of the strictest on the continent, with no constitutional right to bear arms, although that had not helped the victims of the *Charlie Hebdo* magazine shooting. As a result, firing ranges were difficult to find, as were semi-automatic weapons whose serial numbers had been filed off, and whose provenance thus could not be traced.

That's why he had brought this assembly with him, a Ruger SR22 with a ten-plus-one capacity chambered in the common and inexpensive .22 rimfire ammunition, with decent front and rear sights, if he'd needed them. Comfortable and sympathetic, like an old drinking friend.

The gun barely kicked in his hand as the subsonic bullet drove into Gabrielle Lamoines' skull. It burrowed through her forehead at a point directly between and slightly above both eyes, instantly obliterating her entire universe as the contents of her skull were voided onto the down pillow, and the headboard behind it.

"I'm so sorry, *mon cherie*," he lamented as he examined his handiwork, his voice no louder than a puff of wind. A very cold wind, as if sweeping down the steep ravine of a glacier.

He stood there a moment, studying her in the near-darkness, knowing she was dead but needing to make sure. Once he was certain, he retrieved the spent casing from the luxurious carpet but decided to leave the mangled slug where it had driven into the plaster wall. He moved back across the room and slid the gun and silencer into their leather satchel, then snapped a pair of blue nitrile gloves over his hands before retreating into the bathroom in search of towels, soaps, and whatever cleaning solutions the dead woman on the bed might have kept on hand.

Five minutes later he was finished. He opened the front door, finding himself engulfed by the thick odor of noxious cigarettes coming from a tenant who had recently passed by in the hallway. He sensed a sneeze coming on but pressed the back of his gloved hand against his nose to suppress it, not unlike suppressing the roar of exploding gas being forced from the barrel of a gun. Then he silently slipped out of the apartment, confident that he hadn't left a print anywhere, not one telltale hair, not a strand of DNA. There was not one trace of his presence, not even a drop of fluid from the evening's particularly amazing sex.

In that regard, Gabrielle Lamoines had definitely lived up to the details of her dossier, and had more than met his expectations. Such a shame he hadn't met her under alternative circumstances.

Chapter 2

Another perfect sunset on the island of Cyprus painted thin strokes of violet across the horizon, barely defining the darkened edge of the Mediterranean Sea to the west.

Declan Russell sat at the edge of a massive sectional couch, shoes off, toes digging hard into the thick carpet as he worked the five-hour flight from London out of his joints. He began with his feet, then moved to his knees and thighs before working all the way up to his shoulders. Which, at the moment, felt as if the weight of the entire world was resting on them. He crooked his neck right—*crack*—then left—another *crack*—eventually letting his eyes settle on the Breitling Heritage strapped to his wrist. Time was, he owned both a Patek Phillipe and a Vacheron Constantin and wore them on alternate days of the week, but that was before the start of his troubles, the end game of which was why he was here.

Here being a suite he could hardly afford, waiting to meet with a man he had never wanted to see. Specifically, he was in one of the top-level suites that crowned the Phoenician Horizon Hotel and Casino, an integrated resort located just steps from a secluded beach at the edge of the city of Limassol. It was eight hundred square feet of the type of pampered luxury to which he at one time had been accustomed, but which now seemed no more than a fleeting memory. Sixteen floors down were a couple dozen world-class gaming rooms and private salons designed to accommodate the pleasures of high-rollers from Vegas to Macau, and just about everywhere in between.

A decade ago, he easily would have dropped a hundred grand here in one evening, content with the prospect of losing because he enjoyed the social interaction, the energized repartee with the other players seated around the baccarat table. He reveled in the camaraderie of the dealers, the cocktail waitresses, the spectators and hangers-on watching the high-stakes derring-do. His win-loss ratio was abysmal, but long ago he'd come to grips with the fact that he possessed the tenacity and focus to become proficient at anything that had to do with business, but not gambling.

Russell stood up from the sofa and retreated to the well-stocked bar, where he poured yet another measure of Hendrick's into his glass, no ice. He let a taste of it wash over his tongue, savored the familiar hints of rose and cucumber as he again considered why he was here, on this night, in this place. He'd been summoned by a voice on the phone that belonged to a man he had never before met, inviting him to a private dinner downstairs at Samarra, a Michelin-starred restaurant that served incredibly pricey haute cuisine in unbelievably minuscule portions that did absolutely nothing to satisfy one's appetite.

He knew this because he'd checked the menu, once again thinking about the cost of all things. A sure sign of a man on the brink of financial devastation.

The proposal had been initiated a week ago via a late-night call to his home in Kensington that had yanked him out of a dream, one that evaporated as soon as he'd checked the screen on his phone. *Unknown number.* He'd almost ignored it, then remembered his daughter was traveling again and she might be trying to reach him from a borrowed cell or otherwise unfamiliar device. Thus, he'd picked it up and answered with his customary "Yes," a greeting most family and colleagues found offensive and cold, rude to the point of being comical.

"Mr. Russell?" the voice on the other end had said.

"Who is this?"

"Who were you expecting?"

Russell had shifted the phone to his other ear and glanced at the clock: one-twelve in the morning. "No one, not at this hour," he said. "What do you want?"

"To offer you an opportunity for personal redemption."

"What the hell are you talking about? Who the fuck are you?"

"It is said that true redemption is realized only when you accept the future consequences for your past mistakes," the voice had replied.

"What? Who says that?"

"Google it later." The voice waited a beat for dramatic effect, then continued: "The point is, Mr. Russell, your life has fallen into grave disrepair. Your very being has been tossed on the trash heap of financial ruin, and there's no one left in your orbit who gives much of a damn what happens to you. Such is the fleeting nature of a superficial life."

"I'm asking you again, who the fuck are you?"

"Consider me your own version of Jacob Marley," the man on the other end explained—smug and self-satisfied, and damned full of himself.

"Dickens is highly overrated," Declan Russell shot back. The throbbing pain in the back of his head had returned, as it did whenever he'd overdone it with the gin—as he did on most nights. "But I'll bite. Are you here to warn me of the visits of three ghosts, some attempt to get me to atone for past lapses in judgment?"

"Your lapses are none of my concern, and only serve as a reminder of why you have no one of any importance in your life," the voice had said. "No one who cares, no one who gives a rat's ass about you. Except maybe your daughter, but she really only contacts you when she's in need of money."

"You leave my daughter out of this," Russell warned him.

"She's been out of this—out of your life—for years," was the response. "And I'm afraid we're veering off on a tangent, so let me bring you back on point."

"Or I can just hang up."

There was a sigh on the other end, almost as if this response had been predicted. "Go ahead, but if you do, I won't call you back," the voice said. "And then you'll never know what *this* was, and what I can offer you."

A long silence followed, after which Russell found himself saying— almost as if he had no control over his thoughts— "Go on."

There was another dramatic pause that lasted a second or two, then: "You asked me a moment ago what I wanted, why I'm calling. Fact is, I want nothing from you, other than to inform you that an opportunity has come up for you to redeem yourself. Not completely; that would require much more than I am prepared to offer, and considerably more than you deserve. But definitely enough to pluck your life out of the gutter and set it on a steady course again."

"You're insane—"

"You might want to withhold judgment until you hear the details," the voice had replied with an icy chuckle.

Russell had no idea what the fuck the guy was talking about, but his curiosity had been piqued. Redemption? An opportunity to redress his life? Atonement for past sins, of which he knew there were many more than he cared to admit? Lord knew there were enough buried secrets with which he could be blackmailed, if he gave enough of a shit to keep his prior misdeeds out of the news—and if he had enough cheddar to make them all go away.

He liked to think he wasn't rattled easily, but what bothered him was that this guy knew about his daughter; knew the two of them had fallen out over the years, knew they now maintained only the barest of contact, and usually initiated only when she was in need of funds. All of this told him the guy probably knew a lot more about his life than he was letting on—and now that he thought about it, that's what troubled him most of all.

In the end he had acquiesced and accepted the man's offer, which was what brought him here to this luxury suite at the Phoenician Horizon Hotel and Casino tonight. All of it had been gratis, including his first-class airfare from Heathrow.

Sixteen floors down, Rōnin Phythian set his fork on his plate, savoring the last taste of his eggplant risotto. It had come with pickled samphire, coconut wasabi dressing, griddled baby gems, and a drizzle of black olive oil. None of it was food he would have put anywhere near his mouth when he was younger, but he'd spent close to the last eight years of his life watching a daily parade of mammals meander through his African compound, nibbling leaves from the tops of his acacia trees or stalking small game at night. Living that close to God's creatures can induce a person not to want to eat them.

He smiled at the young Cypriot server who approached his table to remove his plate. She was tall and thin, mahogany eyes, just a dusting of rouge on her cheeks. Black hair curled up in a loose bun per order of management—beautiful in any country in the world, but troubled by personal issues nonetheless. Over the past forty minutes he had gleaned just enough from her mind to know she was worried she most likely was pregnant, terrified what her father might do if he learned of her plight. Even more worrisome was whether the father of the baby that could be growing inside her might not return to her after his tour of duty.

"Would you care to see our dessert menu?" she asked him. From the outset they'd worked out that English was the best language for both of them, and she showed a passable adequacy for it.

Under normal circumstances he would have asked for a snifter of Armagnac to be brought to him, but this was not one of those times. "I'm afraid I'm a bit pressed for time," he told her. "Just the bill, please."

"Of course, sir," she said, then glided off to the kitchen.

He checked his watch: eight more minutes to go. The man he was meeting in the Presidential Suite upstairs had checked in earlier that afternoon, still baffled by what he was even doing on this remote Mediterranean island, why he had even agreed to attend this *tête-à-tête* with this cryptic and arcane man he had never met. He hadn't really bought the pitch about finding personal redemption and salvation but, in the end, he'd had no real choice in the matter.

In the two years since Phythian had destroyed the power core of the Greenwich Global Group, he'd arranged nineteen of these meetings. All had been with former G3 clients who, at one time or another, had found the murder-for-hire outfit via word of mouth or on the dark web, and had invested a sizable sum in exchange for the elimination of an adversary. Whether it be a business competitor, political enemy, ideological opponent, or romantic rival, the reasons why a patron placed a contract were never asked, the rationale never questioned. A price was arranged, a time frame set, and a freelancer would be brought in to complete the task.

On one hundred-two such occasions, that freelancer had been Phythian.

Possessing a natural knack for what colloquially was known as "wet work," he'd shown exceptional skill and efficiency in its execution. Over time, new and repeat customers alike had asked for him not by name—that was known only to a select few—but by his reputation and success rate. Never once did he fail in a mission, and his hands never got dirty. Word of his handiwork spread within those circles where such things were discussed, and he'd come to be known as "the most dangerous man alive," until the day he'd taken it upon himself to orchestrate the death of a Cardinal whom he'd found had been involved in a nasty bit of sexual perversion within the Vatican. The *prince of the church* had inexplicably stepped in front of a truck, and had died instantly.

To redress this unsanctioned assassination—a strict violation of Phythian's terms of employment—the G3 concocted an elaborate plot to kill him. The connivance they devised was doomed to failure from the start, and Phythian had used the resulting debacle to disappear as far off the global grid as humanly possible. From that moment forward he had peacefully existed in self-exile, living in harmony on the continent of Africa with the marvelous menagerie of life that coursed through the restored camp he had named Utuliva, Swahili for serenity. Serenity was what his life had transformed into, until a discovery in a remote corner of the world the year before last raised the distinct possibility to the G3 executive committee that he had not been terminated as previously thought and, in fact, was very much alive.

Over the days that followed, Phythian had methodically orchestrated the deadly downfall of the covert group that had been around since the final days of World War Two. It was not something he had strategized or intended, nor had he been possessed of any particularly altruistic motive—other than to save a young woman whose life was in peril because of his own actions. It was simply a convenient end to a persistent problem and, once he'd assumed the reins of the firm, he'd used the G3s sophisticated resources to shift its business model to one focused more on atonement and reparations.

All of this led to his meeting with the man upstairs—no religious euphemism intended—scheduled for just six minutes from now.

The restaurant was equipped with only one security camera, unlike the visual surveillance that covered the hotel's enormous gambling hall. Phythian had made sure to keep his eyes to the floor as the maître d' guided him into the dining room, and he'd asked to be seated at a table he determined would be out of range of its lens. The Phoenician Horizon Hotel and Casino was brimming with gaming tables, and most of the digital vigilance was trained on the grifters, cheats, and scammers who gravitated to them. One could never be too sure, however, who was watching what.

The waitress returned with a smile and his check, which he paid with paper Euros that he handled only at the edges, leaving no prints, and a minimal trace of touch DNA. The same sense of caution had led him to wrap his cutlery in a napkin and slip it into a pocket in his jacket, having secretly replaced it with a clean fork and knife before his plate had been whisked off to the kitchen.

No one must ever know that he'd been here, and that nothing of a questionable nature that might occur tonight could ever lead back to him.

"Whatever is left is yours," he told her. "No change."

"Thank you, sir, and have a great evening," the waitress wished him. She flashed him that smile again, appreciative of the generous gratuity, since tipping was not generally expected nor common.

"Same to you, and may all your concerns work out for the best," he replied. Then he pushed his chair back and rose to his feet, brushing any crumbs from the particularly delicious olive bread from his lap.

It was time to get upstairs.

Declan Russell stood at the slider that led to the massive terrace and stared at the expanse of black, dotted with lights from mega-yachts and fishing boats twinkling out on the dark sea. Racking his focus slightly to take in his own reflection in the glass, he studied the man he had become: a thin frame of wrinkled skin and tired bones, slightly stooped from the six-foot-two rugby frame that at one point caused all heads in any room to turn his way. He was the one and only Declan Russell, financial tycoon and hedge fund manager whose personal net worth had once topped ten figures, the mogul and magnate whose business tactics at times were considered cutthroat, and at other times ruthless—as if there was much difference between the two.

Now here he was, older than he wished and younger than he felt: a withered and ruined man nearing his seventieth birthday, wondering if that landmark might induce Beatrice to get in touch, wherever in the world she might be. In less than two years his life had turned upside down. Investments died on the vine, clients dried up, and bank accounts ceased to exist. Lawsuits were filed, an ongoing scandal mill destroyed his reputation, and friends became ghosts.

Another taste of gin trickled down his throat. He again glanced at his Breitling, which told him he had about twenty minutes before heading downstairs for his appointment in Samarra. The irony of those words was not lost on a man who had been quite fond of the American writer John O'Hara during his years at university.

Russell turned away from the glass at the same instant a bell chimed. It took him a moment to realize someone was at the front door, an oddity since he wasn't expecting any visitors. He'd expressly told the desk clerk that he wanted no room service, and by no means was anyone to come in and turn down his bed and leave mints on his pillow, or whatever the Cypriot equivalent of hospitality might be. Only one person even knew he was at the Phoenician Horizon, and that person had already arranged to meet him downstairs in less than half an hour.

The bell chimed again, and Russell realized his feet seemed to be frozen to the carpet. A peculiar feeling of dread caused his throat to swell, and he felt a clammy chill to his skin. There was a time, before his troubles began, that men and women would line up in the corridor outside his office, their constant entry and egress seeming like a revolving door. Deals, contracts, bond offerings, equities, handshakes: they were all in a day's work, and all with lucre at their root. The reference to Jacob Marley on the late-night phone call seven evenings ago caused a shudder to rattle through him now.

This was how far he'd fallen, to cause his body to tremble at the presence of an unknown specter out in the hallway, one whose only breach thus far was to press a button.

Russell knocked back the last of his Hendricks, then got his feet moving and padded across the lush carpet. He checked his wiry gray hair in a mirror as he passed, brushed a strand away from his face. Tried not to notice the liver spots that seemed to be spreading like some form of pox on his skin. Then he grabbed the brass door handle and gave it a turn, feeling as if the devil incarnate was standing on the other side.

Chapter 3

The man out in the hallway immediately seemed familiar, as if they were schoolboy chums. But that was not possible, as Russell was confident they had never before met—not in his business dealings and definitely not in his personal life, nor had he ever seen a picture of the man. A distinct sense of *déjà vu* gripped him, however, one that he found both troubling and disquieting, while at the same time inexplicably engaging.

Phythian had waited a full thirty seconds before making his presence known. Caution being one thing and courage yet another; he wanted to make sure the hotel guest on the other side of the door was alone. Declan Russell had no wife and one partially estranged daughter, and a quick assessment determined that she had not accompanied him on this trip, nor had anyone else; of that he was certain. He detected just one set of brainwaves inside, those of a despondent and dejected financier pondering his recent fall from grace.

"May I help you?" the man named Russell asked as he assessed his visitor: a good ten years younger than he, late fifties maybe, approximately the same height but without the weary stoop, a face naturally tan from living in a land that saw sun all year round, dark eyes that seemed the color of charcoal. A linen cap was perched on his head, and he held a *faux* leather portfolio in one hand.

"I believe it is I who's here to help you," Phythian said.

"And you are?"

"I go by many names, but most people know me as Phythian."

Russell turned the name over in his head, silently pronouncing it *FITH-yun*, then said it aloud: "Phythian. Would that be your first name or last name?"

"Last. My first name is Rōnin, but it tends to be a bit of a distraction. May I come in?"

"Well, you see, I'm stepping out in a few minutes," Russell replied. "I have reservations for dinner downstairs."

"Indeed you do," Phythian said. "Eight o'clock, if memory serves."

That jacked up Russell's vigilance another notch. "Correct," he confirmed. "But how do you know this?"

"Because that was me on the phone the other night."

"You...how—?"

Phythian raised the hand that was not carrying the portfolio, a gesture of recompense. "I apologize for the subterfuge, and I hope you didn't have your heart set on ordering anything from that pretentious absurdity that serves as a menu. Besides, I believe your suite is much more suited to the confidential subject of our conversation."

"What the bloody hell are you talking about?" Russell asked.

"Don't trouble yourself...it will all become very clear, and very soon," Phythian assured him. "Now, may I come in?"

That was the last thing Russell wanted, but this man's very presence in the doorway seemed to make it impossible for him to say no. It was as if he'd lost his willpower, and was being guided by some sort of invisible hand. With no other alternative at hand, he stepped aside and waved the formidable man inside.

"Please...*mi casa es su casa*," he said.

The man named Phythian stepped across the threshold into the foyer, peeled off his jacket and draped it over a chair by the door. He glanced around the living room, taking in the contemporary styles and muted tones—Chelsea gray couch with cream colored chair, offset by a chrome and glass table between them, a potted ficus tree in a corner. Carpet seemed to flow everywhere, a light and subdued hue that some interior designer probably referenced as *oyster mist*. One wall was fitted with an electric fireplace framed by stacked rock the color of London fog, while another was an assemblage of floor-to-ceiling glass panels, each one sliding in on the other so the entire thing could open out to the balcony.

An ample wet bar occupied a corner of the enormous space, liquor bottles arranged on a granite counter whose ingrained pattern resembled a drift of sand on a windswept beach. On it was set a collection of wine glasses and cut crystal cocktail tumblers, one of which Phythian picked up, as if this were his suite—which, since he was paying for it, it sort of was.

"Would you care for another Hendricks?" he asked his host, as he helped himself to a healthy splash of Armagnac.

"How did you know what I was drinking?" Russell wanted to know. "There's three kinds of gin there."

"Chalk it up to a good guess," Pythian replied. He poured a couple fingers into a fresh glass and handed it to him, no ice. "Or maybe it was because the seal on this bottle has been cracked, and the others aren't."

Russell studied him, continuing to feel terribly uneasy about this whole thing—wondering how much of the story he'd been given on the phone was truth, and how much was misdirection. All of it? Doubtful, since this Mr. Phythian had at least kept his word about their arranged meeting, even if it wasn't going to be in the restaurant downstairs as planned. No problem with that—he'd been correct in his assessment of the menu—but what did he mean by this suite being more suitable to the context of their meeting, or however he had put it?

"Shall we sit down?" he nonetheless invited his guest.

"The view from the terrace looks spectacular, don't you think?" Phythian replied. "And there doesn't seem to be much wind tonight. I say we bring our cocktails outdoors and enjoy some fresh air."

"My thinking exactly," Russell agreed, without giving it much thought at all. His brain seemed to be on autopilot, like the self-driving feature of the electric car he'd bought back when he was still flush but had never had the nerve to engage for more than a few seconds. He wandered over to the massive glass panels and slid them into a pocket in the wall, then waved Phythian through. "After you."

The night was, indeed, warm, hardly a breath of a breeze. It was dry, too, compared with the rain that was blowing across most of Europe tonight. Phythian lowered himself into an oversized chair, plush and sumptuous with soft cushions, low enough to afford a view of the dark Mediterranean through the waist-high glass wall that served as a railing. Lights from the swimming pool sixteen floors below provided just enough contrast between the exterior walls of the suite, and the nothingness beyond. Despite the proximity to the city of Limassol, the black sky was a canvas for thousands of points of light, and his eyes quickly located Orion in the heavens, just as he always had as a boy back home in Rhode Island, before a freak incident had changed his life forever.

He took a sip of Armagnac, then cradled the glass in his hands. By this time Russell had taken up position in the chair on the other side of a low patio table, gripping his tumbler of warm gin. He had a strong urge to pound the thing in one long gulp, knowing such a move would settle his turbulent nerves. But it also would betray his desire to get to the bottom of whatever this was and be done with it, the reason he had agreed to this visit now all but lost on him.

Phythian knew all this was buzzing through Russell's brain because…well, he was Phythian. He was a man imbued with intuitive competencies beyond all comprehension, a mental skillset that bordered on metaphysical, and which commanded both respect and fear among those acquainted with his talents.

Without saying a word, he opened the portfolio and pulled out a manila envelope. He unfastened the metal clasp on the flap, and slid out a sheaf of papers held together by a paperclip. He took a quick glance at the cover page, a standard memo that noted the subject matter simply as CASE FILE 4059, then passed it across the small patio table to Russell.

"What's this?" the former billionaire from London asked.

"Your unredacted past," Phythian replied. "I've already taken care of your present, and the future is up to you."

Russell appeared to mentally deflect the ambiguous response as he allowed his eyes to roam over the top sheet of paper. He then turned the page, and began reading through several paragraphs of text, highlighted with bullet points. For the first thirty seconds he seemed confused by what he was seeing, but the bewildered crease of his brow shifted to discomfort as he began to grasp the enormity of what he held in his hand. He shot a spooked glance at Phythian, then turned his attention back to the narrative, turned the page, kept reading until the very end.

"Where the fuck did you get this?" he asked when he had finished, letting the thin stack of papers settle in his lap.

"So disappointing," Phythian replied. "And so predictable."

"What the hell kind of answer is that?"

"The kind that means that nine out of ten times, the first response someone makes after perusing their own file, is to question its origin. Which I totally understand, since not only is it incontrovertibly damning but, for obvious reasons, was never meant to see the light of day."

"Still, it's a question to which I deserve an answer," Russell pressed.

"Then you don't deny its veracity?" Phythian said.

"Would it make a difference?

"The truth is the truth, no matter how much effort might be expended trying to disprove it." Phythian rose to his feet, wandered over to the glass railing and looked down. Approximately two hundred feet to the pool patio below, or three and a half seconds in free fall. He knocked back another swallow of Armagnac, then turned and faced the ruined British businessman. "As you've probably already figured out, those pages came directly from the archives of the outfit to which you paid two million dollars to have one of your closest business competitors killed."

Russell closed his eyes and chewed on his lower lip a moment before setting his glass down on the table beside him. He equivocated mentally for a moment, as if unsure whether to admit or deny what this Mr. Phythian was saying. Then he said, "That two million dollars included a stipulation that nothing I *allegedly* paid for ever could—or would—be traced back to me. Which begs yet another question. Several, in fact."

"The asking of which I will spare you, for the sake of time and dignity," Phythian replied, cupping the bottom of his glass in one hand. "As I introduced myself to you earlier, my name is Rōnin Phythian. That fact should be important to you because half of those two million dollars you coughed up were wired to a numbered account in a very friendly island nation, made available to me only after I completed the business arrangement you set in motion."

"You're the bloody bugger who—"

"Correct. I am. And for the record, the other half went to the Greenwich Global Group, also known as the G3, which you hired through the dark web just over a decade ago to take care of all the details."

There was no point in arguing the point, and Declan Russell found he couldn't dispute what this oddly disquieting man—*assassin*—was saying, even if he wanted to. It was as if he had lost all free will, and now was simply a puppet in a horrid Punch and Judy show.

"How did you get your damned hands on it?" he asked. "Like I said, my payment came with the guarantee that my identity would never be compromised or revealed."

"There's been a change in upper-level management," Phythian explained, with a slight lift of his shoulders. "A hostile takeover, to couch it in terms you should well understand."

"I'm not following you," Russell replied, shaking his head even though he sensed an icy dread settling in. "What do you mean, hostile?"

"Regime change, in its simplest form. The G3 has ceased to exist, at least as a going concern. There's a new sheriff in town."

The bewilderment on Russell's face was unmistakable, but after a few seconds reality of what Phythian was saying began to set in. "You're talking about...*you*."

"At a wavering instant the swallows gave way to bats."

"What in bloody hell are you blathering about?"

"D.H. Lawrence," Phythian explained. "And don't get all imperious and snooty. We both know that the people who took your money were anything but swallows—which, of course, is inconsequential to our discussion. In any event, I invited you here to make you a one-time offer."

"What sort of offer?" Russell asked.

"A very simple one," Phythian said. "And one that's rather befitting a man in your circumstances. The deal is, you make an additional disbursement in an amount equal to the original—two million dollars—and the file you just read is deleted permanently."

"You're fucking *blackmailing* me?" Russell snapped, momentarily forgetting the man sitting no more than a yard from him was a highly trained professional killer. "It's nothing short of extortion."

"I prefer to look at it as a term life insurance policy."

"*You greedy cold-blooded butcher—*"

"The money wouldn't be going to me," Phythian said, stopping him. "I already banked my cut the first time around. It would go to someone who has suffered greatly at the hand of your avarice and greed."

"What is this, some sort of crusade of conscience? Are you trying to expunge your sins—*your guilt*—for causing Mister Lamoines' death?"

"Like the man once said, 'guilt is regret for what we've done; regret is guilt for what we didn't do."

"Meaning what?" Russell snapped. "I have no regrets."

"If not, then your soul is already lost," Phythian said.

"Fuck that shit. I'm broke, something you bloody well should have figured out before wasting your time on this bullshit scheme. I don't just happen to have two million lying around at the moment. Pounds, dollars, or Euros."

"Your financial circumstances are of no interest to me," Phythian said with a weary sigh. "I take it your answer is no?"

"And what if it is?" Russell countered. "What are you going do to?"

Phythian was still standing at the waist-high glass railing, glass of Armagnac still in his palm. "I'm going to time your descent," he said.

"My *what*? Just what the hell do you think I'm going to do?"

"What they all do, when it comes down to it."

"*They*? How many others have you tried this bullshit on?" Russell asked.

"In the world's two oldest professions, it never serves to keep count."

It took a moment for Russell's confused brain to make sense of what Phythian was saying. "How many imbeciles actually fall for this scam of yours, cough up your ransom?"

"Just enough to keep it interesting."

"You're nothing but a common thug and ruthless murderer," Russell huffed, trying to appear confident while the opposite was true.

"Perhaps I am." Another shrug. "But you might want to consider how it's been possible for me to come here to your lovely suite, sip some of your magnificent vintage Armagnac, and hit you with a financial offer I knew you would have no interest in accepting. You keep thinking you're in control of this situation, but you lost it the second I stepped through that door."

"You have no idea what I'm thinking—"

"But I do, Mr. Russell," Phythian said, his voice calm to the point of annoyance. "And on some level, you've been aware of it from the moment you opened the door."

"Get the fuck out—"

"Totally my intention, and all in good time. At present, however, I want you to focus on the only true option you have remaining to you, something that's been burrowing through your brain like an earwig, laying its eggs as it passed through."

"This is not an episode of *The Twilight Zone*—"

"*Night Gallery*," Phythian corrected him. "And I mention it only because you wouldn't be the first person to go for door number two."

"Do *what*?"

"Choose the path of least resistance, to mix metaphors. The thing is, Mr. Russell, since the moment you let me in, a dark hole has been forming inside your mind. You've been obsessing about how you squandered your life, trying to come to terms with how your physical existence on this planet has been a waste of space. How you've contributed nothing of any lasting value. You made it all about amassing dollars and pounds and Euros, piling wealth upon wealth with no regard to the greater good. Building your empire, no matter the expense, doing whatever needed to be done to add to the pile."

What he spoke was the truth: Declan Russell had never given much thought to the human cost when it came to measuring his personal achievements. Business was business, and on the rare occasion something or someone got in the way, he usually was able to negotiate his way to a beneficial conclusion. Occasionally, in the rare case that he found such an outcome not possible, he took more drastic measures. Andre Lamoines, an arch-competitor who mysteriously had jumped to his death from the first level of the Eiffel Tower ten years ago, was one of them. An outcome, as this disturbingly prescient Rōnin Phythian had said, that had been arranged through a dark web outfit known as the Greenwich Global Group.

In any event, Russell now sensed a peculiar heaviness coming over him, as if a weight were pressing down on his bones, squeezing the last threads of life from his body. Like a cancer on the prowl for viable cells, he could feel it spreading through every artery, vein, and nerve ending, a swelling up through the base of his skull and into his brain, where every synapse felt dull and sluggish and filled his mind with an unbearable mental gloaming from which he saw no escape.

"The guilt, the regret you're feeling must be intolerable," Phythian prodded Russell, who had no idea that his entire being was being manipulated by a trained master who had pulled these same strings countless times before. "There is only one way to free yourself from its grip."

Russell nodded and slowly rose to his feet. Without saying another word—not even thinking of penning a short note to the daughter who certainly would be left wondering what had come over her father, and whether he'd bequeathed anything of value to her—he shuffled across the patio to the waist-high tempered glass wall. He stood there a second, not bothering to look down, just figuring out the logistics of getting his feet up over the top and then tumbling in the right direction. The matter was solved when Phythian mentally suggested that he drag a nearby chaise lounge across the deck for assistance.

He did, and once that task was completed, the rest was easy. He stepped up onto it, his feet momentarily sinking into the thick, luxurious cushion.

Such extravagance and richness: the designers of the Phoenician Horizon Hotel and Casino really had considered everything when it came to the comfort of their guests.

He lifted his left foot first and slung it over the railing, then set it down on the narrow lip of copper coping that protruded on the other side. His right foot followed. He extended his hands behind him as he leaned outward, his fingers grasping the polished top of the glass wall. His entire withered frame teetered at the edge as he stared off at the lights twinkling in the distance, still not daring to look down as his brain convinced him this was his only true course of action. Then he released his hold and he tipped out into the darkness—here one moment, gone the next: the last breath of a human spirit freed from its earthly encumbrances, disappearing into the bosom of the night.

Three and a half seconds start to finish, Phythian counted.

He was still the most dangerous man alive.

Chapter 4

Eight minutes later in Rome, a Fiat 500 with a hand-lettered dashboard placard designating the largest ride-share company in the world rolled slowly along Corso Vittorio Emanuele. The driver craned his neck to his right and upwards, searching for the address that had been scribbled on the scrap of paper he held in in his hand, puzzling over the lack of signage on the doorways on both his left and right.

"*Sei sicuro dell'indirizzo?*" he inquired over his shoulder to the passenger sitting directly behind him.

"*Si*...it's along here somewhere," Carter Logan said, peering through the glass at the unmarked masonry structures offering no markings, no visible sign of an address anywhere—just closed shops, metal doors covered with graffiti rolled down to the sidewalk, signs announcing Tabacchi, Vendita, and VIP. Very Italian Pizza. "*Uno cinquantaquattro—*"

He knew very few words in Italian, and those he did speak came out horribly, like a rookie reading directly from a language translation app he'd downloaded onto his phone—which, in fact, he was.

"*Si, si,*" the driver replied, still studying the buildings with obvious frustration. They edged further down the block, then he finally said, "*Ah... lo vedo,*" using a free hand to point at a pair of dingy doors with weathered brass knockers on them. "*Proprio qui.*"

Logan's cellphone translator program wasn't equipped with voice recognition, but he thought he understood what the driver was telling him, hoping the guy wasn't just trying to dump him on a random sidewalk in Rome, miles from his Air BnB, the night before the start of a global economic conference. Hundreds of government leaders, cabinet ministers, dignitaries, and groupies had descended on the city over the last forty-eight hours, and hotels and taxis had been scarce. He'd had to wait a good half hour for the summoned Fiat to show up at the thread-bare studio apartment for which he was being gouged unmercifully, and now he was late. Not appreciably so, but he didn't want to keep the subject of his interview waiting unnecessarily. Not when the young man had already vocalized his reluctance to talk, and this might be the only chance for the two of them to meet.

"*Uno cinquantaquattro,*" the driver confirmed, pointing at the doorway to indicate they'd finally arrived at their destination

"*Eccellente,*" Logan said, reaching for the small briefcase on the seat beside him. "*Grazie.*"

"*Prego.*"

Logan typed "I'll add a good tip" into the translator program, then relayed the words that appeared on the screen: "*Aggiungo un buon consiglio.*"

"*No, no... questa è Roma,*" the driver said. "*Contanti.*"

"What?"

The driver briskly rubbed his thumb against his other fingers, the global gesture for *cash only.* Logan hated to part with the paper money he'd picked up at a currency exchange stand at the airport just five hours ago, especially since he'd already lost fifty Euros to a ticket scammer at the Termini train station. He reluctantly pulled out his wallet and asked, "How much?"

The amount the driver quoted seemed way too much, but how could he quarrel? He peeled off more than he knew he should have and handed them over, then popped the chrome handle and began to push the door outward, into the street.

"*No, no, signore,*" the driver said, his voice animated as he gestured wildly with his hands. "*Dovete uscire dall'altra parte.*"

Logan had nowhere near the grasp of the language to understand what he was being told, never figuring the driver was explaining that he needed to exit the car on the sidewalk side, rather than directly into traffic. Ignorant to local customs and oblivious to the whine of a five-speed engine roaring up behind them, he thrust the door open as far as it would go.

At the same instant a speeding black motorcycle slammed into it, ripping it from its hinges in a scream of torn and twisted metal. The bike's driver crashed head-first into the closed window, his forward momentum catapulting him through the air in a flailing somersault before he landed a good five yards in front of the Fiat, his unprotected skull striking the pavement with a nauseating thud.

Two other things happened at the same time, in one fluid movement. The Benelli TRK 502 X flipped onto its side and skidded into the crumpled and motionless rider, and an object that looked very much like a gun spiraled through the air and landed in the middle of the street, before skittering under the bumper of a parked Citroen.

"*Idiota...cosa hai fatto*," the driver yelled, smacking the ceiling of his car with both fists, which were encased in brown fingerless gloves. "*Scemo. Stronzo.*"

Logan was out of the car in a flash, checking to make sure no other motor vehicles—cycles or automobiles—were bearing down on him. They weren't. The cheap car door seemed to be hanging from one twisted hinge, and he made his way around it and rushed up to the fallen rider. The young man's arms and legs were twisted at impossible angles, and the hoodie— no helmet—that encased his head was now soggy from an abundance of blood—and, probably, brains. The man had to be dead, but Logan didn't dare touch him. He thought he detected an almost imperceptible rise and fall of his chest, gasping for breath just once, but he couldn't be certain.

There was nothing after that.

"*Dio mio...Dio mio*," the Fiat driver screamed as he charged out from behind the wheel, arms waving wildly. "*L'hai ucciso—*"

Logan could only guess what the man was saying. "Holy shit—" he muttered to himself as he stared at the contorted side of what appeared to be the man's lifeless face. He thought about touching a finger to his neck to check for a pulse, instead lifted his wrist and used his thumb to find any sign of life.

"*Mio dio... l'hai fatto tu*," the driver blubbered as he rushed up, holding his hands to his head. "*Mio dio.*"

The *polizia* were on the scene within seconds. The first vehicle was an electric BMW i3 that raced up from behind the accident scene, from the same direction the motorcycle had been traveling. It seemed to Logan that the EV with the flashing blues must have already been chasing the speeding Benelli, and had just caught up to it.

The police car slowed and cut toward the curb as it approached the accident scene. As soon as it came to a stop, an officer jumped out from behind the wheel and ran up to where Logan was still crouched over the cyclist's motionless body.

"*Cos'è successo qua?*" the police officer snapped. "*Che cosa hai fatto?*" What happened here...what did you do?

Logan had no idea what the uniformed man was saying, just shrugged and explained, "I'm American…I don't speak Italian."

The officer rolled his eyes and turned to the driver of the Fiat. "*Come è successo?*" he asked again, fewer words this time. Then he bent down, touched his fingers to the motorcycle rider's throat, then shook his head. *Deceduto.*

The driver appeared not to know what to do. The man in the hoodie was dead, and by law he—Bruno Ricci—was responsible for his passenger's actions. It was the American's fault, of course, opening the door on the street side, but ultimately Ricci would be held accountable. An incident that ended in death could cause him to forfeit his license, cost him a hefty fine, and conceivably even land him in jail. All these possibilities seemed to tangle in his mind as he launched into a frantic explanation, wildly gesturing at Logan the entire time, laying the blame on the dumb-ass American tourist.

His words came out like water through a firehose and, at some point, the *poliziotto* spotted the gun lying on the pavement under the bumper of the parked Citroen. He edged over and crouched down, looked as if he might pick it up, but didn't. Instead, he unclipped a radio from his belt and made a call for back-up, then rose to his feet and said, "*Nessuno esce di scena.*"

Logan assumed the cop—a word that didn't translate well in the language program—was explaining that neither of them was to leave, not until back-up arrived. Which truly sucked, because by now he was more than just fashionably late for his appointment in the building *right over there*. It was an interview with a skittish source he'd spent weeks trying to arrange, a major story that would send shockwaves around the globe if it proved to be true. Emails and texts had flown back and forth across the Atlantic just to arrange this sit-down, and now it was at great risk of completely falling apart.

He typed a few words into his cellphone app, waited for the translation, then said to the officer, "*Ho un appuntamento lì dentro.*" He showed him the words on the screen, just in case there was any confusion. I have an appointment in there.

"*Può aspettare,*" the policeman replied. He snatched the device out of Logan's hands and typed in his response, which translated to: It can wait.

As if to punctuate his words, another police vehicle raced up the street and braked to a halt. This one was a black Alfa Romeo Giulia, a swarm of blue lights flashing from the roof bar. Two officers got out and huddled with the first uniform on the scene, as well as the ride share driver named Ricci. They spent the next few minutes debating what had happened, focusing on how the biker had ended up dead on the pavement. A lot of accusations were hurled at Ricci, who angrily deflected them, and repeatedly pointed at Logan as he explained his version of the events. Eventually the three officers nodded, indicating they understood how this mishap might have occurred, and the discussion simmered down.

"*Lo stupido Americano non parla Italiano*," Ricci said in an exasperated tone.

"*Nessun problema*," one of the officers replied. "*Parlo Inglese*." I speak English.

He then peeled himself away from the others, made his way over to where Logan was leaning against the fender of the mangled Fiat.

"You caused this?" the English-speaking officer asked as he approached.

"You speak English?" Logan replied, his nose catching an abundance of aftershave.

"Better than you speak Italian, from what I'm told," he said. He was dressed in black trousers with blue shirt, two silver stars indicating his rank of tenente—lieutenant—in the Arma dei Carabinieri, the Italian national police force. He had clean-cut hair and sideburns, black cap on his head with a chromed metal badge and side buttons. He was a little under six feet, average weight for his height and still in solid shape, not enough time on the job yet to relax his diet or physical condition. A gun and several other tools of the profession were strapped to his belt. "Two years exchange with the Boston PD," he added. "My cousin lives there."

"Good," Logan said. "I'm really late for an appointment, in that building." He gestured at the double wooden door with the number 154 above it, the one that had contributed to this entire mess in the first place.

"Cancel it," the tenente said. "You're not going anywhere, not for a while."

"But I have business—"

"In what language did you hear me make a request? I said 'cancel it.'"

Cops, Logan thought. *All the same the world over*. "Yessir," he said, then started to compose a text on his phone.

"What are you doing?"

"Sending a text."

"I didn't mean this very second," the officer told him.

A brief stare-down followed, eventually ending with Logan slipping his phone back into his pocket.

"For the record, I'm Tenente Foschi," the carabinieri introduced himself. He did not extend a hand to shake; this was not going to be that type of acquaintance. "The driver of the car you were riding in says you're responsible for what happened here. An accident that resulted in the death of a man on a motorcycle."

"I didn't mean to," Logan replied, his response sounding pathetic as the gravity of the situation began to sink in. He had made an impulsive error, opening a door on the wrong side of the car, and a man was dead because of it. The fact that said man appeared to have a gun in his possession seemed immaterial, at least at this point. "It was completely unintentional."

"Yet the result is the same. Perhaps you can tell me what happened."

Considering there was no real alternative—and now that his appointment was out of the question—Logan took a deep breath and looked the tenente in the eye.

"I'm here for the conference," he said, meaning the G20. "Sort of a last-minute decision, and I had a bit of a problem finding a place to stay. Ended up getting a room out near the Catacombs."

"Which catacombs?" Foschi asked. "There's a lot of them."

"Priscilla, I think," Logn replied. "Anyway, the owner of the place I'm staying speaks a little English—her name is Maria—and when I told her I needed to be somewhere tonight, she arranged an Uber for me. Called a cousin of her husband's, something like that, and he showed up." He cocked his head in the direction of the driver. "I gave him a slip of paper with the address of where I was going on it, and he brought me here."

"That Fiat is not an Uber," Foschi said. "And that man is not an Uber driver."

"What are you talking about? Maria said—" Logan's voice trailed off, realizing his desperation to get a ride to his appointment had superseded his sense of judgment, particularly in a city he did not know and whose laws and customs he clearly had yet to fully appreciate.

"Uber is not the same here in Rome as it is in America," Tenente Foschi said. "Taxi drivers are against it, so it is not allowed. Except Uber Black, which is expensive, with expensive vehicles. Audis, Alfa Romeos, BMWs. No Fiats. And let me guess—he demanded to be paid in cash, right?"

Fuck, Logan thought, taking great care to make sure he contained the word to his head. "He ripped me off—"

The officer lifted his shoulders in a shrug and said, "That is not the issue here. The issue is that a man is dead because of you. Passport, please."

At which point the interrogation began. *Really began.* Dozens of questions came from the young carabinieri lieutenant, followed by countless more from the homicide investigators who eventually arrived on the scene. Their inquiry was direct, and to the point: When did Logan arrive in Rome? What was his business here? Why was he attending the G20?

He patiently explained he was a member of the media, a former reporter with the *Washington Post* who had left the venerable newspaper to write and edit a highly respected blog read by tens of thousands of people around the world. He was in Rome to add some color to the otherwise tedious politics of the global summit, provide a more human backstory to some of the major players who would be participating in the conference. The person he'd been planning to meet in the building *right over there* was a confidential source and no, even if they took him to jail, he would not reveal his or her identity.

When they finally were done with him, he was ordered to remain at the scene, standing on the sidewalk out of earshot of the polizia, whose words he could not hope to understand anyway. It was only then that he was allowed to send his text, in which he expressed his sincerest dismay that an incident had occurred and he was unexpectedly delayed. Maybe he could reschedule for tomorrow, at whatever time was most convenient.

Not surprisingly, no answer was immediately forthcoming.

The curb and sidewalk were too low for him to sit comfortably, so he found a tree to lean against while he watched the forensics team go to work. The two focal points of their scrutiny were the deceased victim and the weapon he appeared to have been carrying. From where Logan was standing it looked like some sort of military-grade pistol, the type he'd seen in action films where black ops soldiers rappelled from helicopters with guns firing hundreds of rounds a minute.

Several hours into the investigation, the body of the deceased cyclist finally was loaded into the back of a blue-and-white high-top van. A tow truck eventually arrived and the crumpled Fiat was winched onto its short flatbed, along with the mangled door, and it was allowed to depart, presumably to a location where additional examination would be conducted.

A little before midnight a black Maserati Quattroporte with tinted windows and no writing on the side glided up the street. Low and sleek, the sedan's wheels thumped up onto the granite curb and came to a halt in the illuminated halo of a street lamp. It sat there for a moment before a woman wearing what appeared to be an official state uniform—blonde hair streaming out from beneath a matching black cap—emerged from behind the wheel. She circled around the front of the car, and when she approached the rear she hesitated just a fraction of a moment, then opened the door.

Street side, not curbside, Logan noticed.

A man in a long, dark coat climbed out, his commanding presence drawing immediate salutes—and respectful silence—from everyone present. The man returned their gestures—*at ease*—then made his way over to an officer who had three red-and-silver stars on his epaulet, and seemed to be in charge of the crime scene.

"*Dov'è?*" the man asked in a demanding tone suited to his apparent stature, both physical and authoritative.

A bit of confusion followed as the *comandante in capo* gestured at Logan, who knew just enough Italian to understand the response: "*Quello è lui.*" That's him.

The government official clarified his question while shaking his head, saying, "*No, no...intendo quello morto.*"

That seemed to straighten things out: the man from the Quattroporte was looking for the deceased crash victim, not Logan. *Not yet.* The poliziotto cocked his head toward the coroner's van and said, "*Lì dentro. Seguimi.*"

The Roman equivalent of an EMT opened the rear double doors, and the man in the overcoat climbed inside to take a look. Given his position across the street, Logan couldn't see what was going on in there, but after a good fifteen seconds the man backed out and stood up, dusting off his threads. Then he gave a backhanded flip of his hand, and said, "*Portalo via.*"

The doors closed again, and a few seconds later the death wagon rolled away. No lights, no siren; the deceased man in the back was in no need of prompt medical attention.

Only after it had disappeared around the corner did the new arrival—he had to be some sort of cabinet-level minister or police chief—turn his attention to where Logan was standing. He shot him a long, hard look, then pointed directly at him and said to the nearest Carabinieri, "*Viene con me.*"

Come with me: three words that, no matter in what language they were spoken, did not sound encouraging in the least.

Chapter 5

Martin Beaudin silently padded down the carpeted hallway, dark and stuffy and reeking with the odor of a Gauloises that had been smoked earlier.

Known for years throughout the intelligence trade as *Le Serrurier,* he actually was a locksmith by training, a line of work that had served him well many times in the past when his intention had been to gain quick access to an office or residence without the benefit of a key. Rarely did he travel without his professional gear, which featured a generous array of the highest quality German spring steel picks, snakes, and tension tools, along with a wallet-sized credit card set that included a Euro Bogota quad and a Christina Palmer spoon.

He hadn't expected to resort to any of these implements tonight, since the woman who lived in apartment 506 had told him to ring the button downstairs, and she'd buzz him up. He'd done that—three times in fact—but there had been no response. Maybe she had lost track of time and stepped out for a moment, or had changed her mind and decided not to see him at all. He doubted there was any confusion over the hour, since she had expressed profound interest in why he wanted to talk to her, and had personally suggested ten o'clock. It was much later than was his habit, but he was just the messenger here.

Whatever the reason she wasn't answering, he had easily slipped past the lock downstairs and had taken the lift to the top floor. It was a rickety old thing with a steel cage only large enough to fit three adults, and by the time he stepped off on the fifth floor he'd made up his mind to take the fire stairs when he was set to leave.

He had noticed only one surveillance cameras in the building, in the downstairs vestibule. He trusted that his identity was properly concealed—tinted contact lenses that made his eyes appear blue, rather than brown, and a bad hairpiece that looked as if it had been fabricated from a dead rodent. Tortoise shell glasses completed the disguise, although there really was no reason to mask his true identity. No one was looking for him, and he had done nothing unseemly for a great many months.

Beaudin stopped in front of the specified door and knocked. It was now several minutes past their appointed meeting time, and he figured if the woman who lived on the other side hadn't answered the downstairs buzzer, she wouldn't respond now. He was correct; there was no reply, so he tried once more…then a third time.

He briefly considered coming back in the morning, but just as quickly put that notion out of his mind. Experience dictated that when plans fell apart, apparently for no reason, much more often than not there always was a simple and honest explanation.

Not always, however, and that's the trepidation he was sensing tonight.

Merde: he'd been hanging around Rönin Phythian too long.

It was Phythian who had sent him here, with the express instructions not to come away without making personal contact with Gabrielle Lamoines. After a bit of nasty business a couple years ago, during which Phythian had relieved the Greenwich Global Group of its entire brain trust in a matter of days, he'd thought his head also was on the *billot*. His life, fortunately, had been spared, a courtesy granted because Beaudin alone possessed the knowledge to access Equinox. That was the G3's proprietary database that also was linked—through digital back channels—to a host of intelligence networks around the world. As a poet once said, the entire sum of existence is the magic of being needed by just one person.

His train had arrived at Gare du Nord in the center of Paris shortly after noon, and a taxi had taken him to his hotel in the Latin Quarter. He had busied himself walking around the city where his father had been a celebrated war hero so many decades ago, at an hour of history when Europe had fallen to the darkness of evil and all had seemed so desperate. Alas, such bravery and courage seemed to have skipped a generation, although Beaudin believed he had contributed to the balance of good and evil in his own inimitable way.

He stood in the hallway and studied the lock. It appeared to be a basic pin tumbler mechanism that consisted of an outer cylindrical casing that housed a small plug and a pair of pins that corresponded to the notches on a key. He gently inserted a tension wrench from his collection of picks and at the same time lifted each of the pin sets, applying just the right amount of torque on the plug.

Thirty seconds later the lock clicked, and he quietly pushed the door open just enough to slip inside. He returned the tools to his pocket as he waited for his eyes to adjust to the darkness, just a glimmer of light reaching up from the streetlight five floors below. Four decades of clandestine operations had instilled in him a natural sense of vigilance as he entered, the Sig Sauer 365 in his pocket helping to ease his heightened sense of caution.

From the entryway he listened for the steady breathing of a person asleep, but heard nothing. Warily, as if steeling himself for a sudden attack from the shadows within, he reached a gloved hand around the jamb and flipped the wall switch. Instantly the room was bathed in a warm glow that came from a floor lamp set in the corner, on the other side of a sofa, which was a neutral cream with brown piping, with a few throw pillows placed at either end. A couple chairs that did not match were set on opposite sides of a table with a beveled glass top, which held a stack of magazines and an onyx figure that looked like an Egyptian sphinx.

The room was neither large nor small, nor particularly well-appointed; it was just a typical Parisienne apartment, home to a woman in her thirties who seemed to have neither the interest nor inclination to make it a showcase. It was a place to be lived in, with homey knick-knacks set on a shelf there and a bookcase here. Framed art posters, prints from such galleries as Laurent Godin, Perrotin, and Bugada & Cargnel, crowded the walls.

Finding nothing in the outer room, he bypassed the small kitchen and quietly entered the bedroom. It was illuminated by a sliver of light from the bathroom that gave form to the shadows and dark angles that sliced across the bed—the same bed where he could see a woman lying on her back on top of the sheets, naked, her wrists gently but firmly bound to the headboard in a tangle of silk. She was not moving, and definitely not sleeping. In fact, there was a neat hole in her forehead, and the telltale spray of red on the wall behind her confirmed what his eyes were telling him: Gabrielle Lamoines was dead.

Beaudin inhaled a quick breath, blinked his eyes rapidly as a natural response to the revelation that the woman he had been scheduled to meet—no matter what hour of night he had come to the door—was deceased. Death was certainly no stranger to him; he'd encountered it many times during the course of his life, in many varied settings and circumstances. Still, he was struck with sudden sorrow at the sight of the lifeless woman he had never met, whom he had come here to share the truth of why her father had fallen to his death ten years ago.

Beaudin pulled the drapes closed and flicked on a light in the corner. Then he quietly moved over to the bed and compared her face with the image he'd downloaded to his phone: same chestnut hair and dark eyes, same chin and high cheekbones—even if they did appear sallow in the elongated shadows of her immediate afterlife. A sense of total disbelief and confusion appeared to be locked into the lines of her face, while her eyes reflected the wide-open surprise of the last second before death had taken hold. Using his gloved hand, he tried to close them, but her skin was already losing its pliability. Instead, he gathered up a sheet from the floor and covered her body, tampering with the evidence of a death scene the furthest thing from his mind.

Once Mlle Lamoines appeared in a more respectable repose, he stepped back from the bed and glanced around the room. It was large by Parisian standards, maybe four meters by five, high ceilings defined by intricate crown molding and wallpaper that depicted a variety of fruits on a light beige background. The furniture appeared to be a blend of various woods and styles, some dating back to the early part of the last century, others more art deco or even Bauhaus in style.

Plush carpeting covered the floor, leaving indentations of bare feet— probably hers—and larger shoes that likely had been worn by her killer, and Beaudin's, as well. He made a note to smooth them out of the tufted pile before he left, which would be soon, since he now realized that his presence on the building's surveillance footage would become a matter of interest to whatever authorities would be investigating this crime scene, whenever Ms. Lamoines' body might be discovered. Maybe by a housekeeper, or a friend or colleague.

Which brought him to her current appearance and condition. Judging from her unclothed body, whoever had put that bullet through her head very likely had tied her up and made love to her just moments before he'd murdered her. Beaudin was convinced the gunman was a he, since he had studied Gabrielle's lengthy file in the Equinox database, and found numerous references to casual liaisons with men, but no women.

Judging from the burn marks on her skin and the size of the entry wound, her killer had shot her at close range, just a foot or two away. It was an action that suggested this was all business, no pleasure—well, maybe a bit of pleasure—before he'd simply walked out of her apartment, and very likely this city.

"Who did this to you?" he whispered to the woman under the sheet. "Why did you let him get this close?"

Mindful of the time and the circumstances, he quietly began poking around the room. From what he could see, Gabrielle Lamoines had planned on traveling—the G20 meeting in Rome, he guessed, since half the news media in the world would be there. A tapestry carryon bag was set on a chair in one corner, and an Amélie Pichard purse had been placed on the floor next to it. Beaudin began with the travel bag, carefully lifting out each article of clothing, inserting his gloved fingers between the folds, feeling for solid objects, files, canisters with hidden compartments, false bottoms. He doubted he would find much of interest, since most women typically didn't carry top-secret or classified documents when they traveled. Still, judging from the placement of the hole in Gabrielle's head, someone had paid good money to have her killed.

The reason for that might just be found in her personal belongings.

The tapestry bag was clean, however. Nothing had been slipped between the few garments that had been tucked inside, nothing slipped into inside pockets. Nothing was sewn into the lining of the bag itself. It was the same thing with the purse: just typical woman stuff like a wallet, lipstick, a roll of mints, a compact, a case of cotton swabs. There was another case for a contraceptive diaphragm, which caused him to glance back at Gabrielle lying there naked on the bed. *Curious*, he thought. He opened the plastic box, expecting to find it empty but instead he found an SD card inside, the kind usually used to store photographs in a digital camera. It was a little more than an inch square and the width of a wafer, with a label that read 4TB. He slipped it into his pocket and continued searching the contents of the purse.

Eventually he set the handbag back on the floor where he had found it, and turned his attention to the wooden dresser set against the far wall. There he found a jewelry box, a dish that held several rings, and a framed photograph of a man who appeared in his late thirties, standing beside a girl of about ten. He knew from the Equinox file that Gabrielle had been very close to her father, who had died when she was in her early twenties—maybe a decade after this image was taken.

Also set on the dresser surface, in front of the picture, was a rectangular card a little over three inches by five and a half inches, with a surrealistic illustration on it. It depicted a woman dressed in a blue robe and headdress, clenching a rolled-up scroll in her hand, and a figure of a cat at her feet. "The High Priestess – Roman numeral II," he read aloud, without touching it.

Beaudin snapped a quick photo with his phone, then turned his attention to the bathroom. Unlike the rest of the apartment, it appeared to have been recently remodeled, with a large shower, double vanity, toilet, and bidet. No medicine cabinet, but several drawers in the vanity contained a variety of toiletries and medicines he suspected a woman might have. A mobile phone was charging in a wall outlet, but it was thumbprint-protected and would not respond when he tried to get past the home page. Gabrielle had been dead far too long for the heat from her skin to unlock it; instead, he used the pointed end of a safety pin to pop the SIM tray, then removed the memory card inside and slipped it into his pocket, along with the memory device he'd found earlier.

A small toiletry kit held a variety of creams and lotions and perfumes, plus a bottle of Ambien, and some anti-anxiety pills. Also, he found two small hand-rolled joints in a Benadryl bottle. He left everything where it was—even the pair of doobies—and moved back out to the bedroom, where he bent down and began to physically buff his footprints out of the thick carpet with his gloved hands, taking care to leave those of Mlle Lamoines and her killer where they were.

Sixty seconds later he had worked his way through the living room to the front door. He carefully rose to his feet and supported his weight on the sides of his leather-soled shoes, not wanting to leave even one traceable imprint behind. He gave the room one final glance, then gently pulled the door inward and slipped back out into the hallway, his left hand automatically reaching for the Sig Sauer in his pocket, just for comfort and reassurance.

Beaudin kept his eyes to the floor as he softly made his way to the fire stairs, trying to shut out the noxious fumes of those ghastly cigarettes that still lingered in the musty air.

He was dreading the phone call he had to make, knowing the person on the other end would not be pleased with the news he was about to deliver.

Chapter 6

The officer from the low-slung black Maserati Quattroporte turned out to be the *generale di corpo d'armata* della *Guardia di Finanza*, which roughly translated to the Corps General of the Finance Police.

It was a rather lofty position for a man who had been called out to personally investigate the death of a random motorcycle rider who had crashed into the door of a Fiat on the Corso Vittorio Emanuele. In fact, it made no sense to Logan that the incident had attracted so much attention from the police when the entire thing clearly had been an accident. Surely the Italian authorities had a human-resources crunch because of the G20 summit, so what was it about the victim in the hoodie that was such a big deal...and the *Finance Police*? What did they have to do with this?

These were all questions Carter Logan had been asking himself ever since he'd been bundled into the back seat of the Maserati and transported across town to the Guardia's headquarters at Viale Ventuno Aprile, where he now sat in a second-floor interrogation room in dire need of a lavatory and seriously dehydrated. It was sparsely furnished, just a conference table with chairs pushed in around it, but the wood was polished and the padded seats covered with fabric. Lighting came from recessed cans overhead, not too harsh, and there were no mirrors on the walls, which meant no team of investigators leering at him from a dark closet behind one-way glass, studying every movement and inadvertent facial tic. There was a camera, however, nestled into an upper corner where the walls joined with the ceiling.

"Why were you in that particular neighborhood at that particular time?" the general asked him, not for the first time.

"I've already told you," Logan answered. "I had a meeting."

"What you've told me was that the nature of this meeting is none of my business," replied the general, who earlier had said his name was Lionetti, who spoke remarkably good English. "And as I keep telling you,

I'm making it my business. We can do this all night long, but eventually I'll get the information I want."

"As a reporter, I know my legal rights, and that includes protecting the identity of a confidential source." Much of what Logan was saying was bluster, and the rest mostly a poor guess, because he actually had no idea what sort of laws protected journalists in Italy, or any other country outside the U.S., for that matter.

Lionetti glanced at the other man in the room, seated next to him, wearing a uniform with three stars that meant nothing to Logan. They seemed to share a moment of mutual mirth, and then the general continued. "Perhaps you should speak with Carlos Silvestri."

"And who is he?"

"A good question, one you perhaps should have asked before coming to our beautiful city to practice your journalism. But to enlighten you: Signore Silvestri was a reporter for a national newspaper who was investigating a financial scandal at a bank in Siena about ten years ago. During the course of his research, he met with several employees who were under government surveillance, and he refused to answer questions about those meetings. He was arrested for obstruction of justice, interference with an ongoing investigation, and other infractions of the law. A decade later, he's still sitting in jail."

"I'm not obstructing any sort of justice," Logan pointed out. "The person I was planning to meet with is of no concern to your investigation of the man who died. Especially since I never actually had a chance to meet with him."

"All the same, it remains a matter of great interest to us."

Logan was beginning to comprehend that he had no leverage here, nor did he have any idea how long General Lionetti of the Finance Police could hold him for questioning before Italian law required that he be turned loose.

"Perhaps you could enlighten me as to why?" he asked.

Lionetti and the three-star put their heads together and shared some inaudible mumbling. Then the general looked up and said, "The victim of your careless actions tonight has been known to us for some time, for reasons that need not be explained. We find it interesting that a reporter from America refuses to divulge the nature of his business that placed him in that neighborhood at precisely the same time that he died. And actually had a hand in his death."

Logan tried to make sense of what he was being told, finally realized the police somehow were thinking he and the deceased motorcycle rider had been in cahoots; some sort of scheduled hand-off gone bad? A payout? Ambush? Drugs or guns? The dead guy had been carrying a firearm, an ugly thing the forensics investigators had collected as evidence—and who knew what kind of substances might have been in his bloodstream, or on his person?

"I don't know anything about that," he insisted. Wondering if he was going to need to bring in a lawyer, an expense he could ill afford. If he still worked for the *Washington Post* he would have access to dozens of corporate attorneys, but he'd parted company with the paper at the end of last year. Amicably, which was a good thing, but his friendly departure wouldn't do much to help him now. In other words, he was shit out of luck.

"I don't even know the guy's name, and you won't tell me," Logan continued. "Which I totally understand. It's an ongoing case, a person is dead, and you're not authorized to speak on the record. Something of that nature. After the Amanda Knox debacle I can understand why you'd be reluctant to talk to the news media."

The mention of the young American woman who had walked away after a murder conviction did not sit well with either the general or his sidekick. The top dog was on his feet in a second, screaming something in Italian, totally breaking with the overall decorum of their conversation that had been maintained up to this point.

"*Fanculo*," he raged. "*Dannato puttano.*"

Logan had touched a nerve, a very raw one. It probably was not a smart move, especially when he didn't know the extent of this man's power, nor what he personally was up against. After all, a man was dead and Logan apparently had been the cause.

In a gesture of contrition and equanimity, he raised his palms off the table and said, "I apologize, and I didn't mean to bring up what I understand could be a sore subject. The thing is, I've already conceded my complicity in the collision, but it was not my intent to injure or kill anyone. My only real crime was to get out of the wrong side of the car in front of a speeding motorcycle. Clearly a case of being in the wrong place at the wrong time. Both him and me."

"You're sticking to your story that you don't know the deceased?" General Lionetti pressed him, his dark eyes boring directly into Logan's.

"Like I keep saying, I don't even know his name. I only just arrived at the airport a few hours ago."

"And you didn't recognize him?"

"Of course not," Logan insisted. "Is there a reason I should have?"

The scowl on the senior officer's face suggested Logan was pushing his luck again. "The identity of the deceased is strictly a government matter," he said. Both of his hands were resting on the table in front of him, and now the little finger of his left hand began to tap gently on the wood surface—some sort of tell, a subconscious indication that something was going through the man's mind.

After a silence that lasted maybe ten seconds, the two officials again put their heads together to confer—hushed, in Italian. Another fifteen seconds passed, and then double that. Eventually General Lionetti drew his glance back to Logan and folded his fingers together, flexed them with a crack that resembled the snap of a twig.

"We're done with you," he announced. "For now."

"Seriously?"

"Do I look as if I'm joking? You are free to go, pending further inquiry."

"You're not going to arrest me?"

"Not at this time. Amanda Knox, like you said. But we have your address, and we know where to find you, so don't make any hasty decisions to leave the city. If you do, we will find you."

"Does that mean I can have my passport back?"

"At the property desk, downstairs."

"And my phone?" Logan asked.

"Sì, signor Logan," the general said. "Everything."

"Is this where you tell me not to leave town?"

The general shot him a dour look that suggested he approved of neither sarcasm nor insolence. "That would be a given," he said.

First thing he did when he hit the sidewalk was check whether he'd received a message from his skittish source that might suggest he was amenable to setting another meeting.

No surprise; there was nothing.

As fate would have it, Logan's Airbnb near the Catacombs of Priscilla was located just over a mile from the Finance Police headquarters. Close enough to walk, which was a good thing because he had not been offered a ride home. "*Non siamo un servizio taxi*," General Lionette had duly informed him, and he'd learned the hard way there was no such thing as a real Uber in the city of Rome, a painful lesson he'd learned the hard way. Still, it was a nice evening and the tree-lined neighborhood looked relatively safe, although he knew from his years in Washington, DC that these things could change from one block to the next. BMWs and Audis parked in front of trendy townhomes could change in an instant to burned-out Buicks on cinder blocks with no wheels.

Graffiti was everywhere: walls, trees, sidewalk, windows. It was an art form that typically was perpetrated at night, which meant taggers with spray paint and lacquer and markers, and Lord knew what else, could be roaming the shadows, practicing their craft—and possibly shaking down naive American tourists stumbling home after a long night on the town, or after hours of grilling at police headquarters for unwittingly causing the death of another man.

Logan had never thought of himself as a killer but now, as he put one foot in front of the other, his eyes darting right and left for any flicker of moment, any hint of sound, the reality began to hit him. He had taken the life of another human being, a painful truth he could never undo, and one that would be with him as long as he lived.

He followed the GPS on his phone as he zigged and zagged his way back to his Airbnb on Via Ostriana. Unlike the streets of the American capital, which Pierre Charles L'Enfant had so thoughtfully laid out in a functional and easy-to-follow grid, many of Rome's older vias and corsos all seemed to curve and wind with no discernible reason. Vespa scooters and tiny cars that could have been manufactured by Tonka straddled the curbs on both sides, leaving just enough room for a single lane of vehicles to pass. Fortunately, there was no traffic at this hour, no high-pitched motorbikes whizzing past. Logan detected the scent of fresh paint, heard the muffled sound of footfalls on pavement. Someone had been interrupted laying down a new tag.

Despite the app on his screen, he looped around several blocks before finally finding the street on which his short-term rental was located. The neighborhood looked different in the pre-dawn darkness, but he finally found the building: a beige brick structure four stories in height, with balconies that extended along the front and the two sides that were visible from the street. Wall AC units groaned as they pumped cold air inside individual flats, and a few lights were visible in the windows of several units higher-up. A large steel door opened into a locked vestibule from a small stone courtyard, and Logan remembered this was where he had met Maria, the hostess of the rental studio he'd reserved for the duration of the summit, and who later lined up the non-Uber ride with her cousin, or whatever.

At a little after four in the morning she was not there to greet him, nor was he expecting her. Nor was he expecting to find his suitcase and carry-on backpack stashed behind a fatigued palm tree that appeared in desperate need of a drink.

As was Logan, especially after his phone app translated the note that was taped to the handle of his rollaboard:

Rental terminated. Leave key in mail slot, per favore.

Chapter 7

Phythian's phone rang ten minutes after he settled into the back of the taxi he'd hired to take him to Paphos International. By no means was it the largest airport serving passengers traveling in or out of the island of Cyprus, nor did it have as varied a selection of departures as the one in the capital city of Nicosia. However, it was much closer and more convenient to the Phoenician Resort and, as a second-tier facility serving mostly cut-rate airlines, it meant fewer cameras mapping and identifying every face in a crowd.

Same with Paris Beauvais Aéroport, where his non-stop was scheduled to land shortly before noon local time. Its location ninety minutes outside the city in the Hauts-de-France region of France made it a bit inconvenient for impatient travelers itching to join the queue at the Eiffel Tower or see the Louvre, but its size and status as a hub for cut-rate air carriers made it more attractive to him than De Gaulle and Orly. Again, there would be fewer cameras and AI algorithms and facial recognition programs to deal with.

He dug his cell out of his jacket pocket, recognized the +376 country code for Andorra, even though the device was a cheap burner.

"I trust you met with Mlle Lamoines?" he asked, getting right to the point. There were no subtleties, no pleasantries.

"Yes, but we did not make our acquaintance quite the way you or I anticipated, sir," was Martin Beaudin's restrained reply.

"What does that mean?"

Beaudin had been dreading this conversation from the moment he'd found Gabrielle Lamoines' body. Phythian could be capricious and arbitrary and, as his deadly reputation suggested, overly punitive to those he suspected of crossing him—or who yielded results less than desired. He cleared his throat, and said, "What it means, sir, is that she's dead."

This was not the response Phythian was expecting, although it did not surprise him. His previous line of work had taught him never to be shocked by an unexpected turn of events, which often led to an unscripted change of plans. Yet Beaudin's words hit him hard, for personal reasons he had not shared with the locksmith from Andorra, and did not intend to.

"Fuck," he said, his words followed by a brief silence, maybe five seconds. Then: "How the hell did this happen?"

"Someone got to her before I did." Beaudin took a short breath, then offered a thumbnail sketch of what he'd found and what he'd done. "What do you want me to do?" he asked when he finished.

Phythian took a second to process what Beaudin had just told him, then said, "Where are you now?"

"Still in Paris, at a place I know."

"Have you been seen?"

"I took deep cover precautions, but you know security these days. There's cameras just about fucking everywhere."

"What about witnesses? This place where you say you are…could anyone have seen you when you arrived?"

"Not likely. It's an old G3 safe house, from before. No one knows it exists."

Phythian interpreted *before* to mean predating the events of two years ago, when he'd put the Greenwich Global Group out of his misery and initiated the regime change he'd mentioned just hours ago to Declan Russell. "Still, I suggest you get yourself anywhere else but there, and as soon as you can."

"I'm catching the first train from Montparnasse," Beaudin replied. "Should be home by mid-afternoon. Meanwhile, what do we do about Ms. Lamoines?"

Good question, to which Phythian had several answers, and none of which Martin Beaudin need concern himself with. "You leave that to me," he said. "And Martin?"

Addressing him by his first name? That was a first, and not necessarily a good sign. "Yes, sir?"

"In no way was this your fault, and I don't hold you to blame. You had no way to know any of this would happen."

"No, sir, but it doesn't erase the fact that it did," Beaudin said, exhaling a minimalist sigh of relief. "Who would want her dead, Mr. Phythian? She seemed like such a bright, beautiful woman, even in death."

"You leave that to me, as well." Phythian closed his eyes, tried to settle the sense of helplessness and complicity that was roiling inside him. He couldn't help but think Gabrielle's death somehow was his fault, that if he had not been directly responsible for ending her father's life, she very likely would still be alive. "Meanwhile, lose the phone and get a new one."

"Consider it done, sir," Beaudin replied, and ended the call.

Isaac Melancon, the very rich and very powerful chairman-slash-chief executive officer of the Clear Bank of Luxembourg, awoke to the unmistakable blast of a train in the distance. He blinked his eyes open, glanced over at his nightstand, and saw the screen of his cell was lit up in the darkness of his bedroom.

Goddamned locomotive ringtone. Never should have let his young nephew download it into his phone.

He recognized the name on the screen and hit the "talk" button. "Is there any remote possibility you have any Goddamned idea what Goddamned time it is?"

"In fact, I do, sir," the man on the other end said, having already anticipated Melancon's sharp rebuke. His name was Noah Wenner, the CEO's executive assistant, and he'd experienced the full wrath of his boss more than once. He glanced at his Rolex—a gift from Melancon for twenty years of faithful service—and ignored the fury on the other end of the call. "In fact, it is five-fourteen in the morning, sir. Eleven-fourteen in New York. Eight-fourteen in L.A."

"Do you place any value whatsoever on your job?" Melancon demanded.

"That's why I'm calling, sir," Wenner explained. "The day you hired me you made it very clear about contacting you at any time, no matter what hour of day or night it is."

"What I believe I told you is you'd better have a damned good reason to call me in the middle of the night—"

"Precisely," Wenner said in a calm and indifferent tone. "And the fact that it's almost five and one-quarter hours after midnight on most of the European continent tells you what?"

Isaac Melancon exhaled a deep, exasperated breath and closed his eyes. Wenner could be such a tedious and annoying prick; he should have fired the asshole years ago. "It tells me you have what you think is a good reason to be risking your employment while I could be trying to rid myself of this God-awful headache."

"They have medications for that, sir."

There was a weary silence on the other end, then Melancon said, "Out with it, Wenner. What's the problem?"

"The problem, sir, is that we've experienced a breach."

"What do you mean, breach?" Melancon turned his head and studied what he could see of his wife, who was gently snuffling on her side of the king-sized bed, curled up in a cave built of pillows and blankets. She usually was a heavy sleeper, but he didn't want to run the risk of waking her with an early morning business issue, so he gently pivoted to an upright position. His toes found their slippers, right and left, and he eased out of the room, quietly closing the door behind him. "You mean a break-in, as in burglary?"

Wenner had always believed that, by the time he hit forty-eight years of age, he would be running his own bank somewhere, not serving as an executive toady to a dreadfully rich and pompous asshole like Isaac Melancon—so much for aspirations and ambition. Some men have the entrepreneurial spirit and the ability to make their dreams come alive, while others seek the security of a comfort zone. In Wenner's case that comfort came with a six-figure salary, profit-sharing plan, and eight weeks holiday each year—and the forfeiture of any sense of initiative he may once have had.

"Not in the strictest sense of the word," he replied. "Security is much too tight for that sort of thing to occur. But it appears that the bank's digital defense system has been compromised, in a major way."

"What do you define as major?"

Wenner mentally braced himself for the tirade he knew was coming. It was part of his job description, something to which he had grown accustomed during his years at the venerable financial institution, particularly when he'd been promoted to his current position. At first, he had believed Melancon's anger and rage were directed at him personally, and that his employment and all those precious benefits were in constant jeopardy; day by day, week to week, and paycheck to paycheck. Over time, however, he came to realize it was just the intractable nature of the imperious dick who occupied the three-thousand square-foot office suite at the top of the steel and glass structure located on Boulevard Royal in the city center.

"Well, sir, I received a phone call about a half hour ago from Gustave Duprel, our chief of information technology here at headquarters. Seems he was performing some routine server maintenance on the storage drives down in D2 when he noticed...well, he found an irregularity that, in his words, defied explanation."

"What kind of fucking irregularity?" Melancon barked into the phone.

"The thing is, sir, he was replacing a board in one of the computers, and noticed an empty slot that shouldn't have been empty."

"And I presume this isn't just some regular slot?"

"No, sir. It's for a high-capacity memory appliance on which highly confidential information is stored in a proprietary way such that it cannot be accessed via any means of interactive or networked communication without our detection."

"I assume what you just told me has a translation—"

Breathe in, breathe out, Wenner told himself. Repeat.

"Yessir," he said. "What I'm trying to tell you is that someone took a memory drive on which several trillion bytes of privileged, restricted information are stored. It was so secure that not even the best hackers in the world could access it without physically removing the thing from the mother board."

"Which you're telling me has been done."

"Unfortunately, yes," Wenner conceded. "And to make matters worse, if that memory card were to fall into the wrong hands...well, it could be exceptionally damaging to this institution and some of our very best depositors."

"What kind of damage, Wenner?"

"We're talking about detailed, encrypted financial data for thousands of numbered accounts. People, companies, even governments that trust us to keep their banking activities private. That's why we made a point of isolating it from any sort of online network."

Melancon fell silent for what seemed like forever, punctuated by the flushing of a toilet. Then he said, "You're telling me that this memory device with all this proprietary information on it has inexplicably gone missing?"

"Not inexplicably, sir. Someone physically entered the computer vault and pulled it."

"You're certain of this?" Melancon demanded, his voice more of a growl now.

"Absolutely. And what's more, we know who did it."

"Tell me."

Wenner arranged his hastily scribbled notes on the desk in front of him. Every evening Isaac Melancon was driven home in a bulletproof Rolls Royce Spectre to his luxury two-story penthouse on the edge of Limpertsberg, with all its gilded antiques and Oriental rugs, while Wenner practically lived in his office at the bank. It even had a couch that folded out, with sheets and blankets and two reasonably comfortable pillows.

"At exactly one minute after midnight yesterday—Saturday morning—someone with a top-level security clearance gained entry to the room housing the central servers," he explained. "This individual removed the memory card from the motherboard, then exited the area the same way he entered. If the maintenance tech hadn't been running a random back-up tonight, the card's disappearance would have gone undetected until the next routine security check."

"That means it's been missing for over twenty-four hours—"

"To be precise, twenty-nine—" he checked his watch "—and four minutes."

"And you said we have a suspect?"

"We do, sir. A video camera recorded the unauthorized entry to the computer room, and the ocular scanners confirmed the break-in. The only person to go into that room during the time in question is a programmer in the cybercurrency department at our Paris branch. A young Polish man named Xenon Gorski, twenty-eight years old."

"Xenon? Isn't that some sort of inert gas or something?" Melancon asked.

"Yessir," Wenner confirmed. "It's one of the elements on the periodic table. But this one is from Gdansk. Graduated from the University of Warsaw with degrees in biochemistry and computer science. Plus, he's fluent in at least five languages. According to his recruitment file, he passed all of his security clearances without a hint of a problem, and he's been a model employee ever since he came on board."

There was a distinct silence on the other end of the phone as Isaac Melancon sorted this out. Eventually he said, "Do we know if anything else is missing?"

"Nothing, sir. Just that one memory card, it appears."

"Good. This Xenon Gorski…if he lives in Paris, why was he here in Luxembourg?"

Wenner again glanced out the window at the lights of the street six floors below; not much to see down there at this hour except the occasional drunks and prostitutes making their way home. "Our records show he was up here last week to serve as a translator for a meeting of Turkish businessmen interested in establishing a corporate account for a holding company. He lives in a flat in a suburb outside Paris, commutes into a branch of the bank Monday through Friday. Rarely late, never sick."

"And he's there now?" Melancon wanted to know.

"Well, that's the thing, sir," Wenner replied, anticipating the wrath of Kahn. "As soon as we learned of his involvement in this…incident…we sent someone to look for him. He hasn't shown up since his expected train arrived back in Paris early last evening."

"Jesus God, man…you have to find him. And that Goddamned card."

"I'm aware, sir. And we will. I've sent one of our top corporate security agents to track him down. Sergei Djokovic. I believe you know him."

"The Bosnia thing," was all Melancon said.

"That is correct, sir."

"Good choice," Melancon said. "Djokovic is a highly persuasive man, and he employs highly persuasive measures. If anyone can take care of this Gorski shit and get that data back, he's our guy."

Chapter 8

"We should have heard from her by now," said the thin man with the absurdly small soul patch that looked like a scrap of Velcro pasted to his chin.

He took a long, slow sip from his bottle of beer—about his eighth or ninth of the night—then wiped his mouth on the sleeve of his blue FIFA sweatshirt. His name was Matthieu Letermé, which sounded infinitely French, even though he had been born and raised in Bruges, Belgium. "This isn't like her at all," he added, nervously running a hand through his stringy black hair.

"Call her again."

This order came from the brawny Swede sitting across the table from him in a basement flat on a narrow street just a few blocks from Parc Josephat in Brussels. Unlike Letermé, he had blonde hair pulled up in a bun, a round face devoid of hair, and wire-rim glasses borrowed from John Lennon. He also had a scar that he claimed was the result of a razor slip years ago, but actually had been caused by the fingernail of a woman who preferred her sex to be consensual. Friends and colleagues simply called him Sten, since his last name—Gustafsson-Jeglum—was far too long for anyone not of Scandinavian descent to try to articulate.

The walls of the dimly lit room were crammed with computer servers and routers and monitors. There was a constant hum of electricity as the latest digital technology reached out to all the distant corners of the globe, their communications securely scrambled and completely untraceable… so far, at least.

Sten took a long sip of the coffee he'd been drinking all night, by now totally wired by the caffeine surging through his bloodstream, quite the opposite of his friend and partner. His *business partner*, as he liked to clarify for anyone who might get the wrong impression about them; in other words, *he/him*.

"Her phone is turned off," Letermé said. He swirled the contents of his bottle as he concentrated intently on the foamy dregs that churned around inside. "I already tried it twice. No—three times."

"That was hours ago," Sten countered. "She might have turned it on again by now."

"If she'd done that, she would have called. I'm really getting worried that something serious has happened to her."

"Nothing has happened. Gabrielle understands the risks, and she takes special precautions whenever she's working a project." Still, Sten was worried about Gabrielle, concerned that this time she had run into unexpected resistance.

"Then where is she?"

"She'll call," Sten assured him. "We know she received the thing, and we'll hear from her when her part of this is done."

"Why didn't you go down to Paris as you usually do?"

"Last-minute change of plans," Sten said, feeling a pang of guilt. "Gabrielle said she had it covered."

That's when Letermé's cell rang, a particularly noxious Amanda Seyfried vocal from *Les Mis*; the movie, not the play.

"You're kidding," Sten said to him, nodding at the phone.

"The ringtone came with it," Letermé replied defensively as he glanced at the screen.

"Is that her?"

"No name; just a number."

"Answer it anyway."

Matthieu punched the connect button and said "*Oui.*"

"*Où est cela?*" Where is it? the man on the other end wanted to know.

"Xenon?" Letermé asked. "Where are you?"

"Waiting for the metro to open," said the multi-lingual programmer who thirty hours ago had boosted a memory card from the Clear Bank of Luxembourg. "I watched the drop for five hours. She never showed."

"She never called here, either," Letermé told him. "Something's wrong."

"I need that drive back," the Polish man with the odd name said. "If I don't return it this morning, I'm as good as dead."

"How often does the bank do a security check?"

"There's no regular schedule, but definitely by noon today." Xenon was mortally wrong about the schedule, but correct in his assessment of his own personal danger. "If that thing is missing when they run the update, the trail leads right back to me."

"That sucks," Letermé mumbled as he took another swig of beer.

"You guys promised me," Xenon whimpered. "You said everything was going to run smooth as silk."

"Are you going to be at this number for a while?"

"What do you think? It's my mobile."

"I'll call you if we hear anything."

"You're not listening to me. I need—"

"You worry too much," Letermé said, cutting him off. "I'm sure there's a reasonable explanation; with Gabrielle there always is."

"Yeah, you're right," Xenon agreed, but the tone of his voice suggested he wasn't convinced. "Call me if you hear from her."

Letermé clicked off and looked at Sten, sitting there across the table from him, keeping his hands warm with his mug of coffee. "Our Polish friend is starting to go ape-shit," he said.

"I wouldn't want to be in his shoes," Sten replied. He swiveled his chair until he was facing the three-screen array connected to his computer, the triple monitors scrolling through tens of thousands of pages of digital documents that had been hacked from a server at the World Court less than twenty-four hours ago. He tapped a couple of keys, then leaned in close and stared at something that had grabbed his attention.

"What're you doing?" Letermé asked him.

The Swede didn't respond right away, just tapped more keys and then scrolled through endless pages of seemingly random code that appeared. "Someone's trying to access our servers," he finally said.

"Someone's always trying to do that," the Belgian reminded him. "Every government agency and news outfit in the western world, twenty-four-seven."

"True. But this one's new, possibly coming out of Luxembourg."

"The bank, you think? Maybe connected to Xenon's drive?"

Sten lifted a shoulder in a slight shrug. "Could be anything, but coincidences scare me."

"Our fearless, paranoid leader."

"Fearless, yes. Paranoid, no." Sten leaned back and scratched the side of his nose, then took another sip of coffee. "We live in a sick world with lots of sick people running sick companies and sick countries. Making obscenely sick amounts of money on the backs of impoverished, sick children, and raping what's left of an already-sick planet. Greed is the scourge of the earth, the real virus that's killing us all. And we—you and me—are the vaccine that's going to cure this very real global pandemic."

"Right," Letermé said absently as he reached into the dorm-sized fridge for another beer.

He'd long ago grown weary of hearing Sten recite his personal mission statement, expound on the *raison d'tre* for hacking into government and financial servers across the globe, then locking them down and demanding a hefty payment to free them up again. Some of their targets coughed up big bucks to regain access to their secrets, while those that didn't suffered dire consequences—and in all cases, terabytes of compromising data were mined and sorted by a rack of servers in the basement room in this run-down neighborhood of Brussels.

"But in the meantime," Letermé continued, "I'm worried about Gabrielle."

"I can't tell you enough how much I appreciate this," Carter Logan said, for the umpteenth time. He was stretched out on a king-sized bed with a mussed duvet and scattered sheets in a hotel room that was not his. A dozen throw pillows were scattered about, along with the contents of a suitcase that had been emptied in a great hurry. "I had nowhere else to turn."

The room, in fact, belonged to Raleigh Durham, who was standing in front of a large mirror fastened to the wall. She was scouring away the remnants of makeup she'd failed to remove from her face last night, in an effort to put on a new face for the day.

"That's what best friends are for," she told him, also for the umpteenth time. "And I'm glad you called. I'll hang the *do not disturb* sign on the doorknob when I leave so you can get some sleep."

Raleigh's nonstop from Dulles had arrived yesterday morning, a few hours before his, and she'd been able to check in to her hotel early. It was a quiet four-star place a block off Via Sistina with a façade of burnished limestone, diamond-shaped panes of glass in the ground floor windows. A simple yet elegant brass plaque with black lettering announced its name: Albergo delle Colombe, which translated to Hotel of Doves. She had managed a few hours of jet-lagged beauty sleep—not that she needed it, as Logan often reminded her—before covering an impromptu state dinner for a handful of America's closest economic allies. As a result, she had worked until close to midnight before staggering back here and tumbling into bed. Then, barely five hours later, had been awakened by Logan, his weary voice asking—*begging*—if she might find it in her heart to let him crash in her room for a few hours.

"I promise I'll be gone by the time you get back," Logan assured her as he examined the curves of her body through her silk bathrobe.

"Like I said, I had to be up early anyway, and this just gives me more time to dry my hair after I take a shower."

"Would you like some company doing that?"

"Any other morning my answer might be yes, but President Mitchell's hosting a prayer breakfast at seven, and I've got to do live cut-ins. After that, I'm on the run for the rest of the day. No telling when I'll be back."

She untied her belt and let the robe fall to the floor, then slipped into the bathroom, giving him just enough of a peek before she kicked the door shut with her heel.

"Maybe you can put two dollars on Rain Check to win?" Logan called after her, wondering if his attempt at humor would fall on deaf ears.

It didn't. "I'll call my bookie," she shot back.

He was sitting on the edge of the bed, the lack of sleep stinging his eyes as if someone had tossed garlic into them. He was thinking how he could always count on Raleigh Durham to come through in a pinch, also thinking about all the pinches he'd needed from her over the past couple of years. There were far too many, yet the hits just kept on coming.

They had met four years ago at a random media event in Washington. After a rubber chicken dinner, they'd enjoyed a few drinks in the hotel bar, then tumbled into bed for what they both naturally assumed was to be a short-term thing; short, as in maybe eight hours; ten if they'd slept in. Their plan might have worked had they not actually found each other entertaining and enjoyable, and it had taken a month or so to come to the mutual conclusion that their relationship was not sustainable. Lubricious, maybe, but that was a distant cousin to heartfelt grand passion, and they both were wise enough to stop trying to be romantic and instead focus on being friends; and maybe, on occasion, enjoy some friendly benefits, if and when the moon and the stars and very busy work schedules aligned.

And yes, her real name was Raleigh Durham—something her parents thought was clever at the time, not giving much thought to the ridicule she might face growing up. Then again, it was nothing compared to being a mixed-race girl raised in the Carolinas, the child of a black father and white mother and thus the target of ignorant bigots who still were furious that long-entrenched miscegenation laws had been overturned, and who'd been force-fed a meal of Jim Crow.

Logan heard her turn on the water in the shower as he stretched out on the bed. He kicked his shoes off and let them tumble to the carpet. Then he closed his eyes and inhaled a deep breath, let his mind travel down a dark desert highway where a cool wind blew the smell of colitas in the air, the mangled words of an old Eagles song cycling through his head until he drifted to sleep. He remained that way for the good part of five minutes, until the water in the bathroom stopped splashing, signaling that Raleigh had finished with her ablutions.

He awoke with a start, momentarily confused by where he was and how he had come to be there. Then it all flooded back to him, and his mind sped through the highlight reel of last night's events. At the top of that lineup was: who was the deceased guy, and why had he been racing along a narrow street in the heart of Rome at a high rate of speed? With a gun? How had the polizia arrived on the scene so quickly? Had they already been chasing him when the accident occurred? Had he committed a crime, maybe some sort of theft? That could explain why—and this was something was really bothering him—the big wigs had become involved and taken over the investigation.

"I figured I'd find you dead to the world out here," Raleigh said as she emerged from the bathroom, stark naked.

It was yet another benefit of being more than just friends.

"I think the rain is stopping," Logan hinted, a lewd gleam in his eye.

"I told you: I have a breakfast," she told him as she ran a soft towel over her mocha skin that a previous boyfriend had regrettably associated with a shade of Pantone brown. "After that, who knows how the day's going to go. Are the cops done with you?"

Logan didn't recall saying a thing to Raleigh about his experience with the polizia, nor did she ask why he'd shown up at her hotel at five in the morning...sober, in fact. Mutual trust was like that, and right now she was preparing for her first big day of the global summit. As members of the fourth estate, he and she traveled parallel tracks in the same business, although Raleigh was totally mainstream and Logan always seemed to work on the fringe of twilight. A couple of years ago, they both had been involved in the same national political incident involving an attempt to kill the president, and Raleigh's live coverage of the event had caused her to be promoted to White House correspondent for a major cable network. By contrast, he'd been arrested as part of the assassination conspiracy, until he eventually was able to prove that he'd actually chased down and tackled the real culprit. All charges against him ultimately were dropped, and he'd had a good run with the *Washington Post* after that, but the innuendos and whispers remained.

Now here she was, rushing off to a prayer breakfast being hosted by an opportunistic president who craved photo ops, while he—Logan— crashed on her four-star hotel bed after he'd been kicked out of a cheap rental studio at the start of the conference because he'd gotten into some kind of flap that had killed a gunman on a speeding Benelli, destroyed a Fiat, and caused another guy who wasn't really an Uber driver to probably lose his shirt, if not his license.

It wasn't all that dire, in fact. He'd had the opportunity to work at one of the finest bastions of journalism in the country—twice, in fact— and welcomed both the challenge and the paycheck. He began to build a reputation for solving unsolved fatalities, settling the unsettled. In the process, various police agencies had been forced to re-open cases and medical examiners reluctantly identified a number of instances where cause of death had been mistakenly attributed to natural causes. He was building a name for himself and the paper, which should have been good news.

But his editors at *The Post* became increasingly concerned about the anonymous tips that were fueling Logan's investigations. The imprecise answers he provided them did not assuage their concerns of accuracy, nor did they fit their strict journalistic requirement of corroboration from two independent sources. In fact, his obfuscation only fueled suspicion on the top floor, causing the paper's legal team to get involved.

The writing on the wall was much plainer than graffiti on the streets of Rome. After much deliberation, he was released from his employment situation—a polite term for being sacked. Fortunately, an independent news organization with fewer concerns about reportorial exactitude jumped at the chance to syndicate his column three times a week, with a slight decrease in base compensation, and a modest travel stipend that made up for it. The deal enabled him to land an agent who was in the process of negotiating a book contract, and a management firm in Hollywood was shopping a concept for a possible streaming docuseries or—*a real long shot*—a feature film.

Meantime, he was still living on the cheap, rooting out the truth wherever a story needed rooting out. In this case, it was Rome and—only by chance—the G20 forum.

"I think they're done with me, at least for now," he said.

Raleigh wriggled into her bra and wandered back into the bathroom. Again she tapped the door closed with her heel. "Well, try to stay out of trouble," she called out as she turned on the hair dryer.

Anything else she said after that was drowned out by the roar of hot air, and this time Logan was sound asleep before she stepped back out.

Chapter 9

Warm croissants and the sweet aroma of fresh butter filled the boulangerie, blending with the scent of freshly brewed coffee and chocolate.

The rain had stopped hours ago. Through the window of the small bakery, Gabrielle Lamoines' killer kept watch on the empty street while the city awakened and patches of clear sky opened up in the early morning clouds. He sat at a round bistro table, his back to the bakery counter, and watched the first early risers rushing past on the sidewalk. Men in suits and thin ties carried umbrellas they probably wouldn't need, while women bundled up in jackets and scarves hustled by on the sidewalk. Taxis and motorbikes and automobiles glided through the narrow street, churning up water from the gutters, horns blaring as they raced toward their destinations.

The hitman took a slow sip of espresso, hot and thick with steamed milk. It scalded the roof of his mouth but he hardly noticed as he allowed his brain to drift back to last night. As with most "mornings after," he felt indifferent to the career choice he had made, other than to momentarily wonder what had caused the target to be put on a hit list. There was always a reason for these things, but the grief and despair suffered by loved ones was not something he tended to be concerned with. He was neither judge nor jury, victim nor witness.

Simply the executioner—although he'd allowed last evening's encounter to cross over the red line of intimacy, and for that he found himself oddly troubled. Not overly so, however; just enough to cause him a wistful moment of poignancy.

He'd only killed one other woman prior to last night, a Russian sparrow who had sexually compromised a German minister of trade and thus, he supposed, fully knew the risks involved in her line of work. He'd felt no remorse when he'd tailed her from the Hungarian Parliament building in Budapest, followed her down Id Antall Jozsef until he found the opportunity to approach her from behind and plunge his Härkila Oder hunting knife through her spine. Once he'd ascertained that she was, indeed, dead, he'd tipped her into the Danube, allowing the current to carry her downstream several miles to a highway overpass. Her body was found several days later washed up on a sandbar, the blade still protruding from her back—and a soggy tarot card in her pocket. *The Tower.*

But Gabrielle Lamoines had been different. She was a known entity, a popular French television personality widely acclaimed for her in-your-face investigative techniques, and her incisive questioning of her guests. Her take-no-prisoners approach had publicly embarrassed a number of pompous corporate executives and government diplomats, and had led to the early retirement of more than a few CEOs and council ministers. Perhaps that was the reason someone had chosen to have her killed, mused the man Interpol referred to as *Le Magicien*, the French translation of the English word "magician."

Not because of his sleight of hand techniques or ability to make a target disappear, but rather in reference to the tarot card he'd left behind at the scene of the first contract he'd fulfilled for his new employer.

"*Monsieur, votre croissant est prêt,*" a voice behind him at the counter said.

He snapped out of his mental fog and retrieved his croissant from the bakery counter. He checked to make sure there was plenty of brioche cream and apple jam, then returned to his table by the window. He settled in and spread a little of both on the tip of the pastry, then mentally replayed the phone conversation he had received just four days ago.

"Good morning," the robotic voice had greeted him, fed through many layers of digital filtering and relayed several times around the world through a complex network of random computers until there was no way to track the call. "There's a movie showing this week, an older film featuring a major French actress. I'd like you to be my guest at the opening."

"Does this film have a title?"

"*Amelie.* It's a classic about a young Parisienne woman who has developed her own sense of justice."

"Sounds interesting," *Le Magicien* had said. "What are the details of the screening?"

"I will send you time and directions, if you're interested. Regular price, as always. Half up front, half when the show is over."

"*Merci*," he'd replied. "I look forward to seeing it."

Twenty-four hours later he received a text message notifying him that a half-million Euros had been transferred into one of his numbered accounts in the Caribbean, and the other half would join it, pending the verified success of his mission.

It wasn't until the evening before last that he'd received the final phone call informing him of the actual identity of the target: Gabrielle Lamoines. He was puzzled but not surprised, having spent some time in Paris over the last few years. Like most residents in the city, he knew who she was, and also knew she had political sympathies that were not necessarily appreciated among the capitalist set. Her television reports had become increasingly critical of business and government, and it was evident she had cultivated high-level sources that made people with money or power exceptionally nervous. Since she was a smart woman and obviously aware that upsetting the status quo engendered significant personal risk, she inherently would know that she posed a threat to certain individuals and institutions.

Despite the last-minute nature of the assignment, Le Magicien's handlers had provided a remarkably comprehensive dossier detailing Mlle Lamoines' daily habits, photos included. It specified where she lived, where she worked, strengths and weaknesses, proclivities and practices, friends and family, favorite restaurants, hangouts—particularly an intimate cocktail lounge in a hotel near her flat that appeared to be a regular rendezvous spot for casual assignations.

That was where he'd decided to make first contact. He would play with her a bit before determining whether he should simply opt for a quick resolution there, or find a more secure place to act. Relax and enjoy the evening, lure her into the comfort of one of his many personas, then escort her willingly back to her apartment.

It was an easy train ride from his chateau outside Montreux, just over four hours via a peculiar dog-leg stop in Chambéry. He'd arrived in the city just before noon yesterday, and he settled on an action plan while savoring the Burgundy snails and beef tartare at his favorite bistro in Rue Cler. He kept his consumption of wine to a minimum, bearing in mind that he would probably imbibe several cocktails later, as he and his target got to know each other. Once she'd fallen for his charms and succumbed to his hypnotic proficiencies, she'd lose all resistance, and would have no choice but to invite her back to her place.

He recalled how she'd asked him about the gun as he softly walked back across the carpeted floor and pointed it at her. She had threatened to scream but of course she hadn't, because by then she was already dead. It hadn't taken him long to then cleanse both the room and her body, thoroughly enough for an initial investigation, but probably not for a subsequent—and probably much more thorough—forensics exam. No matter: he'd been told by someone who knew such things—alas, now deceased—that his DNA profile had yet to be entered into any of the global databases designed for just that sort of thing, and, even if it were, he was already wanted on four continents for activities that warranted a "shoot on sight" directive from a dozen intelligence agencies.

He could have lifted her cellphone and the SD card he'd found in her otherwise empty diaphragm case, but he had no interest in running a side hack. Other contractors made a tidy sum pawning stolen belongings of their victims or auctioning them to the highest bidder, but he considered double-dipping a gross violation of the job…and too risky.

At the root of it all, Le Magicien was a man of principle, content to bide his time at this lovely *boulangerie*, sipping his coffee and nibbling a croissant, waiting until the bank in Grand Cayman opened and he could talk to an actual, live human being. He'd already confirmed that the second installment of a half million Euros had been sent via digital transfer from the Clear Bank of Luxembourg, but he didn't trust computers. Didn't trust people, either, but when important matters were on the hook it was best to go for personal verification.

The rain that had dampened the streets of Paris last night had cleared out by the time Phythian stepped off the passenger shuttle at the Porte Maillot bus terminal.

The public transport from the airport into the city was a minor annoyance, but it allowed a degree of anonymity that trains and other means of mass conveyance didn't necessarily provide. Phythian had squeezed into a seat beside a middle-aged man in a threadbare suit with a single piece of carryon luggage, who seemed just as disinclined to engage in conversation as he was. A quick mental probe indicated he was on a singles vacation, having lost his wife a few years earlier after a long bout with lymphoma. In other words, sad and depressed, and definitely not a threat.

As often was the case when he had time on his hands and no easy way to spend it, Phythian retreated into his past and contemplated how he had come to be where he was, and *who he was*—a former contract killer on the run, wanted by at least a dozen countries and acronym agencies that existed on the darker side of legitimacy. He'd completed countless missions during his years with the Greenwich Global Group, each and every time using the extrasensory powers that his handlers at The Farm had sharpened in his mind. He'd had no idea at the time—although he should have—that the vitamins and supplements they were feeding him from the day he arrived also served to dull the threads of conscience that would prevent any normal man from taking another life. Thus, over the ensuing years, as he went about his new line of wet work with methodical precision, he never gave his new profession—or his employer—much thought.

A random occurrence on a street near the Vatican in Rome had changed all that. One morning he'd found himself standing at a crosswalk next to a Cardinal whose mind kept drifting fondly to the young boy he'd raped the night before, and the night before that. Without warning, and much to the horror of the onlookers around him, His Eminence inexplicably had stepped in front of an oncoming truck and was killed instantly. As was bound to happen, the G3 executive board quickly learned of the incident, as well as Phythian's presence at the scene and, after a short meeting, its five members determined that the non-sanctioned execution was a gross violation of its code of conduct. In a closed session they unanimously decided to sever his employment and terminate all ties with him, in the strictest sense of the word.

Their plot failed in spectacular fashion, and his liberation from their grip gradually permitted Phythian to reclaim his moral compass, one new marvelous day at a time. It had taken the warmth of the African sun, the parade of elephants and giraffes and zebras through his camp, the give-and-take of the seasons for him to gradually understand all that had been seized from him, and all he stood to regain. Each morning he awoke to the lush Serengeti and its fresh scent of grass, just a trace of dust in the gentle wind, and found himself one day closer to returning to the man he had been before his first encounter with the G3 more than two decades ago, on a BART train racing through a tunnel under San Francisco Bay.

There he had remained in harmony with the earth until the past caught up with him. Then, two years ago, an innocent woman had accidentally stumbled upon a deadly secret, one so poisonous that the G3 and all its ancillary partners decided it must be protected at all costs. And which, in the process, necessitated her immediate death. In his previous life Phythian wouldn't have given the matter a second thought, but years of personal reflection—and thousands of days experiencing the cycle of life in his remote corner of Tanzania—had imbued him with a renewed sense of being.

Five days later the Greenwich Global Group had ceased to exist, along with its entire governing board and its nonagenarian Chairman.

Now here he was, revisiting the transgressions of his past, methodically meting out retribution to those clients who had hired him—through the G3—to assassinate a government official, business competitor, or a personal rival, whoever was worth the hefty price tag that went with a clean and efficient hit.

Such was the case with Declan Russell last night. The erstwhile billionaire had paid two million dollars for the execution of Andre Lamoines, and now that the G3 was under new management—taken private, one might say—it had been his turn to atone for past sins.

Phythian was abundantly aware that his purpose was duplicitous at best, and hypocritical at least. By all counts, he should have been at the front of the line of trespassers, been the first one to take that fatal step. The spiritual detritus of his murderous actions haunted him day and night, and he had made a personal pledge to deal with it, in its own time and its own way.

But...first things first.

After getting off the shuttle, Phythian made a point of blending in with other passengers as he navigated his way through the crowded bus terminal. The station served the nearby Palais des Congrès de Paris, and was at the center of a traffic roundabout centered by a small park that offered a glimpse down the Champs Elysees to the Arc de Triomphe in one direction, and the arches of La Defense in the other. An app on his phone told him that he could catch the 1 line into the heart of the city, whereupon a change to the 4 would bring him to Gabrielle Lamoines' St. Germain neighborhood.

His cellphone pinged as he was crossing Boulevard Pereire: Martin Beaudin again, announcing that his train had just pulled into the station in Bordeaux and he was taking a cigarette break.

"Since when do you smoke?" Phythian pressed him.

"I don't, but everyone on the train smells of the damned things."

"Is this a new phone?"

"One of six I purchased before I boarded," Beaudin assured him.

"Were you followed?" Phythian asked, his eyes fixed on the sidewalk as he made his way to the limestone structure that housed the entrance to the metro station.

Beaudin was the only living holdover from the now-defunct Greenwich Global Group. As one of the former key executives within the organization, he easily could have been part of the purge, but he'd showed a clear understanding of Phythian's vision for regime change—appreciated it, even—and had assisted him in shifting its focus to one more attuned to philanthropy and beneficence. Even if it did mean the occasional termination of a former G3 client.

"Not a chance," he assured Phythian now. "I'm quite certain."

"And the items you mentioned before?"

"Safe. I'll let you know their contents as soon as I'm home and have the opportunity to go through them."

"Do that. And Beaudin?"

"Yes, sir?"

"I appreciate you coming all the way to Paris to take care of this, even if the outcome wasn't as planned."

"The sword of justice has no scabbard," Beaudin replied.

Gabrielle's flat was located on a narrow one-way street a block from the Saint Germain des Prés metro stop. It was an upscale neighborhood in the Sixth Arrondissement, the heart of the city's Rive Gauche and cluttered with quaint boutiques, patisseries, wine shops, and corner cafés.

As Phythian emerged from the station he inhaled the thick aroma of coffee, mixed with warm bread and onion soup. The distinct two-note wail of a police siren announced an official Peugeot several seconds before it veered around the corner, lights flashing. It skidded to a stop in front of the entrance to her building and two uniformed officers got out. He watched as they approached the double wood doors, which appeared to be locked, and one of them started hitting the buttons for residences upstairs. A tenant must have answered because the *policier* leaned close to a speaker and began explaining to whoever was listening that the police were downstairs, trying to get in. The person must have believed them, because the two officers pushed through the door and disappeared into the darkened vestibule.

A minute later a second vehicle pulled up behind the first and two more officers went through a similar routine. None of them noticed Phythian lurking in the darkness of a doorway just ten meters away on the other side of the street, his collar pulled up around his neck against a morning that couldn't decide if it wanted to be chilly or warm. He'd hoped to be able to take a quick look through Gabrielle's home before the gendarmerie arrived, try to get some sort of idea about her killer that Beaudin might have missed, but someone must have discovered her body—a friend or colleague, perhaps, or maybe a housekeeper—and called in a report. He appreciated that Beaudin had made a thorough sweep, but he would have liked to have given the flat his own personal examination. An opportunity that, with the arrival of the authorities, now was out of the question.

Phythian lingered on the street while the four cops made their way upstairs to Gabrielle's flat, which he knew was tucked under the rafters on the top floor. Beaudin had located the address online, then cross-referenced it with an old real estate listing that included a dozen photos from the last time it was on the market, about three years ago. He also had provided a floorplan that Phythian had committed to memory, so he knew where the front door was located in respect to the bedroom, as well as the most likely position of the bed where she had died.

A few moments later he was able to isolate the brainwaves of the four officers from the surrounding mental chatter and penetrate their cerebral processes. He'd learned years ago at The Farm that the frontal lobe of the cerebrum was the region of the brain responsible for most higher cognitive skills, including thinking, planning, problem solving, and organizing, as well as certain aspects of personality and emotions. The parietal lobe— separated from the frontal by the parieto-occipito sulcus—was critically involved with sensory processes, attention, and language, although other regions of the brain contributed to these functions, as well.

The doctors and researchers at The Farm—part of a clandestine government program known as MINDGAZE—had conducted a full range of MRIs and SPECT scans to help them understand Phythian's unexplainable extrasensory abilities, all of which tested way off any spectrum they might have devised for such purposes. As they studied his brain and mapped his paranormal skills, they discovered a unique and puzzling aptitude to connect with specific bundles of neurons in the frontal lobe where basic cerebration originated, prior to its conversion to linguistic communication. In other words, his clairvoyant ability allowed him to perceive cognition before it ever was translated into the spoken word, which was critical if he wasn't conversant in the language of the person whose mind he was tapping. It didn't matter if a person spoke English, Russian, or Swahili—or French.

When he'd still been employed by the G3, his tested range of sibylline perception—aka remote viewing—hovered around a thousand yards. The officers upstairs were well within that range, which meant that as he isolated their thought patterns, he could process Gabrielle's death scene through their minds. This was not as effective as being in the room himself, but this was neither the time nor place to intrude on an official investigation. He was risking enough just being here in this city of over two million people, where several dozen operatives from various intelligence agencies—aided by twenty-five thousand lenses positioned just about everywhere—would love to get their hands on him.

That was, if the rumors of Phythian's existence proved to be true.

Best to remain in the shadows and tune in to what was being said— and, much more important, being thought.

Chapter 10

In another time and possibly another life, Georgy Sokolov would have been a happy and content Russian.

Many men would have given their left nut to have what he'd had: assets topping twelve figures in U.S. dollars, luxurious estates and penthouses in exotic locales all over the world. Lovely women less than half his age wandering around his villa in swim wear that left nothing to the imagination, his just for the asking. The villa itself was fifteen thousand square feet of post-modern living space situated in six buildings on eighteen oceanfront acres on the exclusive southwest shore of Ibiza. Stone and glass and tiles, an expansive horizon pool inset with glass jewels that reflected the sun and glimmered like the Milky Way at night. Full staff and an on-call Michelin two-star chef, exclusive satellite hook-up for secure communications with anyone on the planet. Nothing could be finer in the world of the successful Muscovite billionaire, nothing except for the fact that it was his *only* world. Most of his liquid assets had been frozen over a decade ago when the then-American president took action over the Kremlin's annexation of Crimea. Then, the subsequent ill-advised invasion of Ukraine had all but wiped out his equity positions and off-shore accounts. Gone were his properties in Bellagio, Miami, London, and St. Barth, and he had no idea where his luxury yacht was—or his collection of rare and priceless automobiles. He still had his four passports, but what good would they do him if he had nowhere to go?

What really ate at his brain—every hour of every day—was the death of his son. It had been over two years since Vasily had been felled by a sniper's bullet, estimated by the forensic pathologist who performed the autopsy as a .50-caliber round, although it had never been found. Thirty-two years old, his life snatched from him by a single pull of the trigger. No matter that he'd been illegally hunting elephants in Tarangire

National Park; he was a good man and heir to Georgy's vast fortune and business entities.

Since that day he'd received no word about the *ublyudok* who had pulled the trigger. He'd paid two million dollars up front to a trusted associate who had promised to take care of the matter but, so far, he'd heard nothing; not from his own security team, nor from the associate herself who, mysteriously—*conveniently?*—had disappeared into the ether without leaving a trace.

"Has been two fucking years," he yelled into the phone; in Russian, of course, although he had long ago come to the conclusion that he should cut his ties to the mother country. Loyalty to the nutjob in the Kremlin had gotten him nowhere, and four of his closest friends had inexplicably taken flight from the windows of their hotel rooms. The Russian flew, as it had come to be known. "No one simply disappear like that. Must be *some-fucking-where.*"

"Like I've told you before, the two spotters were last seen renting car in Mombasa," the voice on the other end replied. His name was Galkin, and at one time he'd been a high-ranking security officer in the FSB. Now he was a private thug for hire, and Sokolov was paying him far too much money to have gotten absolutely no results in his attempt to track down his son's killer.

"And where is Mombasa?" Sokolov demanded. He was seated on a step in the shallow end of the pool, a glass of untouched orange juice set on the stone apron beside him.

"Is coastal city in Kenya."

"And what of my contractor?" the oligarch pressed him. "Woman named Diana Petrie."

"Last spotted at Nairobi Airport, two years ago. Got in cab, has not been seen since."

"Goddammit," Sokolov fumed. "I want her found. And the man who killed my son."

"*Da ser,*" the facilitator named Galkin said. "I will make happen."

The former billionaire made a guttural grunt, then ended the call. He felt like hurling the phone over the edge of the massive pool patio onto the rocks below. Two years and millions of dollars he could hardly spare, and still nothing to show for his investment. He glanced at the glass of juice, was about to take a sip when the phone rang again.

"What?" he snapped, assuming it was Galkin again.

"*Georgy, moy tovarishch,*" the man on the other end greeted him, using almost all the Russian words he'd learned since he'd come to know Georgy Sokolov. The caller's name was Allesandro Bortolotti, and over the past year he'd grown indebted to the beleaguered Russian in ways he was beginning to regret. Switching to English, he added, "How is life in paradise?"

Paradise was hardly the word for it, since the Russian oligarch felt like a prisoner within his own home—grand and glorious as it was. He had an image to protect, however, one that he must not reveal to be either spiritually or financially bereft, so he replied, "As fine as life can be, Signore Bortolotti. I presume all is proceeding according to plan?"

"A few moving parts still getting settled, but everything will be ready. All will go as clock work."

"You have the official details?" Sokolov asked.

"Minute-by minute, and all travel routes," Bortolotti confirmed. "Got them from a friend in AISE."

"What's that?"

"Agenzia Informazioni e Sicurezza Esterna. Secret Service."

"And the product?" the Russian asked. "To cover my investment?"

Sokolov was not a man one ever wished to misdirect with a lie, and those who did so tended to meet with tragic circumstances. "Safely tucked away in a shipment of bananas," Bortolotti replied. "Arrives tomorrow night."

"Make sure that it does," the Russian oligarch said. "You're cutting close as is."

"As I said, clockwork."

"Good. Talk later."

Sokolov hung up, sensed a turning point at hand. If the western powers wouldn't return to him what was rightly his, it was up to him to get revenge on their politics and self-righteous bullshit.

This time he did take a sip of juice, as an old Russian proverb came to mind: "A lucky man can stumble upon a treasure while an unlucky one can't even find a mushroom."

Allesandro Bortolotti summoned up every measure of restraint not to throw his phone against the wall. Furious didn't come close to describing how he felt—furious and distraught, even fearful, because he had just lied to the Russian, who was known for his brutal temper, as well as the lengths he would go and the measures he took to make an example of those who crossed him.

Not everything, however, was a lie. Indeed, he had procured the moment-by-moment schedule of the official events at the G20 meeting in Rome, starting with a prayer breakfast held by the U.S. president that very morning...and yes, he also had been given the travel route for all participants to and from their respective hotels to the Nuvola Congress Centre and the nearby Palazzo dei Congressi. The city's entire EUR district had been designated a "red zone" for the global summit, and Italian security had sealed off a 10-square kilometer area and had stationed armed police snipers on strategic rooftops throughout the area; twenty-four/seven, until the gathering ended.

It all amounted to a strategic challenge for anyone planning what Bortolotti had in mind. His scheme would work not only because it was foreordained, but because he had everything in place to ensure it would be a resounding success...except for one thing.

Just before he'd spoken with Sokolov, he'd again tried the number of the man with whom he had arranged the delivery of a great quantity of methamphetamine and fentanyl from a facilitator in Moldova. The shipment was to be delivered that morning to a secure warehouse at the port of Pescara on the Adriatic Sea, two hours east of Rome, with a street value of twenty million Euros, almost exactly what he owed the Russian prick for advancing the funds he'd needed in order to buy the guns and the uniforms and coms equipment. It was all critical to the success of his scheme, and the glorious victory he'd worked for years to achieve.

"*Dove cazzo è finito?*" he screamed at Mateo Tufino, his personal attaché who held a rank similar to that of major within Bortolotti's ad hoc militia. His words translating to "where the fuck is it?"

"I'm working on it, sir," the young man standing next to him responded in Italian, holding his arms and hands tight against his body in an effort not to show how much they were trembling. Bortolotti's rage was legendary, as was his hair-trigger inclination to use the Beretta 92 FS holstered at his waist to cause significant harm to those who delivered unacceptable news.

"I need that shipment today," Bortolotti raged on. A thick vein in his neck—maybe the carotid—looked as if it were about to burst, and if that happened…well, such a thing could create a new set of problems for Tufino, but possibly solve many at the same time. "Understand?"

Tufino nodded quickly; yes, he understood. But he also was faced with a more immediate issue that could cause heads to roll, his very likely being among the first—a head he rather liked, covered with black hair slicked back like that singer-turned-actor Michele Morrone who had over a million YouTube followers. And only God knew how many women fawning over him.

"I've made some calls, and there seems to be a development, sir," he ventured.

"What sort of development?"

"While you were on the phone with the *Tsar*—" Tufino's private nickname for the insufferable Russian "—I spoke with my source inside the Guardia di Finanza."

"What the fuck do they have to do with this?"

"Just hear me out, signore. It appears that a person of great interest to both of us met with a freak accident last night."

"An accident?" Bortolotti asked. "What sort of accident?"

"A motorcycle ran into a car that was double-parked on the street. I'm told the biker died at the scene."

"And this has to do with our immediate problem, *why*?"

"Well, sir, they're not releasing the man's name yet. Next of kin, and all that. But what I'm hearing—unofficially—is it's Santoro."

"*No, mi prendi per il culo!*" Bortolotti seethed. "That can't be—"

"I'm just telling you what I'm hearing, is all," Tufino said.

"*Cazzo!* You're sure of this?"

"The driver had no license on him, but they ran his prints at the scene."

Bortolotti took a moment to throttle down his blood pressure and get his bulging vein under control. Then he said, "How did this 'accident' happen?"

"Looks like he drove into a car door just as someone was getting out. Head crushed like a melon."

"*Cazzo.* What the fuck do you think he did with my shipment?"

"I'm afraid I don't know, sir," Tufino replied. "But I'm working on it."

"I need that delivery. Today."

"*Si, signore.*"

The unspoken backstory was that Stefano Santoro was an inconvenient yet necessary intermediary for anyone who was trying to move a large quantity of illicit goods, without the government or the many tendrils of organized crime getting wind of it. He had disappeared a few years back during a raid in the southern region of Calabria, and hadn't been seen alive—or in pieces—since then. State police had arrested hundreds of politicians, lawyers, and even a local police chief in an operation that took down a crime syndicate known as 'Ndrangheta, and there were rumors that several not-so-loyal members of the organization had been flipped as confidential informants. Several cousins in Santoro's family had been found dead in the weeks that followed, various random appendages missing and one victim unceremoniously ripped open from stem to stern with his intestines spilling out.

"Do they think this freak accident last night could have been a hit?"

"I don't know, but it was only a matter of time before fate caught up to him," Tufino replied.

"I don't give a fuck about Santoro," Bortolotti said, spittle forming on his lips. "Just find my goddamned drugs."

He massaged his forehead with his fingertips while Tufino hustled out of the room, then crossed to a window set deep into the thick stone wall that offered a one-eighty view of the valley and the woodlands beyond.

This time of year, the poplars and lindens and birches formed a green quilt over the rolling hills, framing the meadows where deer and rabbits roamed, and pheasants furiously pounded their wings to take flight. This hunting camp had been in his wife's family for as long as the house and outbuildings had been here, at least three hundred years, until ownership had conveyed to him when she had passed away two winters ago.

His eyes fell on the dirt road that wound along the edge of a shallow ravine in the distance, out near the main road that led to Anghiari. A cloud of dust was rising in the air where vineyards once produced an abundant harvest of Sangiovese grapes, very earthy and rustic, but now the terraced land lay fallow and yielded a harvest mostly of weeds and rocks. Bortolotti had been anticipating the arrival of the man in the Alfa Romeo that was kicking up the soil, angry that there wasn't better news to share with him.

Five minutes later the visitor from the black car—a Giulia, not too different from what the local polizia drove—entered the upstairs library Bortolotti had converted to a temporary staging area.

A large table occupied the center of the room with a massive map of Rome spread out on it. Colored markers indicated where security forces had been positioned in and around the city: red was for military troops, black was for police snipers, yellow meant tanks and other heavy artillery. Set to one side were two laptop computers, each of them connected to a satellite uplink behind the house, camouflaged by a thick wall of cypress near one of the stone outbuildings. Individual flat-screen monitors were tied in to the computers, independently tracking the progress of several dozen vehicles that were working their way southward across the Italian countryside—plus, two boats crossing the Adriatic Sea, one each from Croatia and Montenegro.

Each of them was transporting volunteers who would be participating in tomorrow's activities—and none of them, alas, carrying the drugs that Sokolov had spoken of.

"Allesandro," the newcomer said as he strolled through the open doorway, removing a stylish Homburg from his head and holding it carefully in his hand. The hat was blood red, the color matching that of the cloth square tucked into the breast pocket of his hand-tailored sport coat, a weathered brass skeleton key tucked into the band. "Tell me the good word."

It was his standard greeting, reflecting a typically congenial frame of mind and self-possessed outlook on life. But this morning Bortolotti was in no mood for folksy banter, so he said, "I was rather hoping you'd be bringing that yourself," he said.

"I detect uneasiness in your voice, my friend. That would be very unlike you, on this day in particular."

The man's name was Renato Azzone, and when he wasn't driving several hours north of Rome on a weekday morning at the start of a major global economic summit, he served as Deputy Secretary General of the Governate for Vatican City State. This was a long title to describe what essentially was equal to vice president in many countries, or lieutenant governor in one of America's fifty states. A native of the city of Bergamo in the Lombardy region of northern Italy, he was a lawyer by profession, although he was not visiting his friend Bortolotti out of any immediate legal concerns. Nor was this an official visit, as indicated by the fact that he was driving his own automobile. One that was badly in need of a tune-up and new tires.

"This particular day is a good reminder that if something can go wrong, it will," Bortolotti replied. "But I did not invite you all the way out here to this remote stretch of our beautiful country to bother you with trifles."

"No, sir," Azzone said as he carefully set his hat on the back of a wooden chair. "In fact, it was a pleasant drive, and quite refreshing to get away from the problems at the palace." Referring to the Palazzo del Governatorato, the seat of the Pontifical Commission for Vatican City State located in the private gardens just a stone's throw from St. Peter's Basilica.

"And everything is still on schedule?"

"As well as you might expect with any government. The Church has many working parts, all moving at their own independent pace." He allowed his eyes to settle on a tumbler of amber liquid that was set on a table near where Bortolotti was standing, next to the window. He tried not to judge his friend, who was carrying on his shoulders the weight of Janus, the Roman god of new beginnings and transition—the fulcrum between the great dualities of light and dark, love and hate, or, in this case, peace and violence. "But yes," he said at length. "It appears everything we have spoken about is advancing according to design."

"And His Holiness?"

"The Pope is preoccupied by his own minutiae, as you know. What he doesn't care to know cannot possibly hurt him."

"Yet, it would be reassuring to have his blessing," Bortolotti pressed his friend of many decades. "Or at least his tacit support."

"He'll come around if and when he sees how your triumph benefits the Church," Azzone assured him. "We're pressing for him to give his support in his Sunday address. By that time the outcome will be known, and people will be cheering your ascendancy in the streets. Meanwhile, I've kept our plans very close to the vest, since the Vatican tends to leak from the top down."

Bortolotti let out a low chortle, but it did little to ease his mood. Someone, *somewhere*, had to have leaked information about the shipment of drugs that now was missing, a snafu that somehow, in *some way*, he now believed was connected to a deceased mafioso traitor.

"The Sabbath is a long way off," he said. "A lot can happen between now and then."

Azzone nodded, but said nothing. The room seemed so quiet, so unassuming as the computer drives uploaded and downloaded data, shifting information around a small private network that was designed to avoid spilling any "chatter" into the global intelligence funnel. It was of paramount importance that there be no cracks, no seepage, not one hint of what was coming in the next forty-eight hours.

Xenon Gorski, the multi-lingual computer programmer from Warsaw had a big problem, and he was spiraling out of his mind with fear.

He had done far more than simply pilfer a memory device that housed several terabytes of highly sensitive transactions for thousands of numbered investment accounts. That was bad enough, but he'd physically broken into the bank's cloud vault, using his own ID and his own retina for the scanner. It was the only way he could have accessed the mainframe and removed the portable drive without soliciting the assistance of someone from the IT department. He'd had no choice but to leave a trail of digital breadcrumbs that would have made even Hansel and Gretel happy, and now those crumbs would lead right back to him, and probably already had. He'd planned on erasing all traces when he replaced the card he had given to Gabrielle, but when she hadn't shown up at the drop to return it to him...well, *merde*.

At that moment he was sitting on a bench inside Gare St. Lazarre, wedged in between an old woman in a dirty cloth coat with a scarf pulled tightly over her head, and a disheveled drifter in soiled jeans and sweatshirt who smelled like a public toilet. After reluctantly concluding last night that Gabrielle was a no-show, Xenon first had thought he would just go back to his grungy flat out in Gagny, figure out a plan to deal with the fiasco at the bank.

As soon as the Metro opened, he had boarded the first train that pulled into the station, then immediately realized the idiocy of that decision. His home was the first place anyone would look for him, and it would be suicide to go there. Instead, he transferred to another line and headed for the train station where, after consulting a timetable, he bought a ticket to Grenoble. He had an old flame from university who lived there—or she had, the last time he'd seen her—and she might take pity on him. It was a place he figured no one would think of looking for him, and he could disappear for a while...at least until his money ran out.

He'd been waiting on the platform for almost an hour, impatiently listening for the dispatcher to announce from which track the 10:04 to

Lyon would be leaving. He would have preferred to be traveling back to Warsaw, put this whole Goddamned mess behind him, but returning to Poland wasn't an option; not anymore, not after the business with the Turks.

"*Monsieur Gorski,*" he heard a voice say behind him. In fact, he'd almost missed it because he wasn't expecting anyone to recognize him—or to find him so damned fast. "*Vient s'il vous plaît avec moi.*"

Gorski didn't move, didn't say anything. There was nothing to do or say.

"*Monsieur Gorski, écoutez-moi,*" the voice said again, almost a whisper in his ear.

That's when he felt the gun pressed directly into his spine.

"Come with me," the voice insisted, still speaking French. "I don't wish to shoot you here in the train station, but I will if I have to."

Xenon Gorski did all he could not to urinate in his jeans as he slowly stood up. The man behind him was gripping his shoulder firmly with one hand, holding the barrel of the gun firmly between his T7 and T8 with the other.

"Please…what's this about?" Xenon finally managed to say. "Who are you?"

"A man you don't want to fuck with. Let's go."

No one paid any attention to them as they left the train station, but as they were pushing their way through the double glass doors Xenon heard the overhead sound system announce, "*le train pour Lyon part comme prévu huit.*" The train for Lyon is leaving on track eight.

Instead of boarding the train, instead of escaping this personal hell he'd dug for himself, Xenon Gorski ended up in the back seat of a panel van. The man with the gun was pressed up beside him, the hard barrel now jammed into his ribs. Another man, this one in a black leather jacket and a gray beret, was sitting up front, periodically glancing at him in the rear-view mirror as they drove up Rue de Rome, then hung a right on Rue de Dames.

Double merde. He had been so close to getting out of this damned city, and now he was a dead man. Of that he was quite sure.

Xenon lost track of how many left and right turns they made. He did not recognize this part of Paris, and his usually accurate sense of direction quickly got turned around. He had lived in the city for close to a year, appreciated the cosmopolitan style and the food and the women, but he still didn't think of it as home. Fluent in five languages, he'd had a good job at the bank, but he'd royally screwed that deal. The burly Swede named Sten had promised him twenty thousand Euros, which had sounded like a lot of money at the time, for one small memory card that he'd return the following day. It would have allowed him to make a fresh start: no more card games, no more drugs, and no more Turkish thugs pounding on his door at two in the morning demanding that he pay up now, or else.

"What's this about?" he asked the man with the gun. "Where are we going?"

"Why do you care?" the man answered, his breath stinking of sauteed onions. "No one will miss you."

"Is it about the money?" Xenon pressed, again feeling as if were about to pee his pants, thinking, *please, not here. Not in the car. They'll kill me for sure.*

"In the end it's always about money."

"I have what you want," Xenon pleaded. "Back at my place." Hoping beyond hope this was about his mounting debts and not the theft at the bank.

"It is better to die for the truth than to live for a lie," the man said, pressing the gun even further into his ribs. "No more lies."

This time Xenon's bladder finally did let go.

"Wake up," Sten Gustafsson-Jeglum said, shaking Letermé's shoulder. "You need to see this."

Matthieu Letermé was sleeping off the two six-packs he'd consumed overnight, having finished the last bottle just as his chin finally dropped to his chest in a giant snort of sleep. The sound of glass clattering to the floor did not rouse him, and now—almost five hours later—he still seemed impervious to noise.

"Matthieu—wake up!" the Swede shouted at him again, this time cuffing the side of his head with the palm of his hand. "Now!"

Letermé's head rocked from the force of Sten's blow and his eyes flicked open. He blinked several times and put a hand to his ear, wondering why it all of a sudden was ringing. "What the—?"

"Take a look at the screen," Sten said, swiveling his hungover friend around in his chair. "It's Gabrielle. She's dead."

"What? Gabrielle's dead? When...how—?"

"Check it out," Sten told him, pointing to the story that was open on the browser in front of him. His finger was visibly shaking from the shock of seeing her name in the lead sentence of the article.

Letermé still didn't know what was going on, what Sten was talking about—or why his head was throbbing. He kneaded his temples with his fingertips, then leaned forward and stared at the headline that jumped out at him from the middle screen of the three-monitor array.

FRENCH TV REPORTER FOUND DEAD IN APARTMENT

PARIS – Well-known television reporter and French media celebrity Gabrielle Lamoines was found dead in her Paris home this morning, a police spokesperson told the BBC. Ms. Lamoines, age 35, worked for France 365, and recently had been promoted to noontime anchor at the network. Police said she died from a single gunshot wound to the head and, since no weapon was found at the scene, authorities strongly suspect foul play was involved...

"*Mon Dieu*," Letermé said as he rubbed his eyes with the heels of his hands, as if that might somehow alter the horrific news. "See? I was right... something was dreadfully wrong."

"Seems like," Sten conceded. He squeezed his eyes shut to press back any hint of a tear, then said, "But there was nothing we could do. By that time, she most likely was already dead."

The scrawny Belgian said nothing as he tried to sort through his thoughts, no easy feat because of all the alcohol that still coursed through his veins. He finished reading the article, then said, "It's all because of that fucking memory card."

"We don't know that—"

"Shit, man...a single shot to the forehead? You think that was just some lover's spat?"

The color had drained from Sten's face and he chewed nervously on his lower lip. He prided himself on not being an emotional man, but the news story had sent his system into shock.

"Could be anything," he said absently.

"You were banging her, right?" Letermé asked.

"Shit, man...don't put it like that—"

"Yeah, I'm sorry. It's the beer talking. But if it wasn't for that card… well, who the fuck do you think killed her?"

At this point Sten didn't know what to think. He should have been with Gabrielle last night, but she'd texted him about a change in plans. She'd assured him it was a simple job: copy the contents of the card and email him the contents, then get it back to Xenon in plenty of time for him to put it back. Now Gabrielle was dead, there was no sign of any text or email, and Xenon Gorski was up to his Polish ass in trouble.

He leaned back in his chair and shook his head from side to side, as if trying to make sense from such a senseless act. "Information is the currency of democracy," he eventually said. "But you ask me—and you did—whoever did this must have had a line on what we were doing."

"*Oui*. Which means that we could have red laser dots targeting us, too."

"I've been thinking about that," Sten conceded. "Thinking maybe it's time we put a lot of gone between us and whatever shit is starting to come down."

Chapter 11

"I apologize for making you push me like this," the overweight woman said, glancing over her shoulder at the man whose hands were wrapped around the rubber grips of her wheelchair. "This damned diabetes, it has taken my life away."

Her name was Jantine Hamel, and Rōnin Phythian knew it was a lot more than diabetes that had made her life so miserable over the decades. A former working girl from De Wallen, the largest and best-known red-light district in Amsterdam, she had arrived in Paris more than thirty years ago. She quickly had become a fixture in the sex trade, running girls of all nationalities and types in the Pigalle neighborhood of Paris. Genetics, a weakness for dark chocolate and white Russians, and a prolonged bout with a particularly nasty STD had caused her to lose both her feet, then her legs below the knees. Now she was relegated to a sedentary existence in a rolling chair that could barely contain her ample girth.

"Nothing in the world could ever take away your exquisite beauty and elegance, madame," Phythian told her.

They both knew he was lying, and that was okay. Mme. Hamel had given up on beauty of any form many years ago, and now passed her waning years by watching the long days drag by through the window of her ground-floor flat in a small alley a half block from Boulevard de Clichy, not far from the famed Moulin Rogue.

A thick cough rattled deep in her chest, and she said, "I heard you were dead."

"A lot of people were misinformed, it seems. Would you like to go a little faster?"

"I have moved quickly my entire life," she observed dryly. "There is no need to hurry things now. I'm assuming you've been dead for a reason?"

"It wasn't my choice at the time, and now it's a rather convenient cover," he told her. "The less you know, the better."

"Better is fine with me," she replied. "Now, are you going to tell me to what I owe the pleasure of your company? This can't possibly be a professional visit."

Phythian had first come to know Jantine Hamel not long after he had been dispatched to Paris for one of his initial assignments after joining the ranks of the Greenwich Global Group. The target of his mission was a former KGB agent named Vladimir Antonov, who controlled a sizeable share of the narcotics business in Paris and, by proxy, much of the skin trade as well. Word on the street was that Phythian needed to meet Mme. Hamel, who had been put out of business by the Russian overlord and his Mafiya thugs, and would gladly do anything if it meant making life miserable for the fat KGB prick. Back then Jantine had weighed a hundred pounds less than she did today, and had made it possible for Phythian to achieve his first European success. While most of the drugs and guns and girls in Paris remained controlled by Russian interests, Vladimir Antonov no longer was one of them.

He chuckled at her insinuation and said, "Not professional in the way you or I might mean it, no. But I do have a small favor to ask of you."

"What could you possibly want from a woman with such a fat, legless body?" she asked.

"Not that sort of favor," he told her. "And I understand if you choose not to be associated with someone of my particular trade."

"That could be said of both of us," Mme. Hamel said with a snicker. She glanced up over her shoulder and fixed him with eyes as gray as a cool mist rising from the Seine at dawn, as if probing for some deep, hidden truth. "I've never known you to be bashful, Mr. Phythian. Whatever it is you want, the answer is yes."

"The fact is, madame, I'm looking for a place to lay low for a day or two. Just a room with a bed where I can come and go unnoticed."

A smile crossed her lips and she said, "I know a place with lots of beds," she said. "And plenty of coming and going."

"It's not what you're thinking," he said.

"You can't possibly know what I'm thinking," she laughed.

She had no idea, of course, just how wrong she was. Phythian had never revealed his skillset to her, and there was no reason to do so now.

At the moment all he wanted was a quiet place to disappear from closed-circuit cameras and facial recognition software and the general buzz of the city's streets, a place to sort out what he'd learned eavesdropping down on the street as the police conducted their investigation inside Gabrielle's *appartement*. The exercise had yielded little more than what Martin Beaudin had already told him, except the news that she had engaged in sexual intercourse not long before being killed. She had been washed rather thoroughly post-mortem, leaving behind scant evidence that might prove useful in identifying her killer. The forensics experts had swabbed just about everywhere, and had gathered whatever touch DNA could be found, including trace fluids, skin cells, and pubic hairs.

Whoever had put a bullet through Ms. Lamoines' brain clearly knew what he was doing, which strongly suggested he was a professional. It also posed a problem he hadn't figured into his original equation, and was the reason he could not leave Paris; not until he found the person who had done this to her, and sentence the motherfucker accordingly.

Phythian's original plan had been for Martin Beaudin to set up a private meeting with Gabrielle, whereupon he would plead his case for clemency. It was something he clearly didn't deserve, nor was he so naïve to think she would accept one word of his apology. No amount of money could buy her forgiveness or bring back her *père*. She would tell him to go fuck himself or, better yet, jump off The Eiffel Tower himself, and rid the world of his murderous presence.

He had not pursued this path of forgiveness in any of the other eighteen G3 cases he thus far had dealt with, but Gabrielle was an isolated instance. His chance encounter with her on the street just shortly before he'd caused the death of her father had linked a real face to his job. The face of a beautiful woman who was young and alive and full of promise, and who had love for all that had been in her life. For a brief sliver of time, he had seen the human suffering that came as a result of his livelihood, and it had etched a deep *samskara* of sorrow he'd never been able to shake.

Her murder had eliminated the pain of that confrontation, and now his mission of redemption—a battle driven by guilt and remorse—had abruptly turned into a search for her killer.

"If it's not too much trouble, I would like a private entrance, perhaps through an alleyway or patio," he told Jantine Hamel. "And clean sheets on the bed."

"Washed and changed on the hour, if you so desire, *mon ami*," she assured him with a wink. "Up there at the corner at Rue Houdon, let's take a right."

Carter Logan was awakened a little before noon by a housekeeping cart clanking out in the hallway.

Unlike when he had arrived at the crack of dawn, a swath of light was now angling across the floor from a gap in the thick blackout curtains. Raleigh had not drawn them together tightly last night, and he'd been too exhausted by his interrogation by the Guardia di Finanza to pay attention to such details. All that mattered was that he was in the hotel room of an amazing friend whom, under other circumstances, might still have been here next to him, thinly covered by the crisp cotton sheet that somehow had been bundled into a knot.

As his eyes slowly adjusted to the light, he realized he'd spent his first twenty hours in Rome doing virtually nothing of any substance. The young man he was supposed to meet had gotten spooked when Logan failed to show, and most likely had gone to ground. Arranging last night's meeting had involved a good deal of persuasion and personal guarantees, to protect not only his identity but also his life. Logan worried that his failure to keep their appointment—along with the police presence down in the street—had caused him to lose his nerve. Couldn't really blame the guy, since his potential role of informant had the potential to blow the lid off a worldwide scandal and place him directly in the crosshairs of some of the most dangerous men in the world.

Logan, too, but he'd been there before.

He glanced around, found his cellphone on a small desk that held a handful of tourist flyers and a pad of paper with the hotel's logo on it. He checked his texts, emails, and missed calls, found nothing from the whistleblower he knew only by a pseudonym: *Il Testimone:* The Witness. Of course, he wasn't expecting anything, figured the young man had somehow ducked out the back door of the building on Corso Vittorio Emanuele last night and had hustled to the nearest metro station.

Logan quickly prioritized his day. He couldn't remain here in Raleigh's room; she had been a true princess allowing him to spend a few hours to catch up on much-needed sleep, but he had to move on. Now it was time to find another place—no easy feat, considering how crowded the city was because of the G20 meeting, on top of the usual swarm of tourists that invaded the city in early June. Truth was, he had no real reason to be in Rome if he couldn't meet up with his reluctant contact; he was here chasing down a lead that was ephemeral at best, and if the story eluded him, it was time to pack it in. Head home empty-handed.

It was something he was loath to do.

He dug his dopp kit out of his carryon bag and dragged himself into the bathroom. He studied his tired face in the mirror, then ran a brush across his teeth and gargled with a travel-sized mouthwash he found in the bathroom. Half the men in Rome seemed to have day-old stubble on their chins, so he figured he could shave later. He swept his hand through his hair, then went back out into the bedroom and grabbed his phone, along with a spare key card Raleigh had left behind. After checking the peephole—the housekeeping cart was still out there—he unlocked the door and stepped out into the hallway. Raleigh had already placed the *Non Disturbare* notice on the outer handle, and he decided to leave it there just in case she didn't like housekeeping going through her things.

The concierge downstairs seemed happy to call him a cab, and twenty minutes later he was rolling down the same street as last night. This driver possessed a modest knowledge of English which, combined with the translator app on Logan's phone, enabled him to provide directions to number one-fifty-four on Corso Vittorio Emanuele. He suspected going there was a lost cause but, having nowhere else to be, he was left with little choice.

The mangled Fiat had been trucked away last night, but diamonds of shattered glass remained scattered on the pavement as a reminder of what had happened; same with a dark stain where the motorcycle rider had come to rest on his head, and bled out. Strips of red-and-white police tape were still affixed to nearby trees, blowing lazily in the wind.

Unlike last night, however, the street was crowded and the sidewalk teemed with pedestrians. The shops that had been locked tight were bustling with business, and the aroma of marinara sauce and cheese drifted out of the VIP pizza place down near the corner. The scent battled with the smell of laundry that had been freshly starched at the Lavanderia next door to the tobacco store.

Logan's meeting with Il Testimone had been scheduled to occur in an apartment on an upper floor of the building. At least, he assumed it was an apartment, since the street looked to be residential and there was nothing to suggest there might be offices upstairs. His instructions had been to enter through the heavy door that opened off the street, whereupon he would find a small vestibule with another door, this one locked. He was to press the button for number three-oh-four, wait five seconds, then press it again. Five seconds more and another press would cause whoever was upstairs to hit a buzzer, which was coordinated with a lock that would allow him inside.

He tried that now, doubted it would work. He waited a few moments after his third attempt at the button, sorting through his options. There weren't many, and he hated going back to the original source who had set this whole thing in motion. The same mysterious benefactor who, for the past two years, had been feeding him far-fetched tips that, when he dug into them, exposed the dark secrets behind a flurry of random, unexplained deaths in a half dozen countries over the past twenty years. A lot of men and even a few women were now serving long sentences because of what he'd dug up, and several had even chosen to take their own lives rather than face a lifetime behind bars.

Logan knew he should have felt more indebted to the anonymous information that had helped kick-start his career, but he had good reason to suspect the tip-offs were coming from the very same person who had caused the death of his fiancé eight years ago. Katya Leiffson, the love of his life who had been killed in the crash of a small plane in a top-secret incident he still didn't fully comprehend, and had come to grips with the idea that he probably never would.

It was a tacit arrangement made in hell, and the less contact he had with the cold-blooded killer, the better. All he knew about the man was that he signed his emails "RP," and they came from a server that appeared to be impossible to trace. At some point—maybe today, maybe next week or next year—they would meet face-to-face. Of that he was absolutely certain. And when it did, Logan liked to think he would be prepared to take care of the bastard, once and for all.

Then he heard a voice ask, "*Chi è la?*"

He glanced back at the array of buttons, realized the question was coming from a small speaker set in the plaster wall. "My name is Logan," he replied in English. "I'm sorry...I was supposed to be here last night."

"*Parola in codice, per favore.*"

Code word, please. He thought for a second, recalled the phrase he'd been given in case he found himself in this situation, and had to verify who he was. "It always rains on Sundays," he recited, in Italian. It was a line from Vittorio de Sica's classic post-war drama *Bicycle Thieves*, possibly a favorite of the young man he was supposed to see.

A short silence followed. Then the voice—it sounded as if it belonged to a woman, but filtered with static like a fast-food drive-up unit—said, "*Aspetta, per favore.*"

It was not a request, and Logan waited, as she'd requested. Any reply that was not an immediate "no" got him that much closer to "yes." At least, that's what his older brother had told him years ago when Logan had sought his advice on how to ask Allie Sims to the senior prom.

Eventually the voice—definitely a woman—was back, with another question. "Why were the polizia out in the street last night?"

"There was an accident," Logan explained. "A man died. I was detained and couldn't come upstairs."

Yet another silence followed, and he got the impression that the woman upstairs was communicating with someone else, either in the apartment or via cellphone. The next response confirmed his suspicion, as she said, "Be at the Trevi Fountain in one hour."

"Sì signora," Logan replied. "He'll be there?"

"If he feels it's safe."

"It's a crowded place. How will I recognize him?"

"Leave that to him," the voice said.

"How will he know me?" he asked, but there was no response. The woman was gone.

Chapter 12

Deputy chief inspector Francois Fourgét—pronounced *forjhay*—paced the well-worn vinyl tiles in the investigators' room, stretching his hands outward and cracking his knuckles as he drew his eyes from one detective to the other.

They were on the second floor of the Commissariat de Police at the corner of Rue Bonaparte and Rue de la Montange, a cream-colored limestone building secured from the street by a tall iron fence topped with sharp spikes. The June morning was unseasonably cool, and warm air was cascading from a vent in the ceiling, heating the crown of his bald head. He momentarily wondered why an industrial engineer would try to force hot air downwards, when everyone knew that it rises.

"*Y at il quelque chose d'utile des caméra?* he asked the officer standing beside him, sipping coffee out of a stained ceramic mug. Is there anything useful from the camera in the vestibule?

"I wouldn't get excited," replied Alain Dupont, one of the inspectors who had worked the murder scene earlier at the appartement in St. Germain. He was a tall man, thin, with dark hair and a poor attempt at a mustache clinging to his upper lip. He was sitting in a folding metal chair behind a gray metal desk, working the computer keyboard in front of him. "It's an older analog set-up we don't see much anymore."

"How good is the footage?" Fourgét asked.

"Pretty grainy, and the angle of the lens is rather poor. A person would have to look right at it in order to get a useful shot."

"What about the neighbors? Did anyone see or hear anything?"

"There was only one other resident home on the top floor," the third investigator said. Her name was Madelyn Rochefort, ivory skin and green eyes, a scattering of freckles on both cheeks. Platinum blonde hair du jour cut just above her collar, blue designer glasses, dark skirt and lacy blouse buttoned at the neck. "The victim's next-door neighbor said she had the radio on all evening, tuned to France Musique. She swears she didn't hear anything out of the ordinary."

"And no one saw Mademoiselle Lamoines enter the building?" Fourgét pressed.

Rochefort shook her head as she consulted a spiral notebook she held in her hand. "No one that we've been able to speak with," she replied. "There's another team doing follow-ups this afternoon."

"And nothing from the grainy camera?"

"Just a man in a hat, arm around her," Rochefort told the chief inspector. "Staring at the floor until they got on the elevator."

Fourgét rolled his eyes in exasperation and said, "What about her workplace?"

"Garnier and Kaplan are there now," Dupont offered, looking up from his screen. "Knowing how protective France 365 is of freedom of the press, they won't get much."

"Have you gone through her cellphone?" Fourgét inquired.

"That's actually caused a bit of a delay. Her sim card is missing."

"Missing." Fourgét said it like a statement, not a question.

"It wasn't in her phone, and nowhere in her apartment."

"Orange has a back-up for all that data. Get them to pull it."

"Just got access to it," Dupont assured him, indicating the data scrolling by on his screen. "It's possible that whoever took that card may not know that they back up all that data."

Fourgét looked doubtful as he scratched the top of his balding head, then sat down on the desk that was nearest to him. "Tell me again about the bullet."

"Twenty-two rimfire," Rochefort explained. "Subsonic, probably a suppressor of some sort, which could explain why her neighbor didn't hear anything. We dug it out of the wall behind the headboard, but no sign of the casing. She was shot at a slightly downward angle, meaning the killer was standing over her. And she couldn't move because of her restraints."

"The scarves?"

"Right," Rochefort said. "No signs of a struggle. Indicates she'd been tied up voluntarily, most likely had no idea what was coming."

"When you say no signs of a struggle, we're assuming no sexual assault, then?" the deputy chief inspector wanted to know.

"Sexual activity, yes, but no indication of violence. Except for the bullet, of course. Fired at close range."

"How close?" Fourgét asked.

"About eighteen inches," Rochefort replied. "And get this: judging from the presence of antibacterial soap, it appears she washed herself."

"What do you mean, washed herself?"

"You know...down there," she said, her freckled cheeks growing a bit rosy.

"Before or after she had sex?" Fourgét asked, cracking his knuckles one more time.

"Madeleine Bouchard did the prelim exam, said she'd had a sponge bath that wiped away any external trace of fluids or pubic hair."

"And then she let herself be tied up?" the deputy chief inspector asked, not buying it.

"Maybe she didn't do the sponge bath herself," Dupont suggested.

"You're thinking the killer washed her, after he shot her?"

"That's one possibility," Dupont said.

"There's another?" Fourgét asked.

"Let's take a step back here," Rochefort suggested. "Forget the sex thing for a moment. Let's start with the entry wound itself. A single shot, almost perfectly placed equidistant between her eyes, right in the center of her forehead. "

"A professional hit."

"What if she'd had sex with someone earlier in the evening," Dupont asked. "Whoever he was, he left. And then later the killer showed up—"

"Doesn't work," Fourgét said, shaking his head. "I don't see her lying there willingly, still tied to the bed after her man leaves. She would have made some kind of ruckus to get him to undo them."

"Or, whoever she slept with actually killed her," Rochefort proposed. "But for professional reasons, not personal."

"And he washed up after he was finished?"

"Why not?" Dupont asked. "If there was any way he could be linked to the victim, he'd want to eliminate the trace evidence. Meanwhile, I think we should check out these names in her phone's 'recents' list." He pivoted the computer monitor slightly so Fourgét could see the screen. "Michel Belisle. Philippe Brun. Gustav Allard. Lawrence Reese—"

"It appears our victim knew lots of important people in high places," Fourgét said. "Isn't Michel Belisle a deputy minister of something?"

"Finance," Rochefort said as she peered closer at the screen. "And Philippe Brun ran a pharmaceutical company until he sold it to that Swiss firm, the one that's been swallowing everything up."

"Helsinger-Koch," Fourgét told her. "She did a story about them a few weeks back."

"And Gustav Allard." Dupont scratched his head at that one, then said, "If I'm not mistaken, he's in oil, maybe natural gas."

"He's vice chairman of the FEC," Fourgét corrected him. "France Energy Consortium."

"What about this Lawrence Reese?" Rochefort asked. "Sounds like he could be British."

"Or American," Fourgét pointed out.

"I don't know the name offhand, but I'll check him out," Dupont replied. "Judging by the caliber of Mlle Lamoines' friends, he must be somebody."

"And this Sten Gustafsson-Jeglum." Fourgét said, indicating another name on the screen. "That sounds awfully familiar—"

"It should," Dupont said. "He's the computer hacker that Interpol says is behind a bunch of ransomware attacks. Their latest briefing says he's responsible for the theft of digital files from the World Court in The Hague just last week. I'd put a hundred Euros on him being behind half of Mlle Lamoines exclusive reports."

"I think we need to pay this Monsieur Gustafsson-Jeglum a visit," Fourgét said.

"Get in line," Dupont told him as he leaned back in his hard metal chair. "A bunch of countries, including his homeland of Sweden, have been looking for him for years. He's a slick bastard, always a step ahead of everyone else."

"A legend in his own mind," Rochefort added.

Fourgét rotated his shoulders to the left, then back to the right. "His servers have to be somewhere," he said. "Find those fuckers, we'll find the sonofabitch. Meanwhile, dig out whatever you can from Mlle Lamoines' phone history."

"What are you thinking?" Dupont asked him.

"I'm thinking we've got a deceased television celebrity and social media influencer who had a 'Who's Who' of power and politics in her contact list. One of them is a French government official with access to the most confidential of this country's financial secrets, while another is a big-time oil executive. Then there's this hacker who's wanted across half the developed world for all sorts of alleged ransomware attacks. The bottom line is, Gabrielle Lamoines knew a lot of important people, and at least one of them probably had a good reason to want her dead."

Allesandro Bortolotti continued to rage at the world, and all the fucking things in it. At the top of that list was Mateo Tufino, who had one hand on his phone and the other on the wheel of the Mercedes G 63 SUV, almost a quarter million dollars of German steel that looked like an oversized milk crate on over-inflated tires. The fact that it was black was more than fitting, considering *Il Capo's* inexorable mood.

Tufino finished his call and dropped the mobile device in the cup holder. "*Quasi in orario*," he mumbled as he swerved to avoid a chunk of retread rubber that had spun off a truck tire. The initial leads he'd spoken of earlier had yet to produce any useful information on the whereabouts of the waylaid meth and fentanyl, but now he had a sliver of a reason to hope.

"What did you say?" Bortolotti snapped at him, clearly paying little attention to what his young major was telling him.

"Just that the carabinieri now suspect Santoro hit two known smugglers last night, before he died," Tufino explained.

"How does this connect to us?"

"Too early to tell," Tufino admitted, wishing he had better, more conclusive news to deliver. "Maybe it doesn't."

"Then why do you mention it?"

"To keep you informed, up to the minute." An explanation that sounded altogether better than, "So you won't feel tempted to punish the messenger."

Bortolotti waved off Tufino's very real concern and said, "These smugglers he may have hit: who were they?"

"One Sudanese, the other Bulgarian," Tufino said. "What I'm hearing is, they had ties to the 'Ndrangheta."

"What sort of ties?" Bortolotti wanted to know.

"The sort of ties that smugglers would have." More of a guess than an answer, but it was all Tufino had to work with. "Women. Guns. Drugs."

"*Our drugs*?"

"Could be."

They were ninety minutes south of Anghiari, rolling along in the fast lane of the E45 about fifty minutes east of Rome. Their destination was an industrial neighborhood just outside Tivoli Terme, where several truckloads of weapons and uniforms had been delivered over the weekend. The vehicle's twin turbocharger V8 was chugging gas the way a Russian chugs vodka, and they were going to have to pull off the main highway soon to fill the thirsty beast.

Bortolotti was puffing a fat cigar, a pricey La Casa del Habano, the tip glowing like leaves burning on a cold autumn day. Tufino had rolled the window down to let the smoke out, but that had lasted about two minutes before *Il Capo* hit the button and the glass slid up again.

At that moment Tufino's phone buzzed in the cup holder. It was a number he did not recognize, most likely a burner. This indicated the possibility of some good news on a day when nothing of any good had come his way.

"*Pronto*," he said as he picked it up.

"Gioia Tauro," came the one-word response.

"Say again?" Tufino said, recognizing the voice as that of a man named Faraldo, a part-time snitch and Bortolotti loyalist.

"Gioia Tauro. It's a port not far from Sicily, about twenty-five miles."

"I know where it is. What about it?"

"A panel van has been parked on a dock there for the last twenty-four hours," Faraldo explained. "With two men in it who haven't moved."

"Am I supposed to wet my pants over this?" Tufino inquired, momentarily glancing over at Bortolotti while keeping an eye on the road.

"Aren't you at all curious why they're sitting there, what they're waiting for?"

"Only if you already know the answer to that question."

"I do, and getting it cost me a hundred Euros. And when you pay me a thousand, I'll tell you what I know—"

"Fuck that shit, Faraldo," Tufino snapped at him. Why was it that the runts of the litter always believed themselves to be *cane superiore*? "Time is of the greatest importance here, in case I didn't already explain that to you. But if what you tell me gets me that shipment, I'll give you two."

That brought a silence that lasted a good ten-count. Then the man presumably named Faraldo said, "Crystal, fentanyl, and heroin, is what I heard."

"And these guys are just sitting there?"

"Waiting for delivery, apparently. Now tell me that isn't good enough for two thousand."

It was worth far more than that, if it was the hijacked shipment Bortolotti was waiting on…and maybe even if it wasn't.

"Here's what we're going to do," Tufino said. "If it works, I may even give you three."

Chapter 13

"Get out and unlock the chain," Sten Gustafsson-Jeglum said as he shifted into neutral and set his foot on the brake. "Combination is two, twenty-eight, thirteen."

Matthieu Letermé looked down the long drive that stretched out before them, then opened the door and stepped down from the van. An old Vauxhall Vivero diesel, decent mileage but man, did the exhaust stink. At the far end of the long drive was a large structure that looked as if it had been cobbled together over the centuries from brick, stone, tile, and hand-hewn timbers. Shutters were closed tightly over all the windows, and he could see a jungle of roses and forsythia and ivy that had not been pruned in a very long time.

He walked over to a stone pillar at the side of the unpaved lane and fiddled with the lock on the chain that stretched across the drive to an identical stone pillar. He thumbed in the combination and lowered the chain to the ground. After Sten drove over it, Letermé raised it again and refastened the lock, then climbed back into the passenger seat.

"Whose place is this?" he asked as the Swede shifted into gear and drove the vehicle up the dirt road lined with mature beech trees on either side.

Sten didn't answer right away, just pulled up in front of the sprawling house and cut the engine. The two men sat there for a moment before he opened his door and stepped down to the gravel parking area that was littered with weeds and leaves left over from last autumn. He stretched his arms and rotated his shoulders, loosening his muscles after the long drive from Brussels.

"It's owned by a friend of a friend," he explained, without explaining much. A small lie, in fact, since the shuttered chateau had been in his father's family for over a century, and had belonged to his parents until they had been killed in a terrorist act over ten years ago. As their only child, Sten had inherited a fortune that was far too vast for a young man to manage properly, and thus he'd let the property slip into disrepair. Not the equities and bonds and other financial assets, however; those he'd been quite fastidious about. "C'mon—let's unload this stuff and get to work."

Letermé got out and followed him to the rear of the van, once more assessing the large structure as he shook road cramps from his legs. The front of the building towered three stories above the ground, and a steeply pitched tile roof with four sets of dormer windows—also covered with shutters—rose up another floor above that. A large field sloped away from the front of the chateau several hundred meters down to a line of trees and a crumbling stone wall, and several outbuildings in various states of disrepair were set off to one side of an old pear orchard.

"This friend of yours…have I met him?" he inquired again as Sten unlocked the rear doors and swung them open. "Or her?"

"The less you know, the better," he replied as he tugged a large cardboard box toward him. "Let's just say it's a safe place to set up shop for a while."

Sten could be like that, evasive but direct at the same time, and Letermé had learned shortly after they had met two years ago at a computer conference in Cologne not to press him.

"Where do we put this stuff?" he asked, picking up a box of servers and trailing behind him to the front portico.

Sten set down his carton and unlocked a large wooden door that swung inward on ancient iron hinges. "Follow me," he said.

The rugged, hard-carved slab opened into an entryway that held a pair of unmatched chairs and a small table. Slivers of light angled in through the ancient shutters, and Letermé could see the walls were bare except for picture hooks hammered into the plaster that at one time probably displayed artwork but now served no purpose.

"We'll open the shutters after we get the equipment upstairs," Sten said as he flicked a switch that instantly bathed the room with a soft luminescence. "This way."

Letermé followed him through a door, which led into another room that was equally spartan in its decorating, and then through yet another. Beyond that was a rickety staircase that most likely served as the servants' upstairs access at some point in the history of this house. Sten punched another light switch and they trudged up to the second floor, then turned right and found another flight that took them to a landing on the third level. Three doors opened off the right side, and an oak door was at the far end. Next to it, a metal device was set into the wall, a single LED glowing bright red.

"I'm already lost," Letermé said.

"Just give me a second to deactivate the locks."

Sten set his box of hardware on the wide-board floor and touched his thumb to a small pad. He waited a moment while the light changed from red to a steady green, then slid a card into a slot while simultaneously punching in a six-digit code on a small keypad. There was a brief hum, followed by a chime of five steady notes that sounded like someone tapping a knife on the edge of a glass.

"We're in," he said as he retrieved his box.

What lay beyond was a vast contrast to the rest of the bare, dimly lit house. The room was about twenty feet square, and every inch of wall space was occupied with floor-to-ceiling racks of computer equipment—mostly servers, power units, and switchers. A dozen large wall-mounted screens appeared to be running a steady stream of code, and in the middle of the room a large table held keyboards, drives, smaller monitors, and other assorted hardware.

"What is this place?" Letermé asked, massaging his temples and cursing all the beer he had consumed the night before.

"*Ce, mon ami, est la Maison de Quantum,*" Sten said, a noticeable touch of pride in his voice. He unloaded the box he had brought up from the van and arranged the pieces of equipment in one of the few vacant spaces on the table. "Quantum House. Otherwise known as 'ground zero' to the governments that are trying to shut us down."

"Then it does exist," Letermé said, reverence and awe in his voice. "In an empty chateau in…well, wherever the hell we are."

"As the Americans would say, 'an undisclosed location.' Fortunately, you were so hung over you slept most of the way down here."

"These are the central servers?"

"The heart of the TruthCorps cloud," Sten confirmed with pride.

"This explains why no one has been able to shut us down—"

"Bring 'em on," Sten replied with a Mona Lisa grin.

Letermé nodded as he looked around the room. "How do you keep it all off the grid?"

"Solar panels on the south facing roof, and hydrogen cells in the basement, with tandem back-up propane-fired generators."

"What about connectivity? You can't be going through Big Orange out here."

Sten shook his head, said, "Independent satellite connection, with direct upload and download capabilities provided by a very generous benefactor." In other words, the Gustafsson-Jeglum family trust.

"I feel privileged," Matthieu said, only halfway sarcastic. "How do you know we weren't followed down here from Brussels?"

"We were," Sten told him. "I lost the bastards in Lille, after we crossed the border. You were sleeping."

"And you're certain they didn't pick us up again after that?"

"They met with some temporary misfortune, and after that they were in no condition to continue on," Sten assured him with a wry grin. "Come, let's go get the rest of the stuff."

Nataliya Moisei reveled in opulence, and all the crazy extravagance that went with it. Hers was an abundant world encrusted with diamonds and rubies and emeralds, celebrated with lavish quantities of Cristal champagne served in hand-cut Waterford flutes. It was relaxing in the sumptuous comfort of a private jet, flying to private resorts in the Seychelles and Bali and Thailand. Racing a Bugatti Chiron along the winding roads of the French Riviera, sipping Nolet's gin martinis on the aft deck of a private Amels yacht in Monaco. It was glamping on a private safari in Botswana with a red-haired prince from a European island nation who, alas, went and got married to an American actress whom her high-brow in-laws seemed to despise.

The former prostitute from Moldova had experienced all these things, at one time or another, mostly when she was much younger than her current forty-two years, although many of those years had treated her very kindly. She was the same weight, same measurements as when she was first turned out at age sixteen, and the few signs of age that had begun to appear had thus far been buffed out or enhanced by surgery. These days her hair was dark, done up in a French braid even though this was Rome. Her corrective lenses were a cornflower blue, a new color she believed made appear look five years younger.

This morning she had awakened in her suite at the Grand Hotel Palace on a fashionable block of Via Veneto, luxuriating in the high-thread count Egyptian cotton sheets before treating herself to a bubble bath enhanced with eucalyptus-mint Epsom salts. She experienced both these things alone, an occurrence that was happening more and more these days, and which didn't bother her nearly as much as it would have in the past. Perhaps she would treat herself to a massage and a manicure later, if things went well.

This afternoon she was seated at a small table in the shade of a sycamore, in a secluded garden patio of a restaurant on Via Ludovisi, with white linens, blue napkins, a single rose in a crystal vase. There was no prosecco, however, since this was a work lunch and she had learned long ago not to imbibe alcohol while conducting business.

The man seated across from her seemed out of place...*was* out of place. She knew him only as Alberto, and he claimed to be from Athens, although she knew for a fact he was an Albanian. No matter; he was tall, dark, and handsome—a pleasing but clichéd combination that had always worked for her in the past. They had never slept together—a distinct complication in her constantly evolving line of work—but she had thoroughly fantasized about it more than once.

It would not be so today; today she had an emergency request, brought on by a particularly nasty incident no one—not even she—could have foreseen.

"What happened to the other girl?" Alberto asked, after she'd told him what she needed.

"That is none of your concern," Nataliya replied. "Can you help me or not?"

Alberto tasted a sip of Lambrusco, clearly not sharing Natalie's rules for drinking when business was being discussed. "Of course," he said with a deferential nod. "This new untouched flower, as you put it...when do you need her?"

"Tomorrow," she replied. "At the latest."

"Short notice."

"That's why I came to you."

He could have considered her words a form of flattery, but he knew she would say—*do*—just about anything to get what she needed. "Same as before, I presume?"

"Yes. Pretty and innocent, of course. Fair, preferably blonde hair. Blue or brown eyes, doesn't really matter. American would be good, French or German as well."

"Not British?"

"In a pinch, if you must."

Alberto nodded as she spoke, committing her specs to memory. "Does language matter?" he asked.

Nataliya raised a single eyebrow, as if that were a stupid question. "No one's expecting her to say much," she replied.

"What about age?"

"Fourteen or fifteen. Just like the last one."

He considered all that she had told him, then said, "Fifty grand. Wire transfer, no crypto."

"That's double last time."

"Last time you gave me a week."

They both smiled, neither for the same reason. Fifty thousand dollars was more than Alberto had ever earned for one job. But he was right: this was a last-minute thing, and well worth the price. Plus, it was a drop in the bucket for Nataliya's employer, particularly considering what the sick bastard had in mind for the naïve young thing.

"Deal," she said. "But there's one more thing."

"And what's that?"

"Make sure this one isn't the type to go and kill herself. You do not want to go up against the wrath of the Russian."

"Wait...*what*—?"

"See you tomorrow night," Nataliya said with a tight grin. "Don't disappoint me."

Alberto froze for a moment, his eyes shaken by a sudden fear that seemed to tighten around his heart. "No worries, *signora*. Same place as before?"

"See you there."

She dismissed him with a wave of her hand, and he hurriedly downed the rest of his sparkling wine. Then he rose to his feet and, with a bow of his head, slipped out of the restaurant.

Her business concluded, she glanced around the patio, caught the attention of the server and motioned him over to her table. "Prosecco," she said with a smile. Such sweet, green eyes he had, and an athletic, young body she could just melt herself into, given half the chance.

Chapter 14

Why meet at the Trevi Fountain, of all places?

When they first began exchanging texts, the young man—Il Testimone—had agreed to meet with Logan only if it could be arranged discretely. An apartment on a quiet street in a quiet neighborhood in Rome would do, no prying eyes or distractions or interruptions. Total secrecy and tight security—understandable, given the subject matter and risk involved. Dangerous, too, if the wrong person got wind of it.

But now that their initial meeting had fallen through, he'd selected perhaps the busiest tourist trap in the entire city. Cameras and police were everywhere, thousands of people milling about at all hours of the day and night, tossing coins over their shoulders into the water in the hope that they once again might return to Rome, or maybe one day would even get married here. How in hell would he be able to find Logan amidst all these sightseers staring at the great carving of Oceanus, being hauled out to the sea in a shell-shaped chariot pulled by winged horses?

Even if they did meet up, what then? Would the two of them simply walk around the pedestrian piazza, nibbling on gelato cones while talking about yet another scandal that would send seismic shockwaves through the Catholic church? If so, they'd be in full view of all these visitors, including over a dozen polizia and an untold number of plainclothes security personnel.

Whatever the thinking, despite the risk, Logan had taken the metro to the Barberini station and arrived at Fontana di Trevi ten minutes early. The woman he'd spoken with on the phone had indicated that the man would contact him, so he found a position at the perimeter of the crowd and studied the buildings around him. Most of them were three or four stories high, commercial space on the ground floor housing a pharmacy, a bar, shops selling leather goods and shoes and T-shirts. Offices or apartments were on the upper floors, probably *molto costoso*, although there was not enough money in the world that could get him to live anywhere near these crowds and all this street noise.

Lacking a concrete plan, he began to stroll leisurely from one end of the fountain terrazzo to the other. His eyes drifted from romantic couples walking arm in arm, to parents pushing strollers, to older folks well past the age of the person he was looking for. Finding no one who fit the image in his mind of what his contact must look like, a sense of defeat began to settle in.

In the end the woman was right: the guy found Logan, slipped up behind him and tapped him on the shoulder.

Logan whirled around, found himself face-to-face with a young man he guessed to be in his early twenties. He had dark hair that fell in limp strands past his ears and mirrored shades, apparently the best disguise he could manage without standing out from the multitudes. He was dressed in faded jeans and a Timberland T-shirt, and had a small backpack slung over one shoulder.

"Il Testimone?" Logan asked.

"Carter...*sei tu?*," the young man said. He flung his arms around Logan, drew him close with an enthusiastic man hug. At the same time whispering into Logan's ear, in passable English, "Make like we're old friends."

Generally quick on the uptake, Logan hugged him back and replied, "My God...how long has it been—?"

"Too long," the young man. "Of all the places in all the world, imagine running into you here. What are the odds?"

They ended their friendly embrace and Logan took an awkward step backward. "You have no idea how good it is to see you."

"Same here," Il Testimone said. "Walk with me."

"Where?" Logan wanted to know.

"I lead, you follow. Meantime, tell me what you've been doing since you arrived in Rome." They kept up the old-friends charade as they began walking toward the edge of the piazza, past a souvenir shop and a café that had a line out the door.

"A little of this, a little of that," Logan told him, keeping his answer vague. "I'm only here a couple days, so I don't have time for all the tourist things."

"No one can come to Rome without visiting the Trevi," the young man said. "All a part of the Roman adventure."

They were strolling around the far side of the sparkling pool now, the bottom littered with glittering coins. There were fewer tourists here, the piazza ending at a narrow street where only a few folks were coming or going. A vendor was standing watch over a fruit cart, and a trio of young girls giggled while balancing on the edge of the granite curb, as if they were navigating a dangerous obstacle course. A man in a straw hat tugged low over his face seemed to be assisting his inebriated girlfriend, dressed in shorts and a midriff blouse, down a narrow alleyway away from the crowd.

"Well, I've been here less than twenty-four hours and already I've caused an accident, somehow gotten a man killed, and been kicked out of my Airbnb," Logan replied. "That's enough adventure for me."

"There are adventures of all kinds," the young man said. They slowed a bit in front of a battered red door set into a stone archway, stained and weathered by time and the elements. "This is where mine began. Remember that for later."

Later meant another twenty minutes, much of it spent hustling through the maze of streets leading to and from the fountain, squeezed into the backseat of a car. It was another Fiat, this one smaller with only two doors, easy to maneuver through the narrow alleys and around the other cars, and to park in a city where such an activity seemed to be an impossible feat.

The "old-friends" chit-chat ended as soon as the car sped off, a woman sitting up front behind the wheel. Logan could only see the back of her from the shoulders up, and all he could make out was a dark gray jacket and piercing eyes studying him from a corner of the rear-view mirror. She probably was the same woman he'd spoken with on the phone earlier, but he didn't ask and she didn't say. In fact, she didn't utter one word the entire time they were in the car.

He tried to count the left and right turns, but lost track somewhere after they crossed the Tiber. Eventually they pulled down a narrow alley and stopped in front of a small shop where brightly colored dresses and blouses were hanging from wheeled racks. Several roll-down security gates were locked tight on either side of it, suggesting other businesses had been here at one time, but had long since closed. An unmarked door further to the left had a mail slot cut into it, and this was the one to which the young man in mirrored shades led him.

There was no elevator, only a set of lopsided wooden stairs that let out a painful groan with each step. Still no meaningful conversation, a finger held up to the young man's lips reinforcing the need for silence. Three flights up they came to a landing that offered a view all the way down the stairwell to the ground floor. If one were to fall over the railing, it would be a long and painful descent.

Four doors were on their left, and the young man led him to the third of these. At one time it appeared to have been painted blue, but now all that remained were specks of color that reminded him of an unfinished pointillist painting, something perhaps by Georges Seurat or Paul Signac. Instead of knocking, he inserted a key into the tarnished brass lock, then pushed it open and motioned Logan inside. He made a show of turning an array of deadbolts, presumably to keep unwanted visitors out, but also reminding Logan that there was no quick escape for him, either.

He found himself in a sparsely furnished room. A pair of wood chairs with stained burgundy cushions faced each other, a table positioned between them, and a clump of candles had melted to the wood surface. Drapes were pulled over a single window so Logan couldn't make out what was out there, but his inner GPS told him it faced away from the street, perhaps an inner courtyard where laundry dried in the afternoon breeze and TV antennae were attached to small balconies.

"My name is Alvize," the young man finally introduced himself, only after once he seemed to be comfortable. "I apologize for the—" searching for the word "—*sotterfugio*."

"I understand, and please call me Carter," Logan replied. "And I want to offer you my sincerest apologies for the mishap last night. As I mentioned earlier, I was involved in an accident, and when the police showed up, they wouldn't let me use my phone."

"I know. I watched it from a window. I was worried that somehow you had been followed and they…well, you can see the measures I have to take to ensure my safety."

"And I greatly appreciate you placing yourself at risk," Logan said. "But rest assured, I am not being followed. You are safe with me."

The young man named Alvize let out a wary sigh as he settled into one of the chairs. He seemed familiar with the place, and Logan wondered if this was his apartment, or maybe that of a friend. He could make out a small kitchen through an open doorway, with a small European-style fridge and a cook plate set on a badly scarred Formica counter. A door led to what he presumed was a bedroom, but it was closed and he had no reason to inquire about it.

"All right then," Alvize said, finally removing his shades and setting them on the table in front of him. "Let's get this done."

"Absolutely," Logan replied. "First, I want to thank you for agreeing to discuss your personal trauma, expose your tragedy in the name of justice."

"*Si, si*...we covered all that in the emails. As you might guess I'm a little skittish about this, so let's just…well, as you Americans like to say, 'cut to the chase.'"

Logan nodded, then took his phone out of his pocket and tapped an icon. "As we previously discussed, I'd like to tape this," he said as the digital app opened. "Off the record, for background only."

Alvize gave a wave of his hand, indicating that was fine. "Tell me again how you learned about my…situation," he asked.

"I have an extremely reliable source who mentioned to me the death of Cardinal Giudice, and he seemed to be familiar with your circumstances," Logan said.

"Does this source have a name?"

"I've never met him, and we've never actually spoken. We communicate by email only."

Alvize didn't offer a protest, just nodded and said, "Continue."

"Okay, then," Logan began. "Let's begin with how old you were when… well, when your ordeal started."

He studied Alvize carefully. The young man swallowed hard, maybe realizing for the first time that this might be more difficult than he'd anticipated. He would be putting himself out there for millions of people to read about, telling the story of how he'd been enmeshed in a horrific sex trafficking network inside the Vatican.

"It was ten years ago," Alvize replied. "I was twelve."

Now it was Logan's turn to swallow, thinking back to what he'd been doing when he was that same age: playing pick-up basketball, listening to Green Day and Gorrilaz on the radio, dreaming about Lizzie Ryan from health class in a string bikini. It was a world away, in more ways than one.

"And how did that begin?" he ventured.

"You know that place with the red door I pointed out to you on our way here?" Alvize reminded him.

Logan nodded, but said nothing. He just flashed his eyes at the phone on the table between them, the app indicating it was recording.

"Ok, then…I'm going to tell you a story."

Alvize tipped his head back and stared at the ceiling for a moment, as if to let the memories slip into place, like sand sifting through an hourglass. Then he said, "I was born and raised in the north of Italy, near Milan. My mother worked in a library at the university, and my father had a sales job in the fabric business. I was the oldest of four children, and the only son. My parents were into art and science and history, and made sure we learned languages besides our own. French and English, which is why I can speak with you now. One day *Papà* had a buying trip here in Rome, and at the last minute he invited me along. Wanted to show me what he did, maybe thought it would change my mind about wanting to play *calcio* for the Italian national team. Pursue a career, rather than a dream."

Logan had no idea what *calcio* was, but he could look it up later. Didn't want to break the young man's stream of consciousness.

"Anyway, we took the train down here to Rome, where he had some meetings set up. Two days and two nights, and at the end of the second day we had a few hours to do some sightseeing. Il Colosseo, il Panteon, and San Pietro. We finished up at la Fontana di Trevi, and by that time he decided he needed a drink, Campari being a regular part of his work routine. He left me outside while he ducked into a small bar at the edge of the piazza; it's still there today."

This brought yet another nod from Logan; yes, he had noticed it earlier.

"Anyway, while Papà was inside I wandered around, looking at the fountains and the overpriced shops, and all the people from around the world. It was all so different from what I knew in Milan, and I think I was in some kind of daze. I knew my father wouldn't stop at just one drink, but that didn't matter. I was in Rome, and for the first time ever I felt as if I could do—*be*—just about anything I wanted."

Alvize's voice trailed off and wistful look fell upon his eyes. Dark and disgraced, he averted them to the floor, as if in shame. He kept them there, seemingly unfocused on the hardwood floor that hadn't been sanded in half a century, and continued.

"At first I thought I'd been stung by a bee," he said. "If only that had been the case. But it wasn't a bee—it was a needle—and at that moment my entire world changed. No more dreams of *calcio*—what you Americans call soccer—or even a career, like my father. All I remember is that my brain switched off, like flipping off the lights in a room. And then waking up in the depths of hell."

"You're saying someone drugged you and snatched you off the street at the Trevi Fountain?" Logan asked.

"Not a common occurrence, which is why the polizia actually thought I'd run away," Alvize replied. "Something I didn't know until years later."

"And much easier to explain to the media than a kidnapping in broad daylight," Logan suggested.

"One must not disrupt the flow of tourist dollars," the young man agreed. "Anyway, I woke up on a bed in some dingy room that smelled of wine and piss, my hands and feet tied up and my mouth taped shut. I lay there thinking I was going to die. My father didn't have the kind of job where he could afford to pay ransom, if that's what this was all about. I was terrified that when they figured that out, they would kill me."

"But they didn't."

"No." Alvize began fidgeting, nervously pinching the tips of his fingers. "The next twelve hours were like being in Dante's *Inferno*, except the anguished screams he wrote about were coming from inside my own head. I truly felt like one of those lost souls."

Logan sensed no sorrow or despair in his colorless voice; he seemed well beyond any sort of emotion or attachment to life. He hated to think what the young man had been put through ten years ago, and tried not to imagine the unspeakable cruelty he must have endured.

Still, he asked, "When did you realize what was really going on?"

"Didn't take long," Alvize replied. "That filthy *stronzo* made it pretty damned clear."

Logan didn't need the language app on his phone to translate the curse word; there was no doubt in his mind what it meant. "And after that?"

"I was left lying there in my own blood. I still thought I might die if the bastard returned, but when he came back, after dark, he was with someone else. A man who was bigger and looked tougher, and I thought…well, I figured dying would only be better than the pain. But he didn't touch me. Didn't say a word, in fact. The two of them just rolled me up in a rug, leaving only enough room for me to breathe, and carried me downstairs."

"What happened next?" Logan gently guided him.

"Everything you can imagine. I was beaten, assaulted, invaded, and humiliated. Broken down until I was empty, like cracking a walnut and picking out everything inside. Nothing of me was left at the end. I wanted it all to be over, and I couldn't help but think what Papà was going through. Mamma, too."

Logan had already given considerable thought to the agony his parents must have endured at the time. Problem was, he knew so little of the case—not even Alvize's name until a few minutes ago—and had no way to do any advance research. There were no newspaper archives, no police records; just an email from his usual innominate source that referenced how a Cardinal had stepped in front of a truck near the Vatican, and a follow-up message that had led him to someone who could put him in touch with a person known only as Il Testimone.

"Go on," he said.

Alvize closed his eyes and brushed a strand of hair away from his face. He took a deep breath, then spent the next twenty minutes describing his humiliating descent into the depraved underworld in which he had spent the next nine years. He began with the journey from the filthy room near the Fontana di Trevi, and ended with his eventual escape just over six months ago. All of it again told with a detached indifference that Logan guessed was a coping mechanism, a way to mentally distance himself from the horrors that had been inflicted upon his mind and body.

It surely would haunt him for the rest of his life.

After being smuggled out of Rome, he'd been transported to an old stone farm house in the remote countryside: cold and damp, with a bitter wind slicing through it at all hours of day and night. Outside there seemed to be nothing but stands of naked trees and fallow fields, which only seemed to feed his desperation and growing depression.

"How long were you there?" Logan asked. "This farmhouse."

"Long enough for them to strip me bare," Alvize said. "And I don't mean just my clothes. I'm talking about everything. My dignity, my identity, my self-respect. From the moment they brought me to that place, I stopped being a twelve-year-old boy and became nothing more than a…a lifeless thing. They brought me there to break me down, cut away everything that was me."

Logan knew that reliving the experience had to be excruciating, the trauma nothing short of horrific. "I can't imagine how brutal that must have been," he replied, unable to think of any better words to say.

"The place was a slaughterhouse, and I was nothing but a hog. When that *mafankulo* was done there was nothing left but bone, and a faraway recollection of a boy who had a mother and father, and at one time had dreamed of playing football with the national team."

Logan said nothing for a moment as he let the impact of Alvize's words settle in. "Let's talk about the Cardinal," he finally said. "When were you introduced to him?"

"I'm not sure exactly when it was. There was no such thing as time at the farm house, just the passing of days and nights. I remember the woods were mostly gray and barren when I arrived there, and the trees were full of leaves when I left. One morning, not long after the sun was up, a car pulled up in front. Black, with dark tinting on the windows. From my window upstairs I saw two men get out, and the fucker went down and talked to them. One of the men handed over a thick envelope, and a few minutes later I was brought downstairs and pushed into the backseat."

"Do you know what was in it? This envelope?"

"I assumed it was a payment, but I didn't know how much I was worth," Alvize said. "Two hours later I was inside the Vatican, in a dusty room in la Biblioteca Apostolica."

"The library?"

"Right. Besides books and records and a ton of secrets, it contains a number of living quarters. And that's where I stayed for the entire time I was there."

"Under the tutelage of Cardinal Giudice."

"In the beginning, until he died. *Grazie Dio*. Then others came along. But yes, mostly *Quello Feroce*." Logan shot him a blank look, and Alvize added, "The Fierce One. That's how he was known by most of the other Cardinals, and it was a recognition that was well-earned. In public he had a very mild demeanor, but you didn't want to cross him in private. Or disappoint him. Something I learned the hard way, and pretty quickly."

"And you lived there? In the library?"

"Slept, ate, and studied there. On occasion I was allowed to go outside after dark, as long as I was accompanied, but otherwise I became the resident mouse."

"You say you studied while you were there?"

"*Quello Feroce* was a fanatic about education. I didn't know it at the time, but he had grown up in Desio, not far from where I was born. Just like Achille Ratti before him."

"You'll have to forgive my lack of knowledge of Italian history," Logan said.

Alvize nodded, but again did not reveal even the slightest emotion. "Achille Ratti was the son of the owner of a silk factory. He was ordained a priest and embarked on an academic career within the Church. He eventually became Pope Pius the Eleventh and worked along separate but parallel paths of power as Mussolini before the war. Anyway, Cardinal Giudice took me under his wing and…educated me."

"He groomed you."

"I believe that is a term they use these days, si. To me, it was just a continuation of the assault that began that first day near the fountain. I learned a good many things while I was in residence at the library, much more than I was taught while going to church as a boy." If he was trying to be cynical, it was lost in the lack of emotion.

"You mentioned other Cardinals?" Logan said, trying not to press him too hard.

"They came along after *Quello Feroce* died. As you know, he was hit by a truck while crossing Via Gregorio VII."

Yes, Logan did know. The email he'd received two weeks ago from "RP" had suggested that the Cardinal's death had been accidental, although it was phrased in such a way that suggested the circumstances were more deliberate than the authorities believed: direct retribution, in fact, for the cruelties the bastard had perpetrated within the Vatican walls.

"How did you finally escape?" he asked.

"Trust," Alvize replied. "And patience. About six months ago my most recent captor mistakenly left a door unlocked, and I made good on the opportunity to take my leave. By that time, I was quite familiar with the hallways and passages, and I simply made my way to an exit and found a crowd of tourists. I walked out when they did."

"And you've been running ever since."

"With an eye over my shoulder every second of every day."

"Why not just leave Rome?"

"And go where? This is the only place I know."

"Have you tried contacting your parents? I'm sure they'd love to know you're alive."

"Barely alive, and definitely not the way they would want to remember me. And they wouldn't want to see me, not after what was done to me. They were strict Catholics. In their minds—and the eyes of God—I'm a sinner beyond absolution."

Logan didn't wish to get into a debate of what Alvize should do, or not do. He wasn't equipped to offer advice to a young man who'd been beaten, raped, and emptied of all dignity for the past ten years—for almost half his life. That sort of trauma was better left to the experts, if even they could help him.

"A minute ago, you mentioned that you escaped from your most recent captor," he asked. "Would you care to tell me his name?"

"I also said I've been able to stay ahead of him for six months," Alvize reminded him. "I intend to keep it that way."

"What about the next boy, or the one after that? The ordeal you were put through didn't begin with you, and it won't end with you, either."

The young man gazed deep into Logan's eyes, and for the first time since the phone on the table had started to record their conversation, he displayed the slightest touch of feeling. Just a small one, in the form of a glistening bead of moisture forming in the corner of one eye.

"You think you can stop this?" he asked, not so much a question as a challenge.

"That's why I'm here," Logan told him. "But only if you give me a name."

Alvize inhaled a deep breath, let it out slowly. Again, he picked at the tips of his fingers, finally said, "Renato Azzone. He's the Deputy Secretary General of the Governate for Vatican City."

"That would mean he's an associate of the Pope."

"Correct. And there's something else, something I heard mentioned the night before I managed to get away. That fucker whispered it to me while he was…well, you know…"

Yes, Logan knew. "And this thing," he replied. "Do you remember what it was?"

"A name," the young man said. "Vivaldi."

"You mean like the Baroque composer?"

"That's all I know," Alvize insisted. "Just *Vivaldi*."

Chapter 15

At that very moment, in a musty room no more than a hundred yards from the Trevi Fountain—Abigail Evans was petrified.

Her memory was so impaired that she had no idea where she was, or how she had ended up there. Her brain felt thick and heavy, her vision so diminished that she couldn't make out any features other than the blurred outlines of what she presumed was furniture: a chair here, a table over there, a lamp with a faded brown shade on top of it? An oblong brightness suggested the presence of a window, maybe shrouded by curtains, but she couldn't be sure.

What she was certain of was that she had not come here of her own choice, wherever *here* was. She had no memory of how the day had begun, what she had done, or where she had gone.

She knew her name was Abby—that's what most people called her, at least—and she recalled that she had traveled here to Rome with her parents. That was three, maybe four days ago, a lame-ass idea they had cooked up to get her away from home for a week or ten days to maybe make her forget. Forget what, she did not know. Only that there was something—*someone*—a bad influence whose name she could not recall, from whom they had wanted to isolate her. Getting her away from San Francisco seemed to be the answer.

She was lying on a bed with a spongy mattress, no sheets or comforter or blanket covering her. Her head was on a pillow that smelled of dust and mold...urine, too. She attempted to rub her nose with her hand, but found that was not possible. She had no muscle control over her limbs, either because her arms and legs had fallen asleep, or some kind of paralytic medication had been injected into her bloodstream. Plus, her wrists were bound behind her with duct tape, which explained the hard knot she felt against the base of her spine.

The realization of these things had a very predictable effect: she attempted to scream, which was when she realized a strip of tape had been affixed across her mouth. It was positioned so she could breathe through her nose, but only if she relaxed her body and didn't attempt to inhale great gulps of air. Nasal passages weren't equipped to handle that, a lesson she quickly learned when her brain began to grow faint because of the interrupted supply of oxygen.

She struggled again to move her hands, rolled back and forth on the bed as she tried to dig her heels into the mattress to gain traction. That was not happening, because the same kind of tape binding her wrists was wrapped around her ankles, tightly adhered to her bare skin. It seemed funny, because she now recalled that she had been wearing socks—a new pair with horizontal pink, blue, yellow, and green stripes she had thrown into her suitcase at the last minute before heading for the airport. At school she was known as the Sock Princess because she had so many of them, and if there ever was an occasion for her to receive a gift from friends or family, inevitably she got socks.

Now that Abby remembered this small detail, another came to mind. She had so much wanted to send a selfie to Jagger—that was the nickname he liked her to use—and she remembered now that he was the "bad influence" back home. She had managed to slip away from her parents during their visit to the Trevi Fountain to snap a really cool shot for him: kissy-kissy fish lips, so typical for a girl who wouldn't turn fifteen for a few more months.

"You're too young to be dating someone his age," her father had argued when he'd found them kissing in the parking garage beneath their condo on Nob Hill.

"He's nineteen, for Chrissakes," her mother had added, when she'd found out.

"Dad's five years older than you are," Abby had shot back.

"It's not the same thing, and you know it."

To prove their collective point, they had flown her across one continent, an ocean, and halfway across another continent to remove her from what they insisted was a *bad situation*. This was clearly because they believed the old adage *out of sight out of mind*, while Abby was more than certain that *absence makes the heart grow fonder*.

She had been in the middle of typing a lovey-dovey text to accompany her selfie when she'd felt the sharp sting of a bug on her neck, just below her right ear...a bee, perhaps some sort of weird European gnat. Instinctively she had swatted at it, at which point two things happened: her fingers touched something pen-shaped that had been stuck into her skin and felt nothing like the probiscis of an insect, and then her consciousness dropped out from under her.

How long ago had that been? An hour? Yesterday? Sometime before that? Who had done this to her, and for what reason? The panic she already was feeling only intensified and caused her to struggle even more against the duct tape that constricted both her hands and feet—not a good idea, since all that twisting and tugging seemed to tighten the ligatures that bound her. At least she was still clothed, same shorts and tank top she'd put on in the hotel room before heading out with her parents on their well-intentioned self-guided sightseeing tour.

And now for the first time she was able to actually think about them and knew they must be worried sick, their not-quite-fifteen-year-old girl smiling and tossing coins into the fountain one minute, gone the next. How long would it have been before they noticed she was missing? Five minutes? Ten? It couldn't have been longer than that, even with hundreds of tourists milling around, doing what tourists do. It was one of the most famous attractions in all of Europe, featured in more movies than she cared to think. *Roman Holiday, Three Coins in the Fountain, La Dolce Vita.* Even *Sabrina Goes to Rome* and *The Lizzie McGuire Movie.* All of them were made before she was even born, and she'd never seen any of them, but she remembered the titles from the in-room tourist brochure, which was another good sign that her brain was recovering.

Back to her parents: by now they knew she was gone, but what would they think had happened to her? Had she somehow gotten lost in the labyrinth of streets around the fountain? Could she have run away, still pissed that they had disrupted the start of her summer with this crazy holiday, or maybe she'd wandered off to get a dish of gelato? Or maybe she had tried her luck at the bar on the corner.

How long would it take for them to realize the truth, that she'd been snatched off the street and was being held against her will?

Abby wondered how they—*whoever they were*—had gotten her away from the crush of tourists? Vehicle traffic wasn't permitted anywhere near the fountain, and the streets had been cordoned off with temporary bike rack fencing. She remembered seeing police cars, mostly for crowd control but also probably as a counterterrorism measure. It couldn't have been easy to drug an American teenager and then squirrel her right out from under the collective nose of Italian authority…and her parents, who had been only a few yards away.

Had they done this sort of thing before?

The blurred outlines of her surroundings were beginning to take shape, as if some *avant garde* filmmaker was slowly racking the lens into focus. The farthest objects achieved clarity first, beginning with a window, draperies open just enough to let in a column of light. Next to it was the chair Abby had made out earlier, the wall behind it covered in yellowed paper that was peeling at the seams. Closer to the bed was an old steamer trunk much like the one in her grandmother's attic, the one that held the old scarves and boas and hats she used to play dress-up with as a girl.

By now the pharmaceuticals in her system were wearing off rapidly, and she came to realize she was in no dream or movie. Her predicament was very real, the sort of story she'd occasionally heard about from the news, considering how little of it she actually watched or read. Hundreds of thousands of teenagers went missing for one reason or another every year, and that was only in the United States. Add in major cities across Europe and the figure swelled into the millions. Some of them ran away of their own accord—usually because of some sort of physical or psychological trauma within the family—but many simply disappeared and were never seen again. Those were the victims of psycho killers, random sadists, and sex traffickers—all of them guided by one variation of depravity or another.

None of it looking good for Abbigail Evans.

That's when she heard a noise—footsteps, approaching from what probably was a hallway beyond the solid wood door to her left. It was secured by what appeared to be three heavy locks, plus a metal bar that could be swung down on some sort of hinge, and seemed more useful at keeping people out, rather than keeping her in.

Then she heard a key being inserted in the lock, the sound physically jolting her body as the bolt clicked.

Despite the panic, despite the duct tape, despite the intentions of whoever was on the other side of that door, Abigail Evans decided at that very moment that whatever was about to happen—whatever her captors had planned for her—she would fight with every ounce of courage, every bit of resolve she could dredge out of her very soul. She was going to survive this place, this entire ordeal—even if it turned out to be the last thing she did. What she did not realize, and had no way of knowing, was that every other girl—and, yes, every boy—who had faced the very same fear in the very same bed, with the same duct tape and same dismal fate, had sworn to do the exact same thing.

Part II

Vivace

Chapter 16

The mattress was small and lumpy, but at least the sheets were clean and there were no suspicious stains or bugs. Not that Phythian could see much of either in the subdued light from the single bulb that seemed to be dusted in a light brown sheen, the table lamp perhaps a holdover from the bygone days of sepia.

The room was tucked around the back of a sagging hotel that was not visible from the street, and whose existence was known only to the working women who met their inebriated customers there. It was relatively quiet, the only sound being the occasional squeaking of bedsprings in the rooms next door, or banging rhythmically through the rafters overhead—every hour on the hour, it seemed. Still, the address was well off the grid, the lodging was cheap, and his neighbors paid him no mind as he went about his business and they conducted theirs.

Besides the bed, the room also held a small table and wooden chair with a painfully hard back that seemed way too straight to accommodate the human spine, constructed long before the word *ergonomic* was invented. Nonetheless, Phythian was leaning back in it, his head almost touching the wall behind him, feet propped up on the bed. He cradled a snifter of Armagnac in his hands, inhaled the tamed aroma of vanilla and roasted nuts as he allowed his eyes to slip out of focus. He slowly took a sip, the smooth glow warming his tongue before the liquid slid down his throat. Somewhere he heard a few bars of music and people chanting something, but at that moment his mind was far, far away.

He remained positioned that way, a delicate feat of balance as he allowed his body to relax and let his mind void itself of the rigors of the day. After a few minutes, the internal rhythms of his heart and lungs eased, and he sensed the neurons in his brain relax to the point of shutting down, like a garden of flowers closing their petals up for the night. If he'd been connected to medical monitors, they would have shown that his respiration had slacked off to four breaths per minute, and his heart rate hovered just above fifty.

The pinging of his phone changed all that the instant the screen of his phone lit up: Martin Beaudin. No one else knew the number, nor had any reason to be calling him.

He allowed a deep breath of air to enter his lungs before answering it. "You made it home to Andorra?" he inquired. He gave no greeting, no chit-chat: business only, as usual.

"I got in an hour ago," the locksmith replied. "Wanted to do a little digging before I gave you a call."

"Tell me what you found," Phythian said, lowering his voice. The walls of the hotel were annoyingly thin, which meant if he could hear what was going on next door, the same could be said for his room.

"I went through Mlle Lamoines' phone card first," Beaudin told him, getting right to it. "As you may know, a SIM card is an English acronym that stands for subscriber identity module, and it stores all the identification that allows a smartphone to connect to specific mobile network. In this case, Orange S.A. It also contains things like user identity, phone number, network authorization data, personal security keys, and contacts."

"What about access to cloud storage?" Phythian asked. He pictured him sitting in his second-floor drawing room above a locksmith shop on a quiet side street in Andorra la Vella, the capital city of the tiny Pyrenees principality. He would be sipping a glass of Bordeaux, a window cracked open to in the late spring breeze, laptop open on the table in front of him. Phythian had visited him there once, found it to be four floors of narrow rooms burdened with dark walls and heavy drapes and leather-bound books that hadn't been opened in decades, plus a well-stocked wine cellar that even a sommelier at a Michelin three-star restaurant would envy.

"*Certainement*, if one has the password."

"And I assume you do?" he asked. "Have the password."

"Your lady friend made it easy by storing it in a folder."

Interesting choice of word—*friend*—since Phythian would not in a million years have used it to describe his relationship with Gabrielle Lamoines. They had only met once, when she was about twenty and he had accidentally brushed past her on the street several blocks from the Champs Élysées in the Eighth Arrondissement. He had been conducting reconnaissance in the neighborhood where her parents lived, in advance of his scheduled assassination of Monsieur Lamoines later that week, a death that was to appear as either an accident or suicide.

"*Bonjour, mademoiselle,*" he had said to her, and she had just offered him a polite smile and moved on her carefree way.

So…*friend*? Hardly; it was Phythian who had caused her to lose her father, a horrible and unexplained tragedy that had thrown Gabrielle into an eddy of depression from which only self-prescribed medication and a turnstile of men had eventually helped her cope, just barely.

He had not given the passing encounter the slightest consideration at the time, and only recently had revisited that brief moment in his mind.

As with most moral and true Americans, he'd been raised to believe that "thou shalt not kill" was a noble imperative punishable by death. His subsequent training as a Marine had confused that notion, however, when his superior officers decreed that killing the enemy not only was an expected part of military life, but something to be rewarded with medals and accolades. He'd willingly succumbed to the soldierly message of duty and honor, as most impressionable young men do, and readily accepted that the missions he was being trained to fly were assigned in the name of global stability and the common good. In other words, it was for mother, country, and God, and not necessarily in that order.

His handlers at The Farm in western Virginia had extended that ingrained mindset of fealty to include whatever missions the G3 required him to fulfill. Whether on the battlefield or in the air space above it, he was not to question the motivation or rationale behind any command. To disobey a direct order would be considered a violation of the code of conduct, and would be dealt with in the most severe way possible. There was no distinction between the military and the private sector: the enemy was the enemy, and he had but one job to do. The whys and wherefores were none of his concern.

This daily catechism had been pounded into his head during his indoctrination, and over time his mind had succumbed to the blurred edges.

"Are you there?" he heard Beaudin ask, yanking him from the past back into the present.

"Of course. Go on."

"Yes, sir. Anyway, it appears Mlle Lamoines apparently used her phone for both business and pleasure. From what I've been able to determine, she had a lot of both going on. Her contacts folder has a couple hundred names in it, some with company names after them, some just with email addresses. I haven't had time to go through them all and verify which is which, because I wanted to focus on recent texts and calls first."

"What did you find?" Phythian asked.

"Nothing that seems to lead directly to whoever killed her. Mostly just confirmation of upcoming appointments, quick exchanges with people at work. That sort of thing."

"But…"

"Right. *But.* There were a couple things that struck me as odd."

"Odd in what way?"

"In the way that made me cross-check them back to her contacts, as well as her sent-and-received emails. The SIM card doesn't retain all that information, although most of it's in the phone company cloud. Nonetheless, there were a few high-powered names that seemed to stand out. And a lot of texts with a fellow named Sten Gustafsson-Jeglum."

The name meant nothing to Phythian, but he asked, "How recent?"

"There's an entire thread from yesterday," Beaudin replied. "Looks like she had to break off their plans, because of her trip to Rome. And there's a mention of some kind of hand-off."

"What time was this?"

"Crack of dawn, it seems. I just copied it and sent it to you."

As if on cue Phythian's cell pinged again, and he found the exchange of SMS messages Beaudin had just forwarded to him. "Hang on while I read it," he said.

"Take your time," the locksmith in Andorra replied.

Phythian heard him take a long, slow sip of wine, then turned his attention back to the text conversation:

Gabrielle: Sorry…can't make it. I have a plane to catch first thing.

Sten: Something always seems to come up.

Gabrielle: Nature of the job, mon ami.

Sten: You'll still be able to do the hand-off?

Gabrielle: Of course. Midnight, at the L'AIR par Aristide Maillol.

Sten: When will I see you?

Gabrielle: Not sure. I'll be in Rome all week, and after that I don't know.

Sten: Will you be back for the weekend?

Gabrielle: My plans are open-ended, but I'll make it up to you. ☺

Sten: Just promise me that you'll be careful.

Gabrielle: I always am. Au revoir et belle rêves.

That was the end of the text string. As Beaudin had speculated previously, Gabrielle Lamoines was set to fly to the G20 meeting in Rome this morning, a trip her death had unfortunately prevented. The exchange between her and the fellow named Sten hinted at a relationship that mixed business with pleasure, although Phythian got the distinct impression that the personal aspect of it might not have been fifty-fifty. And yes, there had been a mention of some sort of hand-off, at a sculpture he knew was located at the Jardin des Tuileries not far from the Louvres. What was that all about? he wondered.

"Anything else of note?" he asked.

"Well, there is one more thing I found a bit odd," Beaudin replied. "A few hours after Mlle Lamoines died, she received a few calls from a number that doesn't appear to be in her contact list."

"What time are we talking about?" Phythian asked.

"They started a little after midnight, and the last one was around six this morning. Whoever it was seemed desperate to reach her."

"Have you called that number?"

"It seems to be turned off," Beaudin replied. "Or out of service."

Made sense, if the caller was the person involved with the hand-off. "What about the memory card, the one you found in her bathroom?"

"It's next on my list. Meantime, there's something else that may turn into nothing."

"Let me be the judge of that," Phythian said. "What is it?"

"Well, there was an item in Mlle Lamoines' room that looked…well, out of keeping with the rest of the place," the locksmith replied.

"What sort of item?"

"An illustration, a little larger than a playing card. I found it on the top of her commode, and it shows a woman wearing a blue robe and headdress. The words 'The High Priestess' are written on it."

"You took this card with you?" Phythian asked.

"I didn't want to disturb it," Beaudin said. "But I did snap a picture."

"Good thinking. Send it."

After a few more questions he ended the call, let another taste of Armagnac flow over his tongue. The broad mouth and deep body of the glass had allowed the aroma to open up, and now he tasted a hint of pear and caramel, in addition to the vanilla and nuts.

His phone *pinged* one more time: Beaudin's photograph had arrived. Phythian opened it, found an illustration painted with thick blue and black strokes. It depicted a woman draped in a flowing cloak, standing in front of a stone archway, a rolled-up scroll clenched in what appeared to be her left hand. A large cat—real or statue he couldn't tell—was positioned at her feet. As Beaudin had said, the words *The High Priestess* were written at the top of the card, and at the bottom it read *La Sacredotisa*, the Spanish translation. A quick Google search explained that the image was from a set of tarot cards designed by the late surrealist painter, Salvador Dali.

Beaudin had said he'd found the card on Gabrielle's dresser, but there was no way of knowing if it had been placed there by her or someone else...or perhaps her killer. He closed the image on his phone, then again read through the text exchange between Gabrielle and the fellow named Sten. Were they friends or colleagues, or maybe lovers? Possibly all of the above?

Phythian next typed "Sten Gustafsson-Jeglum" into his phone's search engine, which told him the guy was a proficient hacker and online data pirate whose ransomware activities continued to infect government and corporate computers across the globe. His loosely knit organization went by the name TruthCorps, and the list of charges filed against him covered a wide range of serious crimes: fraud, money laundering, conspiracy, and even cyber terrorism. At least a dozen countries repeatedly had tried to shut down his servers and nail his Swedish ass, but thus far he'd managed to elude all efforts to capture him. Interpol had a long-standing Red Notice out for his arrest and ultimate extradition, and he was a permanent fixture atop the FBI's list of wanted international fugitives.

Phythian decided right then that he wanted to meet this man of Gabrielle's texts.

In the end, Xenon Gorski was given a Hobson's choice: his thumbs or his manhood. He elected to lose his thumbs; in the thirty-odd years that Sergei Djokovic had been in this line of work, he had never met a man who had chosen otherwise.

The crude surgical procedure was performed in a windowless room inside a darkened brick warehouse located just outside the Peripherique in Croissy Sur-Seine, wet floors and dripping walls and an underlying stench of decaying flesh. Windows that at one time let in shafts of light had been painted black, and now only little slivers where the paint had peeled off allowed in orange and violet speckles of the setting sun. Sergei mercifully kept the job short and sweet, the rusty pruning shears taking no more than ten seconds total.

"You chose wisely," Sergei said as Xenon cradled his hands, rocking back and forth in agony. The stumps where his thumbs had been only moments before now were covered with strips of cloth torn from an old T-shirt. "I would have done the same."

Xenon wanted to spit on him, just as he had done earlier, but he suspected these people—a generous word for whoever they were—were not quite done with him. They'd probably take his tongue as punishment, or possibly resort to selection Number One, just to make a point. In fact, it may have been the spitting that had caused this bastard to lop off his thumbs to begin with. Judging from the looks of this place, and the dark stains that had dried on the concrete floor, a number of other prisoners had screamed and lost similar appendages in here…which convinced him even more that the worst was yet to come.

"They're going to get infected," he found himself moaning, the pain searing his hands and his arms. While his wrists were free, his feet and torso were taped tightly to the chair on which he was seated. "These rags—they're filthy."

Sergei said nothing, just pulled a metal chair around and straddled it, facing Xenon from what he determined to be a safe distance. He stared at his thin Polish prisoner for what seemed like the longest time, but said nothing.

"Please…" Xenon finally said through his pain. "Tell me what…this is about."

Sergei seemed in no mood to be hasty. He took a cigar out of his pocket, trimmed the tip with his clippers, and stuffed it in his mouth. He lit it from a disposable butane lighter, then took a deep breath, holding the smoke in his lungs before slowly letting it out in Xenon's face.

"Tell me what I want to know," he finally said.

"I have money…back at my place. I told you this already…in the car."

Sergei took another draw on his cigar, shorter this time. "Yes, you did," he said, his words coming out in little puffs of smoke. "Thing is, we already went there. Before we picked you up."

"You went to my apartment?" Xenon said, trying not to look alarmed.

"Then you must have found it."

"We didn't find shit," Sergei snapped at him.

"The money's inside my computer," Xenon said with a whimper. "There's a compartment in the back. Please...take me there. I'll get it for you."

"Too late." Sergei shook his head, using the lighter to give his cigar a little more flame. Turning the flint wheel with his thumb, just to remind Xenon what he no longer was capable of doing. He drew another deep breath, said, "We torched it."

"You what?" Xenon's eyes opened wide, and he thought, *you fucking idiots, you have no idea what you've done.*

"Place went up like a pile of matches." Sergei sounded almost proud of the fact, the way he said it. "But let's forget about that, okay? A smart guy like you must have figured out by now why you're here."

No, Xenon hadn't figured anything of the sort. In fact, he had suspected it was the eighteen thousand he owed the Turk on account of the gambling and the drugs...and the women. His mother had warned him about such things when he had gone off to university, but he hadn't listened. The vices of a young man out on his own for the first time have no ears or voice of reason.

Then it occurred to him that the Turk probably had nothing to do with any of this.

"The bank?" he finally said, almost blubbering. Thinking he could not let the man see his fear or his pain.

"That's right," Sergei nodded. "Talk to me about *the bank.*"

"It was nothing, really," Xenon said. "I only borrowed the card for a day. Two at the most. So I could pay back someone I owe. Çelik."

"You mentioned this Çelik in the car." Sergei tapped his ash to the floor. "I don't give a shit who he is, and he's not involved in this. Now, focus on the bank."

Xenon did focus on the bank, the words coming out fast now. He explained how he worked in the programming department in the Paris branch of the Clear Bank of Luxembourg, and as such he had access to the mainframe servers where information regarding thousands of anonymous numbered accounts was stored. He had been offered a pile of Euros to remove a small memory card, and the only way to get it out of the bank was to physically remove it, then read it with an external device designed for just that purpose. He spilled everything to this man, Sergei, who looked like he was former KGB, Xenon thinking he'd already lost his thumbs, and didn't want to press his luck.

"Who paid you to do this?" Sergei asked. "And don't tell me you don't know."

"But I don't," he insisted, his voice almost a whimper. "It's the truth. One day last week I got a text. Said if I did this thing, I would be paid twenty thousand Euros. Half of it up front. I found an envelope under my door that night. Ten thousand Euros was in it. I hid it in the back of my computer."

"We checked your phone," Sergei informed him. He reached behind him, produced a pair of garden loppers that were used to cut small branches off trees. "There was no text like that. Stop lying."

"If you have my phone, then you know I'm not lying," Xenon pleaded. "The text disappeared within minutes. There's an app for that now."

Sergei considered this, decided not to press the point. "You know what was on that card?" he finally asked.

"Names of people and companies who hide their money in numbered accounts so they don't have to pay taxes," Xenon explained. The bandages around his hands were soaked through with blood, and he was starting to feel weak.

"That's right." Sergei picked up the bloody pruning shears, opened the sticky blades as wide as they could go. Wide enough to slice a small limb in two, easy. Then he glanced at the shadow of a man standing behind Gorski in the darkness. "Hold his arms again while I pull down his trousers," he said.

Xenon screamed, tried to wriggle his feet loose as he rocked his chair from side to side. "Please, no—"

"Then give me the name."

"But I swear—"

"The truth, Gorski."

The young Pole closed his eyes so he couldn't see the hungry blades that this oaf was holding less than ten inches from his groin. He let out a little snivel, then said, "Sten Ingebretesen-Jeglum."

"Who's that?" the man with the shears asked.

But Xenon Gorski just shook his head, realizing that he probably had sent not only his own soul to hell, but that of his Swedish friend, as well. "A guy I know," he said.

Sergei waved off the man in the shadows, said, "Where do we find him? This friend of yours who paid you to steal the card."

"You can't," Gorski told him. "He finds you."

Sergei opened and closed the shears rapidly, several times. *Snip-snip.* "Give me the fucking address—"

"I don't know where he lives," Gorski said, his voice resolute, darkened by pending doom. "No one does."

Sergei thought on that for a minute, figured the Polish prick was probably telling the truth—amazing what a little pain and fear will do to a man. "So where is it now?" he demanded. "The card?"

"I gave it to someone else, to copy. She was going to give it back to me last night, but she…she never showed."

"Ah…a woman," Sergei said, moving the bloody shears closer to Gorski's crotch. "Does she have a name?"

Xenon Gorski again closed his eyes, tried not to think about what this monster might have in mind. Not for him, but for Gabrielle. He didn't want to rat her out; he was not that sort of man, even though she hadn't shown up at the drop, and even though he had just snitched on his friend Sten. He didn't want to think what other body parts he might lose if he didn't cooperate here, so he took a deep breath, and let out a long sigh that made the name "Gabrielle Lamoines" sound as if it were traveling on a breeze.

Chapter 17

Shortly after four o'clock local time Logan inserted an old-fashioned key into an old-fashioned lock and opened the door to his new digs. In this case, it was a small but clean room in a small but tidy hotel that came with a two-point-seven (out of five) Trip Advisor rating and a private bathroom (no bidet) on a one-way street across from a shop that had been boarded up. Scorch marks from a recent fire suggested the reason for this, and the walls on both sides of the narrow lane were covered with graffiti, some of which showed signs of either being scoured away or painted over.

He'd stayed in rooms that were much worse, but he still yanked down the sheets to make certain no bed bugs had taken up residence. He'd encountered the nasty critters once before, in a squalid hotel near Penn Station in New York that no longer existed, and remembered them from the British movie *The L-Shaped Room*, starring Leslie Caron. Finding none here, he parked his carry-on bag in a corner, then retreated to the *gabinetto* to run a blade over his two-day growth of beard.

The bathroom was a study in minutiae and unintended whimsy. A black porcelain toilet was partially situated beneath a pink porcelain sink, while a turquoise metal shower no larger than a phone booth—back when those were still were a thing—took up most of the Lilliputian space. But it was a place to hang his hat for the next few days. Euphemistically speaking, since there were no hooks, no hangers, and no closet. But it was dry, it seemed to have hot water, and it was near the center of Rome and close to the Republicca metro station. Wifi was free and adequate, a small mercato and a ristorante were at the end of the block, as was a place to buy bananas and tangerines, if he so desired. So were a half dozen dumpsters for recycling, which the good people of Rome seemed to take very seriously.

After his quick shave he sat down on a plastic chair that was pushed under a laminated desk. After digging an adapter out of his bag, he plugged in his laptop and called Raleigh Durham while he waited for it to boot, figuring she'd be up to her ass in work and he'd just get her voicemail.

But she answered on the first ring, and said, "How's the jailbird?"

Logan couldn't remember how much he'd spilled last night—this morning—when he'd shown up at her door, so he replied, "What did I tell you?"

"More than you should have, Mr. Capone. Did you get a good nap?"

"In fact, I did. And the day has turned out better than I'd hoped. I just wanted to let you know that you won't be coming back to a squatter tonight, whatever time you get in."

"Which will be late. And that's too bad, because I'll miss your witty repartee. Although not necessarily the smell of your aftershave."

"I don't use aftershave."

"Hmmm…maybe that was my point." He heard her giggle on the other end, and then she said, "By the way, you know that man you killed last night—"

"I actually mentioned that?"

"You pretty much spilled your guts, Cart," using her term of endearment for him. "And for what it's worth, it turns out he's not just any old gunman on a motorcycle."

"What are you talking about?"

"I'm talking about a former Mafioso soldier turned government snitch who's suspected of killing two arms dealers earlier in the evening. Goes by the name Stefano Santoro. Or at least he did before you killed him."

"How do you know all this?"

"It's what I do."

Logan thought back to the nasty pistol he'd seen spin up into the air just after the guy had plowed into the Fiat door, and said, "That must be why they grilled me all night."

"Seems you bagged yourself a big-name dude, my friend, which is either good news or bad news."

Shit on a stick, he thought. Good or bad, if even half of what Raleigh was saying was anywhere near the truth, the next few days of his life could be the stuff of nightmares.

"You sure know how to brighten up a man's day," he told her.

"Keep that in mind," she replied. "When the day is gone, and all its sweets are left… sweet voice, sweet lips, soft hand, and softer breast."

"Shakespeare?"

"Keats," she corrected him. "Or his cheap bastard stepchild. Goodnight."

She hung up, leaving him sitting there, thinking *what the hell just happened?* He also was wondering if some romantic inuendo had just sailed way over his head like a triple hit high up against the center field wall—and, if so, how he'd misjudged it entirely.

Two minutes later he was connected to the hotel wifi, and ran an internet search on Renato Azzone. He was the Vatican government official from whom Alvize had escaped six months ago, and from whom he'd been running ever since. More than just a top deputy within the city-state's government, the bastard was a close confident within the Holy See and supposedly had the ear of the Pope.

Appointed to his current position two years ago by His Holiness, Azzone was born in the Lombardy region of Northern Italy in the mid-'60s. A devout Catholic, he'd earned a law degree at Bocconi University, then continued his studies in canon law and missiology at the Pontifical Gregorian University in Rome. His faith and oratorical skills caught the attention of a prominent bishop and, upon graduation, he was invited to serve as a librarian at the Vatican Secret Archives. While the name had always suggested vast mysteries and conspiracies perpetrated within the Catholic Church, the word "secret" actually was derived from the Latin lexeme *secretum*, or private. In reality, the Archives primarily housed the See's paperwork and correspondence related to the Pope, and other materials typically of little interest to those outside the Church's governance.

Described as highly intelligent and loyal to a fault, Azzone rose through the Vatican ranks, serving on the Pontifical Council for the Laity before a previous Pope named him to the Roman Curia. A few years later he was elevated by the new Pope to the Pontifical Commission, at the urging of Bishop Maximillian Klaus, an Austrian and fellow member of the Legion of Christ. When Cardinal Giudice stepped in front of a truck outside the Vatican, Klaus—in his new role as Vice Secretary General, and with Azzone's counsel—formed a conclave that embraced a strict theocentric nationalism.

Logan's Google search also referenced a close friendship that dated back to Azzone's adolescence in Lombardy. A family acquaintance had come to stay with his parents for a few weeks one summer—reason unspecified—and the two men, while far apart in age, had maintained a casual correspondence ever since. Now in his mid-sixties, that friend—Alessandro Bortolotti—had risen to become a major player in the neofascist movement that was sweeping across Europe. Drawing inspiration from the Italian Social Movement that had simmered in various regions of the country during his younger years, he began to hold rallies in towns where he knew strong neofascist sympathies lay. He would whip attendees into a frenzy, railing against the injustices committed by politicians and the "foreign invaders" who stole the jobs and bastardized the traditions of true Italians.

As attendance at these gatherings grew—first in the hundreds, and eventually in the tens of thousands—his message became increasingly extreme. Initially vowing to change the system through the ballot box, his doctrine had evolved in recent years to encourage the overthrow of western democratic entities by whatever means necessary. The election of Giorgia Meloni as the first fascist Prime Minister of Italy since the days of Mussolini did little to dissuade him from his political ambition; after all, she had been chosen via a semi-democratic process, which Bortolotti abhorred and against which he continually railed.

In fact, each of his rallies increasingly called for disruption of the deep state government, and ended with a straight-armed, pumped-fist call-and-response from the closely packed crowd that demanded violence through power by tearing things apart, or, as loosely translated into Latin:

Violentiam. Valeo. Diripio.

Which, Google now told him had been abbreviated to a neofascist right-wing political battle cry: *ViValDi.*

Which raised the question: what was he up to? Did Bortolotti have an end game? Agitators rarely agitated just for sport; they had a vision of how their efforts would play out, how their goals could be achieved.

"Your delivery is a day out, signore," Mateo Tufino said over his right shoulder. His eyes were glued to the reflection of Bortolotti, who now was sitting in the backseat. A dark gloom seemed to have settled in on the man, like an approaching storm that was about to let loose a crack of lighting any moment now. "Two days at the most."

"You sure of this?"

"I have good ears on the ground, and that's what they're telling me."

"Well, tell your ears that's playing it Goddamned close—"

"Yes, sir," Tufino agreed. They were on the E80 now, the four-lane highway that circled the eastern edge of Rome, heading to a destination that *Il Capo* had not yet divulged. "The boat was delayed leaving Tunisia, another official needing a bribe. But it's in international waters now, and there shouldn't be any more trouble."

Bortolotti didn't respond, just massaged his cheek bones with fingers the size of small tree roots. No revolution of any consequence ever was truly won without the spilling of blood. For that he needed weapons, which he'd financed on the come. To be paid for with the sale of the drugs that were sitting out in the middle of the Mediterranean, which Tufino was telling him was still a day out from delivery...maybe two. The Russian might allow him that much time, but not much more.

"Take *uscita venticinque*, up ahead," he finally said: Exit twenty-five.

"And after that?"

"That's on a need-to-know basis," Bortolotti replied. Despite his annoyance—frustration—with the missing drug shipment, he trusted Tufino implicitly, but he also knew that even the tightest institutions could spring a leak. This close to zero hour and the promise of triumph, he wasn't taking any chances.

"Si, signore."

Bortolotti glanced at Tufino's reflection in the rearview mirror, found no malice or artifice in his eyes. Satisfied that his strategy was safe, he sat back in the plush seat of the quarter-million-Euro Mercedes and picked up his pen. He stared at the empty page in front of him, and began to write the first rough draft of his victory speech, scratching out words as more appropriate ones came to mind—in Italian, of course, confident that it would be translated into every language of the continent, plus a special Americanized version for the United States.

The world has just witnessed the power and the will of the great people of Europe. Through incredible determination and bravery, we brought an end not only to this year's ~~meeting~~ coven of globalist ~~leaders~~ swindlers, but also the defeat of the democratic elites who seek to destroy not only the sanctity of our nationhood, but also the very heritage of the proud people across this great continent.

As I speak to you right now, [NUMBER TO BE DETERMINED] heads of state are dead, and another [INSERT NUMBER] have been critically wounded. While it may seem proper to mourn the loss of life and limb, we must not forget that these despots and charlatans were traitors to our customs, our morals, and the laws that draw us together as a people. As such, they are not worthy of our tears.

In their unbridled quest for profit and riches, they invited a stream of immigrants from regions that have no rooted interest in our land, our people, our languages, or our values. They have weakened the natural defenses of our countries, crippled our borders, undermined our currency, diluted our laws, and depressed the dignity of our people. They've conspired to restrict our freedoms, repress our livelihoods, and restrain our very sustenance as they welcomed more and more outsiders into our towns and neighborhoods, swelling the very streets on which we live.

In the past our protests fell on deaf ears, and our pleas were ignored. Well, I am standing before you at this hour to tell you: NO MORE! We have won. We have made ourselves heard, and it is time to regain the liberty and justice that these deep state imposters took from us. Finally, we can—we will—change this runaway expansion of the global human threat by putting our beliefs into motion.

The American President Theodore Roosevelt once implored his country's leaders to speak softly but carry a big stick. Well, today we stopped speaking and instead wielded that stick—swiftly, fiercely, and with finality.

Violentiam. Valeo. Diripio.

Just let the fucking shipment arrive on time, Bortolotti thought as he set the pen down, gazing at the ancient hills of Rome passing in the distance, calling on the power of God to draw him into the bosom of power. Sensing the courage and resolve of all of the great city-state's kings, dictators, and emperors awakening deep inside him.

He pulled his phone out of his pocket and punched a number at the top of his "recents" list. It was a conversation he'd been postponing but knew was imminent, the price he'd paid when he'd sold his soul to the devil himself: the treacherous Russian into whose lair he'd crawled to make this all happen, to ensure the events of tomorrow would happen as planned—and cement his rise to power.

"*Da*," the man on the other end answered.

"Signor Sokolov," Bortolotti said in a voice as bright and chipper as he could muster. "Everything is in place. Vivaldi is a go."

• • •

"I'm calling for Sten Gustafsson-Jeglum, please," the voice on the phone said: male, easily American, most likely white, but with a regional hitch the Swede didn't quite recognize.

The young hacker who was wanted in a dozen countries hesitated a second, then inquired, "*Vem fan är det här?*" Which translated loosely to, who the fuck is this?

"I'm afraid I don't speak Swedish," Phythian replied. "But I got this number from a mutual friend, who suggested I call if anything ever happened to her."

"And who might this mutual friend be?" Sten asked, switching to English, already knowing the answer to his question. Of the six prepaid phones he owned, only two people had the number for this one.

"Gabrielle Lamoines," Phythian said.

Sten again fell silent for a moment, his eyes drifting to the bank of monitors on the makeshift desk in front of him. Most of them had *Matrix*-like lines of code scrolling down them, but one was playing a chase scene from one of his favorite movies: an American thriller starring Gene Hackman and Will Smith, and loaded with paranoia and conspiracy.

"And how is our mutual friend Gabrielle doing?" he eventually asked.

"I believe you already know the answer to that one, Sten," Phythian replied.

There was a brief silence; then the Swede said, "Regrettably, you are quite correct. It's a sad day, very sad. May I ask you a question?"

"Save your breath. My name is Rōnin Phythian."

Another brief silence followed, then Sten said. "The last time I heard that name used in a sentence, it was in the past tense. As in, 'Phythian is dead.'"

"As Mark Twain once famously said, 'the report of my death was an exaggeration.' And don't let it distract from the fact that we need to meet."

"I don't do meetings," Sten countered.

"You'll want to do this one," Phythian assured him. "Your name was all over Gabrielle's phone, and you're already wanted by just about every nation around the world. The last thing you need is more trouble."

"Even if what you say is true, I fail to see how a meeting would be beneficial to me."

"Your benefit is none of my concern. My business is only with Gabrielle, and whoever killed her. I believe she was involved with something bigger than she was, and it led to her death."

"And you think I know what that thing might be?"

"Based on the flurry of texts and calls between the two of you yesterday, it's a logical conclusion. One I'm sure the police have already made."

"Gabrielle knew that what she was doing carried its risks," Sten insisted.

"And this time those risks likely cost her her life. And yours very well could be next."

"Still too risky," Sten insisted, but Phythian detected a softening in his voice, as if the guy might be coming around to his way of thinking. Not that he really had any choice in the matter.

"For you and me both," Phythian said. "But given the status of our deceased friend, I'm willing to take a chance if you are."

The Swede mulled this over, the various scenarios and risks playing out in his brain in a flash of a second. Then he said, "Where are you now?"

"Paris."

An icy shudder caused Sten to shiver; *too close for comfort*. "Very well," he said, despite his better instinct. "We can meet tonight."

"When and where?"

"I'll call you later with further directions."

"Make sure you do," Phythian warned him.

"I will," Sten replied. "And you make sure you turn off your GPS."

"I don't have GPS. Big brother is not my friend."

"Makes two of us," Sten replied. "One more thing—"

"Yes?" Phythian asked, even though he knew what was coming.

"You screw with me, you're dead."

"If you've read even a single page of my curriculum vitae, as I suspect you have, you know you have even more reason than me to be worried," Phythian told him. "See you tonight."

Chapter 18

Logan clicked the stop button on his laptop and the video froze on a final frame. He'd just finished watching an eight-minute clip extracted from a much longer address Allesandro Bortolotti had given at a rally in Budapest last winter. The image on his screen depicted a man with his mouth wide open in a moment of fury, his closed fist pumped high in the air—a gesture repeated by everyone in the crowd pressing up against the stage.

Thousands of people had attended the gathering in Hero's Square to hear him and other neofascists from Eastern Europe applaud the besieged Nazi soldiers who escaped from the Russian-encircled city at the end of World War II. Almost all were dressed in black and carried flags depicting various far-right movements as they marched in honor of National Socialist "heroes," while perpetrating the lie that the holocaust was nothing but a fabrication of far-left Jewish sympathizers.

Bortolotti's message was passionate yet simple. It called for a return to the principle of "blood and soil"—*blut und boden* in German, and *sangue e terra* in Italian. The slogan initially was used to evoke the idea of a purified "Aryan" race ruling over the land that was their God-given birthright. Stealing directly from Heinrich Himmler's playbook, he laid into the immigrant parasites who had swarmed throughout all of Europe, and were responsible for the near-extinction of its culture, its values, and its very identity.

Logan could not possibly understand the language, but subtitles at the bottom of the video translated the fiery rhetoric that had caused the crowd to erupt with cheers. "We must not remain docile while those in power continue to corrupt, and be corrupt," he exhorted the throng. "We are the people in the streets, the people in the markets and the factories and the mines. We are the workers who see our jobs being stolen by outsiders, populating our cities and towns, and spreading their foreign ideas and their alien gods. Those intruders are not us. They do not represent who we are, nor what we stand for. It is a full-fledged invasion, and we must stop it now, before our blood is corrupted and we no longer have a homeland. We must achieve victory at any cost. *Violentiam*. We must assume power above all else. *Valeo*. And we must tear apart their plot to destroy our way of life. The very plot to destroy who we are. *Diripio. ViValDi.*"

The man's planning a Goddamned coup, Logan thought. *Fucking lunatic.*

His hotel room was small, but he still had to stand up and cross the room to retrieve the bottle of Montalcino he'd purchased at the corner store. It came with a screw cap, which he twisted off and then poured a healthy amount into a glass he'd found—and thoroughly washed—in the minuscule bathroom. He took a tentative sip before he sat back down; at six Euros he'd expected it to be the equivalent of Italian rotgut, but instead was surprised how smooth it tasted going down: cherries and cranberries, with an underlying layer of vanilla and a hint of earthiness.

He picked up his phone and dialed a number he'd been given two days ago by a friend who worked in the Georgetown University Department of Theology, and who had helped him out on a religious ethics story a while back. The number was for the direct cell of a retired G.U. professor and provost, a specialist in Catholic systematic theology and expert on ecumenical dialogue and biblical hermeneutics. *Whatever they were.* His most recent book on the role of the Church in the Italian government had won him the Pulitzer Prize, and he now divided his time between Bethesda and an apartment just north of the Vatican.

Logan let the phone ring and ring, figured it eventually would just go to voicemail. Eventually there was a click on the other end and someone answered, "This is David Vaughan. Whoever you are, how the fuck did you get this number?"

"No one followed me," Phythian assured the Swede with the blonde man-bun sitting across from him in a booth in the *Hypermarché* food court. Just like in the movies, Sten Gustafsson-Jeglum had sent him scurrying from the blue line to the red line to the green, eventually directing him to a newly constructed station way the hell out in the working-class suburb of Aubervilliers.

"How can you be sure?"

"Over the years I developed a knack for these things."

"Can't ever be too careful," Sten said, his eyes nervously darting from right to left.

They were seated at a small Formica-topped table near the rear of a pizza joint. Sten was positioned with his back to the wall so he could see anything or anyone out of the ordinary, either coming or going. Phythian had arrived at their rendezvous first and had ordered a glass of Beaujolais before selecting a table and sitting down. Predictably, Sten had picked a different one, insisting it provided a cleaner escape route if either of them had to make a fast move.

"This is your life?" Phythian asked, using his hands to indicate that he meant this entire way of living on the lam, paranoid and suspicious and distrustful. "Always looking over your shoulder, I mean."

"Not much different from yours, I suspect," Sten said.

"When I'm not on the move, my surroundings couldn't look more different." His mind briefly drifted to the herd of Masai giraffes he'd watched grazing in an acacia grove not far from his secluded camp the evening before he'd left on this trip. An itinerary that had included a brief check-in at an island off the coast of Scotland before his flight to Cyprus. "But you're right: freedom comes at a steep price."

"And a lot of powerful people don't appreciate it when freedom has the upper hand."

"Or when pirates hack into their computers and hold them for ransom."

"In our diseased world there are many variations of justice," the Swede said.

"Certainly not to be confused with justification," was Phythian's retort.

At that moment two men in long, dark coats appeared at the edge of the food court. Sten's eyes shifted from one of them to the other, then darted to the emergency exit. Eventually the two men dropped into a booth and started talking in hushed tones, and when Sten was satisfied they were not there for him, he drew his gaze back to Phythian.

"But you did not come all this way to engage me in a discussion of ethics and morality," he said. "As I recall, you said this was about our mutual friend, Gabrielle Lamoines."

"Yes, I did," Phythian agreed, his eyes lingering on the two newcomers a moment. "It appears you figured quite prominently in her life."

"And you want to know if I figured just as prominently in her death."

Phythian shook his head and said, "You didn't kill her. I already know that. But you're just as concerned as I am about who did, and you may possess information that could provide answers to both of us. You also rightly believe that I might prove to be a safer partner than the police in bringing her killer to justice. Of which you speak so highly."

Sten appeared to bristle at the jibe, tried not to let it show. "As I mentioned earlier, I know a great deal about you, Mr. Phythian. In fact, I ran a deep dive into your life."

"As I'm doing with you right now."

Sten shot him a wary look, but didn't let his words interrupt his train of thought. "You worked for the Greenwich Global Group," he said.

"Past tense," Phythian replied.

"The most dangerous man alive."

"The file still says that?"

"Over a hundred kills."

"I lost track years ago."

"But they didn't. And that's why they tried to kill you."

"They did that because I went off-script and facilitated the death of a pervert," Phythian corrected him. "The G3 didn't appreciate it when their contractors went rogue on them."

"Whatever," Sten said, rolling his eyes. "Your file also includes a lot of bullshit about noetic sciences, intuitive reasoning, and mental visualizing. All of which is referred to as an exceptional extrasensory skillset. Quote-unquote."

"But, as you said, bullshit."

The Swede grinned at that, and said, "I'm a strict empiricist, Mr. Phythian. I deal in facts. Bits and bytes, zeroes and ones. I like science and certainty and things that are beyond a reasonable doubt. So go ahead and prove to me that you can do what your Greenwich dossier says you can do."

Phythian couldn't help but return the smile as he thought back to all the demonstrations he'd been obliged to give to cynical feds and academics and intelligence officers who doubted the truth about his unique abilities.

"The old dog and pony show," he replied.

"Show me what you've got," the Swede pressed him.

Phythian exhaled a deep breath out of tedium, then lifted his glass to his lips and drained it. "All right, if you insist," he finally said, clearing his throat. "It took you just under an hour to drive here from your country house near the town of Ajou, out in Normandy. More of a chateau, really, a property you inherited when your parents were killed in the Madrid train bombing. You call this place *La Maison de Quantum,* because the third floor houses the servers and uplinks that keep your illegal hacking organization running. That third floor—the quantum core—can only be accessed via a steel reinforced door, secured by both an optical scanner and a six-digit electronic lock. The combination to that lock is 2-9-3-2-8-1. The number has no meaning in your life, just a random series you selected."

Sten sat there across the table from him without reacting for a good ten seconds—hard to do, since he was experiencing a complex rush of anger, curiosity, mania, and disbelief. "Very impressive," he finally said. "And, I concede, very dangerous in the wrong hands."

"Even the right ones," Phythian said, nodding slowly. "Now will you trust me, or do you need more proof? Such as what you were doing the evening before last, just before midnight."

Sten cocked his head, still in denial over the display of extrasensory ability he had just experienced. "As I said, very impressive. But what I really want to know is what you need me for. If you have access to everything in my head, why bother asking questions?"

"No bother, really, and I've come to enjoy the sport of it," Phythian replied. "I can find my way into every one of your thoughts and memories—millions of them—just about any time I want. But just like one of your precious computers, that information doesn't mean shit if there isn't some sort of app than can make some order out of it. There are several ways to do that, some much more convenient than others. And verbal communication tends to be the most efficient pathway to comprehension."

"But…what you just did, about the house and the server room and the entry code. I didn't tell you any of that."

"Not in actual words. But your brain put it in a structured order anyway, probably because it was top of mind, and something you really didn't want me to know. Just like trying not to think of something will always make you think of it, like the time when you were twelve and your cousin walked in on you fantasizing over the pages in the Miss Mary catalog, right? Once it gets stuck there in the forefront of your mind, it's almost impossible to unstick it."

Sten started to object but saw there was no point, so he just nodded slowly, resigned himself to accept what Phythian was telling him. What he had just witnessed contradicted every empirical cell in his body, but there was no other way the freak could have known about *La Maison de Quantum,* or the entry code…or the lingerie pics.

"Does it work in every language?" he finally asked.

"Language is immaterial, for complex reasons that would take the rest of the night to explain."

"I stand corrected," Sten Gustafsson-Jeglum said. "You really do learn something new every day."

"And now I want to learn a bit about Gabrielle."

"Go ahead—ask questions, if you really must."

Phythian watched as a nerve in Sten's upper lip twitched, most likely because he had no idea which of his thoughts and memories the freak of nature sitting across from him might pull out of his brain. "Let's start with your appointment with Gabrielle," he said. "The one she broke off with you yesterday, because she was going to Rome."

"How do you know about—" Sten cut himself off; there was no point in denying it. "Just tell me what you think you know," he said.

"I know it had to do with some sort of hand-off that was to occur later, near a sculpture in Jardin des Tuileries," Phythian replied. "Tell me about that."

"It was something she was helping me with," the Swede said. "A memory card that was stolen from a bank based in Luxembourg."

"And worth a lot of money, I would guess."

"Your guess would be correct, but it's not about the money. Never has been. It's about the free flow of information in a global society, where justice depends on open communication and the dissemination of truth."

"To quote your own words, *bullshit.*"

"Don't ask a question if you can't accept the answer," Sten said with a sneer.

"Acceptance isn't the issue here. My questions just make it easier to get at the truth."

Sten Gustafsson-Jeglum's face lost several shades of color as he again realized that Phythian was still in there, rummaging around in his private thoughts and memories. "Gabrielle liked to live on the sharper edge of life," he allowed.

"Was she aware of all the larcenous things you're involved with?"

"I think I want to end this conversation right now—"

"Give it a rest, Sten. I'm not interested in whatever your game is, other than Gabrielle's involvement in it," Phythian assured him. "Doesn't matter to me how many corporate servers you crack, or what computers you hold up for ransom. Most of them probably deserve it. But I do believe that something our mutual friend either knew or did resulted in someone wanting her dead. And you believe it, too."

"I don't give a damn about beliefs, just facts," Sten snapped. "Like I said, zeroes and ones. But since you insist on doing this, here's the deal. I met Gabrielle a couple years ago in Prague. She was covering an IMF meeting, and I was there trying to hack their servers. Not being French I had no idea who she was, and she didn't give a shit what I did, or why I was there. But she was lonely, and...well, it was only after we got to really know each other, that we spoke about our respective modes of employment."

"Do you know what she was working on most recently, anything that might have caused someone to kill her?"

Sten frowned, trying to keep his thoughts focused on what was being asked, and nothing more; definitely no mental wandering. "Anything and everything, really," he said. "Bank fraud, pharmaceutical cover-ups, oil greed, government corruption, the military complex, political scandals, terrorism. Gabrielle was nonpartisan when it came to poking her nose into things."

"But nothing specific that you knew about these last few days."

"I'm sorry, no," Sten insisted, another lie, even though there was no point.

"Tell me about Xenon Gorski," Phythian pressed, changing the subject.

Fuck, this bastard is good, Sten thought, also thinking, *I've got to end this, get away from him now, before he raids my entire brain.* "I never actually met him, but he's a Polish dude who was helping Gabrielle with something," he said.

"The card from the bank in Luxembourg you mentioned, right?"

Feeling a sense of total defeat settling in, he nodded. "Xenon called me a half dozen times last night, wondering if I'd heard from her. The last time, he seemed to be freaking out from fear. Then he stopped calling altogether."

"Do you know where this Gorski fellow lives?"

"Like I said, I never met him. I know Gabrielle did, but it's too late to ask her."

"Yes, it is." Phythian studied his empty glass, decided it best to keep it that way. He'd already absorbed enough information from Sten for one evening, and he needed to keep his brain in a reasonably functioning order so as to process it all later.

"Are we quite through here?" Sten asked, as if reading Phythian's mind, for a change.

"I believe so," Phythian said, but made no motion to stand up. "I want to thank you for meeting with me, and I would suggest it would be best if this visit never officially happened."

"For both of us. And don't take this the wrong way, but I hope I never have the chance to ever see you again."

"Understandable." The Swede started to collect his pizza trash, but Phythian put out a hand to stop him. "One more thing. Tell me about Allesandro Bortolotti."

Sten shot him an annoyed look and said, "I really have to go—"

"No you really don't, not for a couple minutes. But just to help your memory along, Gabrielle mentioned him to you the last time you talked."

The Swede hesitated, his eyes carrying the look of a chess player whose king has just been mated. "Since you're asking me about her, you probably already know."

"Come on—don't make me poke through your brain any more than I already have. It's not a very enjoyable place, and you really don't want me going there."

Sten appeared to cringe at the prospect of prolonging such an intrusion. "All I know is Gabrielle was working on something that had to do with the rise of right-wing nationalism in Europe," he said. "She was always chasing this lead or that clue, and then a couple weeks ago she blurted out the name."

"Bortolotti."

The Swede nodded; there was no use lying about it. "She asked me to put out feelers, learn what I could about him. Who he was, where his funding was coming from. What his end game was."

"And did you?"

"Like still waters, my connections run deep."

"And what did you learn?" Phythian asked him.

"Well, since you're asking me, and not just pulling it out of my head as if you were pulling weeds, it appears he—Bortolotti—has a major thing planned."

"What sort of major thing?"

"If I knew that, we wouldn't be sitting here," Sten said. "And Gabrielle might still be alive."

Chapter 19

Xenon Gorski's body was found just after midnight under the Pont des Arts on the right bank of the Seine.

A young man and his girlfriend quite literally stumbled upon him on the cobbled walking path, dumped there in the darkness. At first, they both thought Xenon was either drunk or homeless, or maybe both. It was only when they noticed the bandages on the victim's hands, and all the fresh blood on his clothing, that they realized this was more than just some vagrant who had passed out from too much absinthe or cheap red wine.

The phone beside deputy chief inspector Francois Fourgét's bed rang six times, almost going to voicemail before he rolled over and picked it up.

"*Que le fait de baiser est cela?*" he growled into the receiver.

"*Je suis désolé de vous réveiller,*" inspector Alain Dupont replied. "*Mais il y a eu un autre meurtre.*"

Fourgét sighed with exasperation, turned on the bedside lamp. "So now you're going to wake me up in the middle of the night whenever there's another murder?"

"No, monsieur. But I thought you'd want to know right away about this one."

Dupont explained how the body of a drifter had been found beneath the pedestrian bridge that crossed the Seine. His thumbs had been removed crudely and his left eye had been put out by a bullet before his body was dumped to the pathway below.

Fourgét grumbled and rubbed the corners of his eyes. "And you thought I'd want to know about this poor soul, in the middle of the fucking night, why?"

Inspector Dupont had worked with Fourgét for six years and was accustomed to the deputy chief inspector's temper, especially when he'd been roused from a deep sleep. "The victim had no identification on him, no wallet or money or anything. But he did have a telephone number scribbled on his left forearm."

"*My* number?" Fourgét snapped into the phone. "Is that why you called me in the middle of the night, to see who answered?"

"No, monsieur," Dupont answered patiently. "I called because I knew you'd want to know whose number it was."

"And?"

"And ironically, we have the phone downstairs in the evidence room. It belonged to Gabrielle Lamoines."

Fourgét said nothing for a moment as the last drips of sleep drained from his mind. Then he swung his legs over the edge of the bed and said, "Where are you?"

"Still at the bridge, inspector."

"I'll be there in twenty minutes."

After again checking for insects, Logan collapsed on his bed. Except for the short nap he'd managed in Raleigh Durham's room that morning, he hadn't slept since his plane was thirty-eight thousand feet above Greenland forty-some hours ago. His eyes burned as if he'd just stared at an eclipse, his head throbbed, and his throat was parched. He knew he needed to hydrate more, but the water from the tap had a beige tint to it, and the mercato down the block was closed.

The Montalcino he'd consumed earlier in the evening hadn't helped much. Neither had the hours he'd spent hunched over his laptop, scrolling through hundreds of Google hits about Vivaldi. The baroque composer from Venice occupied most of the first thirty pages, but he'd had better luck when he added "Bortolotti" to the search parameters.

Particularly helpful was an article titled "The Nationalist Drive That Brought Fascism Back to the Mainstream." It detailed how, before the turn of the millennium, the young revolutionary led a small group of rebels to seize a cold and barren warehouse in Milan, just a few blocks off a street known as Via Padova. As the multicultural heart of the city, it was known as a particularly dangerous neighborhood because of the continual clash of Latinos, Asians, Muslims, and Africans. Bortolotti and his followers had inhabited the building for the next eight years, fondly referring to it as *Casa Benito* in honor of Mussolini, their ideological hero. Agitators came and went, the cause waxed and waned, but he remained dedicated to his particular brand of nationalism and made impassioned speeches about the need for a one-party state led by a powerful and forceful leader.

It was during this time that he first coined the phrase *Violentiam-Valeo-Diripio*.

He first foray into politics was as a candidate for the Senate, representing the *Partito Nazionale Fascista*. He lost. He ran again, and lost again—but by an even larger margin. Realizing that he would never prevail as a minority candidate in a democratic system, he channeled a more populist ministry: social media. There he built a solid following on all the usual digital platforms—Facebook, Twitter, Instagram, Tik Tok—but YouTube was his favorite, and he quickly built a fan base in the millions.

Bortolotti also reached out to other nationalist and neofascist groups inside Italy and across all of Europe. The influx of refugees from Syria, Iraq, Afghanistan, and Yemen was already fueling anger and resentment among countrymen who were feeling increasingly disenfranchised, and he used this growing rage to fan the flames. Such instruments of persuasion as rocks and bottles had escalated to pipe bombs and stabbings, and there was an elevated level of internet chatter calling for violence and destruction as being the means to the end of sham democratic elections.

The YouTube excerpt Logan had viewed earlier had been recorded at a rally just four months ago. Clearly the hyperbole was intensifying and Bortolotti was ratcheting up his rhetoric, itching for a showdown.

At some point he closed his eyes and succumbed to sleep, even though a new morning was already making its presence known on the other side of the curtains. Soon delivery vans and motorbikes would be barreling down the street below, and the city would begin to awaken to the second day of the global summit. Within hours, presidents and prime ministers would be meeting to discuss mutual priorities and set goals that would benefit the planet, their individual countries, and their political careers, although not necessarily in that order.

And, somewhere out there, a nihilist named Allesandro Bortolotti was plotting an act of violence designed to shake the status quo to the core.

Violentiam. Valeo. Diripio.

Morning was just beginning to break over Paris. Clouds had moved in during the night, pulling a dark veil over the stars and the moon, and a hint of rain hung in the air. The first streaks of sun began to backlight the flying buttresses of Notre Dame Cathedral that remained encased in scaffolding, even though it had reopened for tourists.

Chief deputy inspector Fourgét stood on the pathway beneath the bridge at the edge of the river, his cellphone pressed to his ear as the medical examiner gave the go-ahead to remove the body from the scene.

"I see," Fourgét said into the device. Thirty minutes ago, he had sent a scan of the victim's remaining prints to FAED, the French database housing the records of convicted criminals and those suspected of committing serious lesser *délits*. "Gorski, first name Xenon. What do we have on him?"

While Fourgét was talking, Inspector Dupont continued to examine the crime scene. Despite the fact that the young victim's thumbs had been recently removed, cause of death clearly was the single gunshot to his left eye. Burn marks, gunshot residue, and the abrasion collar around the wound indicated that the deadly round had been fired at very close range, probably within a few centimeters of the skin.

Furthermore, it appeared as if he'd been tortured and killed elsewhere, then transported to this bridge and dumped over the rail. Dupont figured the suspects—there had to be more than one in order to move the body—had not known that a pathway traversed the shore of the Seine along here, and likely had expected the body to splash into the river. Had the killers panicked when it had not, or did they even care? They'd been particularly careful not to leave any evidence of themselves behind, and likewise had stripped him of any identification he might typically have carried with him, including his wallet and anything else he'd had on him.

Fourgét ended his conversation, came over to where Dupont was standing. "We have an ID, and an address. It could be an old one, but it's where we start."

"What's his name?" Dupont asked, his eyes trailing after the two medics who were maneuvering the wheeled stretcher bearing his body up the stairway to an ambulance on the Quai de Conti, above.

"Xenon Gorski."

"What kind of name is that?

Fourgét shrugged, then looked up at the sky as a drop of rain hit his head. "I'm told it's not uncommon in Poland. No police record, but his prints were in the database for his work card. He was employed by The Clear Bank of Luxembourg, Paris branch. Lived out in Gagny. Or at least he did when he applied for the permit."

"I got a call-back while you were on the phone," Dupont said. "Rochefort checked Gabrielle Lamoines' phone records, found that someone repeatedly tried to reach her the night she was killed. Before and after time of death."

"Do we have the number of the person who called her?"

"Forensics is working that now," Dupont told him. "What do you want to bet it's a burner that belonged to this Gorski fellow?"

Fourgét thought a moment as he seemed to contemplate the outline of the cathedral in the distance, then said, "They took his thumbs, Alain. His thumbs. Haven't we had a couple of bodies in the morgue with the same type of wounds?"

"Last fall, a couple weeks apart," Dupont replied. "Never found a connection between the two victims, and there wasn't enough to go on to solve either one."

"Do you recall if we identified the victims?"

"I'll have to check the files. You think there's a connection to Mr. Gorski?"

"Could be. Are we done here?"

"Nothing much more to see," Dupont replied.

"Then I say we grab some coffee and drive out to Gagny for a visit," Fourgét suggested.

Arnaud Clément was already seated at a small table by the plate glass window when Phythian arrived at the boulangerie. A small cup of espresso sat in front of him, as did a plate holding a fruit tart the man hadn't touched. Phythian glanced at his watch and saw he was four minutes early, causing him to wonder how long the man had been waiting for him.

"Monsieur Clément," he said as he came up to the table and pulled out a chair. "I hope I haven't kept you too long—"

"Nonsense, Monsieur Phythian," the man replied, not rising from his chair. He seemed consumed with grief, which was understandable given the fact that Gabrielle Lamoines had only been dead for thirty-six hours. He wore a button-down shirt open at the collar, and a suit coat but no tie. A thick crop of hair with salt and pepper streaks seemed in need of a trim, and his skin carried the pallor of someone who hadn't slept in a long while. "I arrived early and already ordered. I hope you don't mind."

"Please, go ahead and start." Phythian nodded at the pastry, then sat down. He'd called Clément at the crack of dawn, based on one of numerous threads he'd pulled from the Swede's brain last night, and immediately sensed the man was guarded about something he didn't wish to discuss. Nor could he understand why he had agreed to meet with this complete stranger who had called him out of the blue so early in the morning. "I want to thank you again for being so gracious to share a cup of coffee, particularly so soon after Mlle Lamoines' passing."

Clément dipped his head in a nod but didn't say anything, not right away. He picked up his tart and nibbled a corner of it, then set it down. His eyes followed a young woman steering a bicycle down the street, a pack strapped to her back as if she was on her way to work. "It's all…such a shock," he eventually said. "So sudden."

It was then that Phythian picked up a truth he'd initially suspected when they'd first spoken. Not only had Clément hired and mentored Gabrielle at the television network; he'd been having an affair with his young protégé. His heart was swollen with loss, but he couldn't share his pain with anyone: not his wife of twenty-two years, nor his three marvelous children—and certainly not his colleagues in the newsroom, who must never learn of their intimacy. Even though most of them suspected it anyway—office gossip being what it was.

"From what I understand, she was a remarkable woman," Phythian observed.

"She truly had that *je ne sais quoi*," he conceded. "Everyone at the network is utterly bereft. As are thousands of viewers. She's the top trending topic on Twitter this morning."

Phythian nodded, taking the moment to go fishing through the man's memories. He'd learned years ago that doing so was particularly easy when a person was emotionally vulnerable, and this morning there seemed to be plenty of low risk, high-return rewards to be had. He quickly learned their relationship had turned from collegial to intimate fourteen months ago, when they had both traveled to the World Economic Forum meeting in Davos, Switzerland. The Alps tended to get mighty cold at the end of January, and an abundance of champagne and brandy led them back to her room, where they kept each other warm for much of the duration.

While Clément secretly thought of himself as a sexual dualist—sleeping only with Gabrielle and his wife—she had made it clear that she was of a different mind. He reluctantly accepted that he had no right to demand her fidelity, and as long as she agreed to use adequate protection, and keep her random dalliances to herself, he could live with her lifestyle. It was not that such things didn't keep him up late at night, wondering what—*whom*—she might be doing.

"I assume you've spoken with the police?" Phythian asked.

"They talked to just about everyone at the network, and I hope they catch *le fils de pute*." Clément again picked up his fruit pastry, but this time it didn't get anywhere near his lips. He seemed to study it with great interest, but it was only to give him time to frame a question: "Might I ask, Monsieur, what your interest is in her death?"

Wondering, *was this man one of her many liaisons over the years*?

"I knew her father, a long time ago," Phythian replied. "He and Gabrielle were very close, and after he died, I kept an eye on her, from a distance. I somehow feel responsible for much of what happened to her since that tragedy, and now…well, I want to make right by her."

"You're not working on behalf of anyone's interest?"

"Not for many years," Phythian assured him.

"And you don't believe the police are adequately equipped to find whoever did this?"

"Do you?"

Clément made a *who-knows* gesture with his hands and said, "The police are the police."

"*Exactement*," Phythian agreed. "Hence my personal interest in finding her killer."

Arnaud Clément studied him for a long moment as Phythian deftly caused the man's brain to blindly accept what he was saying. "In what way might I be of assistance?" he finally said.

Phythian leaned forward and folded his hands on the table. "When you spoke with the police, did they explain to you the circumstances of Mlle Lamoines' death?"

"I know she was shot," Clément replied. "Am I to presume you have more details?"

"I'm privy to a bit of information that has not been released to the public," Phythian told him. He had such a powerful grip on the man's mind now that nothing he said or implied would be questioned. "Information that leads me to ask if she had any enemies."

"You're saying she was murdered because she crossed the wrong person?"

"Someone clearly wanted her dead," Phythian explained. "I just want to know if there was anything she was working on, someone who might have taken offense at being exposed by her. Maybe worried that she was getting too close to an inconvenient truth."

"That doesn't narrow things down a lot," Clément said. "Gabrielle was fearless and courageous in her work."

At that moment a server came over to their table. He was thin and pale, dressed in black trousers and a white shirt, with a jaunty black cap perched on his head. Phythian ordered a coffee and a chocolate croissant, then waited for him to move out of earshot.

"Did she ever mention someone named Xenon?" he asked, once he was certain he wasn't being overheard.

"Xenon? Isn't that an element on the periodic chart?"

"Number fifty-four. But the Xenon I'm talking about is a young man from Poland. I don't know much about him, except that he recently was working on something with Gabrielle."

"Is that a fact?"

Phythian caught his cynicism and quickly added, "I don't believe their contact was of an intimate nature. In fact, it probably involved the bank where he worked."

Clément gave a doubtful shake of his head, said, "The name means nothing to me. I was Gabby's boss, but many times I had no idea what she was really working on."

How quickly he'd gone from Mlle Lamoines to Gabrielle to Gabby. "Is there anything you can think of that seemed different about her the last few days," Phythian asked. "Or weeks?"

"That's the problem, Monsieur. Gabby always seemed different, every hour of every day. She was a changing spirit, and that's what her fans loved about her. She hated tedium and routine, thrived on change. Almost to the point of revolution."

At that moment the waiter returned with Phythian's coffee and croissant. He politely thanked the young man, then picked up the white porcelain cup but did not take a sip.

"What about someone named Sten Gustafsson-Jeglum?" he asked.

Clément blinked rapidly a few times, quickly glanced down at the floor. A typical stall tactic when a person attempted to bury something, if only a nasty memory. After a moment or two he regained his composure and looked Phythian in the eye, said, "In fact, yes, this Sten fellow came up in conversation more than once. What's your interest in him?"

"Whatever Gabrielle's interest was."

"She didn't say, and I didn't ask," Clément replied, a distant coldness in his voice.

Phythian nodded, deciphering the barely nuanced response. "Yet she mentioned him to you," he said. "Why do you think that would have been?"

It hardly required someone of Phythian's unmatched skillset to perceive the jealousy the man was trying to conceal. "I think she and this Sten fellow had some sort of business arrangement," he lied. "Other than that, I really don't know."

"What about the name Bortolotti?"

"Bortolotti?" Clément repeated, his voice almost a whisper as the recognition registered in his eyes. "What does he have to do with her death?"

"So, you do recognize it? The name?"

"Oh, *merde*." Clément lowered his face into his hands, and Phythian detected a gentle tremor as he inhaled several rapid breaths. "You have to believe me, I had no idea things would ever go this far."

Phythian waited for Clément to regain his composure, then said, "Tell me about him."

"You really think that fucking *fascist* was responsible for Gabrielle's death?"

"Right now, he's just a name." It was a gentle lie, since Phythian had spent a good deal of time late last evening looking into Bortolotti's rise from young and naïve activist to powerful foe of the entire European Union. "But judging by your reaction, it seems he's more than that."

Clément closed his eyes as a barrage of emotions seemed to overwhelm his brain. "I'm really not sure I can be of much help," he insisted.

"Please try anyway," Phythian pressed, realizing the reason Clément was stalling was because it involved more pleasure than business, and he still wasn't prepared to admit to his infidelities. "It might provide some insight into why Gabrielle was murdered."

"You really think so?" Arnaud said. Still buying time to figure out whether to continue the charade, or go for the truth. A hard stare from Phythian and an awkward silence ultimately caused truth to win out. "Gabby got an anonymous tip," he eventually said. "Last fall."

"A tip that involved Bortolotti?"

Clément glanced around the restaurant, then leaned closer across the table. "He was holding a rally in Budapest, some sort of neo-Nazi thing. The man's a Hitler fanatic, the sort who would believe the Holocaust was a good thing, if he believed it happened at all. Anyway, Gabby wanted to attend, but she was afraid to go alone. It was probably the only time I ever saw fear in her eyes."

"You agreed to go with her," Phythian said, already knowing his response.

"I did. The whole thing was a vile show of hatred and intolerance, a thoroughly vulgar display of human behavior. I couldn't wait to get out of there when it was over. But Gabby...she was mesmerized by the idea that someone as contemptible as Bortolotti could delude so many people into pledging their unrelenting allegiance to him."

"Right from the playbook of Hitler and Mussolini," Phythian said.

"Exactly. The point is, when we got back to Paris, she couldn't let it go. She produced a segment for her show about the rally, hoping to expose the fucker for what he is. Did a lot of digging, talked to a lot of people. Some of whom didn't appreciate her poking around this thing called Vivaldi."

"Vivaldi, like in the composer?"

"*Non*," Clément said, nervously picking at the cuticle of his thumb. "It has to do with Bortolotti's fascist movement that's been simmering across Europe, ready to boil over."

"Why Vivaldi?" he inquired, even though he'd already pulled the answer out of Clément's brain.

"It's a contraction of the first letters of the Latin words *violentiam*, *valeo*, and *diripio*."

"And she aired this segment?" Phythian pressed him.

He dropped his head in a pensive nod and said, "Several weeks ago. I cautioned her against it but, in the end, it was her call."

"And—?"

"And she didn't get the response she expected. She thought her viewers would be outraged that only eighty years after Hitler's brownshirts occupied this city, so many people would be opening their arms to this new fascist movement. Instead, she got hundreds of letters and emails praising Bortolotti, commending his courage to speak the truth. And berating her for being a traitor to France and the French people. That's also when the hate mail started."

"Did she get death threats?"

"*Certainement.*"

"I presume you mentioned all this to the police?" Phythian inquired.

"Their questions seemed far more parochial in nature," Clément said. "I seriously doubted anyone in our audience would actually go so far as to kill Gabby, but now…"

Given the intimate yet professional circumstances surrounding her death—specifics of which the police seemed to be withholding from the media—Phythian doubted it had anything to do with an impassioned viewer. On the other hand, he knew the feel and nuances of a contract hit, and he trusted Martin Beaudin's first-hand assessment of the scene.

"I'm sure the authorities will follow up on every lead," he replied.

"And you?" Clément asked. "What's your next step?"

"Like I said, I want to make right by her."

"Meaning?"

"Meaning I appreciate all you've shared with me," Phythian said. Confident that in two minutes, the late Gabrielle Lamoines' occasional and grieving lover would barely remember anything the two of them had discussed.

Chapter 20

Abby would have screamed had a strap of duct tape not been fastened across her mouth. A bottom-of-her-lungs, maximum-decibel scream, until someone came running and rescued her from all this madness, which, of course, was the entire point.

There were two men, both the stuff of her worst nightmares. Correction: she had never had a nightmare about vile creatures such as these, since it was impossible for her brain to conjure up evil that was anything close to what she saw in their eyes: demons lurking in the dark fringes of depravity, the embodiment of sin and perversion from which her parents had protected her over all of her almost-fifteen years.

And damn, how she missed both of them right this very moment.

The two men had spoken very little when they'd entered the room and, when they did, it was a language she did not understand. Eastern European, maybe Armenian, even though she had no idea what Armenian sounded like. One of them looked Italian, possibly Greek, with dark hair and a sculpted chin that might have made him handsome had he not been so venal...and menacing. The other was dark-skinned and bald, a Hollywood version of a Somalian pirate, with glossy, hungry eyes that made no secret of his lecherous gluttony.

He'd suggested something to his colleague, words Abby had easily grasped despite the language barrier. Nothing in what he said, or the way he said it, left much to the imagination.

He was going to rape her.

But the other one—*chiseled* was the word that clung to her mind—shook his head sharply and said, "*Voch': na petk' e kuys lini.*"

"*De ari. Voch' vok' ch'i Imana—*"

"*I asats', voch'!*" the chiseled one snapped. "*Mak'ur.*"

That seemed to settle the matter, at least for now. It appeared he was in charge, an observation from which Abby took just a glimmer of promise, if such a thing was possible. Then he said to her, in English, "Time to move, missy."

That had been ages ago. Now she was in the back of a van, her hands shackled behind her back and chained to a strut in the steel frame, just loose enough to keep the blood circulating, tight enough to restrict her from moving around the vehicle's rear compartment. They'd rolled her up in a rug and carried her down the stairs, head first, blood rushing to her brain until they exited out into a street or alley. She couldn't tell where she was, unable to hear a thing because of the carpet layered around her and then, later, the whir of tires on pavement beneath her.

They'd driven for what seemed forever, and Abby could see nothing from where she was positioned on the floor in the rear of the vehicle, just angles of sunlight that occasionally slashed through the windshield as they maneuvered through the streets of Rome. Lots of horns blaring here and there, and at one point she detected a siren in the distance. Police or ambulance, she couldn't tell which.

Eventually the abrupt right and left turns eased up. So did the sudden acceleration and braking. She figured they must have left the city and were out in the suburbs, if Rome had suburbs. The duct tape covering her mouth made it difficult for her to breathe, a problem only made worse because her fear was constricting her airway. At one point she blacked out, and had no idea how long she'd been unconscious. Minutes? Hours? When she awoke, she tried to unclutter her brain, think of things that might relax her and allow her lungs to inhale and exhale.

Finally the vehicle slowed. It thumped over a speed bump, then another. A truck engine rumbled somewhere, and then she heard voices outside, not far away. Again, words she couldn't understand, but at least the murmuring told her other people were around, somewhere. Good or bad she couldn't tell, and guessing didn't give her much hope.

Five minutes later they came to a stop. Abby figured they must have parked in the shadow of a building, because there was no direct light coming into the van. She heard what she thought was the whine of an airplane engine nearby—nothing commercial; maybe a private jet. Her two captors spoke to each other in the front seat, then opened their doors and climbed out. Abby heard them shuffle through some loose gravel as they circled around to the rear of the vehicle, and then she heard the sound of a key being inserted in the lock.

Chiseled opened the door, just wide enough to get a glimpse inside. He glanced back and said something to the Somalian pirate, who stepped forward and crawled up inside the rear compartment. He produced a ring of keys, sorted through it until he found the one that opened the manacles that bound her to the wall. When he was finished, he allowed his hand to wander to a place no one had touched before, and shot her a leering grin.

Then he grabbed her by the hair and pulled her out of the van.

"*Hesht, hesht,*" Chiseled reprimanded him. "I said, untouched."

"*Klirus tstsi,*" Pirate replied, with a throaty cackle.

The two men led her around the side of the van. She could see now they were at the edge of a taxiway at some airport, a half dozen planes parked on the tarmac nearby. Some distance outside Rome, Abby figured, but she had no idea where.

Fifty yards away a jet was parked with its nose pointing toward where she presumed the runway would be: sleek and white, no airline insignia, just letters and numbers painted on the side of the engine. The cabin door was hinged downward, revealing a set of stairs that led up inside. A woman in a loose, white pantsuit cinched with a sash belt was standing beside them. She had dark hair done up in a French braid, and dipped her head in a visible nod of approval.

She stepped forward and barked something at them.

"*Traffico,*" Mr. Chiseled replied, either as an excuse or apology for being late.

Pirate gave Abby a hard nudge forward and said, "*Habkaas.*" Flashing her a lewd grin that left no doubt about what was on his mind. How things would have gone much differently for her had he been the one giving the orders.

Then Chiseled gripped her by the elbow and marched her the rest of the way to the plane. Abby felt her legs grow weak, and a dizzying sensation swept through her entire body as she pushed back a wave of panic. Whose plane was this? Who was the woman in white? Where did they think they were taking her? She almost collapsed to the pavement before her captor caught her and hauled her back to her feet, then continued to prod her the rest of the way across the tarmac toward the waiting aircraft.

When they arrived at the stairs, he handed her off to the woman in white. "This is where we leave you," he told her. "Have a good flight."

Abby shuddered at the words, tried to hold herself together. She refused to let these fuckers know she was scared out of her mind.

"Your payment will be in your account within the hour," the woman assured him. Then she turned to Abby and said, "My name is Nataliya." She placed a firm hand on her new ward's shoulder and guided her to the first step, whispering in her ear, "Give me any lip, even the slightest reason, and I will *fucking* snap your neck."

If Abigail Evans had been terrified before, she now was petrified.

The small room was situated to the rear of the kitchen at the back of a *pasticceria* on Via Viscardi in the Ponticelli region of Naples. *Napoli.* The glass and stone storefront was located half a block from Parrocchia Ss. Pietro E Paolo in one direction, and a full block from the Church of the Holy Cross in the other. It was as if both arms of God were cradling it to His bosom.

A Fiat Punto with the word "polizia" stenciled on the side was parked out front. The vehicle rarely moved, its presence at the curb designed to convey a reassuring sense of law and order in this largely lawless and orderless section of the city. The decaying neighborhood was a stronghold of the treacherous Camorra crime organization that rivaled those in Sicily and Apulia, and by many accounts it was the oldest and most notorious such institution in all of Italy. Structured around loose-knit clans run by a *capo,* or boss, its main profit centers were drug trafficking, racketeering, counterfeiting, and money laundering, while some of its members had strengthened their power base by becoming active in politics, as well.

The room behind the kitchen served as the headquarters of one of these localized gangs and, from time to time, doubled as a safe house for members on the run from a rival group or, less likely, the authorities. It was furnished with a single table, four chairs, and a wall of shelves cluttered with pilfered alcohol and electronics that were earmarked as bribes for local politicians and church officials.

There was also a small television, tuned to a news report from Rome. Something about a young woman from the United States who had vanished from the Trevi Fountain yesterday and her parents were worried sick about her. Tears, anger, heartfelt pleas—even a reward—were offered for her to come home, or for whoever took her to please release her unharmed.

"The funeral is tomorrow," Aldo Scalici announced, ignoring the TV as he glanced at the other two men seated at the table. In his mid-thirties—

black jeans and a black T-shirt—he had thick, black hair that matched his eyebrows and the full beard on his chin. A glass of anisette sat on the wood surface in front of him, but he had yet to touch it.

"Fuck that shit," said the man to his right. His name was Rimiggiu Tuccitto, but he was known to his close friends and associates—including those gathered tonight—as Remy. He was at least ten years older and thirty pounds heavier than Aldo, and had a shaved scalp and a thin mustache that hung down on both sides of his upper lip. He also had Dumbo ears, wire spectacles, gray T-shirt with stains under the arms. "*Bastardo* deserved what he had coming."

"That's what the media want us to think," Aldo replied. "But he was my cousin, and that makes him one of us."

"*Era un informatore,*" Remy snarled, shaking his head. In one hand he held a bottle of Moretti, from which he occasionally took a sip, and with the other he was slowly dealing cards one-by-one from a deck and placing them, face-up, on a growing pile.

An *informatore* was the lowest form of life in any crime outfit, no matter whose side he was on. Camorra, Stidda…whatever. With Stefano Santoro—whose funeral was scheduled for Friday at four—a lot of suspicion lingered following the business of several years ago, and his subsequent disappearance.

"Nonetheless, he's family."

Remy spewed a glob of spit to the tile floor, kept dealing cards from his deck.

If Aldo felt any contempt for this demonstration of familial discourtesy, he didn't let it show. Instead, he glanced at Vicenzu Livrizzi—aka Vinnie, originally from Salerno—who was studying the colored illustrations in an Orfani graphic novel. Hadn't looked up since the mention of the funeral, except once to reach for his tumbler of Valpolicella on the table.

"You're being awfully silent tonight," Aldo said. "*Il gatto ti ha mangiato la lingua?*"

Vinnie remained with his nose glued in his book another second or two before looking up. The youngest of the three, he'd started with the Camorra in his mid-teens and had the scars to show for it. A razor slash on his left cheek, another above his right eye, and a gash that had not healed well on his neck. That one came from a knife fight in which two rival gang members had been killed, and had earned Vinnie his colors.

"Polizia will be there," he said. "Taking photos."

"So what's new?" Aldo replied with a shrug. "We're already in the system. What's a couple more pics?"

"Word is, *Il Boccino* was on the run when he got himself killed," Vinnie said, Boccino being another word for snitch, the moniker that had been pinned on Santoro after the 'Ndrangheta raid. "Hijacked a shipment of meth and fentanyl the night before last."

"And you heard this how?" Aldo wanted to know.

"I have *informatores* of my own. Inside the police."

"And these informants—what else are they telling you?" This came from Remy, who had stopped dealing his cards and was now staring at the young kid from Salerno across the table from him.

"That he was working a job for Cattaneo," Vinnie said. Cattaneo being the name of the *capo* of one of their biggest rivals in the Camorra.

"*Che cazzo dici*," Remy said. "That's bullshit."

"Call it what you will. That's the inside word."

"What kind of job?" Aldo asked, at long last reaching for his anisette.

"They're expecting a shipment from Tunisia, maybe Libya, tomorrow night. Santoro was the point person."

Remy picked up his pile of cards, squared them off against the table surface, and shuffled. "And now that he's dead?" he wanted to know.

"Therein lies the weakness in their plan," Vinnie said.

"Meaning what?" Aldo asked, taking another sip of anisette.

Vinnie cracked a thin smile, glanced at his two older *compagnas*. "Meaning there's about twenty million Euros worth of drugs arriving tomorrow night, or the day after. Thing is, now that Santoro's dead, no one knows exactly where. Or when."

"What's that got to do with us?" Remy asked.

"What I hear is, he was communicating with *il Capo* through a device—an Apple watch—paired to his mobile. The police seized that, but the watch seems to be missing. They believe there maybe was information on it that wasn't on his iPhone."

"Probably lost it," Aldo suggested. "Or wasn't wearing it when he died."

Vinnie poured himself another half-glass of wine and casually shook his head. "My source is in the Finance Guard, on the top floor," he said. "The last time the watch synched to his cell was fifteen minutes before he died, but the cops know he got two calls during that time. And photographs taken at the scene show nothing on his arm, which means it had to have come off during the collision."

"Then what happened to it?"

"What I'm hearing is, the police think the band probably snapped when he hit the car and the thing popped off," Vinnie replied. "No one recovered it at the scene, which means someone had to have grabbed it before anyone arrived. In fact, they're now thinking it could have been the man who caused the incident in the first place."

Aldo poured the rest of his anisette down his throat and set the glass back on the table with a thud. "Do you have a name?" he asked.

"Carter Logan," Vinnie replied. "He's an American reporter, in town for the summit."

"*Cazzo di politica*," Remy cursed, not quite under his breath. Fucking politicians.

"*Figlio di putana*," Aldo said. "They let the guy who killed Santoro just walk away?"

"What I hear is, *il informatore* was nearing the end of his usefulness. No big loss. Besides, they knew where the American was staying."

"Knew?" Remy asked. "As in, not now?"

"My guy says he was staying at an Air BnB, but got booted in the middle of the night."

Aldo tipped his head back, stared at the ceiling for a moment while some sort of bug crawled across it. He wondered how the fuck it could stay there, upside down, without falling to the floor. Or the table. "So, no one knows where he is?" he eventually said.

"They should at least be able to track his credit card," Remy pointed out. "Unless he's been paying cash."

"Americans think in plastic," Aldo replied. "And if he has this Apple watch, he's got to have something up his sleeve."

"What are you thinking?" Vinnie wanted to know.

A crooked smile formed on Aldo's lips, matching the larcenous gleam in his eye. "Find him, force him to give us the watch," he said. "Which will lead us to the drugs."

"Exactly," Vinnie replied, relieved he didn't have to build a case for his plan. "While Signore Logan was being questioned last night, they installed a tracking app on his phone—"

"—And wherever he goes, they'll know it," Aldo finished for him.

"Exactly," Vinnie said. "And so will we."

"Not much to go on, you ask me." Captain Enzo Segreto said, falling just short of rolling his eyes at what he was hearing. A twelve-year veteran of the Finance Guard, he'd earned a reputation for being brash and direct, while keeping his temperament just on the proper side of cocky. "It appears this source of yours isn't particularly forthcoming with details."

"Such is the nature of informants," Colonel Marchetti replied with a wave of his hand. He was a tall man, slightly balding under his hat, his skin carrying a glossy sheen that had worried his wife until the doctor said it was just oil that came from the sebaceous glands that contain ceramides, and actually was a sign of good health. "It's all we have to go with, and we have to treat it as credible."

The two officers were standing in the men's room on the third floor of the Guardia headquarters on Via Vette Settembre, just about the only secure location in the building that was known to be free of surveillance devices. That being said, two sentries were hanging in the hall outside, and Marchetti personally had checked every stall for potential eavesdroppers prior to beginning this conversation. Despite all the precautions, however, he kept his voice to just above a whisper.

Segreto was staring at his reflection in a mirror over one of the half-dozen sinks in the tiled room. He noticed that the light from the fluorescent tube overhead almost made his teeth look blue. "Do we at least know when this thing we're not entirely sure of is supposed to happen?" he asked.

It was the same question Marchetti had asked his own superior just twenty minutes ago, and he had no better answer than the one he'd been given. "Tomorrow afternoon. One o'clock."

"We're certain of the timing?"

"That's what our source tells us."

"And this source, whoever he is: you're sure you can completely trust him?"

The colonel turned on the water, ran his hands under it. Just to create more noise, in case someone actually was listening in. "*Cazzo, no*," he said. "I've been in this job too long to trust anyone completely. But he came to us, out of conscience or ethics. Morals. Whatever. And it seems he's in a position to know."

"Even though he doesn't know the entire plan," Segreto said.

"He either doesn't know it, or is too scared to tell us." Marchetti finished washing his hands and turned the faucet off. "Things don't go well for people who turn on this *coglione*, remember?"

Yes, Captain Segreto remembered. Bortolotti's brutality had been well-documented within the ranks of the Guardia, and had played out on television. "This is all pretty last minute, sir. Have you checked out his story? And his background?"

"His background is well-known to us," Marchetti replied. "You would recognize him by his name alone, but I'm not at liberty to divulge that. The important thing is that we have surveillance teams moving in now, and Generale Lionetti specifically requested that you be brought in to form a tactical presence so we're ready on the ground."

"That's cutting it pretty damned close, if this is all coming down tomorrow."

"That's why he asked for you specifically. He was very impressed with how you resolved that matter at the Palazzo Montecitorio last February." He was referring to a hostage situation at the Chamber of Deputies that could have been tragic for the lower house of parliament, but which Segreto had resolved with the deaths of only two gunmen.

"So that brings me back around to when," the captain said. "And what and where."

"The answer to your first question is, as soon as we walk out of this room," Marchetti said as he slid his hands under the air dryer. "Details about the rest have been sent to your phone. Any questions?"

"I'll let you know."

"And Captain?"

"Yes, sir?"

"Arrests are preferable, but the alternative is acceptable, if necessary. Understood?"

"Completely," Segreto said.

"*Merde*," deputy chief Inspector Fourgét swore as he and Dupont pulled the Peugeot up in front of the burned-out shell of a building that was exactly where Xenon Gorski's apartment was supposed to be. "*Merde double*."

A blue and yellow Renault with the words "*Police de Gagny*" painted on the side was angled to the curb, and two uniformed officers were standing in front of it. They were discussing something with an elderly woman in her housecoat and slippers, white hair piled on top of her head in curlers. The woman was gesturing with her arms, and one of the officers appeared to be growing agitated with her.

Fourgét opened the door and got out of the Peugeot, headed over to where the cops and the woman stood.

"It's what I saw," she was insisting. "A van came by here yesterday morning, early, and two men got out and went inside that building. After they came out, smoke. Then flames, lots of them."

"You're quite sure of this?" one of the two Gagny police officers asked her. His skin was pasty white, his eyes pale blue, his chin almost squared off at the end, with an equally square dimple. "What time did this happen?"

"Around one 'clock," the woman explained. "I was watching a rerun of '*Enquetes et Revelations*,' and it had just ended."

"And you're sure of this?"

Deputy chief inspector Fourgét took that moment to step forward. He showed his badge to the two uniformed officers, then said, "Madame, would you please tell us what you saw?"

The woman shot a look of contempt to the officer whom she apparently thought had been condescending, and said, "I live across the street, there—" She gestured to an old brick building with cracked windows, roof tiles missing, trash in the front yard "—and was watching television when I heard a car drive up. I looked through the window, right there, and saw a van parked in front of that building. Two men got out and banged on the door, and for a second I thought it was another drug thing, so I hid."

"Drug thing?" Fourgét asked.

"*Oui, oui*. Those thugs are here all day and night."

"What happened next?"

"Well, couple minutes later I heard the van start up and drive away, and when I looked out the window, I saw all this smoke."

"Where did you see the smoke?" Dupont inquired.

"Coming out the front door. They'd left it open. Then all of a sudden… whoosh! The place just went up in flames."

Fourgét nodded, then turned to the two Gagny police officers. "I'm deputy chief inspector Fourgét, Paris police. And this is inspector Alain Dupont. Please tell me why you don't believe this woman's story."

"It appears you're a bit out of your jurisdiction, inspector," one of the local cops said.

"Following a lead in a case. And I'm waiting for an answer."

"*Son histoire n'a pas eu de bon sens,*" the officer replied.

"Well, it makes complete sense to me," Fourgét said. Then he turned to the woman and asked, "Do you know the man who lives in that apartment?"

"Not really," she said, shaking her head. "I've seen him a couple times, but this isn't exactly the sort of neighborhood where you make friends."

"How about the two men you saw last night? Can you describe them?"

"They both were wearing black sweatshirts with hoods. Black trousers, too. That's all I could see, really."

Of course it was, Fourgét thought. "Could you see if they were armed?"

She thought for a moment, then said, "One of the men had a gun."

"What kind of gun?" Fourgét pressed, momentarily glancing at the Gagny officers.

"A drug gun," the woman said. "The kind that shoots fast. "

"What time was the fire called in?" Dupont asked, turning his attention to the two officiers de police.

"A little after one," said the one who until now had remained silent. He was tall, thin, young, no more than twenty-five. Wiry, narrow moustache that looked like a thin, furry worm crawling across his upper lip. "It's being investigated as possible arson."

"You think?" Fourgét said, heavy sarcasm in his voice. Then, simply as a courtesy, he said, "We need to go in there."

"For what reason?" the officer with the square jaw asked him.

"For the reason that the young man who lived there was murdered in Paris last night," inspector Dupont said. "Despite the fire, we need to look inside."

The officer thought about it a moment, then said, "Sure. What could it hurt?"

At that moment inspector Dupont's cellphone rang. He checked the screen, mouthed to Fourgét that it was Rochefort and he needed to take the call. He glanced back at the local officer, who clearly didn't appreciate the presence of Paris homicide inspectors on his local turf, then hit the "talk' button and said, "*Oui?*"

Dupont did more listening than talking, only offering an additional "*oui*" as Rochefort provided him with information. Fourgét glanced at him impatiently, and Dupont held up a finger, indicating the conversation was almost over. Finally, he said "*au revoir,*" and slipped the phone back in his pocket. "Looks like all of the men in Gabrielle Lamoines' contact list has an alibi."

"Convenient," was all Fourgét said.

Two minutes later they were both standing on the top step of Xenon Gorski's burned-out apartment. "So...two men in a van come to Gorski's apartment, and a few hours later he turns up dead on the bank of the Seine," Fourgét said as he stepped inside the charred flat. "Our friend in curlers says she saw two men, but didn't mention anything about her neighbor being one of them. You think she's a reliable witness?"

"I think she believes what she saw," Dupont answered as he followed his boss inside. "Give or take a little exaggeration."

Fourgét moved to the edge of the room, said nothing as he slowly edged around the perimeter of the apartment. Eventually he came to a clump of melted plastic and blackened circuit boards that had hardened on a scorched table. He bent down to take a closer look, said, "Take a look at this."

Dupont cautiously walked over to where he was standing. "What do you make of it?" he asked.

"Judging by the circuit boards I'd say it's a desktop computer," Fourgét replied. "At least it was."

Dupont inspected it for a closer look, saw that a plastic panel on the back of the destroyed unit had warped and was ready to pop off. He snapped it loose and pulled a wad of charred paper out of a small compartment. "Banknote, with a little green still visible," he said as he held it up for Fourgét to take a look.

"Hundred Euro note," Fourgét said as he leaned closer and studied the clump of burned currency. "Looks to me like Monsieur Gorski came into a little cash."

"*Oui,*" Dupont said as he rose to his feet. "Cash that maybe cost him some valuable appendages, then got him shot in the head and tossed off the Pont des Arts."

"It took a little digging, but here's your list," Miklos Moravec said in a heavy Czech accent as he pushed a sheet of paper across the table to Phythian. Then he took a sip from a bottle of Pilsner Urquell, a popular beer brewed in his home town of Pilzen but not easily found in Paris.

Phythian had switched from caffeine to mineral water when they sat down, but he had yet to touch the glass that the young woman with the long lashes and glossy red lips had set in front of him. "I trust you didn't have any trouble running this," he said as he took a cursory glance at the single sheet of paper.

"It's what I do," Moravec waved him off. "As you'll see, it's just a basic data merge. Victim's name, line of work he or she was involved in, location and method of death. Along with the specific tarot card found at each scene, and the date of the killing."

The two men were seated at a sidewalk café on a quiet street just a couple blocks from the Czech embassy on Avenue Charles Flouquet. Moravec had not been surprised to hear Phythian's voice when he had called last evening, even though Interpol reports still listed his American friend as dead. Not surprised because it was Moravec who, several months ago, had provided him with new passports—Swiss, Dutch, Canadian, and Irish—and had procured the safety deposit boxes in Athens and Cairo. Boxes into which thousands of Euros in small notes had been stashed.

Phythian gave a cursory glance up and down the street. This being Paris, he assumed he would be within view of at least a dozen surveillances cameras at any one moment. Nothing he could do about that, other than keep his face turned low, eyes shaded by a pair of Ray-Bans and a Basque beret he'd picked up in a thrift shop. He'd also turned his collar up against the afternoon, which had grown chilly, with a steady breeze blowing down the Seine—and if he got really paranoid, he could always use the surgical face mask left over from the pandemic that he always carried with him.

Fortunately, the sidewalks were filled with men and women hustling from one place to another, blocking the AI software from making a positive ID, or so he hoped. He was less concerned with the pedestrians themselves, since none of them seemed to be paying him any mind as they went about their respective routines. If anyone was looking for him specifically, he would know.

He glanced down at the single sheet of paper his Czech friend had given him, studied the names and accompanying information:

- Stephane Kroeger / 48 / President/IMF / shot / Nice / The Magician / Dec. 28
- Alain Geiger / 49 / pharmaceuticals / Zurich / shot twice / The Sun / Jan. 18

- William Hammond / 61 / hedge funds / London / shot twice / Wheel of Fortune / March 1
- Johannes Levin / 36 / software / Palo Alto / shot [sniper, long-range] / The Star / April 12
- Kushtrim Naglayos / 53 / mining / Jerusalem / shot / The Hanged Man / August 20
- Marcellus Messina / 58 / global shipping / Venice / poisoned / The Chariot / Oct. 8
- Lukas Gallegos / 41 / global industrialist / Geneva / drowned / The World / Dec. 5
- Willem Demler / 59 / aerospace tech / Berlin / electrocuted / The Moon / Feb. 13
- Hanna Zaitsev / 30/ FSB agent / Budapest / knifed / The Tower / March 29
- Arjeta Leas / 49/ inherited wealth / Gibraltar / automobile accident / The Emperor / May 1
- Ilya Tesovic / 59 / natural gas / Ankara / shot / Judgment / May 17
- Gabrielle Lamoines / 34 / journalist/ Paris / shot / The High Priestess / June 7

"As I said on the phone, no one has been able to determine any sort of definitive pattern or connection between the victims," Moravec explained as Phythian finally took a sip of his sparkling water. "Not in the manner of death, nor any personal or business relationship to other people on the list. The lone exception is that all the cards were from the same deck of cards designed by the Spanish artist Salvador Dali."

"And all of them appear to have been rich," Phythian said. "Except for Gabrielle."

"And the sparrow." Moravec pointed at the line that listed Valeria Zaitsev, the Russian agent who had died at a much younger age than all the others.

"There's a lot of money in spying. One of the world's oldest professions."

"Still, the evidence of wealth does not necessarily reflect a pattern," the Czech said.

He was in his late fifties and had been a young recruit in the Prague police department when the iron curtain had ripped, and suddenly turned his world upside down. With the pending collapse of the Soviet Union, he had been part of a riot squad called in to quell a student uprising, but in the middle of the demonstration he put down his gun and joined his fellow countrymen. He had been thrown in jail for his actions, but as Czechoslovakia fell in late December that year he was freed and widely hailed as a patriot and a hero. After Václav Havel was elected president of the new Czech Republic, Moravec was elevated to a position within the new government, ultimately being named chief of security at its embassy in Paris.

"Which doesn't mean there isn't one," Phythian replied. "Wet work is a quirky business."

"You would know," Moravec agreed, a thinly veiled reference to Phythian's previous line of work. "But I can tell you, the only pattern Interpol agrees on is that all of the victims most likely were killed by the same person."

"I assume the cards found at each scene are being left out of the media reports."

"Only a few highly placed authorities outside the official channels are privy to that information," Moravec confirmed. "But those who do know concur that the same suspect is directly involved in all of the murders, so we know there's no copycat involved."

"Interesting how the contractor is inconsistent in the ways he's killed his victims," Phythian said. "Six different methods in twelve separate murders."

"Correct," Moravec said. "The first five on the list were shot, but the sixth here—Marcello Matteo—was poisoned, and the one following that drowned. Then there's electrocutions and car accidents; and there's no discernible pattern at all in the cards that the killer had left behind. Nothing that appears to relate to the victims themselves, or their line of work, their means of death. Or each other."

Phythian swirled the water in his glass and watched a riot of bubbles explode. "But there is a pattern here—trust me."

"So, what's your theory on the killer?" Moravec asked. "The man they call *Le Magicien*."

"French for 'the magician.'"

"That's correct. Interpol gave him the name because that was the first tarot card that the killer left behind."

"The first that they know of," Phythian pointed out. "The file says Stephane Kroeger was shot in Nice, about eighteen months ago." He found the timeframe more than coincidental, considering the collapse of the Greenwich Global Group had occurred just a few months prior to that.

"What are you thinking—?"

"I've been out of this game for a long time, but this guy's clearly a pro. The real question is, who's putting out the contracts on these targets?"

"Your former employers?" Moravec asked.

"A relic of the past," Phythian said, shaking his head.

"Meaning what?"

"Meaning they've closed down for good."

The Czech took another sip of his pilsner as he considered what his friend was telling him. "You personally know this to be true?" he finally asked.

"Trust me…they're gone."

"Then it appears there's a new player at the table."

"Nature abhors a vacuum." Phythian had anticipated that another murder-for-hire outfit would take the place of the G3, but unfortunately there was nothing he could do about it. Such was the burden of human history and the curse of fair market economics. "What I want to know is, are all these victims targeted by the same outfit, or is the killer an independent technician who signs each canvas with a tarot card?"

"You don't think he could simply be a serial killer?" Moravec suggested.

"Doesn't fit the pattern," Phythian said, shaking his head. "This bastard traveled to twelve different cities on three continents to do his thing. Hardly the pattern of a psycho nut job."

"No, and you're right: it does have all the patterns of a contractor," Moravec agreed, stabbing his finger at the list. "There has to be some other connection, somewhere, in all this."

"And it's possible Le Magicien himself may not even know what it is."

"So what's next?" Moravec asked him. "Interpol's already looked at this from all sides. Databases, analysts, profilers, experts of every sort. Even tarot card readers. And they didn't come up with shit."

"Sometimes it takes a fish to catch a fish," Phythian said.

Chapter 21

Carter Logan took the metro five stops from his hotel to the Ottaviano station in the Pratti neighborhood, just north of the Vatican. Fortunately, he didn't have to travel through Termini where, if he encountered the ticket scammer again, he might just find himself being questioned by the polizia for assault.

He climbed the eighteen stairs up to the street and glanced around to get his bearings. The GPS on his phone told him to cross through the intersection, walk two blocks straight ahead, then turn right and continue to the next corner. Sure enough, halfway up the block was a cozy local trattoria known as *Cibo e Vino*, which translated directly to "food and wine."

Professor David Vaughan had made it clear on the phone that his schedule that evening was tight. He had an appointment with an unspecified bishop at the Pontifical Council for Inter-Religious Dialogue, followed by a student-faculty reception at the American University, where he was a visiting professor teaching a course on Religions in Times of Conflict. It was bound to be a long night, but he allowed that he could stop for a quick glass of prosecco at five o'clock before heading off to The Vatican.

It was five minutes to the hour now and, as Logan approached the café, he spotted a man seated alone at a table in the corner of a patio that was built out over the sidewalk. As a prosaism of his academic status, he was wearing a tweed jacket, and an umbrella hung by its handle from the railing, even though there was little chance of rain. He appeared to have just sat down, and was rifling through a briefcase balanced in his lap.

Logan dodged a young man whipping by on a Link micro-scooter, then walked up to him and said, "Dr. Vaughan?"

"Mr. Logan," the Pulitzer Prize winner replied. He looked as if he would stand up, were it not for the cumbersome valise, and extended his hand. "Please, sit down. And call me David."

"Only if you call me Carter," Logan said as he settled into the chair across the table.

Vaughan moved the case to the floor, then glanced around just as a waiter emerged from the bistro and hurried up to them. "Prosecco, signore?" he inquired.

"*Si, si,*" the professor said. "And whatever my new friend is having."

Logan quickly studied a wine list and ordered a glass of Sardinian Cannonau. The two men made small talk until the server returned, chatting about the steamy DC summer that was about to begin, their mutual friend at Georgetown, and how the nonstop political chaos only seemed to be getting worse. Time was ticking, and when Vaughan took a surreptitious glance at his watch, Logan shifted the discussion to why he'd asked to meet.

"What can you tell me about Renato Azzone?" he asked.

"Yes, you mentioned him on the phone," Vaughan replied. He was older than Logan expected: mid-seventies, wispy white hair that fell loosely over the crown of his head. He wore Coke bottle glasses, and a hearing aid was tucked into the ear that was visible, and possibly the other one, as well. "Might I inquire why you're asking about the Deputy Secretary General of the Vatican?"

"His name came up with regard to an article I'm working on."

"What article is that?"

Logan had promised Alvize total confidentiality about his story, swore he would keep the young man's identity and whereabouts a secret no matter what. In fact, Renato Azzone was merely a means to get to the heart of an even darker story which, it now seemed, extended well beyond the death of Cardinal Allessio Giudice and the sexual improprieties that had contributed to his nickname: Quello Feroce.

He leaned forward across the table and fixed his eyes on the professor's. "What can you tell me about Vivaldi?" he said.

The question was not what Vaughan was expecting, and it caught him off-guard. He recovered quickly, and replied, "I assume you're not talking about the composer."

"You assume correctly. I'm talking about Violentiam–Valeo–Diripio."

Professor Vaughan lowered in head in a subtle nod, and said, "If you know about that, then you must know about Alessandro Bortolotti."

"I know he's the man behind this current wave of neo-fascism sweeping across Europe. I watched a couple of his speeches, did some background on him."

"Then you also know what a treacherous demagogue he is. The fusion of Hitler, Mussolini, and Stalin in one unstable stick of dynamite."

"You really think he's that dangerous?" Logan asked.

Vaughan gently grasped his prosecco glass by the stem, took a long, slow sip. When he finished, he continued to hold it, studied the bubbles erupting inside. "In order to understand the man, you first need to know the history," he said. "Political scientists will tell you that the rise of this new fascist movement in Europe over the last few decades has come about because of the same forces that were at play in the years leading up to World War Two. Things like ongoing economic crises, lack of jobs, immigration from outside the region, and a pervasive feeling of defeatism. It all created a disconnect among those who felt cut off, at the same time fueling a surge of ethnocentric zealotry. Bortolotti has exploited it all with expert finesse."

"One would think that the legitimate election of a fascist as Prime Minister would ease their hearts and minds," Logan pointed out.

"With Bortolotti, it isn't as much about fascism as it is the power," Vaughan replied. "In my opinion he's more opposed to the concept of democracy than he's attached to any particular ideology."

A squeal of brakes and a blast of a small horn caused both men to look up, just as a Renault nearly collided with a Vespa. This was followed by considerable swearing and much gesticulating, and then both drivers moved on in their respective directions.

"Tempers are ready to erupt," Logan observed.

"The entire city of Rome is on edge this week," the professor pointed out. "Roads are closed and special forces are slowing things down to a crawl. But...back to Bortolotti. He's a very calculating man, and he's using the resentment of the average person to drum up a new brand of right-wing nationalism. While Meloni is content to use the ballot box, he has far different means in mind."

"Plus, he already ran for office twice, and lost both times," Logan pointed out.

"Exactly. Narcissists don't like to lose, and when they do, they either call it a lie or blame it on cheating. Bortolotti refused to accept his defeats, and instead blamed them on a plot conceived and controlled by the Deep State. Despite his ego and pathology, he's an intelligent man, and he knows there's a wide swath of the population ready to jump all over the next conspiracy."

"So, what's his connection to Renato Azzone? And, more important, The Vatican?"

"That's the big question, isn't it?" Dr. Vaughan said. "If you've read my latest book—and I don't blame you if you haven't—you'll know several things about Italy. First, it's actually a pretty new country. It only dates back to the middle of the nineteenth century, and came about through a long-standing battle with the Papal States and Pope Pius the Ninth. He forbade Catholics from recognizing Italy's legitimacy and voting in the country's elections, fueling an internal struggle that continued until Mussolini came to power in 1922. Without boring you with details, *il Duce* managed to change all that."

"Kind of weird, since Italy is such a Catholic country," Logan replied.

"Keep in mind that Catholics only recently got involved in politics. Contrary to what we have in the U.S.—theoretically, at least—the popes rejected the notion of separation of church and state, and actually regarded the Italian government as its enemy. They held a sort of medieval perspective that there should be no freedom of speech, freedom of conscience, or freedom of religion. No freedom of anything. All these things were sort of antithetical to what the church believed in. And, as it turned out, what Mussolini also believed in. When he came to power, he and the Pope worked cheek to jowl, so to speak."

A delivery truck chose that moment to chug by, releasing a belch of diesel exhaust. "What I think you're telling me is The Vatican has a long history of embracing an autocratic frame of government," Logan concluded.

"That's a bit of an oversimplification, but essentially, yes," Vaughan said. The rest of his prosecco went down his throat; then he checked his watch, as if to see if he had time for one more. He did, and signaled to the waiter. "Bortolotti was born and raised in the same region of Italy as Pius the Eleventh, who collaborated with Mussolini in the twenties, before the war. He studied Il Duce diligently, and he hasn't hidden the fact that he holds him in high esteem. In fact, that's what he likes to be called within his inner circle."

"Where does Renato Azzone fit in to all this?"

"Azzone is the right hand to the current Pope, and has his ear in all matters of state. While His Holiness is not as easily swayed as Pius XI was, Bortolotti knows that if he has His blessing, the people of Italy will embrace him with open arms."

"Even though they've already voted a fascist into office."

"Remember what I said about narcissists," Vaughan offered with a wry grin.

"You think Azzone can get the Pope to endorse his power play, whatever it is?"

"Bortolotti does, and that's what really counts," the visiting Georgetown professor said. The waiter wandered up with a refill of prosecco, then drifted off to another table. "That's where this Violentiam–Valeo–Diripio thing comes in to play."

Logan considered what the professor was telling him, then said, "You think he's planning a violent coup."

"It's the way that true fascists often come to power," the professor concurred.

"What do you think he has in mind?"

Mindful of his imminent appointments, the professor downed his sparkling wine in one long gulp. Then he looked Logan in the eye and said, "Whatever it is, it will be big, And, I suspect, very soon."

Georgy Sokolov was doing a lazy man's breast stroke in his horizon pool, pushing water aside with his broad hands, paddling slowly with his feet. He was doing his best to keep his head above water, in more ways than one.

His phone chirped where he'd left it on the tile pool apron, and he dogpaddled over to pick it up. Here his toes could touch the bottom, and he stood with both hands free and answered the call.

"Georgy, darling," Nataliya Moisei said, in English. She'd never seen a reason to learn Russian, which she considered a waste of brain cells, considering the long-range drift of global politics and national influences. "We're in the air."

"ETA?"

"Two hours. The pilot has to fly around an area of atmospheric disturbance."

"And the package?" he inquired.

"On board and subdued. I gave her a little something when I buckled her in."

Sokolov let out an audible sigh as he stared out where the Mediterranean met the sky in a crisp line, the intersection of two shades of blue. Everything was coming together according to plan, even if the price had been steep.

"Tell me about her," he said.

"Not quite fifteen years old, blonde hair. Shoulder length. Fair skin, a few freckles. Blue eyes, good cheeks. American, about five-six. Her name is Abigail. You'll like her."

"Tits?"

There it was: the thing that mattered most to this Russian. Almost every Russian she'd ever met, in fact, which was another reason Nataliya never found cause to learn the language. So many of them were scumbags or thugs, or both.

"Well-developed for her age," she said. "You won't be disappointed."

"It's not me I'm concerned about," Sokolov replied. "We're at fifty-three participants at last count, including online. It's them we don't want to disappoint."

"No, we don't, babe," she agreed.

"And is she…intact?" he asked.

It was a question she'd anticipated, and something she'd already verified before she placed this call. "I examined her myself," Nataliya assured him.

"Good, good. I can't wait to see her. And you, of course."

"Very soon, my darling," she said, making a kissy noise.

She was about to end the call when Sokolov said, "There's one more thing—"

"Yes, Georgy?"

"I'm counting on you to keep this one alive, no matter what."

Phythian found Jantine Hamel seated beneath a horse chestnut tree on the broad promenade that bisected Boulevard de Clichy, almost right on the border between the ninth and eighteenth arrondissements. She had a bag of breadcrumbs in her lap and a flock of pigeons at her feet, pecking at morsels of a day-old loaf she'd been given at a bakery near the corner. An unseasonably cool breeze drifted up the street, ruffling leaves and tossing pieces of trash around the pavement in invisible eddies.

It was not a chance meeting. She flashed him a broad smile as he gently grazed her cheek with a kiss. "*A quoi dois-je le plaisir?*" she asked.

"Why, madame," he replied, feigning shock. "Must I have a reason to seek out the most beautiful woman in all of Paris?"

"I would blush if you weren't so full of shit," she told him. "Sit down, s'il vous plaît."

Mme. Hamel had positioned her chair next to a park bench that had been empty and, she supposed, would remain that way. No one would wish to sit near an old woman with no legs who was feeding a sizable flock of birds. *Mon Dieu*, what might they be forced to talk about? Phythian lowered himself into his seat, and gathered her withered hand in his. A web of wrinkles wove in and around the bruises and brown spots of age, but her nails were painted a bright red, to match her lips.

He said nothing for a moment, then let go of her palm as he dug a burgundy box out of a pocket of his windbreaker. "Are you familiar with these?" he asked as he handed it to her.

Her fingers stroked the soft velvet cover, embossed with gold leaf lettering that identified the contents as the Tarot Universal Dali. "I've heard about them, but I don't believe I've ever seen a set," she told him. "I understand they're quite hard to find and rather expensive. Do you mind if I take them out?"

"Please do."

The box was actually a cardboard sleeve, and Jantine used her finger to gently push out a separate cardboard pack that also read "Tarot Universal Dali." A picture of a card labeled "The Magician" was positioned in the center.

"Where did you get these?" she asked him as she opened it and removed a deck of tarot cards, along with a small booklet.

"At a wonderful little shop on Rue Jean-Macé, in the Seventh," he replied. "What can you tell me about them?"

"This booklet here will fill you in on each individual card and what it means. It's in French, English, and Spanish, see? But if you're talking about this particular deck…well, from what I've heard, each card was designed by Salvador Dali, using images from a number of sources. Each card is signed by him and, as you can see, they're all edged in gold."

"Would it be common for someone to use them in a reading?" Phythian asked.

Jantine Hamel was slowly going through the cards one by one, studying the surreal imagery on each and then setting it aside to go on to the next. "Not really," she said. "The Rider-Waite tarot deck generally is the most popular deck used in English-speaking countries, while the Tarot de Marseille is the most popular here in France. From what I understand, the Dali deck is more of an artistic eccentricity than a practical tool of the trade."

"A collector's item?" he pressed her.

"Since there's no real practical use for them, yes," she told him. "Do you mind me asking what this is about?"

"You can ask, but I'm not sure I can tell you much," Phythian said. "They came up in something here in Paris I wasn't anticipating, and I'm trying to figure out how they fit in."

"Well, whatever it is, it must be pretty important to have dragged you back from the dead," she observed with a smile. She set another card aside, then shuddered visibly when she saw the next one in the box. It was labeled "Death," and bore the image of a cypress tree with a skull embedded in it, the trunk seemingly sliced in two on the bias. "*Tres macabre*, you think?"

"You're the expert," he reminded her. He pointed at the High Priestess card on her lap and said, "What can you tell me about this one?"

She picked it up and studied it a long moment. "To be honest, I don't know what Dali was going for here," she said. "But then, that would apply to most of his work. In a standard tarot deck this card usually shows a woman wearing a blue robe or gown, just as in this card, although the Tarot de Marseilles has her dressed in a blue cape and red robe."

"I'm assuming the symbolism all refers to something—"

"That's why the illustrations are so intricate, yet oddly vague at the same time," she said. "That way a lot is left up to the interpretation of the reader. Typically, the High Priestess card is associated with secrets, mysteries, and revelations, especially when there's a powerful woman involved. It also is thought to mean the perfect woman when enmeshed with a man but, when applied to a single woman, it can mean independence. As I've explained, a lot depends on the individual reader's perception."

Phythian considered what Jantine Hamel was telling him, wondered what message the assassin had been trying to send by placing this particular card at Gabrielle's death scene…if he was trying to send a message at all.

"For what reason might someone acquire this specific set of cards," he asked.

She raised a shoulder in a noncommittal shrug as she continued to examine the deck. "Well, he or she would definitely have an interest in tarot, but not necessarily as a reader," she said. "Probably also a fan of Dali's work, but I suspect there's more than that."

"Such as?"

"Well, I would think the person has a basic knowledge of the history of the cards, and a genuine appreciation of what they mean. They'd make an exquisite gift for the right person. Wife, girlfriend. Lover."

"Do you still read cards for clients?" he asked her.

"With this fat, legless body, it's about all I can do," she told him. "Pretty pathetic, don't you think?"

"Not the words I would use to describe a woman who is so beauteous in so many ways," he said. "Do you think you could make good use of these cards?"

She made an effort to turn her head back to look at him. "Is this your way of asking me to tell your fortune?"

The last thing Phythian wanted was to know what the future held for him. "No," he replied. "This is my way of telling you I'd like you to keep them."

"Keep them? But I can't possibly pay you what they're worth—"

"I want you to have them as a gift," Phythian said. "I have no use for them."

"But you only just bought them—"

"And now I'd like to give them to you, for helping me."

She fixed his eyes with hers, as if probing for some truth hidden deep within them. In her experience, no man ever did anything out of the kindness of his soul. They all wanted something, if not now then at a future date. It was in their DNA, and was how she had done so well in her chosen profession—not that she had actually chosen it. Rather, it had found her, just as it found so many other young women whose circumstances had set them on a path to ignominy.

Finally, she said, "But you do want something. I can tell."

"You have done more for me than I could dream of," he conceded. "The cards are simply my way of thanking you. May I wheel you home?"

"A noble gesture, *mon ami*. But I'd prefer to remain here a bit longer, as the glow slowly fades from the street. Quite a metaphor for the twilight time of an old woman's life, don't you think?"

Chapter 22

"Does the shop have a surveillance camera?" Deputy Chief Inspector Fourgét asked inspector Madelyn Rochefort.

He took a sip of cold coffee from a paper cup, wished it was a light Beaujolais instead of bitter brew with old grounds floating in it. He wished he could be home right now with his wife Claudia, who was preparing her specialty coq au vin that, in his estimation, was better than any Michelin-starred restaurant in the city.

"Out of order," the investigator said, shaking her head. They were back in the same conference room on the second floor of the Commissariat de Police, the blast of air coming from the ceiling vent warmer than usual because of the drop in temperature outside. "No one has thought to fix it in years."

"Then pull all the CCTV footage within a three-block radius. Something somewhere must have picked him up either entering or leaving the shop."

"Already in the works," Rochefort replied. "You think it's coincidence?"

"Coincidence that the day after a woman is found dead with one of those weird cards at the scene, a man goes into an obscure shop dealing in…what was the term that woman used—?"

"Esotericism."

"Right," Fourgét said. "The only shop in the city that had a deck of those very same cards, and he goes in and buys them. I have a gut feel about this, Rochefort."

Le Magicien was sitting alone at a sidewalk table across from the Paris Opera, nursing a glass of cognac while he watched the patrons descend the steps in all their finery. The featured show that evening had been *La Cenerentola*—aka Cinderella, or Goodness Triumphant—an operatic *dramma giocoso* in two acts by Gioachino Rossini. In all his years on the planet he had yet to understand the attraction of this sort of music: the contorted vibratos of the singers, the pinched esophageal screeches, the exaggerated notes. But he did enjoy watching the folks who seemed to appreciate it, quite possibly for the same reasons he didn't.

In all their exuberance he found a certain clamor here that served as a countermeasure to the anger in his head. It was a technique he'd learned during his training at The Farm in Virginia, when he'd been seething with an unquenched rage he could not control, one that had led him down a dangerous and self-destructive path. The violent streak that randomly gripped him for no apparent reason could be traced back to his stepfather, a Welshman who seemed to take great pleasure in beating both him and his Mum, and whom—shortly before he'd run off and joined the British Army—he'd bludgeoned, partially dismembered, and then buried in the rose garden behind their cozy little house near Coventry.

His handlers quickly diagnosed his personality as sociopathic, and his employment with the Greenwich Global Group had done nothing to dissuade him of his brutal tendencies. Instead, they had trained him to channel his fury into a practicable career, one which relied on his natural proclivity toward violence and kept him comfortable and busy. He was both compliant and reliable and, just like a young man who eventually loses track of his sexual conquests, he had no idea how many assignments he'd carried out during his tenure.

Then, two years ago, the work dried up. No explanation offered; no reason given. Months later he learned that the G3 had been dissolved and its leadership exterminated. The Chairman—one of the original founders after the fall of the Third Reich, and who had to have been close to one hundred—had died. Most of the executive board had been killed off, and the second-in-command—a woman named Diana Petrie, who was particularly lacking in charm and charisma—had gone missing. There was no succession plan in place, no process to keep the cogs turning. There was no one to schedule new assignments, no money to transfer to contractors' offshore accounts. No funds to cover assignments already in the pipeline.

Freelancers were left high and dry.

For the first time since his dismissal from the Army, **Le Magicien** had found himself out of a job. Yes, he had a healthy cash reserve stashed away in a half dozen banks, mostly in the Caribbean. Income was not a problem, and he could travel freely on any of his four passports. His career, however, had given him a sense of identity and purpose and—without something to keep him occupied—he could feel the old anger building inside. It was just like two tectonic plates pushing against each other, waiting for the increasing stress to create a seismic rupture.

His reprieve came via a phone call eighteen months ago, a few weeks before Christmas. He'd been riding in a taxi on his way to the airport for a flight to Madrid, and almost let it go straight to voicemail. Instead, he listened as a grotesque, digitized voice on the other end made him a business proposition, one for which he would be paid very well if he could make himself free on a certain date just before the new year.

"You come highly recommended," the scrambled voice explained. "You are reliable, you have experience, and you're already off the grid."

A conversation ensued and details were discussed, after which he had accepted the assignment, under certain mutually agreed-upon conditions. He and "the voice" were never to meet. Each job was to be paid by wire transfer to a numbered offshore account. The method by which he would carry out the contract was his choice, within reason: poison, gunshot, strangulation, drowning: whatever he decided given the target, the locale, and other incidental circumstances.

His first sanction under this new regime was Stephane Kroeger, the acting president of the International Monetary Fund, who had an appetite for fast cars and faster women. The fact that he was on holiday in Nice made the job that much more enjoyable, and the placement of the Salvador Dali tarot card was a purely capricious afterthought, since Le Magicien had found a brand-new deck of them in the target's hotel room—a gift for his wife, or perhaps a daughter? No one ever reported them missing, and they became a signature of his subsequent work, despite the fact that they meant not a damned thing to him, or anyone else—well, maybe to his Mum, but she was already dead. By all regards, he was safe.

After Professor Vaughan bid *arrivederci* and left the sidewalk patio, Logan retreated inside to use the rest room before making his way back to his minuscule hotel room. It was five stops by metro, or a hefty walk back if he decided to hoof it. Either way, his bladder wasn't going to last that long, so making a pit stop at the restaurant's men's room seemed the smart thing to do.

When he was finished, he could have just headed for the door, but he noticed that the café had a stylish bar with a black marble counter, well-stocked with all kinds of booze, and a glass-encased wine closet boasting an abundance of bottles. What harm could one more glass of Italian red do? The television mounted on the wall gave off the feel of a sports pub back home in his Kalorama neighborhood, as the patrons seated on stools or standing around had their eyes glued to the screen.

Logan expected to find a soccer match going on, but instead it seemed to be some sort of news report, with flashing red and blue lights and chaos in the background. A reporter was staring directly into the camera, describing what was happening behind her, but she was speaking Italian—naturally—so he couldn't decipher what she was saying.

A woman seated on a stool nursing a drink in a highball glass helped him with that. She shifted her eyes from the newscast to this strange man standing beside her, gave him a quick once-over.

"*Buona serata*," she said with one of the sweetest smiles he thought he'd ever seen.

Careful, a voice in his head screamed at him. *This is how it started last time, and it almost got you killed.*

"*Mi dispiace, ma il mio Italiano è pessimo*," he apologized. It was one of the few phrases he'd memorized from the language app.

"No problem," she told him. "English is fine with me. And it's gin, sweet vermouth, and Campari, with a slice of fresh orange." Referring to the contents of her glass on the bar.

"Ah…I was wondering what that might be," he said. "And you speak English."

"And you must be American." She flashed him a polite smile, teeth that seemed so perfect that they seemed imperfect. A smile that again made him flash back on the seductive chick who had tried to slash his throat the summer before last, an encounter that ultimately had ended far worse for her than for him.

"What makes you say so?" he inquired.

"Because of your accent, and you look as if you've never seen a Negroni before." She handed him the glass and said, "Try a sip."

He did, and that's how he came to be seated on the stool next to her, his own Negroni with a large slice of orange in a highball glass set on a napkin in front of him. He could get a glass of wine anytime, anywhere, but here he was, sitting in at the bar in a trendy trattoria just a few blocks from the Vatican. Speaking with a lovely young woman named Aurora, her head shaved on one side, a dark ponytail pulled over her shoulder on the other. She wore a full constellation of piercings, rings, and facial studs, all of them looking every bit as painful as possible, plus she had the most gorgeous brown eyes he'd ever seen. Well, perhaps that was a stretch, but she was indeed quite lovely, and he hadn't imbibed anywhere near enough alcohol yet for his judgment to be impaired—not like that last time.

She plucked the orange slice from her glass and nibbled it as she glanced up at the television.

"What's going on" Logan asked, nodding at the screen. "Something big happen at the G-twenty today?"

"No, nothing like that. There's been another abduction from the Trevi Fountain."

He had just taken a sip of his drink, and almost spit it out. "What?"

"It's become a real problem, but the authorities pretend like it's nothing," Aurora replied. "Worried it might hurt the tourist business."

By now he was leaning forward, staring at the reporter even though he had no idea what she was saying. He was thinking about Alvize, whose kidnapping from the very same spot had occurred almost ten years ago.

"This happens a lot?" he asked.

"More than it should, which is never," she said. "This time it was a young girl from America. Fifteen years old. Vanished into thin air, almost right in front of her parents."

"They must be going out of their minds."

"Totally," Aurora replied. "They say they thought she had wandered into a souvenir shop, or maybe had gone off to toss a coin over her shoulder. It's been over a day now, and still no word from her."

"How could she just disappear like that without someone seeing her?"

"Good question, and no one seems to have a good answer," she told him. "The polizia say a forensics team is examining CCTV video, but these people are slick. I guarantee you they won't find anything."

One Negroni turned into two, followed by a glass of Sangiovese that Logan assured himself couldn't hurt. He kept his eyes glued to the screen while Aurora provided a play-by-play of what was going on, and being said. Actually, some of the time he shifted his gaze to her eyes, and occasionally to the plain white top she was wearing, a revealing collar that exposed plenty of skin, deep neckline. As one side of his brain was telling him, he was a single man alone in Rome for the first time, and nothing was off limits. Fortunately, the sensible side kept telling him, over and over, *don't go there.*

Around nine o'clock a man who seemed to be Aurora's boyfriend sneaked up behind her. He kissed her on the back of her neck, and said, "*Mi dispiace di essere in ritardo, amore mio.*"

By now, Logan had picked up just enough Italian—and knew just enough body language—to figure the guy was apologizing for being late. It was an attempt to atone for leaving her sitting there at the bar for hours, fending off lecherous men while flirting with an American stranger.

In any event, when the guy showed up, Logan determined it was his cue to make a graceful exit. Time to bid farewell to his new friend and pay his bill, find his way back to his hotel, and figure out the next step in his exposé about sex trafficking and abductions in Rome, particularly since another one had happened just yesterday.

Logan realized then and there that there was no way to write the story without confronting the corrupt sleazebag whose name was Renato Azzone.

He decided to walk. Riding the metro would have been the easier way to get back to his hotel, but the Negronis had hit him harder than he'd expected, and the additional glass of wine seemed to contribute significantly to the rotation of the earth. However, he believed the fresh air of a brisk walk would do him good, allow him to clear his mind so he could get a fresh start on tomorrow—which, either way, was going to arrive a lot sooner than he wished. Along with a sledge-hammer headache that he should have thought about when he'd come out of the men's room—such as it was—and had made that detour through the bar.

"That's him," Vinnie Livrizzi said, gesturing with his head toward the man in dark khakis and windbreaker who just moments ago had stepped out of the trendy bistro they'd been staking out.

He was riding shotgun in Aldo's Mercedes, an older 560-S model, silver with turbo V8 and missing a rear bumper and front medallion. Aldo was behind the wheel, while Remy had remained home in Naples to look after his pregnant girlfriend, the daughter of a rival capo who was ready to pop a baby any day. The car was parked across the street and a half block down, the American target teetering up the sidewalk toward them.

"About fucking time," Aldo said as he wiped a lock of hair from his eyes and keyed the engine to life. "Looks like he's had a few."

Vinnie's source inside the Guardia di Finanza had coughed up whatever information had been gathered on Logan, beginning with the fact that he'd managed to find a new room at a budget hotel that catered to tourists mostly from eastern Europe. The GPS tracker that had been activated in his phone enabled the police to follow his every move, and they'd kept him under surveillance ever since. The thinking was that if the he was involved in Santoro's death, he might lead them to whoever ordered it. At the moment they were parked somewhere nearby, keeping an eye on him from a distance.

So were Aldo and Vinnie, albeit much closer. They'd waited what seemed like ages for Logan to finish talking with some guy dressed like an art curator or shrink, before he'd gone inside to use the *bagno*. Where he'd stayed for another age until he finally stumbled back out, apparently *mezzo ubriaco*.

"What now?" Vinnie asked.

"For Chrissakes…do I have to do all the thinking?" Aldo said. "We follow him, is what we do. Eventually he'll get to a dark stretch, and we take him there."

"You don't think he'll notice us behind him?"

"Look at how he's walking. *Quell idiota* isn't noticing a thing."

"You've outdone yourself this time, my sweet."

Georgy Sokolov ran his hands over Nataliya Moisie's breasts, trickled his fingers around both nipples simultaneously. She let out a low moan as her body shuddered at his touch. They both were naked, and she was seated in his lap, gazing out at the dark Mediterranean, the lights of a cruise ship far off in the distance the only sign of life out there. She tipped her head back as far as she could, locked her lips to his, ran her tongue inside his mouth. It was an odd angle for her to sustain for very long, one that stretched just about every muscle in her neck.

"You like her?" she said to her Russian boss, lover, and corrupter of all good things.

He pulled his lips away from hers, momentarily holding her tongue with his teeth, and lightly lowered his hands to a more sensitive spot. "I could not imagine more perfect prize," he whispered into her ear. "Girl will fetch good price."

They were lounging in the dark marble spa, jets turned off and the water temperature set at forty degrees Celsius. Just a gentle wisp of a breeze was blowing through the acacias and olive trees, and a faint strain of music was coming from a villa further up the private road. It sounded baroque, perhaps Teleman or Albinoni.

No, Vivaldi…that's definitely what it was.

Such irony, Sokolov thought.

"She put up a bit of a fuss on the plane when she woke up," Nataliya said. "I had to give her another shot to subdue her."

"That means she is… *energichnyy*," he replied, searching for the Russian equivalent of spirited. "Should raise the stakes."

Nataliya let out a noise very much like a purr, and said, "Without question, my darling."

"Where is *shlyukha* now?"

"Where all the other *shlyukhas* go. Under heavy guard."

"Good. Will keep her there overnight, let her panic grow. Will make her more *derzkiy* when time comes."

"Mmmm," she agreed. "Now, could you maybe do that thing to me again?"

Sokolov's fingers began to move, ever so gently, and he said, "Pleasure is all mine."

"I certainly hope not," she replied.

The place where Abby had been stashed was an unfinished room carved into the hillside beneath the main floor of the sprawling seafront villa: thick concrete walls, no windows, just a narrow air vent set in a ceiling that also seemed to be constructed of cement. All of it was dull and gray, the floor cold and hard.

The only piece of furniture was a bed. Unlike the filthy room back in Rome where she had started this ordeal, this one was fitted with a clean duvet and pillows that seemed never to have been used. They even smelled new and fresh, as if they had just come from Bed, Bath and Beyond.

Her wrists and ankles were still shackled, but thick sheepskin cuffs protected her from chafing. They, in turn, were bound together with a tempered metal chain that allowed for just enough movement to take a few steps toward the steel door embedded in the far wall. A retractable cable attached to a shearling collar allowed her to make it about halfway toward it, teasing her with the prospect of what might be on the other side.

Abby sat at the edge of the bed, wiggling her toes despite the temperature of the floor. The woman who had brought her here had swapped her cut-offs and midriff top for a set of sweats—gray with pink trim, no logo. She'd also replaced her sneakers with some sort of soft shoes that were almost like ballet slippers, but they were tight and pinched her feet. Kicking them off had given her a minuscule sense of freedom, but the overwhelming horror of what had happened to her, where she was, had ratcheted up the panic that had seized her the moment she'd been snatched back at the fountain.

Her mind remained a blur from those early moments, and she wondered what time it was. What day? She knew she'd been drugged again—that bitch on the plane had given her something powerful—and she'd lost track of everything, starting with where she'd been taken. Was she still in Italy, or halfway around the world? And for what possible *goddamn* reason?

That actually was the easy part. The bitch had offered the briefest of explanations once the cabin door had closed and the private jet had lifted off into the air. Her demeanor reminded Abby of that sleazy whore who'd been convicted of sex trafficking a few years back, partner in crime with the billionaire pedophile who'd supposedly killed himself in his jail cell. She didn't have the same appearance, nor did she seem to be of the same nationality—not even the same age, but she possessed that same smug attitude, same *my-shit-don't-stink* arrogance.

And that's the part that worried her the most.

"Say goodbye to everything you know about your life," the woman had whispered in her ear as she'd attached the cuffs to the seat's armrests. "Your new future begins now."

Abby pushed the reality of the moment down in her mind as far as she could, forced a heavy curtain of denial to drop across her consciousness. The drugs that were pumping through her system had helped with that, and several times she'd drifted off to a welcome darkness that momentarily took her away from this living hell.

"We'll be landing soon," the whore-bitch dressed in white had told her. "And just so you know, what lies ahead for you isn't as bad as you might think. You might even learn to like it."

Logan stopped at the corner across from the metro station, waited while a box truck for a furniture company rolled through the intersection. Sirens screamed in the distance, a nuisance he figured had to do with the global summit and the military presence throughout the city. Random protests had been springing up all across Rome, and a stream of online chatter fueled a constant threat of violence twenty-four/seven. In response, thousands of law enforcement officers had been deployed to quell any possible violence, specialized vehicles capable of detecting explosives and toxic materials were on patrol, and military drones and helicopters patrolled a no-fly zone around the commercial airports.

If there was one comforting fact, it was that at no time in the past few years was it any safer for him to walk home than tonight. Not even the taggers would be out.

Halfway through the crosswalk, however, his phone rang. He hurried across the street, where he checked the screen: Raleigh Durham. He felt the same momentary thrill he always felt whenever she called, even though they both insisted they were *just friends*.

"What's up?" he asked as he reached the curb, barely avoiding a man pedaling a bicycle. He checked his pocket for his wallet, just to be sure it was still there.

"Looks like rain," she said, her voice sultry and suggestive. "Quite a bit of it, in fact."

"What do you have in mind?" he replied, a carnal shiver arousing the neuropathways to his brain, and everywhere else.

"My hotel, thirty minutes."

That morning she'd told him she'd be almost definitely working late into the night, occupied with dinners and receptions and marathon meetings. Her peripatetic life always seemed in motion and subject to change, and rare was the occasion when events turned in his favor. And when they did, who was he to argue?

"I'm on my way," he said.

"*Fanculo*," Aldo swore as he watched Logan make an abrupt turn down the steps into the Ottaviano metro station. He thumped his hands on the steering wheel in frustration.

"Where the fuck's he going?" Vinnie wondered aloud, peering through the windshield.

It was a rhetorical question so he wasn't expecting an answer, but Aldo felt compelled to provide one anyway. "How the hell should I know? Follow him."

"What?"

"Go on…see where he's headed."

"He's got a big jump on us—"

"Trains are staggered this time of night," Aldo said, cutting him off. "He'll have to wait on the platform."

"But he's already inside—"

"So why the fuck are you sitting here?"

Chapter 23

"They know you're in Paris," Martin Beaudin said from the second-floor library of his secluded house deep in the heart of the Pyrenees. He was on his third glass of a 2016 Chateau Canon St. Emilion, and savoring the aroma of a Hoyo de Monterrey le Hoyo du Maire imported from Cuba. "The Americans and Israelis both captured your biometrics as you got off the bus yesterday at the Porte Maillot terminal."

Phythian was neither surprised nor particularly worried. After the downfall of the Greenwich Global Group he'd expected the viral spread of rumors that he was still alive, and an increasing number of algorithms had started running his touchpoints through their facial recognition databases.

"An inevitable fact of life," Phythian replied with a sigh. "Is there reason for immediate concern?"

He was strolling up Rue Henry Monnier at a leisurely pace, his jacket collar tucked up against his neck to ward off the evening chill. One hand was in his pocket, the other holding the phone against his ear as he stopped in front of the window of a darkened shop. During the day it sold empanadas, but at this hour—a little before midnight —the display shelves were empty and the patisserie was dark.

"Let's just say it might be a good idea to take extra care the next few days," Beaudin cautioned him. "According to Equinox, there's a steep price on your head."

Equinox was the central server that gathered, sorted, and stored multiple terabytes of data previously amassed by the now-defunct Greenwich Global Group. Even after the organization's demise two years ago, it remained linked to highly classified intelligence databases within various acronym agencies in almost a dozen countries, most of them represented by the nations gathering this week at the G20 in Rome.

"How steep?" Phythian asked, getting back to what Beaudin had just relayed to him.

"Five million Euros. Cash or crypto, contractor's choice."

"Duly noted." He turned away from the window, continued on his way up the sidewalk toward the next corner. "Did you check to see if Equinox mentions anything about this tarot card thing?"

"I did, and whatever is there is anecdotal at best," Beaudin said. As the G3's longtime data master, he'd had unfettered access to its mainframe and knew his way around the system. He literally knew where the bones were buried, and how they got there. "According to the original charter established after the war, all technicians were strictly prohibited from leaving behind any kind of identifying signature that might lead to their capture or death, or could be traced back to management. That meant no cards, no feathers, no coins. No hint of perfume or cigarettes, not even a note. *Nothing*. The rules were very explicit about this, under penalty of death."

"That doesn't mean that whoever killed Gabrielle Lamoines wasn't one of theirs," Phythian replied.

"Don't confuse me with your English double negatives," the Frenchman said. Phythian waited while Beaudin took a long sip of wine, then let out a gentle sigh as he swallowed. "In any event, if you look at that list of victims you sent me—those whose death scenes included one of those tarot cards drawn by Dali—you'll see that those hits occurred after you took control of the G3."

"With them out of the business, it was inevitable that other groups would emerge to fill the void," Phythian said.

"Same thing with all their former contractors," Beaudin replied. "My guess is, Gabrielle's killer has been around for years, and there's a high likelihood that he worked for the G3 before becoming a free agent."

"Any idea what the significance of the tarot cards might be?"

"Nothing definitive. Just one of those anecdotes I mentioned, a brief entry in a file in a folder I found in an old personnel database. I ran a search and it came up."

"Are you going to tell me, or do I have to pull it out of your head?"

"Well, sir," the old locksmith said, hesitating a moment to collect his thoughts. "It's just a throwaway reference, really, but it might mean something to you. It reads, 'When his mother wasn't tending to her small garden of yellow roses, she was reading tarot cards for neighbors.'"

Damn, he thought. What he said was, "Seriously?"

"That's what it says," Beaudin confirmed.

Phythian instantly flashed back to that cold February afternoon at The Farm, the day this entire odyssey began more than twenty years ago. He had been a green recruit at the time, recently discharged from the Marines, almost broke, and contemplating where life would take him next. Rumors of his raw abilities had quickly preceded him to the MINDGAZE facilities in western Virginia, and the G3 doctors were almost foaming at the mouth at the prospect of working with him, anxious to see if the reports about his uncanny skills possibly could be true. A lot of money and more than a few careers were riding on exploring—and then exploiting—his extra-sensory competencies.

He'd arrived at the equestrian facility in horse country by limousine and was introduced to Dr. Andrews, the senior-level shrink on loan from the Pentagon who'd been brought in under the guise of a Defense Department research program to assess his rumored skillset. Within minutes, Phythian had become engaged in an alpha-male battle with his bunkmate, a British Army major with severe anger management issues that had brought him close to a court martial. The guy's name was Thompson, and Phythian had been cajoled into performing a deep data dive into his brain—one that caused the apoplectic officer to hurl himself off a balcony. Phythian had never seen the Neanderthal again, but later heard he'd been reassigned to a different part of the program to ensure they never encountered each other again.

During that brief mental probe, Phythian had discovered many things about the life and times of Major Thompson—including the fact that his mother fastidiously tended a yellow rose garden, dead-heading the buds and pruning the stalks every morning. It was beneath this patch of blooms that her son had hidden the body of his dead stepfather who, after a time, was thought to have run off in the middle of the night.

One other thing he'd learned that day was that the man's mother also dabbled in the occult, reading palms, tea leaves, and tarot cards for her neighbors. She did this for a small fee, which subsidized her fondness for a bottomless glass of sherry every evening.

"Major Richard Thompson, with the British Army," Phythian recalled. "A bit of a loose cannon, as I recall."

"Intermittent explosive disorder, is what it says here," Beaudin agreed. "It appears he was training at The Farm in Virginia the same time you were there, and the two of you had a rather contentious interaction."

"Your personnel report is correct," Phythian said. "I never knew what happened to him."

"In the end he was stripped of his military rank and title, and left Her Majesty's service under a stain for reasons that remain redacted," Beaudin explained. "He worked for several non-government contractors in Afghanistan and Iraq after that, and eventually—during a long drought of suitable candidates—the G3 relaxed its rules and he was deemed employable."

"You're suggesting this Major Thompson with the anger management issues was the hired gun who shot Gabrielle Lamoines?" Phythian asked.

"I'm saying a lot of the dots are there," Beaudin assured him. "I'm sure if they connect, you'll find a way to do it."

Georgy Sokolov couldn't sleep and hadn't slept well for a long time, unable to shake the gnawing anxiety stemming from his crumbling oil empire and all the financial chaos that came with it. He was counting on the arrival of Nataliya to alleviate the disquiet that sometimes bordered on panic, and for an hour or so she had, a beautiful and pleasurable diversion, but one that dissipated as soon as the little blue pill wore off.

After climbing out of the spa, she had invited him to accompany her to bed, the promise of a full-body massage tempting him, but in the end he told her to go ahead without him. "I still have some things to take care of," he'd told her.

His words were not a lie. He retreated to his library, a spacious room furnished with some of the finest antiques from the Far East, and a collection of artwork no one else must ever be allowed to see. He checked emails (nothing of interest), reviewed his financial holdings (big mistake), even watched a little porn (no reaction at all). In the end he closed his laptop and pushed his way out onto the sprawling pool patio, gazed up at the same stars under which he and Nataliya had made love just an hour ago—stars that seemed so infinite, the breadth and depth of the universe making him feel so small. So insignificant.

Well, all that was about to change. Tomorrow was going to be a big day, for any number of reasons, and there was no room for even one of them to get fucked up. He'd been anticipating this confluence of events for years, ever since that *treklyatyy* American president had started squeezing his financial resources after the Crimean thing.

Well, tomorrow would teach them all. The leaders of the world's democracies would be in one place at one time, shaking hands and babbling about climate change and nuclear proliferation, fighting each other for photo ops. For them it would all be over so fast, so much blood in the streets and smoke in the air that they would never know what hit them.

Violentiam. Valeo. Diripio.

ViValDi.

Thirty yards away, far from the stars and the darkened horizon and the luxury of contemplating anything positive about her future, Abby Evans lay on her bed in her concrete dungeon. She, too, could not sleep. Her worries were focused on concerns of a more immediate and fatalistic nature, and no pondering the wonders and curiosities of the heavens would possibly help her.

The overhead light set into the masonry ceiling had no on-off switch, at least not on this side of the door. A few hours ago, a guard had brought her a tray with some kind of tasteless dish made from tomatoes and rice, which she ate. She remembered what her biology teacher had said about animals in the wild: they eat whatever they can, whenever they can, because they never know when they'll eat again. Same thing here.

The guard had checked in every hour on the hour, or so it seemed. At some point a new sentry took over, his dark, leering eyes gazing hungrily at her, his skin giving off the odor of stale sweat and dead fish. He wore loose trousers, dirty army-drab T-shirt, gun tucked into his waistband, and as he left, he made a suggestive gesture to her. She figured he must have been under some sort of order not to touch her, because he didn't.

The woman from the plane looked in on her, as well. She no longer was wearing the white pantsuit; instead, she was draped in what looked like a silk kimono decorated with peacocks that looked far too large on her...a man's robe, she realized.

"Have you eaten?" she'd asked from just inside the doorway, in that same strange accent.

Abby didn't reply, simply stared at her with a sullen look.

"Do you need to use the facilities?"

She gave no response.

"Well, then...sleep well," the woman said with a devilish smile. As she stepped out and closed the door, a heavy lock jolted into place, and the room was engulfed with a ghastly silence.

The light stayed on, however. Abby lay on the bed a few moments after that, her fingers absently toying with the steel tether connected to her collar. She played with it, pulling a length out from the wall-mounted mechanism. She wrapped the steel leash around her hand a time or two, felt the tension as the spring-driven apparatus tried to reel it back in.

That's when the idea struck her. At some point the new guard would return—the vulgar one with the lecherous eyes and rancid smell—which meant she had to work quickly. She climbed up on top of the mattress, kneeled in the center as close to the wall as she could, and pulled out a length of cable. She looped it around her throat: once, twice, three times, just so there could be no mistaken intent. When she released it, she felt the spring-wound cord tighten against her windpipe, almost choking her.

She unwound it, then did it again, this time inserting her fingers between the tether and her raw skin, relieving the tension just enough to be able to breathe. She had no idea how long she would have to hold this position until she heard the sound of the lock again, signaling her hourly check-in, or whatever time frame was the routine here. Sooner or later, she knew, someone would come through that door, and when he—or *she*—did, Abby would release the cable and let gravity and physics take care of the rest.

Part III

Presto

Chapter 24

Abby waited what seemed like forever before she heard footfalls outside her door. They paused, and she inhaled a deep breath, preparing herself for whatever fate dealt her in the next few seconds. Her life very well depended on what transpired when that door swung open, teetering on a fulcrum of her own making.

When she heard the lock shift, she slipped her fingers from beneath the triple loop of steel cable that encircled her neck. The cord bit into her throat and she felt it tighten against her trachea. At the same moment the foul-smelling guard slipped into the room and let out an evil cackle, and said, "*Diavolo, puttana...*"

He stopped mid-sentence as he assessed the situation, frozen by the sight of this young girl who was attempting to strangle herself with her tether. He realized the crazy Russian upstairs would disembowel and emasculate him if his American whore were to die. He cried out "*Oh mio Dio, no, no, no,*" and sprinted across the floor to where she was slumped at the edge of the bed.

Abby felt his arms wrap around her as he tried to lift her up, attempting to relax the tension on her makeshift noose, which actually *was* beginning to choke the life out of her. He muttered to himself over and over as he tried to unwind the cord from her throat, panicked to the point of hysteria. "Please don't die. Please don't die—"

He managed to free her, but Abby remained limp. Was she already dead? "*Merda...*" he said as he gripped her by the shoulders and gave her a shake.

Abruptly her eyes blinked open in a glare of fury, in the same that her hand shot out. She had noticed earlier that he was wearing loose-fitting trousers, and she grabbed his crotch and squeezed as tightly as she could possibly muster—hard and deep, digging her nails through the cloth into his groin.

He howled as he tried to jerk away, but the pain was too much, and her grip was too tight. He rocked backward, but still she hung on, until he managed to swing an arm around and lash the side of her head with his elbow. She was no match for his strength and knew she only had another second or two before the balance of power flipped. She shook off the pain, reached with her other hand to where she'd seen the gun earlier, inserted in his waistband. She pulled it out and swung it up in the same fluid motion, then pressed the barrel under his chin.

Still squeezing with the other hand, but not as tight. And terrified out of her mind.

"Get. Off. Me." she snarled at him, no uncertainty in her voice.

He froze, still gripped with agonizing pain. Abby went rigid from the confusion of what to do next. She hadn't thought this far ahead in her plan, and she was at a total loss. He read the uncertainty in her eyes and made a sudden move to grab the gun, but her hand tightened on his *testicoli* and the recurrent torment stopped him.

"You fucking move, I shoot," she snarled at him.

Despite the language barrier and the agony, he seemed to grasp what she was saying. Maybe thinking he could give her a second or two, then take her by surprise and subdue her.

Abby read this notion in his eyes, slowly shifted her position and released her grip on his privates. She continued to hold the gun against his jaw as she wriggled away a few inches, and came up on her feet on the other side of the bed.

"You're not going to shoot me," the guard growled at her in Italian.

The words were lost on her, but she caught the substance. She was holding the gun in both hands now, aiming at his heart, wondering if he might be wearing a bulletproof vest; or if there was a safety latch she had to flip in order for it to work. She'd never fired a gun in her life—*she was from California, for Chrissakes*—much less ever held one. But for some reason—perhaps his tormented gonads, or his wish to live—he hadn't lunged at her...yet. Which told her two things: he was still in pain from how she'd mangled his manhood, and he was genuinely worried she'd shoot him.

"Stay there," she told him as she slowly edged away from the bed, knowing that the more distance she put between them, the worse shot she'd have. She also knew that eventually she'd come to the end of her tether.

He seemed to know that, too. When she finally got to the end of the line—literally—he made his move, charging at her on legs that were still wobbly with pain. He flung his arms forward and dived for the gun, at the same moment her finger squeezed the trigger.

Allesandro Bortolotti had been planning for this day longer than he could remember.

The initial idea had come to him the morning after he'd suffered his second defeat at the ballot box. His foray into legitimate politics had not yielded the results he'd desired, and he decided to redirect his efforts toward a plan that would achieve a more positive outcome…and much more quickly than a typical constitutional approach.

He would achieve what his childhood idol Mussolini had not been able to do.

He had numerous reasons to be in a good mood this morning. Or at least a better one than yesterday. First, Mateo Tufino had called him before first light to let him know that he'd received a text that his shipment would be arriving in the port of Gioia Tauro just after midnight.

Second, close to a thousand *nazionalista* loyalists from across southern Europe had begun to report in from various locations around the city. Over the past thirty-six hours they had checked in to cheap hotels and rented rooms, or were bunking in with friends or family who were sympathetic to the cause. They were in contact via a loose network of volunteer commanders who utilized burner phones and spoke in code, in order to minimize chatter and reduce any chance of international security forces from detecting their intentions.

Third, a sympathizer who managed a clothing factory outside Milan had delivered one thousand uniforms cut and sewn to the exact specifications of the Italian Army. The finished garments were identical to the original, down to the peaked cap, jacket with five buttons and two inside pockets, matching trousers with two back pockets and two mid-thigh pockets. The shipment also included government-issue footwear, gloves, and a summer-weight jacket. No raingear was needed, since the weather was expected to be dry for the next five days.

The sun had crept above the rooftops to the east and Bortolotti was standing on the balcony of his apartment, rented for the month under the guise of a high-tech gaming company based in Berlin. The firm did not exist, at least not in a legitimate sense, and he was confident the convoluted trail of shell companies would hold up to any governmental scrutiny in advance of the summit, should the need arise. He had selected its location for its proximity to the Nuvola and the media center at the nearby Palazzo dei Congressi, where the G20 leaders were meeting.

The twelfth-floor residence had a panoramic view that extended from the secure "red zone" around the convention center, all the way up to the Rome Cavalieri Hotel in the distance, where most of the symposium's leaders were staying. It had infinitely nicer amenities than this place, but Bortolotti was not in town to experience elegance or the luxury of a fine hotel. Secrecy and privacy had been critical during the lead-up to today's activities, and by nightfall an entirely different tenor would have overtaken the city of Rome.

By then he would be enjoying the fruits of his labors, while the devastating force of ViValDi would be reverberating far and wide, encircling the globe with a new political reality.

He had just taken a sip of espresso he'd brewed using the machine in the kitchen when his phone rang. It was Renate Azzone, an early riser on most mornings and—considering the time was just after six—decidedly so today.

"I thought I might find you up despite the hour," he said when Bortolotti picked up.

"Many things in the works, and much still to be done. Have you received any word from His Holiness?"

"Not directly, and nothing conclusive," Azzone replied. "He's not as inclined to bestow his full support behind the cause until the full impact of the day is known. Unlike Achille Ratti."

Achille Ratti being the name of Pope Pius XI, who had gone all in with Mussolini in the lead-up to World War II. Unfortunately, the Italian fascist's ability to consolidate power and bridge fissures with the Catholic Church eventually was dwarfed by his political weaknesses, particularly his ill-conceived economic policies, myopic foreign policy, and his relationship with the Nazis.

Different times called for different measures, and Bortolotti believed his time had come.

"The Pope's agency would go a long way to instill a sense of calm throughout the country," he reminded Azzone. "It would be wise of him to make up his mind before it's made up for him. As Italy goes, so goes the Church."

"His Holiness is more aware than most people of the longstanding relationship between the citizens of Italy and the Holy See," Azzone bristled. "He is a devoted scholar of fascism and its role in the near-term history of this country, and the Vatican. He also knows that things did not end well for either Ratti or Il Duce."

"It will be different this time," Bortolotti assured his friend. "Everything is in place for a decisive success. Victory is all but assured."

"And when that momentous triumph occurs, I'm sure you will receive the blessing you desire," Azzone said. "*ViValDi.*"

"*ViValDi,*" Bortolotti repeated, ending the call.

The one drawback to experiencing a most wonderful late-night rendezvous with Raleigh Durham was the guarantee that Carter Logan would be awakened by her phone alarm before the sun split the horizon. Thus, at a couple minutes past six, he was lying on his side, chin propped up on one elbow, luxury sheets covering him up to his waist.

"Big day at the summit today," she said to him from the bathroom. She'd just toweled off after a quick shower, and through a crack in the door he could see her applying a dusting of body powder. "Starting with a breakfast in under an hour."

"Can you bring me back a cup of coffee?" he asked.

"Sorry, Sweets. I'm heading over the river and through the streets to the *Cavalieri.*"

"What's that?"

She turned on the blow dryer, spent a minute working it over her hair. When she clicked it off, she said, "It's the hotel where most of the world leaders are staying. They're meeting there this morning in closed sessions before heading down later to the Nuvola for the big closing luncheon."

"Sounds like a fun time will be had by all."

"It's what I do," she said as she clamped a grotesque contraption to an eyelash and squeezed. "What's your day like?"

"I'm going to see if I can scam my way to a meeting with a vile, rotten pervert at the Vatican," Logan replied. "Mind if I use your laptop?"

"I'm leaving in five minutes," Raleigh called to him. "It's coming with me."

"I'll only need it for three," he assured her.

Aldo hadn't remained furious at Vinnie very long. Neither of them had expected the American to abruptly dart into the metro station and give them the slip. The Camorra thug had made a valiant effort to catch up with him, see where the American named Logan might be going, but there was no sign of him anywhere. A train must have just departed the platform, leaving the place all but deserted. He was shit-out-of-luck.

In the end they had camped out near the American's hotel, the name of which had been provided by the source inside the Guardia di Finanza, but not the room number, which had led to much yelling between Vinnie and his snitch. Eventually the two thugs from Napoli took turns keeping an eye on the entrance, but both had slept more than they'd been awake, and would have missed him had he come home.

He hadn't, however, and now—just a few minutes before seven—they both were hungry, and still tired. Even worse, they both had to take a leak.

All that was going to have to wait, however, as Vinnie blurted out, "*Porca puttana.*" It was an all-encompassing Italian epithet that had any number of translations, including "for God's sake," "son of a bitch," "motherfucker," or "holy shit." In this case the rendering included all of the above. "That's him, right there."

Aldo looked where he was pointing and, sure enough, Logan was wandering up the sidewalk; his hands in his pockets, eyes studying the buildings on both sides of the street, certainly not noticing the silver Mercedes parked at the next corner, two gangsters sitting in the front seat, watching his every move.

"That's what he was wearing last night," Vinnie said.

"Must've got lucky."

"Or lost."

"Does he look lost to you?" Aldo asked him.

"No, but he doesn't look lucky, either."

They watched him in silence, waited until he pushed the door open and made his way inside the hotel. Then Vinnie said, "I'll go talk to the desk clerk."

"What for?"

"To get his room number. Then we wait a few minutes, let him get comfortable."

"Don't get creative, not like last time," Aldo said.

"I know what I'm doing," Vinnie assured him.

He opened the car door and slid out, pushing it closed tightly behind him. He swept his hair back with his hand, then started off down the sidewalk at a deliberate gait, glancing from side to side, keeping an eye open for polizia. This was Rome, not Napoli, and he was far from his home turf. Even though he had a contact inside La Guardia, he was on his own here.

Abby was shivering so badly she thought she'd pass out from the chill. The gray sweatsuit the bitch from the plane—she now remembered her name was Nataliya—had given her provided a small degree of warmth, but an unseasonable cold front had crept in, and the breeze that flowed up the rocky cliff from the sea had iced her to the bone.

Just a few hours ago she had shot a man—fatally. Never in a million years would she ever have thought of herself as a killer, but there was no doubt the guy was dead. The first bullet had knocked him on his ass, and when the momentary hysteria had released its grip, she'd unleashed another round clean through his neck.

She remembered dropping the gun, then closing the door behind her when she'd left the room. Most of what happened after that remained a blur. She couldn't recall how she'd made her way out of the dark basement carved into the hillside, except that she'd passed a room barricaded by a door with iron bars. Another dungeon? she wondered, then noticed the racks of bottles behind it: a wine cellar, like the one her father was always talking about building someday, when they could afford a real house in Sausalito.

She thought about him now, and her mother, felt a flood of tears building up inside her, but realized that if she succumbed to them right now, she'd lose all measure of sanity—and any ability to think this through. More than anything, she needed to figure out where she was, and how to get away.

She'd awakened a moment ago in the back of a dark blue vehicle—an SUV with tinted windows, black upholstery, and a new car smell. She didn't remember climbing inside it, but she'd been so panicked after pulling the trigger that she'd lost all sense of time and place.

The vehicle was parked in a circular driveway that also overlooked the ocean. There were two other cars, one a yellow two-seater with the top down, the other a sleek red thing that looked as if it belonged on a race track. One of the SUV windows had been left open, which was how she'd slipped inside following her escape. Very convenient at the time, but now it allowed in the cool breeze that seeped through the light fabric of her clothes…and the stupid slippers she'd been given, making her feel as if her toes were ice cubes.

There was no way to know what time it was. She'd never been a Girl Scout or gone to summer camp, but the angle of the light and the long shadows cast by the palm trees and cacti suggested it was early morning; no birds, no creatures anywhere. Not even a dog roaming the grounds. No human presence, either, at least not out here in the driveway.

Although she assumed that would change as soon as someone found the body behind the locked door.

At that moment she caught a flicker of motion off to her right, spotted a human form coming down a short flight of steps from a side door: a woman, from the looks of her, and not just any woman, she realized as she drew closer. It was the *fucking bitch* who had probed her on the airplane yesterday, when she'd thought Abby was passed out from whatever drugs she'd shot into her: Nataliya.

She was wearing a long, flowing skirt—white again—with a slit up the side, and a white midriff top that exposed a couple inches of belly. Large white sunglasses and a beaded necklace completed the ensemble as she strutted across the driveway, matching white shrug draped across her shoulders, a to-go mug of coffee in one hand.

She headed her way.

Shit.

Abby ducked down, rolled herself into the smallest ball she could manage. Was she coming out to the car just to get something, or was she headed somewhere? Maybe someone had discovered Abby's disappearance and she was looking for her. But that didn't seem right: the dead guard would have sent everyone into a frenzy, and this witch seemed too cold and focused to be panicked.

A moment later Abby heard the driver's side door open, and the woman spent a moment arranging herself behind the wheel. There was a metallic clang as the tumbler was inserted into a cup holder, followed by the grumble of a cold engine grinding to life.

The sound system came on, playing a piece Abby recognized but to which she did not know the name. The *presto e forte* of Vivaldi's "Summer" concerto in G minor, a raging storm that matched the pulsing tempo in her heart. She huddled in the rear of the SUV as the vehicle started to move, circling through the courtyard and down the driveway.

Chapter 25

Donald Poole, the head of President Mitchell's security team, was pacing the floor of the windowless room on the mezzanine level of the Nuvola Convention Center. It was a study in sterility, bright lighting turned up to the max, drab tables and chairs and a cart of bitter coffee set up in a corner—but he wasn't there for amenities, and what the place lacked in comfort it made up for in peace of mind. Well, not exactly, since he didn't have eyes on the commander in chief—codename Keystone—despite the two-dozen forty-inch flat-screen monitors positioned along one wall, four rows of six screens each, floor to ceiling.

Each of these was displaying real-time HD video of the entire motorcade route, beginning at the Aleph Rome on Via di S. Basilio. It was a beautiful hotel, everything luxurious and very presidential, while most of the other world leaders at the summit were staying at the Rome Cavalieri Waldorf Astoria. Also quite nice, but Mitchell wished to play by his own rules, so he and his entourage had reserved the two top floors of these much more centralized digs on the other side of the Tiber River.

The immediate problem for Poole—the one that was keeping him up at night and overloading him with caffeine every day—was that getting to and from the summit took President Mitchell through a maze of narrow streets, none of them remotely straight for more than a few blocks. Line of sight along the route was for shit, with precisely twenty-seven left and right turns, buildings on both sides that could trap the motorcade like a box canyon. It had windows and rooftops everywhere, and far too many trees lining Vialle della Terme di Caracalla. A sniper's heaven. Only when the route finally merged into Via Cristoforo Colombo was it a straight shot the rest of the way, mostly protected by Italian national police forces.

Key word: *mostly*.

Even then, the security chief couldn't allow himself to breathe easily, not that he ever did in this job, particularly after the close call two years ago when the president had almost lost his life to a rogue assassin. Poole had been certain that incident would cost him his job and his pension, but the president had been in a good mood when he'd tendered his resignation, and had actually laughed it off…with a caveat, of course

"Don't ever let it happen again."

Again, due to the nature of his job, was potentially every day after that one, leading up to now. And he sure as fuck didn't like what he was seeing.

It wasn't all his responsibility alone, not by any stretch. Every country represented at the G20 had some sort of armed presence. The larger member nations imported a respectable contingent of security personnel sworn to protect and serve their president or prime minister, while the smaller states, not wanting to be embarrassed by the size of their budgets, still made a grand show of their uniformed detail.

The Italian government had the most at stake, since they needed to prove to the world that they could quell any political uprising or protest, turn back any kind of terrorist attack. Thus, the city of Rome had sealed off a 10-square kilometer section of the EUR district, and had established an armored perimeter around the *Nuvola* and the nearby *Palazzo dei Congressi.* Additionally, a number of roads had been closed, and police sharpshooters had taken up strategic positions on rooftops along the routes where government leaders were expected to travel.

The military also was making a show of force with drones and helicopters in the air, and soldiers on the ground. All of them were prepared for combat in Army fatigues, smartly dressed with peaked caps perched on their heads and freshly pressed slacks. There was no doubt about who they were and that they were there for.

An entire floor of the convention center had been given over to event security, and Poole's advance team had set up surveillance and communications systems according to their unique specs. As a matter of goodwill, he'd pledged to share any pertinent data his team collected with the other seventeen national security directors on the ground, and vice versa.

"Only one more day of this shit," he muttered to himself. He was a lanky, sinewy man in his early sixties, with thinning hair swept back over his crown. Today, as every day, he was dressed in a charcoal gray suit, bland tie with seemingly colorless diagonal stripes, glasses with black frames that made his eyes look bigger than they were. A requisite pigtail device was embedded in his left ear.

He glanced from one screen to the next. So did the four fulltime agents assigned to "the pocket," a football reference that designated the protective bubble surrounding the quarterback. In total, ten eyes scanned constantly for any surreptitious movement or suspicious behavior that might warrant intervention, or a need to switch to an alternate itinerary. Of which there were several, known only to a privileged few, but none that had as many cameras as the main route.

With so many monitors to watch, so many angles on so many streets, so many known and unknown variables at play, Poole easily could have missed it. He almost did, in fact, as his eyes lingered just a moment or two on one screen before shifting to the next, and then the next. But then he spotted something that in retrospect didn't seem all that much out of the ordinary, but just…well, odd. *Different.*

"What the hell is that?" he said, out loud but mostly to himself.

"What?" asked his deputy director of security, who was seated at a table with a digital switching console in front of him. His name was Andy Park, young and ambitious, second-generation son of Korean immigrants. Like his boss, he was keenly studying the live video, methodically shifting his eyes from one monitor to another.

"Back up nineteen," Poole directed him. "To seven-twelve." Meaning twelve minutes after the hour, just forty seconds ago.

Without saying a word Park reversed the footage, hit "play."

"Look for the van," Poole continued, pointing at the screen. The camera lens was pointed up Via Druso through an intersection at Porta Metronia, the infamous arched remains of a 3rd-century waterway gate within the Aurelian city walls. "Right about…*now*."

Park did as instructed, peered closer as if that would help his vision. Then he saw it, or at least *thought* he saw it.

"There," Poole said. "White and unmarked. It stops at the edge of the frame, right under that tree, there."

"People are getting out of it," Park replied. "Five of them. Looks like they're Army."

"Precisely," Poole replied. "Except it's outside the red zone, and not one of the official staging areas. I've seen the Defense Department's plan, and that's why we positioned a camera there, instead of troops."

By now, the other three agents assigned to scan the screens were huddled close, intently focused on the video playing on monitor nineteen. "Go back to real time, and let's keep an eye on the other monitors," Poole went on. "Park, you take the top row. Benson, you get row two, and Donahue, you're on three. Sciuto, watch the bottom six."

"Are we looking for more vans?" Angela Sciuto asked. She was the newest recruit to the presidential detail, just six years out of Georgetown Law.

"If there's one of them, there's bound to be more," Poole said as he felt his stomach flip. "Meanwhile, I've got to make a call."

"The orders come from the top," Captain Segreto said to the nine heavily armed soldiers seated around him on wooden crates and stacks of tires. Each of the ten officers was fitted with heavy-duty body armor and equipped with both an M4 carbine and a Beretta 92FS pistol, plus extra rounds of both 5.56×45mm and nine-millimeter ammo. "I know this may sound very last-minute, but I have it on good authority that this threat not only is very real, but imminent."

Given the vagaries that Colonel Marchetti had relayed to him yesterday in the men's room at Guardia di Finanza, he remained unconvinced of the reality and imminence of what some unnamed source had revealed. His job had been to assemble a tactical response team, and that's what he'd done. Orders were orders and, at the very least, this assignment gave him something tangible to do, rather than stand at a checkpoint with the rest of the international security presence that was protecting the G20 summit.

Marchetti had described it as a code red assessment, which—although Segreto had never heard of the term—he assumed meant critical to the nation's interest.

The nine men and women gathered with him in the shuttered automobile repair shop had been hand-picked because of their efficiency in putting down the armed invasion at the Palazzo Montecitorio last February. They were smart, quick, committed, and all of them highly proficient at the firing range. Two of them had sustained minor injuries during the incident, and another two were credited with the deaths of two gunmen. All were active duty, and—like Segreto—relieved to be rid of the boredom that came with standing at attention all day, expecting the worst during the global meeting but figuring the entire deployment would turn out to be another lesson in tedium.

"We will form up in two teams of five each," he went on. "Audio and video surveillance has already been established, and we will move out immediately if and when action is warranted. On my orders, and my orders only. You've already been briefed on the target, whose identity should be no mystery to any of you. Any questions so far?"

Segreto drew his glance across nine pair of eyes, all gazing back at him from beneath their bullet-resistant helmets: six men, three women, each of them shaking their heads in response to his question. It was not a rhetorical inquiry; since they were putting their lives on the line, they had a right to know what was going on. Up to a point; after all, this was the military, which was not known for being a free and open institution.

No one had a question, at least none that any of them wished to voice.

"All right, then. We'll be riding to the site in two separate vehicles. You've already been assigned your team—A or B—so roll out and join up with the other members of your squad. While this might turn out to be only a combat readiness exercise, it could become a serious engagement with enemy forces. Be careful and let the hand of God be at your side."

Logan stepped out of the shower and toweled himself off with a small scrap of hotel terrycloth that barely fit around his waist.

He glanced in the mirror, winced at the dark circles under his eyes caused by only five hours of sleep. It was hardly enough, but more than the night before. He gently massaged his forehead, then slipped into the bedroom and pulled on fresh trousers and a short-sleeve shirt, a light blue button-down, and a pair of comfortable shoes. He'd started to charge his cell the moment he'd come in, but it was only at sixty percent. Hopefully it would be enough to last the day, unless he got dragged into overtime.

He slipped it into his pocket, and had just grabbed his wallet and sunglasses when a drum riff alerted him that a text had arrived. He dug the device back out, saw the message was from a local number. It was a reply to the one he'd sent not long after he'd left Raleigh's room, a private number Alvize had given him with great reluctance. After six months, Renate Azzone would still be wondering where his boy toy had gone, and Logan wanted to lure him in: bait the hook to see if anything might bite.

Dove cazzo sei? the text read. Translation, via the language app: "Where the fuck are you?"

A jolt of adrenaline surged through Logan's blood, as he recalled what his Uncle Stuart had told him that summer he'd spent out on Catalina. Many years ago, back when his teenage sense of invincibility was leading him down a self-destructive path, and his parents had shipped his sorry ass out to California for a lesson in tough love, and mostly so they could be rid of him for a couple months.

"Don't be too quick trying to reel the fish in, Carter," the old *L.A. Times* reporter had said. "Give him plenty of time to get a good taste. His priority here is different than yours, so you have to be patient. Then, when you feel him tug on the line, pull it just a bit to set the hook. Only when you truly know you've got him should you start to reel him in."

It was an invaluable lesson which, over time, he realized applied to much more than old men and the sea—just about anyone and anything, in fact. With that in mind, he texted back a two-word response: Intorno a, or one word in English: "Around."

He knew he had to play it carefully here: short sentences only, since no phone-based translation app would get the colloquial subtleties of a particular region, much less the repartee of a personal relationship. The program had earned four-point-eight stars out of five, but some of the reviewers had left such comments as, "Great for navigating your way through the streets of Rome or Venice, but not so useful if you're trying to hook up." Or, alternately, "Good for getting around, but don't be surprised if you order an avocado and a lawyer shows up instead."

The phone indicated that the person on the other end was typing something, and a minute later a reply appeared. Logan copied and pasted the message into the app, which translated it from Italian: "I've been worried sick about what happened to you. I thought you might be dead."

There were several ways he could proceed, but he needed to sound legit. The number Alvize had given him was for Renate Azzone's personal cell, but the young man had also explained—his voice trembling with fear—that *il bastardo* was cunning and slippery. One wrong move and he would see through whatever ruse Logan might have in mind.

So, he typed back, I felt dead. In Italian, of course.

Which, after a few seconds, brought the response, Because of me?

Because of everything, Logan typed.

But we were...are...perfect together.

I've had time to think, Logan wrote back, worried that his translated verb phrasing might be mangled.

And?

And I'm having second thoughts. Fucking verbs again.

Meet me. It was the precise response Logan was hoping for, and much quicker than he'd anticipated. Which meant he couldn't let his guard down.

Not sure, he replied, playing the fish slowly. I need time.

Time for what? Azzone asked.

Time to decide, Logan wrote back.

Then why did you text me?

Logan contemplated his response. He wanted—*needed*—to craft a reply that would appear as if Alvize was writing it. Then he remembered something the young man had told him, something crude that Azzone would whisper in his ear during late-night intimate encounters in the chambers above the Vatican library. Two words that urged him to go slower.

Andante, andante.

Oh, my dear boy, Azzone wrote back. You remember.

How could I forget? Logan typed in return.

There was no immediate reply. Logan worried he'd fucked up somehow, hoped it was only because something had unexpectedly interrupted their text exchange. Five minutes passed, and then a fresh message arrived: Meet me at that place we went that first time. Eleven o'clock this morning.

Shit. Logan had no idea what place Azzone was referring to; it could have been just about anything, anywhere, given all there was to do in Rome. He supposed it was the sort of thing that would trigger an instant memory in Alvize's mind, and probably not something noble. But inquiring about it now would send up a red flag.

I'll be there, he typed in response.

Then he called Alvize's number, hoping the wary young man would pick up.

As Deputy Secretary General of the Governate for the Vatican City State, Renate Azzone spent most of his working hours at the Palace of the Governorate, located behind St. Peter's Basilica. It was well off the tourist route, a secluded hermitage where he would be free to think and ponder. And plan.

He had awakened early, as could be expected on this morning that Allesandro Bortolotti genuinely believed would mark his transcendence into European history. The imperious bastard also would want assurance that the Pope was on board with the end game, if not necessarily the means by which the win would be achieved. As before, Azzone had demurred by saying His Holiness wished to reserve final judgment until there was something to judge, insisting that God's plans could not be rushed or presumed—not quite what Bortolotti wanted to hear, but there were no alternate truths to play here.

As with most despots, the lunatic was possessed of a wild notion that he was ordained to change the course of world history, destined to impose a new order on a populace that was too complacent to fully comprehend their own collective ignorance.

La pazzia. Madness.

Indeed, Azzone was genuinely worried about what insanity might be in place by the end of the day, including his complicity in it. God surely did not approve of bullets in the air or blood in the streets, not at the hands of a psychopath. He could have nipped this scheme in the bud months ago, but he'd been too preoccupied by the escape of his young *compango* to think of much else. Reporting his disappearance to the police or the Pontifical Gendarmerie had been out of the question, so he'd paid rather dearly for the services of a private investigator whose search thus far had resulted only in the transfer of a sizeable amount of Euros from one bank account to another.

How surprised he'd been, therefore, to have received a text on his private phone from the young man that read, Buongiorno, mio caro signore. The very same words that Alvize would greet him every morning in the secret residential quarters above the library.

His heart had jumped instantly.

Then, just as quickly, it skipped a beat. What if this was a trap? How could he be sure it was his *ragazzo amante*, suddenly communicating with him after all these months?

His mind had gone dizzy, and he'd felt light-headed. Was he being set up, or had Alvize finally come to his senses? Perhaps even missed him, missed *them*...everything they'd had together. His mind had jumped back and forth, one side of his brain telling him to forget the young man and move on. The other side, however—the side that had always been in control of his urges and had landed him in the confessional many times—insisted he reply, but with caution.

After much deliberation, he had crafted an honest response and sent it on its way. He'd received a quick message back, and engaged the sender in a casual but earnest dialogue, one that did little to overcome his excitement, or quell his doubts—until he saw those two words on his screen: Andante, andante.

It *was* Alvize. The boy was alive and, it seemed, willing to come home. What's more, despite the tumultuous events the coming day might bring, Renate Azzone would be seeing him in just a few hours, at that place he'd taken him not long after Cardinal Giudice had abruptly died; run over by a truck, of all things. It was a glorious place from which they were able to look out over most of the city and exult in the power of history, the beauty of Rome.

Il Parco Savello. Also known as Giardino degli Aranci, the orange grove at the top of the Aventine Hill.

How wonderful it would be to hold him in his arms, gaze into his eyes, feel the warmth of his heart pounding so close to his own once again. Then he would slide the sharp steel edge of his snap-blade stiletto between his fourth and fifth ribs, near their articulation with the costal cartilages—deep and steady, with passion.

He would hear him take his last breath, then release his body as he bled out.

Il figlio di puttana.

Chapter 26

Le Magicien—better known as former British Army Major Richard Thompson—was sitting alone on a concrete bench at the edge of a pedestrian walkway just off Voie Georges Pompidou, looking out over the Seine. It was quiet this time of morning and he had a good view of a lithe young yogi in tight leggings holding a provocative tree pose. Earlier, he had picked up a to-go cup of café with a shot of espresso, and had wandered a bit before settling on this place, under the spreading branches of a small grove of poplars—all in all, not a bad start to another day in Paris.

He watched as the young woman subtly and slowly shifted to something that looked like a hood ornament on an old car, balancing on one foot while the non-standing leg raised up, and both of her arms reached forward.

At that moment he felt one of his phones vibrate, the device only one person in the world knew to call. He immediately knew what this was about and for a moment ignored the thing, but it continued to pulse. Eventually he hit "talk" and said, "*Oui.*"

"Where are you?" the scrambled voice on the other end asked.

"Enjoying a beautiful morning at the edge of the Seine," Thompson replied. "It's very pleasant this time of year."

"Good. There's a new film coming to a revival house that we'd like you to see."

Thompson thought a moment, then picked up his paper cup as he watched a young couple stroll by, arm-in-arm. He took a sip of café and asked, "What is the movie?"

"*An American in Paris,*" the voice explained.

"I presume we're not talking about Gene Kelly?"

"No, but equally skilled at his chosen profession. I believe you will enjoy it."

"Enjoyment is never a consideration," Thompson assured him. "When is the screening?"

"As soon as you can manage," the encrypted voice replied. "And there is one thing you should know in advance about the lead actor in this show."

He gazed out at the river as a houseboat chugged up the Seine past the *Pont d'Arcole*. "What about him?"

"He's a brilliant thespian and very adept at deceiving his audience, which means you need to take the utmost care," the voice said. "If you agree, you will receive the playbill shortly."

A few yards further up the pedestrian esplanade a dachshund was taking a dump. Its owner was standing by patiently, his hand enveloped in a waste bag…a dirty job, but someone had to do it. Thompson's mood abruptly shifted from contemplative to commerce, and he said, "Go ahead and send it to me."

"Thompson's definitely in the Equinox database," Beaudin confirmed with an early-morning call, his scratchy throat sounding as if he hadn't been to bed at all. "Worked for the Greenwich Global Group for years, until you closed it down."

Phythian was not surprised that the G3 had employed the angry former British Army officer after investing what he presumed was significant time and money in his professional development. "Under his own name, or an alias?" he inquired in the darkness of his tiny room off the Pigalle alleyway. It was quieter, now that the squeak of bedsprings above, and on either side of him, had finally subsided.

"His and three others. Malcolm Findlay, from Auckland. George Tremblay, from Winnipeg. And Mason Graham, from Malta."

"Any idea if he still uses any of them?"

"All passports apparently are still valid, and Graham's credit card was used to reserve a room at La Pérouse Hôtel on Rue Amélie in the Seventh. He arrived three nights ago, and because Equinox still has a back door to financial transactions, I was able to determine that he's still there."

"Any idea who he's working for now?" he asked.

"I checked around, made a few calls since we last spoke," Beaudin replied. "All indications suggest he's a freelancer for an upstart organization known as J Street."

Clever, Phythian thought; named after the nonexistent street in Washington that French engineer Pierre L'Enfant had curiously omitted when he designed the grid for the nation's capital. There were many stories suggesting why he had done this, but the one that seemed to stick was that he bore a strong grudge against someone whose name began with the letter J.

"What do we know about them?" he asked.

"Just that they're a boutique outfit that came on the scene about eighteen months ago," Beaudin explained. "Not long after the G3 took its final bow."

"It was always expected that other organizations would bridge the gap," Phythian said, almost defensively.

"Agreed. And I hear J Street is making a competitive push to gain market share."

"I assume they're deep web?"

"With a business model similar to the G3," Beaudin confirmed. "Possibly organized by one of its former associates."

"And you're certain the Gabrielle Lamoines hit was arranged through them?"

"Yes, sir. Hired out to Major Thompson, as we suspected."

"Did your late-night calls provide a reason why she was targeted?"

"Not specifically, sir. Nor the identity of the party who arranged it. But my source did mention something peculiar, although I haven't been able to make any sense of it."

"And that peculiar thing was?"

The locksmith in Andorra didn't say anything for a few seconds, carefully choosing his words. Phythian knew he could be prickly when revealing information; after almost four decades of protecting confidential information, it had become part of his DNA.

"Out with it," he pressed.

"All she said was 'Vivaldi,'" Beaudin eventually replied. "I don't think she was talking about the Italian composer, either."

This took Phythian right back to what Arnaud Clément had told him yesterday, about the neofascist nutjob named Alessandro Bortolotti and his nationalist movement.

Violentiam. Valeo. Diripio.

"*Merci beaucoup*," he said. "Is there anything else?"

"Well, sir," Beaudin demurred. "You know that five-million price on your head I mentioned yesterday?"

"Are you trying to make a point, Beaudin?"

"Yes, sir. Just the fact that if Thompson's still there in Paris, there's a good chance he has another job lined up."

Noah Wenner detested coming to this place. He was uncomfortable with the thick steam and the sweaty stench and all the naked men with their fat asses perched on cedar benches, rivulets of perspiration and stale testosterone oozing from their pores. Earlier, when Isaac Melancon called and told him to meet him at Club Athlétique de Lux at eight o'clock, Wenner had little choice but to follow orders. Now they were sitting side-by-side in one of six private saunas, a towel spread across Wenner's lap while Melancon's personal assets were exposed for all to see.

"So, the little Polish turd fessed up to taking the memory card?" the CEO of the Clear Bank of Luxembourg asked.

"He did," Wenner wheezed. He was having difficulty breathing, the moist, hot air swelling his lungs and throat. "When Djokovic questioned him, he claimed someone sent him a blind text offering him twenty thousand Euros to borrow it for it for a night."

"What happened to it then?"

"The original plan was to hand it off to some computer hacker, with the idea that he'd get it back the next day. Instead of doing that, however, for some reason he gave it to a woman. She promised to return it to him within twenty-four hours, but she never showed."

"And our Serbian friend was certain he was telling the truth?"

Wenner nodded, wiped a trickle of sweat from his forehead. "He said he tried to get more out of him, used several different methods that involved significant pain. In the end, though, I think that's all he knew."

Melancon fixed him with a dark glare, said, "This woman he gave it to. Do we know her name?"

"We do," Wenner told him. "Gabrielle Lamoines."

"*Seriously?* The French reporter who was murdered?"

"It appears so."

"So where is the card now?" Melancon asked, so sign of regret or sympathy. "Not in the possession of the police, I hope."

"The answer to that is anyone's guess, sir. It's a very high-profile case, and it's possible the investigators found it. That's the worst-case scenario. Of course, there's every chance that whoever killed her might have taken it, or maybe she gave it to someone else."

"You are aware how valuable that card is," Melancon snapped at him.

"Absolutely, sir. And we are doing everything we can to locate it. As long as it still exists, we will find it."

"I trust you know better than to disappoint me." The CEO stood up in all his naked glory, dripping from the condensation of steam and sweat. "The financial health of this institution—and the privacy of its clients— totally depends upon getting it back."

Wenner followed his boss' lead and rose from the wood slab. He tightened the wet towel around his waist, cinched it with a knot. "I understand," he said. "The good news is, the card was equipped with a specialized sensor. A homing device designed to 'ping' whenever it's plugged into a circuit board with a wifi connection. Known in the trade as a black pigeon."

"And has this 'black pigeon' pinged?"

"Not yet, sir. Which suggests that wherever it is, whoever has it in their possession, they haven't looked at it yet. They may not even know what it is."

Melancon turned and looked at his long-time assistant, his eyes glazed over from the heat. And his anger. "Do I have to tell you again how important it is that we get that card back?"

"I'm already on it, sir," Wenner replied. "There's a person I sometimes use for jobs like this. She's expensive, but well worth it."

"Whatever it takes." Melancon pushed open the glass door and exited the steam room, Wenner following close behind. The change in temperature and air viscosity was an instant relief. "Next time we speak I want this matter settled. Is that clear?"

"Yes, sir."

"And the card back wherever the fuck it belongs."

"Of course," Wenner assured him, knowing that by now the thing was in the wind, almost impossible to locate, and also knowing there was no woman, expensive or not, who could get it back. This meant that by the end of the week he would be without a job, after all those fucking years submitting to the whims of Isaac Melancon.

Of course, it was better than being dead—which was not wholly out of the question, either.

Flaó.

Whenever Georgy Sokolov had a craving for it, that meant he had to have it now. As with most mornings on Ibiza, he'd worked up an appetite after rolling over in bed and making love with Nataliya, but today he couldn't be content with his usual breakfast of *syrnikis* and *kolbassa*. Two of the few fond recollections he still held from his Russian childhood, the traditions of which he seemed to be abandoning more and more since his personal circumstances had gone to shit.

No, it had to be *flaó*, a traditional Ibizan pastry filled with goat cheese and ground almonds and honey. He was obsessed with it, and there was only one place on this side of the island where it could be purchased to go: a cliffside restaurant in the small village of Es Cubells, eight miles from his secluded villa, but thirty minutes by car along the narrow road that, in most places, was a single lane of tightly packed stone.

That's where Nataliya was now. She was crossing the small, dusty lot toward the SUV when her phone chirped. She continued to be amazed that it worked all the way out here in the middle of fucking nowhere, and she felt like letting it go straight to voicemail. The Mediterranean sun was already starting to bake her skin, and her eyeshadow felt as if it were melting down her cheeks; plus, the cardboard bakery box was too big to carry in just one hand.

The phone persisted, however, so she hustled toward the vehicle and set the pastries down on the front fender, then pulled the cell out of the purse that was slung over her shoulder, saw it was Georgy.

Fuck. Now what?

"Hi Sweetie...what's up?" she asked.

"That whore...she's gone!" he barked at her.

"What? Who—?"

"That *shlyukha*, the one for tomorrow night. She's gone. And Dimitri's dead. Killed with his own gun."

Nataliya's blood pressure spiked from zero to the stratosphere in a flash of a second. She could feel it pulsing in her brain, and her heart instantly constricted as if someone had reached into her chest and was squeezing it. *How the fuck could this have happened?* she asked herself as her legs grew wobbly. That *târfă jgheab* couldn't be missing, not today—not after the last girl had gone and killed herself.

She reached out her empty hand to steady herself, knocking the box of pastries to the ground. Then she managed to get a grip, take a breath, and think through what Sokolov was telling her. "Did you check the rocks?" she asked him.

The rocks below the horizon pool were where the last *căţea* had been found, after she'd presumably leapt to her own death in a fit of despair.

"I've checked everywhere. You need to find her."

Nataliya rolled her eyes and glanced upwards toward the heavens. This was the last thing she needed right now. She kicked at a *flaó* that had rolled out of the box, sent it flying across the gravel lot. "I'm on it," she said, like the compliant little twat she was.

"Pre-bidding is up to million and half," Sokolov reminded her. "Get. Her. Back."

"I said, 'I'm on it.' "

She was. Unbeknownst to the former billionaire, she had inserted a tracking chip into Abby's neck at the very same entry point where Alberto from Albania had stuck her with the needle. The pinprick would itch for a day or two, and the girl wouldn't suspect a thing.

"You'd better be," Sokolov said. Then, softening his tone, he added, "And Honeybun… did they have the *flaó*?"

"Yes, Sweetie," she replied. She took a few steps across the gravel lot and gathered up the pastry from where it had come to rest, put it back in the box. "Don't worry…the little skank can't get far."

The bitch named Nataliya was speaking again in that language Abby didn't understand, but the implication was clear: she'd just learned about her escape.

They would have searched the villa and the landscaped grounds first, but of course they hadn't found her; not there, because she'd stowed away in the back of the SUV and by now was here in this tiny village perched on a ragged cliff that dropped off to the sea hundreds of feet below. A good half hour from the place she'd been held captive, some sort of luxury estate in an exotic locale with water and sky as far as she could see. Despite her expensive private education, her knowledge of geography was minimal. She could still be in Italy, or Greece, or Spain. Maybe Turkey? Where was that, exactly?

She'd managed to get out of the vehicle when Nataliya had parked and gone inside some sort of restaurant. The terrain was arid and scrubby, a few palm trees and cactus…aloe, too. A few tables were set off to one side under white canopies, and a couple other cars were parked in the lot. Plus a motorcycle.

She knew all this because thirty seconds after the woman had gone inside, Abby had popped the inside latch of the vehicle's tailgate and opened it just far enough to slip out. Then gently pushed it closed until the lock clicked into place.

From there it was a quick scramble around the vehicle to a low stone wall. She crawled over it, landed in a patch of volcanic-looking landscape stones on the other side. Decorative shrubs had been planted at regular intervals, as if it were some sort of rock garden, but hadn't yet filled out enough for her to completely hide from view…but it was enough cover for her to see what was going on, without giving herself away.

That's when she'd heard the phone ring and the harsh words began. Hushed yelling, both of them agitated about something. The fight didn't last long, just enough for the woman to kick something that had spilled from a box…a donut or something. Then she'd ended the call, tucked the thing back in the box, and climbed in behind the wheel of the SUV.

She started the engine, then stepped on the gas as she swerved through the gravel lot in the same direction from which Abby was certain they had just come.

Chapter 27

"Merda," Aldo swore under his breath. "Polizia."

He and Vinnie had just climbed out of the silver Mercedes and were crossing the street toward Logan's hotel. They'd given him a few minutes to go upstairs and get comfortable in his room, lose track of time. He could take a shower, since he'd been out all night doing...well, doing just about anything: drinking, getting laid...maybe even plotting how to work with the information he'd found on Santoro's Apple watch, and arrange to intercept the drug shipment that was arriving at some unknown destination.

Aldo used his chin to indicate the Maserati Ghibli, black and white, that was pulling up to the curb; no lights, no siren. It lurched to a stop, and two uniformed officers opened their doors in tandem and piled out of the car.

"Shit...that one looks like a *pezzo grosso*," Vinnie said. A big shot. "You think they're here for him?"

"Fuck do I know." Aldo replied.

"What do we do?"

"We wait. If they come out without him, we go in."

"All we seem to do is wait," Vinnie protested.

"You have a better plan?" Aldo asked him.

No, Vinnie did not, and he knew enough to keep his mouth shut. Sometimes silence was enough of an answer.

The loud knock out in the hallway surprised Logan, since no one but Raleigh Durham knew where he was, and possibly the police, even though the last address he'd given them was the Air BnB from which he'd been evicted. He assumed that if they'd wanted to talk to him, however, they'd find a way to track him down.

There was no peephole, so he opened the door a crack and peered out. He instantly recognized General Lionetti from his late-night interrogation the evening before last. The other officer was dressed in a uniform that carried what appeared to be a lesser officer's insignia but, he presumed, still within the Guardia di Finanza.

Neither of them offered even a smile. Just grim faces, arms crossed, two pair of eyes glued to Logan's.

"Signore Logan," Lionetti said. Speaking first because of his rank, and to set the tone of this surprise visit. No nonsense, no bullshit. "It appears you changed accommodations."

"I was forced to leave the other place," Logan explained.

"As I learned," the general said. "You were supposed to let us know your movements."

Logan stole a furtive glance at his watch. He had just over thirty minutes if he was going to make it to Il Parco Savello with a few minutes to spare.

"I apologize," he replied. "I've been busy."

"As have we. And trying to find you only made us busier."

Logan stepped aside and waved the two officers into the room. The one that was not the general began wandering around, glancing at the bed, the small table that served as a desk, the pile of clothing on top of it. Logan's sport coat—actually the jacket from a two-piece suit—was draped over the back of a chair.

"What can I do for you two gents?" he asked.

"You can start by telling the truth," Lionetti told him. "Unlike last time."

"All I've been telling you is the truth," Logan protested.

"You're still going with that bullshit story that you just happened to be on that street, at that exact time, and ambushed that exact person the night before last?"

Jesus Fucking Christ, were the words that coursed through Logan's mind. *Don't these people have anything better to do?*

What he said was, "You're right about the first two things, but I damned well didn't ambush anybody. Especially not some mafia snitch named Santoro who your people were chasing because he killed a couple of arms dealers earlier that same the night."

Both police officers stared at him in surprise; then Lionetti snapped, "How do you know about that?"

"Come on, General," Logan replied. "You're not the only one here with confidential sources. And you could make this a lot easier if you just told me what you really want to know."

Lionetti's nostrils flared and he chewed his lip for a second. He glanced briefly at the other officer, who not-so-subtly shook his head. Whatever he was looking for wasn't there, at least not in plain sight.

"I can't confirm the identity of the victim, but *in via confidenziale*—" off the record "—we believe he was involved in a matter of great international security," he explained. "That's all I can tell you. Except that an item he had on his person seems to have gone missing, and we have reason to believe it's in your possession."

That's when it clicked, or at least started to make sense...an *a-ha moment* if there ever was one. "What item might this be?" Logan asked, delaying the inevitable.

General Lionetti shot him that same dark glare and said, "A watch. Made by the American computer company called Apple."

"And you think I have it?"

"The deceased was wearing it just moments before the accident," Lionetti explained. "It wasn't on his person when we arrived on the scene, and it's nowhere to be found. The driver doesn't have it, so that leaves you."

"I can see why the Amanda Knox thing fell apart," Logan said before he could keep from blurting out what he was thinking.

"And you would make it so much easier—for you, in particular—if you just stopped all this *cazzate* and gave it to me."

Logan had no idea what *cazzate* might be, but figured from the way the general used it in a sentence that it was not something he wanted to step in. "I would, if I had it," he said. "I swear on great Caesar's ghost."

Lionetti and the other officer exchanged glances that suggested they had no concept of the American euphemism. "We can search your room," he said.

"Be my guest. I have nothing to hide."

By now Lionetti's eyes were burning with anger. He fixed them on Logan for an uncomfortably long moment, while his uniformed associate appeared eager to start tossing the room upon his superior's command. Then the general let out a rapid-fire volley of words that wouldn't be permitted anywhere near a church, causing a nerve to quiver in his chin.

"I have a mind to arrest you for obstruction of justice," he seethed, his brow furrowed like a freshly plowed field. "You've impeded an investigation, and caused us to lose two precious days on a case that could have serious worldwide repercussions. In the middle of a major global summit, *per l'amor di Cristo.*"

"That was not my intention," Logan insisted. "I'm just a reporter, doing my job."

"My ass." Lionetti closed his eyes, exhaled a deep breath of exasperation. "How long do you plan on being in town?" he asked.

"I'm scheduled to leave Friday, but I might push it to Saturday."

"If you're not behind bars by then," the general said, stroking his chin. It crossed his mind that maybe he should just haul this American troublemaker down to headquarters right now, just for being the pain in the ass he was. Then again, it probably was better to just let him be, since he was just another American *idiota turista.*

"I've told you the truth, and nothing but," Logan insisted.

"Well, don't for one second believe that's going to keep you out of jail," the general said as he and his silent minion edged toward the door. "That's up to the *pubblico ministere* to decide, and he'd toss Mother Teresa into the hole if he thought she deserved it."

"Mother Teresa is dead," Logan pointed out.

"Keep that in mind," Lionetti said as the two officers stepped out into the hallway. "*A presto, signore.*"

"The mission is a go," Mateo Tufino said into the phone. "All troops have been dispatched and are standing by for orders."

"Where are you?" Alessandro Bortolotti wanted to know.

He was on his third cup of coffee, feeling the energized rush of caffeine course through his blood—that, and raw adrenaline. The air was crisp, and a slight haze had seeped in over the city since he'd first awakened, partially obscuring the view of the city from his balcony. He hoped it would dissipate as the morning wore on, so he might have a clear view of the smoke and fire that was to come.

"Luneur Park," Tufino said. "About a hundred meters from the perimeter."

"Any problem getting through the security line into the red zone?"

"The uniform and documents worked as planned. I am a captain with the carabinieri."

"And the generals? Are you in contact with them?"

"Si, signore," Tufino replied. "I just spoke with Gatti, across the street from the Waldorf. The targets are preparing to leave in the next twenty minutes. Lang called earlier, said your troops are arriving around Porta Metronia per schedule. Infiltrating the streets as we speak. Sadik and Onofre report the same at their checkpoints. All forces are on the scene and blending in."

"Good, good," Bortolotti said. "How about Lavigne?"

"He got delayed at the roadblock at il Giardino della Cascate, as anticipated. Security was tight, but his credentials were in order."

What Tufino was telling him was truly too good to be true. All five of his commanders—from Italy, Austria, Turkey, Catalan, and France—were in place. So were the thousand-plus recruits who had eagerly signed up for this mission from across Europe, as far away as Latvia and Kaliningrad. Over the last few years Bortolotti had whipped up a rabid crowd wherever he had spoken, his message of nativist injustice and unbridled immigration stoking the fear among his disenfranchised countrymen. Then, by manipulating social media and spreading a distrust of mainstream media, he'd succeeding in uniting tens of millions of partisans inside a broad tent of neofascist sympathies. Close elections in France and Austria, and the retention of Soviet-era authoritarianism in Belarus only helped to further the cause. The sham election of Meloni, the far-right poser here in Italy, had only served to reinforce his message.

Now, he was counting on this whipped-up nationalist fervor to come to a crescendo on this, the last day of the global summit.

Bortolotti glanced at his watch: just three hours until the closing luncheon was set to begin in the Nuvola. Thirty minutes after that, in the middle of the soup course—the confidential menu had listed it as *ribollita*, a Tuscan specialty made from beans and vegetables and stale bread—the incursion would begin.

"Make sure all troops are in place at noon," he told Tufino. "Ready to move out on command."

"Rest assured, signore: everything is in place," his personal associate assured him. "Vi-Val-Di."

"ViValDi," Bortolotti echoed, and ended the call.

Major Richard Thompson, aka Le Magicien, didn't care for rush jobs. Too many variables, too much risk involved in the planning process— or, in this case, the lack thereof. While he appreciated receiving another assignment so soon after the last, its timing so close on the heels of the Lamoines hit caused him to be cautious.

Despite his tendency toward anger as a young man, the onset of age-induced patience—coupled with his bio-chemical rewiring at The Farm—had transformed his approach to work. If nothing else, he had become a student of human behavior, and he went to great lengths to know as much about his next target as he could: how they slept, where they slept, and with whom they slept. He knew when they woke up, whether they drank coffee or tea or vodka for breakfast. Whether they did crunches in the morning, or went for a run, what route they took to get to the office, or the market, or the gym, *he knew*.

With this knowledge at hand, he then determined the best way to do the job. His preferred method was always the quickest and easiest: a single shot to the head, direct and definitive, even if it did require that he get closer to his target than he liked. Of course, alternate methods sometimes were better solutions, depending on the circumstances of the assignment. That's why electrocuting the German engineer in Berlin had worked so well; same thing with the Russian agent he'd stabbed in Budapest, and the playboy who'd died in a horrible car crash in Gibraltar, in which the unexpected appearance of a pair of Barbary macaques had featured prominently. Pure genius.

This was why Thompson was troubled when the voice on the phone had offered him his next contract with little advance notice. Not only did he not have time to stake out his target properly; he also was worried that somehow the intended target possessed some sort of mysterious quality that made him dangerous. This, in turn, could make this job particularly risky. Still, a million Euros were a million Euros, no matter how much the politicians had screwed with the value of the currency.

From that moment to this, he had considered all the proven methods he could throw at this particular job. Eventually worked his way back around to the most obvious, and efficient: a short-range shot, just a quick brush with death as he and the target passed each other on a random Parisian Street.

He won't even hear it, just like Gabrielle Lamoines didn't hear it, the former British major thought as he subconsciously caressed the Ruger tucked into the holster inside his jacket, the custom silencer fitted snug against it.

• • •

Logan waited a good sixty seconds for the police to leave the hotel, then slipped out of the room to the end of the hall. From there he took the fire stairs, which ended at the side of the lobby, a modest-sized space with a small registration desk at one end, and a grouping of chairs at the other. All dark wood with layers of aging varnish, floral wallpaper that when new had probably been a light cream, but now was yellow and dingy. The place smelled of dust and cigars and a whiff of perfume from a woman who recently had passed through, leaving behind a hint of jasmine mixed with cumin.

There was no sign of Lionetti or his sidekick anywhere. They weren't in the lobby, and there was no official vehicle parked outside—unless they had come in the silver Mercedes that was across the street, unmarked, with its windows up and no one inside. Probably not; Italian authorities surely would drive Italian vehicles, and in much better condition than that thing.

He started toward the front entrance, then pivoted and approached the clerk behind the registration desk. She appeared to be in her mid-twenties, with ebony hair swept up and clamped at the back of her head. She had dark eyes, and maybe just a touch more rouge on her cheeks than was fashionable. She had been on duty yesterday when Logan had checked in, and he'd found her rather fluent in English.

"Do you have another way out of here?" he asked her.

"You don't like our front door?" she replied with a smile.

"It is quite lovely, but I have my reasons."

"Do those reasons have anything to do with the polizia who were just here?"

"They think I'm someone that I'm not," he explained, without explaining much.

"And who aren't you?" the desk clerk asked.

"Someone who prefers to leave by the front entrance."

The smile returned, and she pointed to a door in a corner, beyond where the chairs and couches were clustered. "That's it, right over there," she said. "*Ingresso di servizio.*"

"Give it a minute," Aldo said as they both watched the two officers exit the hotel and return to their vehicle. "Just in case they come back."

"Why would they do that?" Vinnie asked.

"Because they're polizia. And stop asking questions."

They were hanging down the street in front of the small mercato, studying the oranges and pears in a produce tray that had been set out on the sidewalk. The shopkeeper was keeping close watch on them from inside, just in case their roaming eyes grew fingers.

"What if it wasn't the American they were after?" Vinnie speculated as he picked up a ripe peach, and considered slipping it into his pocket; but this was not Napoli, where half the police were on the pad. Not worth it for a piece of fruit he easily could purchase with the loose change in his pocket.

"Like I said, give it a minute," Aldo said. "Then we go in and find out for sure."

Chapter 28

Nataliya was halfway back to the villa, dreading Sokolov's impending wrath and violence, when she finally picked up wifi on her phone—not much, just two bars. She pulled up the icon that activated the GPS app connected to the chip she'd inserted under the American girl's skin, waited for the program to load while she managed to keep the oversized tires on the narrow road. Not an easy feat, with all the switchbacks and rockslides that kept her pace at no more than thirty kilometers per hour.

As she navigated a sharp turn, she glanced at the screen and saw a flashing red dot that indicated where the target was. An instant rush of adrenaline filled her with hope, thinking *you can't get away from me, you little twat* as she touched her foot just a little harder to the gas.

It took her another full minute to realize she was moving further away from the blinking marker. She smacked the wheel with both hands as she stomped on the brake, causing the SUV to skid too close to the edge of the cliff, a couple hundred feet straight down to the surf below.

How the fuck could that be? she wondered as she inched forward again, looking for a place to make a U-turn. That's when it hit her.

"She was in the Goddamned car," Nataliya cursed out loud. "And I gave her a fucking ride to town."

Phythian pushed his way through the large double doors of La Pérouse Hôtel on Rue Amélie and stepped into a world of 18th century regency.

He was immediately struck by the dark paneling, polished stone floors with black diamond inlays partially obscured by time-worn Oriental rugs. An antique marble fireplace was the centerpiece of the room, a fire crackling inside even though it was June. The main lobby was furnished with leather sofas and wingback armchairs covered in garnet velvet, matching pillows, shiny brass tacks seemingly holding everything together. Cocktail tables that doubled as chessboards were lighted by candles encased in glass globes, while a matching pair of art deco vases on either side of the registration desk each displayed a single red ginger lily.

It was the sort of place in which a baron or duke or a count—or a former major in the British Army, disgraced and discharged because of a violent altercation with a certain colonel—would feel most comfortable in the heart of Paris.

Two desk clerks were on duty, both of them assisting hotel guests. One was checking in; the other appeared to be having an issue with the flush mechanism in the toilet. Phythian was in no particular hurry, and waited patiently while their needs were tended to. Eventually a set of keys was handed over and the new arrival waved off a bellman as she headed toward the elevator, tugging a rollaboard.

"*Puis-je vous aider, monsieur*," the newly freed-up clerk asked. She was young, with copper hair cropped just below the ears with what appeared to be a single chop of the scissors. Large glasses, blue eyes with long, fluttering lashes, she was attractive, in a waif-like sort of way.

Phythian spoke simple guidebook French, which was not enough for what he wanted to converse with her about. He could conduct an entire mental give-and-take without exchanging a word, but instead he said, "*Parlez-vous anglais?*"

"*Ah, oui, oui,*" she said with a winsome smile, holding up her thumb and forefinger a half inch apart. "A little."

Which, he had come to learn, translated to: I do, and actually quite well, but I'm going to make you work for it. This was a vow, it seemed, many French people took in anticipation of speaking with—and irritating— mono-lingual Americans.

"I'd like to leave a message for a registered guest, *s'il vous plaît*," he replied.

"And who would that be?"

"A Mr. Mason Graham, from Malta," Phythian told her.

She tapped a few keys on her computer, studied the monitor for a second. Her face brightened, and she said, "You are correct, *monsieur*. I can't give you his number, but I can ring him, if you'd like."

By now Phythian already knew Thompson was staying on the sixth floor, number six-oh-eight. But he had no interest in meeting with the man—not face-to-face, given what happened the last time—nor, indirectly, on the phone.

"*Non, merci,*" he told her. "A simple note will do just fine. Might you be able to spare a piece of paper and a pen?"

"*Bien sûr.*" The smile returned, and she rummaged through a drawer. She found the two items he had requested, both of which bore the logo of the hotel. She slid them across the marble registration counter to him and said, "Take your time."

He'd already determined what he was going to write—twenty words, total—and scribbled them in blue ink on the cream sheet of stationery. He blew on it when he was finished, then creased it down the middle lengthwise, and once again the other way.

"Please make sure it gets to him," he said. Flashed her a smile of his own, a little crooked. "Room six-oh-eight."

The fake Italian Army uniforms that had been designed and sewn to Defense Ministry specs were virtually indistinguishable from the real thing. They had the same peaked cap, same jacket with the same buttons and pockets, same trousers and shoes, the same Beretta AR70/90 gas-operated rifle chambered for the 5.56×45 mm NATO cartridge, courtesy of the arms shipment that had been hijacked from a warehouse the previous month. The one thousand, sixty-two volunteers who professed unyielding loyalty to Alessandro Bortolotti and his nationalist cause had been measured and fitted weeks ago. Now, as they took up position on street corners and piazzas at the perimeter of the red security zone near the Nuvola, they blended right in with the other security forces.

Despite, and perhaps because of, the presence of other military troops—as well as local poliziotto, Carabinieri, and Guardia di Finanza—no one questioned their presence. Nor did they challenge their authority, something Bortolotti was counting on in order for his plan to succeed.

Over the last few minutes, he'd personally checked in with his five generals—Gatti, Lang, Sadik, Onofre, and Lavigne—for status reports. All troops were on the ground, and their commanding officers had called in from twenty-eight pre-determined checkpoints along both the standard transportation route from the Cavalieri Waldorf Astoria, as well as the maze of streets through which the U.S. presidential motorcade would navigate. All itineraries eventually would merge onto Via Cristoforo Columbo as they made their way to the summit, where the world leaders—sixteen men and three women—would mutually congratulate one another on enacting far-reaching accords designed to achieve far-reaching, worldwide goals.

Then they would pose for pictures, share a meal, and fly home.

From his rented twelfth-floor flat, Il Duce peered through a pair of military-grade field glasses and found the Nuvola Congress Centre and the nearby Palazzo dei Congressi. The haze had burned off, and he could see military vehicles, a few tanks, and a scattering of soldiers on the broad thoroughfare that led to both structures. It was a notable show of power, but no match for the battalion of soldiers that soon would converge on the site of the global meeting.

The violence and mayhem that would ensue would be nothing short of breathtaking, and by the time the news media and political pundits realized what had happened, he would be the supreme ruler of the people of Italy.

At precisely eleven-thirteen Bortolotti called Mateo Tufino on his encrypted phone and asked, "Is everything in place?"

"Locked and loaded," his lieutenant and confidante confirmed. "Waiting for your command."

"Now is the moment for men to rise up and take action," he said. "To deviate from the unchecked sins of yesterday and change the course of mankind for all time."

"Sir?" Tufino replied, not sure whether his words constituted an order, or whether Bortolotti was attempting to make a statement of great profundity as the spotlight of history was about to fall upon him.

"Commence the mission," Bortolotti clarified. "Move 'em out."

Donald Poole didn't like what he was seeing, not one Goddamned bit.

Neither did Olivia Mertens, his counterpart from the EU who had rushed over from the room next door. As a deputy commander of Eurocorp, her job was to oversee every aspect of the international security team for the G20 Summit. Originally from Bruges, at a young age she had joined the Motorized Brigade, a land component of the Belgian Armed Forces, and her swift thinking and intuitive response to crisis situations had quickly led her to her current post, one which she found both energizing and seductive.

There now were eleven known instances of vans distributing soldiers at checkpoints where there should not have been any. She personally counted forty-six *impostores,* each of them dressed and armed as Italian Army troops, a mere fraction of the total number of bogies that were probably on the ground by now.

"What do you make of it?" Poole asked her.

"*Problemés avec un grand P,*" she replied. "And whatever it is, we need to stop it now."

"They have to be coordinating something," Poole said. "Look—there's another one."

He was correct. Another vehicle—this one a yellow box truck with lettering on it—had pulled to the curb. The rear doors had swung open and a half dozen soldata were scrambling out.

"What does that say?" Poole asked, pointing at the logo on the side.

"*Termoidraulico di Caruso,*" she said. "Caruso's plumbing and heating. Those guys look just like real troops."

"That's their plan. Infiltrate, blend in, and gain access to…whatever."

"The Ring," Olivia Mertens said, using the code word for the site of the Summit. That included the Nuvola and the media center in the nearby Palazzo dei Congressi, as well as the shuttle service loop between the two that was operating within a corridor. In other words, the very building in which they were watching the action unfold on the screen, and immediately next door to the hall where the leaders would be meeting. That would be followed by the official closing luncheon—she checked her watch—scheduled to begin just over an hour from now.

All of it was to be protected by hundreds of legitimate troops from the Italian Army.

"Jesus Fucking Christ," said Poole, not one inclined to expletives or hyperbole. "They're planning a total shitstorm."

"How many of them, you think?"

Not something he cared to contemplate. "Anyone's guess," he replied. "But if they're going for chaos and bloodshed, they probably have the numbers. I never thought I'd say it, but we need to activate ICASP."

He was referring to the acronym for Integrated Communications And Security Protocol, the proprietary system connecting all international security forces at the symposium. While hailed publicly as a grand example of cooperation among all the nations participating in the global symposium, in actuality it had been a colossal challenge to coordinate such a bureaucratic undertaking. Poole and Mertens were part of the task force that developed the plan, but both were skeptical that—in a time of crisis—it would prove to be either practical or sufficient.

"Time to see if the damned thing works," she said.

Chapter 29

As often happens in Paris, the light rain that dampened the city just moments ago passed through quickly, and when Major Thompson stepped out of the metro station, he found the clouds had begun to part. An aroma of garlic and warm bread hung in the air, and somewhere someone was broiling lamb. Probably the Middle Eastern restaurant across the street.

Despite his wariness for hastily constructed scenarios, he'd had to chuckle when he received final word on the intended target: a former Greenwich Global Group contractor who eight years ago was thought to have been killed when a private plane disappeared over the Mediterranean after taking off from Israel. *The most dangerous man alive,* as he'd been described in the dossier that had been sent via scrambled email.

Rōnin Phythian.

What a fucking joke, he'd thought when he read it. Dangerous? Certifiable was more like it, when he thought back to their confrontation at The Farm in Virginia, all those years ago. The guy was downright creepy in the way he'd bored into his brain, and exhumed all those old childhood memories—particularly those that involved his Mum, who had gotten remarried to a Welshman who beat the young boy, often on the bottoms of his feet so the bruises wouldn't be noticed. Memories he'd thought he'd buried, just like he'd buried the sonofabitch in the rose garden behind their house outside Coventry.

Phythian had overstepped his bounds that day, and Thompson had ended up with two broken legs and a dislocated shoulder. It would be a pleasure to kill this American psycho, not just for the money, but as payback for that invasive embarrassment all those years ago.

The world was so full of marvelous ironies.

He pushed his way into the lobby of La Pérouse Hôtel, his favorite place to hang his hat whenever he was in Paris. Beads of moisture dribbled to the floor as he removed his wet jacket, and he detected the aroma of pipe smoke coming from the drawing room. He folded the damp garment over his arm, then began to drip his way toward the elevator. He made it halfway across the Persian carpet when a voice called out to him from the registration desk.

"Monsieur Graham—?"

Another of the wonderful amenities he appreciated about this place was how the staff made a point of knowing each guest's name. Thompson stopped and made an abrupt turn, then wandered over to where the desk clerk was standing. He remembered her from when he'd checked in a few nights ago, short reddish hair with large eyeglasses. "*Oui?*" he asked her.

"Message for you, sir," she said.

Warning bells rang in his brain, but he was a master at clouding his reactions. How could there be a message for him, when no one knew where he was staying? He was using his Maltese alias, for Chrissakes. Not even his employer was privy to that information.

"A message?" he replied. "Whoever from?"

"A gentleman who didn't give me his name, nor did I inquire. Would you like it now, or when you next go out?"

Never, was the answer that immediately came to mind. At no time had the man behind the scrambled and encrypted voice on the phone made physical contact, and there was no reason for him to do so now. The contract was in place, and half his payment had already been transferred to an account in a particularly accommodating bank on a tropical island where the water was warm, the liquor cheap, and the lobsters exquisite. There was no reason for the man to send him a follow-up note.

"When was this?" he asked.

The desk clerk shrugged, then turned and plucked a folded slip of stationery out of a slot behind her. "Maybe an hour ago," she said. "He asked for a pen and a piece of paper, then handed me this."

Thompson hesitated a moment before accepting it. He didn't want to look at it; didn't even want to touch the damned thing, as if to do so would bring a world of hurt down on him. His curiosity was too great to let it go, however, so he took it from her, unfolded it, and let his brain absorb the words scrawled in blue ink:

There will be killing till the score is paid. You forced yourself upon this house...now fight your way out.

What the hell? Who the fuck was quoting him Homer's *The Odyssey*? It was certainly not the man on the phone; of that he was certain. That deal was all but done, except for the final act itself and subsequent proof of death. That would be confirmed by placement of corroborating news stories in two separate media outlets, each with a quote attributed to official authorities. Whoever his handler might be, he would not have journeyed to Paris to leave a handwritten note bearing some cryptic passage from an epic story penned well over two thousand years ago.

Then he recalled that day back at The Farm, the moment Phythian had invaded his mind, uncovered all that shit from the past—which caused him to snap, and somehow induced him to believe he was a bird ready to take flight from a mezzanine balcony outside the room they'd been assigned to share. Without thinking, Thompson had climbed onto the railing and pushed off with the grace of an eagle ready to soar into the firmament, then dropped with the gravity of a cinder block.

And while all this was happening, the sonofabitch had said to him, an impish twinkle in his eye: "Fly, dotard fly... With thy wise dreams, and fables of the sky," another fucking line from the same epic Homer poem.

Twice Nataliya veered precipitously close to the edge of the cliff, and once she thought she'd made a fatal error as a wheel lost contact with the road and swung out into the void. But inertia and the three other tires kept the Jaguar on the narrow lane, as she prayed to a god she didn't believe in that she wouldn't encounter another car.

The fates, however, were smiling on her. She met nothing but a wild hare on her race back to Es Cubells, and he just chewed on a wad of scrub as she sped past him in a cloud of dust.

The dot on the GPS app indicated that Abby Evans hadn't moved...at least, not enough to register on the screen. That meant she was still in the vicinity of the bakery, which was both good and bad: good because she was only two miles—eight minutes—away; bad because she might already have met up with some of the local folks—even the police—and had told them her story.

She touched her foot harder on the pedal, and prayed again.

Abby didn't know where she was, or who she could trust. The words on the street signs and buildings around her mentioned Santa María des

Cubells and Restaurante Los Pinos, which she recognized as Spanish—
something she was familiar with in California, since she had taken three
years of it, including middle school.

That meant she had to be in Spain—more specifically, a small village
that appeared to be named Es Cubells—which seemed to consist of not
much more than a few whitewashed buildings at an intersection of twisting
roads, overlooking a sea as blue as the Pacific Ocean back home. She tried
not to think of that, whether she might ever see it again or her home on
Nob Hill—or even her parents, whose crazy idea it had been to whisk her
off to Rome, in an attempt to get her away from Jagger. She hated to admit
it, but she was beginning to think that they were right: he *was* too old for
her, and certainly not the best influence. Fact was, he didn't seem all that
different from the dirtballs who had snatched her at the Trevi Fountain.

Abby hadn't moved from where she'd ducked down behind the low
garden wall after she'd sneaked out of the car. She was leaning against
the bulbous trunk of a tree, partially obscured from view by its weeping
branches and the parched fronds of a nearby palm. From time to time a
car would crawl through town, make a rolling stop at the junction and
then continue on its way. On the other side of the parking lot was the
place where Nataliya had purchased what looked to be some pastries, a
restaurant with a patio that looked out over the main road and then the
sea beyond.

The Mediterranean? she wondered.

Her stomach let out a low rumble and she realized she hadn't eaten
since last night, when they'd locked her in her dungeon and brought her
the tomato-and-rice concoction on a partitioned plastic plate. She'd made
her getaway this morning long before breakfast, so yeah… she was getting
hungry.

Problem was, she had no money and no passport…no ID at all.

Abby realized she was going to have to approach someone, explain
who she was and what had happened to her. Since this appeared to be a
part of Spain and not Italy, she figured none of the townspeople had heard
about the kidnapping of a young girl in Rome. Would anyone believe her?
Would anyone care? She hadn't seen a police vehicle, which caused her to
wonder if there was even a single cop in this sleepy little village.

Then she realized the solution to her problems was right in front of her,
on the other side of the town square: Catedral la Santa Lucia dels Cubells.

It looked more like a church than a cathedral, and right now it was the closest she might get to finding someone who could summon help, keep her safe from her captor who had imprisoned her in *that place*, and only had bad things in store for her.

She screwed up her courage, glanced right and left and everywhere in between. Then she cautiously stood up from her hiding spot behind the rock wall and headed toward the blindingly white building with a single bell positioned in a tower high above its arched entrance.

The door was solid wood with solid iron hinges. She gave it a push, but it didn't move, then tried a harder shove, but it still didn't budge. She heard the engine of a car approaching from somewhere, didn't dare look around. Instead, she glanced at the hinges, realized it opened outward, and quickly gave the handle a tug.

It was heavy, but she pulled it open just enough to slip inside the sanctuary, then closed it behind her...

...Just as Nataliya skidded into the parking lot on the other side of the street. The red dot hadn't moved, which meant the young twat who had become more of a problem than she'd anticipated had to be around here, somewhere.

Abby stood just inside the door, waited while her eyes adjusted to the darkness. The church sanctuary was only dimly lighted, from a few sconces on the wall and an arrangement of candles up front near the altar. She blinked a few times, then began moving up the aisle that transected pews on either side. No one else appeared to be inside; she guessed the day was too beautiful for anyone to worship in the dingy confines of a church—or maybe because it was a weekday—Thursday, perhaps Friday. She actually had no idea.

The place was quiet, the only sound being that of her shoes on the stone floor. It felt as if she could almost hear the flames flicker as they danced around the pools of wax and cast ghostly shadows on the vaulted ceiling. She paused to watch them quiver, and just about jumped out of her skin when she felt a hand on her shoulder.

Abby spun around, her eyes wide with terror. She found herself eye-to-eye with a man not much taller than she was, dressed in black except for a white collar and a cross on a chain hanging from his neck.

"*¿Puedo ayudarte, jovencita?*" he inquired. May I help you, young woman?

She shook her head, backed up a step or two. Ready to bolt, except that he was blocking her way to the door…plus, she had nowhere to run.

"*Por favor, siéntase como en casa,*" he said, inviting her in with a sweep of his hand. "*Todos son bienvenidos aquí.*" All are welcome here.

"I don't understand," she said, in a voice that was little more than a whimper.

He cocked his head and replied, "Ah…English. American, perhaps?"

She nodded briskly, felt the tears starting to stream down her face. "You have to help me, please," she begged him. "I've been kidnapped, and they brought me to…this place. I don't even know where I am."

"There, there, *senorita,*" the young priest said. Rather handsome in a rugged sort of way, he had dark longish hair, eyes the color of those olives her mother put in her Greek salads. "You are safe here in the house of God. Please, come with me and we'll see what we can do."

Il Parco Savello, home to the city's infamous orange garden, was located at the top of the Aventine Hill, near an ancient stone fortress erected toward the end of the 13th century. As with many locales in Rome, it was built mostly on top of the ruins of an even older landmark, a 10th century castle that had belonged to the baronial Crescentii family.

At first, Alvize had told Logan a firm "no" when he'd asked him the location that Renate Azzone was referring to. "*Nessun fottuto modo,*" was how he put it. Too much was at stake, including his freedom…and possibly his life.

Logan had persisted, however, and in the end the young man had relented, albeit reluctantly, and only after Logan swore there would be no blowback on him. He had no idea where Alvize lived or worked, so there was no way he could give up the young man's whereabouts. Even under the threat of physical pain, which Alvize assured him would be considerable if Logan let down his guard.

Eventually he revealed that the reference to *that place we went that time* was the Orange Garden. More specifically, the Terrazza Belvedere Aventino located within its walls, the terrace that held perhaps the best view of the rooftops of Rome. That was where Azzone had brought him just a few nights after Cardinal Giudice had died, when he'd decided to take the boy into his own tutelage. It had been late, and most of the tourists had long since departed to their hotels and dinner reservations. The few people who remained were either savoring the sunset view, or had found seclusion in the darker corners of the park, cloaked by long shadows of trees and the privacy offered by the ancient walls. There they could embrace and kiss and grope with wild fervor, as if sex had a sell-by date.

It was there, on that evening, that the future deputy governor of the Vatican had assured Alvize that the late Cardinal's manner of lending him out to colleagues and associates had come to an end. Instead, he—*Alvize*—now would be Azzone's sole apprentice.

"But your horror didn't stop there," Logan had guessed, trying to draw the young man out further.

"In the words of Jean-Paul Sartre, 'life begins on the other side of despair,'" Alvize replied. "It was right then that I plotted my escape, although I did not know it would take me all these years to summon the courage to actually do it."

When Logan left his hotel he circled around to the street, keeping an eye open for the police. There was no telling if they might change their mind and double back to arrest him. But he spotted no one, except a couple scruffy-looking dudes hanging out by a produce stand halfway down the block.

Because of the global summit, taxis were scarce and, as he'd learned the hard way, Ubers were nonexistent. Public transportation was stretched beyond the limits, and even the Metro had been closed that morning because of the meeting.

All these things conspired against him, and caused him to arrive at Il Parco Savello just five minutes ahead of when Renate Azzone had specified. He had cut it much closer than he'd intended, especially since he'd never been there before. The walk from his hotel was just under two miles on streets heavily laden with tourists, and he did his best to hustle around the Forum and Palatine Hill and Circus Maximus. Logan constantly had to zig and zag around the electric bicycles and tour guides holding colored flags, but he finally made it to the garden's entrance.

Alvize had specified on the phone that he should take Clivo dei Publicii up the hill to the main gate, then fall in with the crowd along the footpath and head toward the terrace perched at the edge of the cliff. If Azzone was going to show up—and Alvize had expressed his doubts about this—that's where he'd be waiting.

An internet search had told Logan that Azzone was in his early fifties, salt-and-pepper hair, slightly ruddy complexion, glasses with black frames, and lips that turned down in a slight pout. He almost always wore some kind of head covering, his favorite being a red homburg with a skeleton key tucked into the band, and a matching square of fabric tucked into the breast pocket of his jacket, if he was wearing one, which today he was.

Logan spotted him standing at the corner of the stone terrace, not far from where he had first assaulted Alvize. The young man had been surprisingly forthcoming about the incident, as well as the fact that the key in the hat band actually was the only one that opened the door to the room where he'd been locked away all those years.

This was where Logan had the element of surprise, at least for a moment or two. He knew what Azzone looked like, knew where he was standing, his head pivoting from side to side as he gave the once-over to all the young men in the park. There were a lot of them—some alone, some with young women, a few with other men. Bicycles didn't seem to be permitted within the grounds, but vendors certainly were, hawking watercolors and selfie-sticks. The sweet smell of orange blossoms hung in the air, even though it was the end of the season.

Logan veered off the path and cut across the grass. He studied Azzone as he approached from the side, appearing to be looking at something on his phone but occasionally glancing up occasionally so he could see where he was going—just another sightseer dividing his time between the lure of a three-inch screen and possibly the most glorious view in all of Rome.

That's how he came to be standing right next to the deputy asshole of the Vatican, and said, "*Non mi stanco mai di questa vista.*" Which, before he'd fed the words into his phone app just a second ago, translated roughly to "I never get tired of this view."

"*Glorioso,*" was Azzone's clipped reply.

"*Niente di simile in tutta Roma,*" Logan continued. Nothing quite like it in all of Rome.

"*Non.*" Clearly he was preoccupied, glancing about, not wanting to talk to this stranger who was slaughtering the Italian language with an American accent.

Logan decided to shift gears: time to get down to business. As he'd been strolling over to the terrace, he'd turned on the record function in his phone, which was equipped with a high-quality omnidirectional microphone—

quite useful in his line of work, although not particularly ethical. Something his former editor at the *Washington Post* had pointed out more than once, even though DC had a one-party consent law on the books.

"Alvize sends you his regards," he said, this time in English, a language the young man had disclosed that Azzone spoke with great fluency.

His reaction was sudden and swift. He spun toward Logan, grabbed him by the collar with both fists. "*Chi cazzo sei?*" he demanded.

Logan backpedaled as he slapped Azzone's hands away. "Answer a couple questions and I'm out of here," he replied.

"Fuck that," Azzone growled. "Where's Alvi?"

"He's not coming. I'm here instead."

"Then you just made one bloody big mistake."

"And why would that be?" Logan asked.

"Because you clearly have no idea who I am," Azzone said, spittle spraying from his clenched teeth.

Logan edged back a step, to avoid the shower and to put some distance between them. "Last I checked you were Deputy Secretary General of the Governate for Vatican," he replied. "And a trafficker of underage children." He was keeping all that he really wanted to say in check.

"You *pezzo di merda stronzo—*"

Logan didn't even see the fist coming at him, just felt it land hard and square on his right jaw. The force of the blow rocked him sideways and spun him around, as sparkles of light flashed in his brain and he crumpled to the ground. He tasted blood and dirt as he tried to push his way back up, but a kick to the ribs put a stop to that. Then he heard what he thought was Azzone yelling—something like "*vieni qui in fretta*"—but he couldn't be sure, as none of this made sense. Well, of course it did—the asshole pervert from the Vatican had just knocked him silly—but there was nothing he could do.

A moment later a pair of hands roughly grabbed him by the armpits and hoisted him to his feet. By then Logan's vision was too blurry to see what the hell was going on, as bright flashes continued to strobe in his skull. Then the two men—Azzone and this new guy—half-walked, half-dragged him toward the gate.

Cristo Santo, the American named Logan walked fast; hard for Aldo and Vinnie to keep up with him without letting him know they were behind him as he marched along at a steady clip. They followed up one hill, down another, taking this left and that right, then another left. The phone in his hand was probably giving him directions as he zig-zagged for two miles in and around the sights of ancient Rome. At one point he stopped and bought a bottle of water from a street vendor but, aside from that, he pounded the pavement like a man possessed.

"Where the hell do you think he's going?" Aldo asked at one point as they advanced up a modest but long incline.

"Beats the hell out of me," Vinnie replied, his voice coming out in ragged bursts. "We should've hit him when we had the chance."

"When was that?"

Vinnie had no answer, so they kept walking, past the Temple of Jupiter and the ruins of the Circus Maximus, then onwards, up Clivo dei Publicii toward the top of Aventine Hill.

"Do you see him anywhere?" Aldo asked, glancing around.

"I think he went in there," Vinnie replied, pointing at a gate a hundred yards ahead of them. "Al Giardino degli Aranci."

They hoofed it the rest of the way so they wouldn't lose him. As they slipped into the park, they quickly scanned the grounds, spotted Logan stumbling toward them, with two men—both dressed in black but one with a red hat—supporting him under each arm as they dragged him forward. They passed within a few yards of each other before the American was escorted back out to the street.

"*Che cazzo*?" Aldo said to Vinnie. "Who are those guys?"

"*Merda*…the one with the hat looks like a priest. Did you see the collar?"

"*Al diavolo*—"

"Now what?" Vinnie wanted to know.

Good question, and Aldo had no good answer. This was an unexpected development, one he hadn't planned on or strategized about. The three men—Logan stuffed between them—crossed the pavement and approached a black Alfa Romeo Giulia, with tinted glass and too much chrome. The man in the red hat climbed behind the wheel, while his compatriot pushed the American into the rear compartment, then piled in beside him. The vehicle pulled away from the curb before the door was even closed, and accelerated down the street.

"*Cazzo. Cazzo, cazzo, cazzo*," Vinnie said. "We lost him."

"Not so fast." Aldo made a jerking motion with his head, indicating a car parked a little further up the one-way street. "Check it out."

"What are you talking about?"

"Right there," Aldo said as he dodged in front of a passing Lancia and stopped at a banged-up Fiat: an older Panda model, small and boxy and easy to park within the tight confines of the city. He peeked through the glass, then over his shoulder at whoever might be watching.

Thirty seconds later they were inside, and the engine was running. "Easiest car in Italy to boost," he said with pride as he stepped on the gas and the tiny engine buzzed like a chain saw. "Hang on."

The black Giulia had a good lead, but there was a global summit going on. It was the last day of a crowning achievement that reflected so well on the preparedness of Rome, and everything had turned on the proverbial dime. Everything except the typically gridlocked streets, made all the worse because many of the metro stations were closed and regular bus routes compromised. That meant more people in cars, more yelling and honking and fender-bending than usual.

All of which combined to make it much easier for the teppisti from Napoli to keep an eye on the Alfa Romeo, already trapped in a logjam of screaming and cursing drivers half a dozen vehicles ahead of them.

Chapter 30

After dropping off his message at Major Tompson's hotel, Phythian staked out a discreet table in the shade of an awning at an outdoor café across the street. Under normal circumstances he would have enjoyed a glass of a dry Chenin Blanc right about now, but at the moment he was on the job. That meant he was sipping a concoction of fresh lemon juice, bitters, and tonic, stirred over ice with a rock candy swizzle stick. All of it was a little too sweet for his taste, but he hadn't chosen the location for its cocktails.

It was the unobstructed view of the front door that mattered.

The rain from earlier had let up, the clouds eased away. A glimmer of moisture remained on the pavement, reflecting the green trees lining the sidewalk, and a tricolor flag riffled in the wind; very impressionistic, much like a cityscape that Renoir might have captured on canvas in another era.

Inside, Thompson had read the handwritten message several times and was clearly rattled. After crushing the note in his fist he'd retreated upstairs, sixth floor corner room, and had spent close to the last hour brooding, scheming, and obsessing. He wasn't quite in panic mode yet, but was getting closer with each passing moment as he worried that Phythian was close—very close—and possibly picking through in his mind right now.

He flashed briefly on something he'd read as a boy, a short story by Richard Connell titled "The Most Dangerous Game." Somewhat of a parable about power and instinct and survival, it was the tale of a big game hunter who found himself the prey in a contest of skills against a sociopathic Russian recluse.

The hunter becomes the hunted.

Phythian absorbed all this while he sat at his table, sipping the too-sweet mocktail, exercising his near-legendary proficiency at what researchers referred to as remote viewing—or, as his old G3 handler Diana Petrie called it, the Vulcan mind meld.

"Not quite the same thing," he'd said once, pointing out some inconsistencies with the old television show.

"Perhaps not," she'd conceded. "But close enough for government work, and close enough for me."

It also was close enough to detect that Thompson had left his room and was on his way down the hall to the elevator—*the lift*, as his British brain was inclined to call it. He'd double-checked that his Ruger and silencer were in the tailor-made holster inside his jacket, then shuffled through his diminishing deck of tarot cards. He looked at each one, carefully considered his options, then plucked one out of the pack: *La Muerte*, otherwise known as the Death card, depicted in this Dali-esque rendition as a cypress tree emblazoned with a skull, next to a single blooming rose. It was a highly stylized image that represented big changes, transformation, endings…and in some interpretations, eternal darkness.

Interesting choice, Phythian mused as he waited for Thompson to leave his refuge, not by the front door but, rather predictably, via a service entrance that opened out onto a rear alley.

No problem: keeping track of Major Thompson was much like placing a GPS tracker on the underside of an automobile. Phythian didn't need to see him in order to know where he was.

The blinking red dot hadn't moved one micron on the cellphone's three-inch screen, but that didn't mean the young twat had stayed put.

Dear God, don't let her be dead, Nataliya thought.

She pulled into the same parking space as she had less than thirty minutes ago, quickly scanned the near-empty lot. There weren't a lot of places to hide in Es Cubells: just a few stores and eateries, and a couple of nearby houses. She tried to imagine what she would have done if the roles were reversed and she was Abby. She couldn't actually blame her for doing what she'd done; for Chrissakes, the last girl had thrown herself off the edge of the horizon pool onto the rocks below, rather than face her fate. While this American child didn't know all the particulars of her kidnapping, she seemed bright enough to grasp what she was up against, and that her life was in grave danger.

Still, killing a guard and escaping her dungeon were mistakes that had to be rectified, dealt with in the harshest of ways.

Sokolov's only stipulation was that the girl's face, and her purity, remained intact. Other than that, all modes of punishment were on the table.

Make contact with someone. That's what Abby would have done, or at least tried to do. There was no way she could know where she was, and she had no phone, no money, no ID. However, she did have a pretty smile and a certain degree of charm, and could easily convince someone what had happened to her—explain that she'd been kidnapped and brought out here to Ibiza in the middle of the Mediterranean, and held against her will at a secluded oceanfront villa. The island was well-known for its over-the-top party and drug scene, which might lead someone to believe her.

Her abduction in Rome probably would be of little interest to the locals but, if she had managed to speak with someone, calls would be made. Stories would be checked out. The police presence on Ibiza usually was concentrated in the more populated towns, where they looked for petty thieves, dope dealers, and smugglers—certainly not sex traffickers like Sokolov and his invited guests, who had forked over an obscene sum just to attend his live auction tomorrow night.

Problem was, the main attraction of that event was on the run here in Es Cubells.

At that moment Nataliya's phone rang. Sokolov again. She cursed under her breath, then answered with a curt, "Yes?"

"Any sign of her?" the Russian oligarch inquired.

"GPS puts her in the middle of this fucking town. I'm close."

"Close not good enough. Find that *suka* and bring back here."

"Yes, Darling," she replied and rang off. Thinking, *I'll find that bitch even if I have to light a candle in church…*

…Just like the one across the street, with the arched door and the single bell at the peak of its roof.

She spun on her heels and marched across the dusty road—no worries about jaywalking in this godforsaken village—to the front door of the cathedral. She didn't bother to knock, just pulled the door open and slipped inside. She glanced around the dimly lit sanctuary, let her eyes adjust to the flickering candles, and the stained glass set high up in the far wall. The aroma of melting wax and mildew touched off the olfactory memories in her brain.

That's when she saw the girl, standing with a man dressed like a priest at the front of the church, near the altar—dressed like one because he was one. Neither of them appeared to have seen Nataliya enter, didn't notice the momentary crease of light streaming through the door as she slipped in, then gently tugged it closed.

Sunteți așa de futut, she fumed as she slipped off her shoes and moved silently down the left wall of the church. You are so fucked.

She stopped beside a hand-hewn wooden buttress and ducked into the shadows. Their conversation was louder here, and she could make out what they were saying:

Priest: "This is a fantastic story, *senorita*—"

Abby: "I swear, it's true. You have to believe me."

Priest: "I believe that *you* believe it's true. But what you're saying makes no sense."

Abby: "I don't even know where I am. I was drugged and put on a plane—"

Priest: "So you've already said. But tell me: who did this to you?"

Abby: "I don't know. Russians, I think. They locked me up in some big house on a cliff."

"She's a guest at Villa Sol y Mar," Nataliya interrupted in a loud voice as she emerged from behind the colonnade where she was hiding. "She got into an argument with her mother and father, then ran off. They're worried sick about her."

Every drop of blood seemed to fade from Abby Evans' face, and it looked as if she might faint. Her eyes gaped wide as the sight of the bitch from the airplane, and she let out a paralyzing scream. "She's lying...they kidnapped me!"

The priest shot a confused glance from Nataliya to Abby, uncertain as to what to do next. "This is all so irregular," he began.

"Don't listen to her...you have to believe me—"

"The girl has a drug problem, and we're trying to get her clean," Nataliya said. "That's why she's here on Ibiza."

"That's not true—"

"Her parents are there, at this villa?" the priest asked.

"Yes. They brought her all the way from America for treatment. The combination of cocaine and meth makes her hysterical. And paranoid."

The priest clearly didn't know what to do, whom to believe: the distraught girl with a look of sheer terror in her eyes, or this lovely woman dressed in white who seemed to have such a calm and soothing demeanor. In his mind he heard the words of the catechism, reminding him that

Christ is the source of the priesthood, the priest of the old law was a figure of Christ, and the priest of the new law acts in the person of Christ. Big help that was right now, trying to determine who was telling the truth and who was lying…like Solomon deciding whether to split the baby.

Nataliya saw the look of discomfort in his eyes, saw he was trying to make the right judgment call here. She realized he might need a little persuasion doing so.

"Just look at her," she pressed him. "You can see the effect of the drugs in her eyes. They've taken over her mind and body, just as the devil possesses the human soul. The poor thing needs medical help."

The priest gazed up toward the heavens, a view that was obscured by the steep, timbered roof of the church. He closed his eyes and his lips seemed to move, as if in a silent prayer for guidance from the Lord. Then he took a deep breath and looked at her.

"Take her," he said, gently nudging Abby toward her. "May Christ be with you both."

Abby let out a tremendous howl, but Nataliya just clamped a hand over her mouth.

"Thank you, Father," she said, offering up a reverential smile as she led the hysterical girl toward the back of the church, fully expecting her to try to bolt any second. At the same time knowing the syringe of succinylcholine chloride she kept in the glove box of the Jaguar would silence her within seconds.

Renate Azzone would have liked to have killed the American imposter right there in the Orange Garden, but the park was too crowded, too public. People were bound to notice, and witnesses would have no problem recalling his appearance when they were questioned by the *polizia*. They would describe the killer as a man dressed like a priest, with a distinct red hat and a key tucked into the band…with a matching color square in his pocket.

This would not be a problem, since he'd already worked out a plan for when—and if—Alvize Sala had shown up. As much as he wanted to kill the young *stronzo* right on the spot, doing so would present challenges. As the Deputy Director of the Vatican Governate, he would be protected by diplomatic immunity, but that would only serve as a Band-Aid considering the trouble that could arise from murdering someone who had been held captive within the city walls.

THE FALL OF VIVALDI • 261

Plan A had been to transport the young man to a seldom-used garage in the Tuscalano Nord area not far from the central railroad terminal. The same scheme would work—with a few modifications—for the interrogation and eventual demise of Carter Logan. That was the name listed on his driver's license, with an address in Washington, DC, the same name on his three credit cards, as well as his passport. His wallet contained a little over three hundred Euros, which Azzone's wingman in the backseat stuffed into his own pocket, thinking he could use the cash to buy his wife a nice pair of gold earrings for her birthday, which was next week.

"Where the fuck are you taking me?" Logan mumbled, the pain in his ribs and kidneys screaming at him as if the end of days were upon him. A length of tape had been affixed across his mouth, so the words came out as, *Whe dufugeru taggig meh?*

"*Silenzio,*" the wingman snapped. "Not a word, or I shoot."

He was referring to the gun that was jabbed into his gut right around where his liver was, an organ engorged with so much blood that it would only take seconds for a bullet to do its thing.

Just then, Azzone's phone rang in its hands-free dashboard holder. The screen told him it was Bortolotti, so he had to answer.

"Il Duce," he said. His usual response whenever the neofascist *tiranno* called—same nickname as Mussolini, and look what happened to him.

"Where are you?"

"I have a bit of business to finish up, then I'll be on my way."

"*Che cazzo,*" Bortolotti told him. "I want you here. Now."

"This thing, it can't wait—"

"What part of 'now' did you not hear? You're late, and you have a critical role to play in the end game.

"I'll be there as soon as I can—" Azzone insisted.

"Now!" Bortolotti shouted into his ear. "Anything else can wait."

The phone went dead. Azzone studied the cars ahead, then glanced at his prisoner in the rearview mirror, wondered again how this *stronzo* had come to know about Alvize, and what else he might have learned. Why he was poking around in this matter at all, since the young man's escape had not been reported in the media, and only two other people within the palace walls knew that he'd even been living there? Such was the nature of the hallways and passages and secret residences within the Vatican, and the code of silence that for centuries had protected a long string of transgressions.

"What was that all about?" the backseat wingman inquired.

"Il Duce," Azzone replied. "Seeking a command performance."

"Now?"

"As soon as we lose this traffic."

Six cars back Aldo wondered where the fuck they were headed. Damned summit meeting had packed the streets, and no one was going anywhere…not any time soon. It was inch forward, stop; forward, stop.

The only food he and Vinnie had eaten since daybreak were the apricots they'd managed to pocket at the produce stand earlier. Damned storekeeper kept his eyes glued to them like a hawk the entire time, as if a couple missing *albicocche* would bankrupt his business. Of course, they could have paid for anything in the store they wanted but, for the *teppisti* from Napoli, it was a matter of principle.

"Where do you think they're going?" Vinnie asked him, nodding in the direction of the black Giulia.

"Nowhere, just like us," Aldo replied.

"Traffic's so slow, maybe we could just get out, walk up to them—"

"And do what? Ambush them and snatch the American in the middle of the street, hundreds of witnesses sitting in their cars?"

"Just a thought," Vinnie muttered.

He reached down, twisted one of the knobs on the ancient dashboard radio. The volume came up gradually as he turned, the station playing a classical piece he recognized from the old phonograph at his uncle's house as a kid in Caltanissetta: Vivaldi. He turned the other dial, in search of something louder, more upbeat, something like electro-dance-rap with a pounding bass beat, a wild music track to accompany what he knew was about to go down—as soon as they broke out of this gridlock.

Just then a siren cut through the symphony of horns outside. The two-note wail was coming from behind them, somewhere back in the infinite clog of vehicles. Aldo glanced in the rearview mirror, while Vinnie swiveled his head and peered over his shoulder. Both reactions were borne out of a near-constant mental state of paranoia down in Napoli, where most of the polizia knew them and the few honest ones might even pull them over for questioning. It was different here in Rome, however. No matter that they were driving a Fiat they'd just boosted from the street in front of the Orange Garden, and were looking to have a talk with an American tourist a few cars ahead of them so they could steal a device that would give them the jump on a stash of drugs that was arriving in some port sometime tonight.

The siren kept wailing. Seconds ticked, tempers flared. Eventually a gap just wide enough for the polizia vehicle to pass through began to open up. It inched forward slowly, pulled up alongside the Fiat Panda, then rolled deliberately past the next few cars, past the black Giulia. As it pressed forward, it created a wake—more of a void waiting to be filled— that Aldo took advantage of. He made a quick flick of the wheel, slipped in behind it, as did the Alfa Romeo, which was now directly ahead of them.

The communications system known as ICASP had cost a small fortune to install, an outrageous outlay for something that would be used for little more than a week before being dismantled, its components carted off and relegated to storage.

There had been much arguing and debating and wringing of hands over the merits of installing the comms program. It was obscenely expensive, and the city of Rome and the Italian armed forces already had a functioning system, so there was no need to run another program parallel to it. Likewise, it was redundant to what the Americans and Brits and Germans would be bringing with them, so why bother? Plus: who was going to pay for it all?

In the end, the fact that it would fully coordinate the international security response in the event of any potential terrorist threat at the summit was what prevailed. The marketing folks from the high-tech firm based in Norway made a superb pitch, hands were shaken, and contracts were signed...and a seven-figure check—dollars, not Euros—was deposited in the bank.

In Donald Poole's estimation, it was living up to its hype. Within seconds of sending out an alert for possible interference from unknown bogeys dressed in fake Italian Army uniforms, every participating branch of the police and military security force was linked in to the conversation. Every legitimate commander—on the ground and in the air—knew of the situation that appeared to be unfolding in the streets. Someone was inserting impostors within the official ranks, with the intention of creating chaos on this, the last day of the global meeting.

This was where ICASP would prove to be worth its investment, or not.

"How many genuine Army troops are currently deployed in the city?" Poole asked Olivia Mertens. She was standing to his right; on his left were the on-site security chiefs from Japan and Canada. Others were crowded into the room behind them, anxiously studying the screens.

"That's need-to-know only," replied a voice through the console speaker—imperious, to the point of arrogant. As typically proved to be the case, the biggest obstacle to official communications often proved to be the officials themselves.

"And we fucking need to know," Poole said. "We're seeing enemy proxies—probably hundreds of them—on their way to the Nuvola. In uniform, and heavily armed. We need to know how much of a threat they are."

There was a brief pause and a click as the microphone on the other end was muted. Ten seconds later a different voice came on and said, "A little more than a thousand Army personnel in combat dress are in the red zone."

"Copy that," Olivia Mertens said. "How do we tell them apart from the imposters?"

"I can answer that," replied a voice from the back of the room. All heads turned to find a lieutenant colonel from the carabinieri pressing his way through the men and women who had begun to congregate, headed toward the array of video monitors. He was tall and lean, Sean Connery as Bond in his early years—not bad English, with a bit of an Italian take rather than Scottish. "Let me take a look."

"Absolutely, sir," Poole said, wondering who the newcomer was.

The crowd parted like the Red Sea and the officer came through. He stood in front of the monitors, arms stiff at his side, eyes roaming from one screen to the next. "Closeups?"

One of the techs who was operating the video control board made some adjustments, and a moment later a large, still image of several impostores appeared on the mosaic of screens. They had just climbed out of a van and were standing on the sidewalk, dressed in full Italian Army combat uniform: shirt, trousers, cap, rifle. "This is from twelve minutes ago, in front of the Hotel Caravel," the tech said.

"*Grazie*," the lieutenant colonel replied. "My name's Rossi, by the way."

"Poole," the head of President Mitchell's security team said. "Secret Service. This is Mertens."

"Eurocorp," she added.

"Right." Rossi closely studied the image imposed on the grid of monitors, nodding his head slowly as he absorbed what he was seeing. "Not a bad facsimile," he finally said. "Professionally fabricated to official military specs, tailored by people who know their craft. Tight stitches, attention to detail. But it appears they messed up."

"Messed up how?" Poole asked.

"Before I answer that, show me another one."

The board operator dutifully replaced the still frame with another, this one captured on Via Tito Omboni about ten minutes previously: a different soldier, identical garb, same weapon slung over his shoulder.

"Are those the same guns as your people?" Mertens asked him.

"Yes, but no surprise. Hundreds of them went missing from the U.S. Army base near Livorno a couple months back. Black market is everywhere. But see that?" Rossi pointed at one of the screens that depicted the soldier's neck and head. "They made a mistake with the collars, see? They're too narrow. And the caps were sewn without the ridging around the edges, which prevents the fabric from fraying over time. It also helps keep the lining inside from bunching up."

Poole checked his watch; time was ticking quickly. "Which means what?" he asked.

"They probably didn't include it," the lieutenant colonel replied. "And see there? He's wearing an earbud, not one of our standard coms pieces." Then he turned and looked at the tech op, and said, "Would it be possible to run through a few more?"

It was, and they did. The tech flashed images of twenty more impostores on the monitor grid, all of whom appeared to be fitted with Bluetooth devices.

"That's our opening," Rossi announced. "They aren't listening to our communications."

"What if their command post is?" Olivia Mertens asked.

"That would be doubtful."

"You sound pretty confident," Poole observed.

"Our system is encrypted, with a new classified code issued every morning," Lieutenant Colonel Rossi explained. "Whoever these people are, unless they received the new cipher this morning, they're out of the loop."

"What if they have someone on the inside?" Poole asked.

"Not very likely," Rossi said. "But just as a precaution, I'll send out a new one. Unless they have a mole deeply embedded in our ops, they're shit out of luck."

• • •

"Did we receive today's code?" Bortolotti asked Mateo Tufino as he rubbed his hands together with childish glee, delighted at how well his strategy was coming together. Only a few more minutes now until all his men would be in position, and the attack would commence.

Not even for a minute did he bemoan the potential loss of life. Brave men on both sides were going to die today, an unfortunate but necessary aspect of any bloody revolution; all a part of the anticipated human collateral, an unavoidable aspect in the ongoing march for nation and liberty.

"Got it early this morning," Tufino confirmed. "Whatever they do, however they react, we will know."

"Unless they've changed it."

"They won't do that. They have no way to know what's about to happen."

"*Excelente*," Bortolotti said, his voice almost like that of a child. "Let me know when everyone is in position."

"Si signore," Tufino said. "ViValDi."

"ViValDi."

Chapter 31

After about an hour of extreme disquiet, Major Richard Thompson began to get his shit together.

He accomplished this first by walking hurriedly to the La Tour-Maubourg metro station, the stop closest to his hotel and typically quite crowded. Tourists, mostly, were on their way from one attraction or museum to the next, but a few locals, as well. He managed to find a seat between a young man with a backpack on his lap and a woman smiling at something on her phone, too preoccupied to pay him any attention, as was everyone else in the car. None of them appeared to resemble what he remembered of Rōnin Phythian.

Nor was Phythian in the car ahead of or behind him. Thompson had cautiously peered through the glass doors at both ends, just to make sure the psycho hadn't somehow followed him down to the platform and sneaked aboard. The dossier he'd received last night via text suggested Phythian's mental skillset was functional up to one thousand yards, and offered a strong warning not to let his guard down if he thought he might be anywhere within that range. That was hard to prevent, considering that Thompson intended to fulfill his contract at extremely close range, and the fact that he'd lost the element of surprise.

He rode the train all the way to the end of the line at Balard, remained on the car while the last passengers disembarked and a new set shuffled aboard. No sign of his quarry during the process, which meant Thompson had either eluded him, or the bastard was playing him like a fish. Either way, he remained where he was, pretending to read the discarded financial section of *La Monde* as the doors closed and he began his return journey on the 8 Line back through the tunnel toward Pointe du Lac. It was the last place he wanted to be right now, and instead thought of the view from the deck of his chateau outside Montreux, holding a smoldering cigar in one hand and a glass of absinthe in the other. The real stuff, with just enough thujone to give his brain a hallucinogenic kick and allow him not to think about any of this shit.

Then someone standing in front of him said, "*Excusez-moi, monsieur. Puis-je m'asseoir ici* ?"

His cold expression and rigid features usually ensured that no one approached him while he was riding the Metro, so he paid no attention to the request at first. Then the young woman standing in front of him tapped him on the shoulder and again inquired whether she might have the seat next to him.

He glanced up and realized he was taking up more than one seat. "*Mais évidemment*," he replied. "*Je suis désolé*." Then he made room for her, and she slipped into the space beside him.

They rode like that for a moment or two, before she opened a tourist map printed in English. "*Pardonnez-moi...pouvez vous me dire comment... arriver à la tombe de* Jim Morrison," she asked him.

This was a typical question, one he'd heard before when he'd visited Paris. Inexplicably, Jim Morrison's grave was one of the top attractions in the city, and this pretty lass definitely fit the demographic that most often trekked out there to leave flowers or bras or panties on the dead rocker's headstone. Her tourist map, though, was printed in English, and the way she seemed to be struggling with her French told him he should switch the conversation to what he presumed was her native language.

"His grave is in the Pere Lachaise cemetery, here," Thompson said, pointing to a location in the 20th Arrondissement. "The easiest way to get there is just to switch to the number nine train at the Republique station, right here. Get off four stops later at Charonne, and follow all the tourists."

She looked on her map, saw where he was pointing. "Am I that much of a cliché?" she asked him, a little embarrassed.

"It is only by accident that Jim Morrison happened to die in Paris," he said with a smile.

She nodded and closed her accordioned map, then offered him her hand and said, "My name is Jennifer."

"George Tremblay," he lied, using his Winnipeg alias.

"You sound like maybe you're from London, or maybe Liverpool."

"Originally from England, but these days I'm a citizen of the world," he replied. "But I was just a few years older than you are now when I first came here. I wanted to write and paint and drink wine. And meet young girls who had similar interests." He could tell she was a little nervous about that last statement so he quickly added, "But now I'm just interested in the wine. And killing time, among other things. As your friend Jim Morrison once said, 'No one here gets out alive.'"

Three cars forward, Rōnin Phythian relaxed in his seat and deftly explored the frontal lobe of Major Thompson's cerebrum.

As a man who forced himself into exile eight years ago, weeks sometimes passed without him coming into contact with another human being. He didn't see one, didn't speak with one, didn't watch them on TV or stream images of them online—particularly since coverage often was spotty in the plains of Africa.

His hand actually had been forced eight years ago, when his former employer had contrived the complex plan to kill him. The G3 did not tolerate rogue agents who acted independently, so the executive committee determined Phythian must be eliminated, both because he was becoming harder to control, and because the Catholic Church had been a trusted customer for many years.

After crashing the airplane that was intended to be his coffin, he'd disappeared to a remote section of the Serengeti in northern Tanzania. Despite the ongoing government oppression in the region, here he was able to live off the grid and enjoy his solitude without constantly looking over his shoulder for the pale rider. Nonetheless, he always kept one eye trained on the horizon for a cloud of dust in the wind, and whenever he had cause to leave his camp for any period of time, he intuitively switched his full range of senses to red alert. Old habits did, indeed, die hard.

At Utuliva he could appreciate the beauty and grace of a world untouched by the hands of humans, even though it was close to where the species first had sprung from the womb of evolution well over a million years ago. It also afforded him a place to take refuge from the global chaos, and appreciate the elegance and majesty of all creatures, great and small, without his mind being cluttered by their cerebral processes. Which, over time, he'd come to believe were intricate and highly ordered, except when the fight-or-flight switch got flipped and panic ensued.

Which was what he sensed was going through Thompson's brain at the moment. The message Phythian had left with the hotel desk clerk had clearly rattled him, fueling a very real sense of alarm. Before that moment, the Major had convinced himself that he possessed both leverage and advantage in his mission to hunt down the over-hyped former hitman and erstwhile adversary. But now…well, he had to concede that Phythian had somehow come to learn that he was in town and, worse yet, knew where he was staying. Not bad; had to give the man credit.

The more he kept trying to convince himself of the flummery of all this, the more he was faced with a grim reality: An assassin who possessed the ability to kill a person just by mentally planting the suggestion was, in fact, a formidable foe. All he required was a swift mental push to sow the seeds of despair and death in the target's brain, then control the outcome.

That was all in the dossier, too.

All of which, Phythian knew, was causing the poor bastard named Thompson fits.

"There's no debating the matter," Azzone said over his shoulder to the guard covering Logan in back seat of the Giulia. "*Il Duce* said 'now.'"

"But we can't just show up there with this…this *succhiacazzi*," the man with the gun replied. His name was Wilhelm Graf, and he was a close associate of a bishop from Munich who had been brought to the Vatican more than a decade before. Fluent in four languages, Italian being one of them, he was most comfortable speaking in the tongue of the Fatherland. As was his old man, and *his* old man before him, a proud Schutzstaffel guard who had served valiantly as one of the first Blockführers at Dachau during the start of the truly Great War.

"That's my problem to worry about, not yours," said Azzone, who really wasn't worried at all. Quite soon there would be so much violence unleashed, so much blood spilled, that one more body in the streets would hardly be noticed.

He'd spent hours last night reviewing the security plans Bortolotti had given him, knew where the polizia checkpoints were, where the Army troops would be the heaviest. Mostly they would be within a four- or five-block range of Via Cristoforo Colombo, but other *ad hoc* sentry positions had been established along some of the major arteries that fed into the main thoroughfare. He'd memorized them all, knew the quickest and most secure routes to the condo high-rise where Bortolotti right now was calling the shots.

What Azzone had not figured on was having an American prisoner bound and gagged in the backseat of his car. The text message this morning from Alvize—*merda*, how stupid he'd been to fall for that ploy—had thrown him off-kilter. He should have seen right through the ruse, but he'd been preoccupied ever since the kid had run away last winter. That caused him to react foolishly, rather than think his actions through in a rational and logical sequence.

"Whatever you say, boss," Graf replied. Just enough skepticism in his voice to express his lingering doubts.

At that moment Azzone made an abrupt left turn down a narrow side street, just wide enough to allow cars to park against the curb, and a single lane of vehicles to squeeze through. A rearview glance at a POS Fiat that followed right behind him confirmed he wasn't the only one who knew the shortcut.

He glanced at the dashboard clock, saw it was just a couple minutes until Bortolotti gave his order, and the ViValDi battle plan went into action. By now at least a dozen motorcades would be heading toward Via Cristoforo Colombo on their way to the Nuvola, with their own national security forces and local motorcycle officers providing protection. How were they to know that the soldiers providing cover along the route were about to raise their arms and unleash a full-scale assault against them. They were sitting ducks who had no idea they were outmanned and outgunned.

Azzone hung a right turn at the next intersection, which fed him into a slightly wider street. Still not much traffic, so he tapped the gas and gained speed. At that point his phone rang and he instinctively glanced at the screen, thinking it was Bortolotti again. Not expecting to see the numeral "1."

The Pope.

Another fucking distraction he didn't need, not now. But it was a call he had to take, so he connected the call and hit "speaker."

"Your Holiness," he said with great reverence, at the same time shooting a sharp glance at Graf in the backseat. Message: keep the *fottuto stronzo* quiet.

"Renate. Such a pleasure to hear your voice."

"And yours. To what do I owe this honor?"

There was a little throat-clearing on the other end, and then the Pope said, "You have been very patient while I have diligently considered your request."

"I recognize you're a very busy man with the weight of the entire world on your shoulders—"

"And after much thought and reflection, my answer is no."

"Excuse me?" Azzone asked, his heart suddenly clenching in his chest.

"I have given great deliberation to this scheme of yours, and the resulting implications it would most certainly have on the Church and its faithful followers," the Pontiff said, his voice steady and measured. "After consulting with the power of the Holy Spirit, I cannot condone what you have in mind. Nor will the Holy See forgive or pardon the actions of anyone involved in the wanton violence planned for today."

Wanton violence? It was a goddamned revolution. "You Holiness—" Azzone said again.

"That is my final answer," The Pope replied. "I urge you to call it off."

At that moment, somewhere a few blocks away, a resounding shot rang out, followed by a volley of automatic gunfire.

A little too fucking late for that, Azzone said to himself.

Lieutenant Colonel Rossi gave the order himself.

"All members of the Italian Army, remove your hats immediately and turn them inside out. I repeat: remove your headgear and turn it inside out."

Donald Poole actually thought it was a simple, yet brilliant, solution. With a thousand impostores making a planned incursion into the ranks of the armed military personnel lining the street, all of them dressed in combat uniforms and carrying battlefield-grade weapons, there had been no way to tell the good guys from the bad guys.

It was Olivia Mertens who had pointed it out, just moments ago. "Their mission is to overpower our security forces," she'd observed. "That means they must know how to tell theirs apart from ours."

The command center fell completely silent for a moment as everyone in the room shared in this epiphany. So simple, so obvious, yet no one said a word. At least not immediately, since no one had a suggestion.

"Probably some kind of badge or medal," Poole suggested. "Something they've been told to look for."

That brought a flurry of murmuring and nodding, but nothing that came close to encouraging. Unless the good guys were in the position to know what to look for, the bad guys had the upper hand.

Then Rossi said, "Their hats."

"Excuse me, sir?" Poole asked.

"Our standard-issue hats have red liners," the colonel explained. "I would bet anything theirs don't."

"Can they turn them inside-out?" Mertens asked.

"No reason why not." Rossi stared at the array of screens a moment or two longer, then plucked a radio handpiece from his much-decorated epaulet and flicked a switch. "Patch me in to central command," he barked at whoever answered. "That's a direct order. *Now.*"

That had been five long minutes ago, three hundred seconds of white knuckles and nail-biting.

"Where do you think they're headed?" Vinnie asked Aldo. They finally were free of the traffic jam and moving swiftly down the narrow street.

"How the fuck should I know?" Aldo replied. "Wherever they end up."

"Then what?"

"We'll figure that out when we get there."

"They probably have guns—"

"So do we," Aldo replied.

"Yeah, but wherever they're going, they've probably got more of them. Probably more people, too."

Aldo eased his foot off the gas, allowing a little distance to form between the Fiat and the black Alfa Romeo about twenty meters in front of them. "You chickening out?" he said, glancing at Vinnie crowded in the shotgun seat beside him.

"*Cazzo no, amico,*" was Vinnie's response. "I just want to come up with a plan for when we get there, wherever we're going. Not get blindsided. Or killed."

"I already thought about that. Who do you think I was texting while we were stuck in traffic back there?"

"Maria, I figured. Or maybe Viviana." The former being Aldo's wife, while the latter was his most recent *amante*.

"Leave them out of this. And just so you know, it was Remy. He sent me a message and I was getting back to him."

"Did Livia finally pop?" Vinnie asked.

"Little girl, couple hours ago," Aldo replied. "They named her Emilia. Anyways, he got bored, sitting around the waiting room while she pushed and screamed. And then when her family showed up...well, he couldn't wait to get out of there, so he's on his way. With Cos and Ricky." Short for Cosimo and Enrico, respectively, two of Remy's cousins on his mother's side; hot-headed little bastards, both of them.

"On his way where?"

"I'll let him know when we know."

"How will we know?" Vinnie asked.

It was a serious question, but Aldo simply brushed it off as inconsequential. "It'll probably be the place with all the guns," he said.

Nataliya literally dragged Abby by the hair out of the SUV, where she'd strapped her in with a half dozen bungee cords she found in a rear hatch. The short-acting narcotic she'd administered had begun to wear off after a few minutes, but the threat of the gun in the uncooperative twit's face kept her quiet the rest of the way back to Sokolov's villa.

"No scars, no bruises," the Russian oligarch quickly assessed when they got out of the car. He'd come out to the cobbled dooryard to greet them, delighted that his prize objet d'art had been retrieved from town, and without serious injury to her person. "Nothing visible."

"Bitch needs a good lashing," Nataliya seethed as she forced Abby to move.

"She get more than that," Sokolov said with a tight smile. He turned, motioned for a guard standing at the far side of the circular dooryard to approach. "Escort this *shlyukha* back to her room."

"*Da*, Mr. Sokolov," the sentry said, a glint in his eye.

"And let me remind you, you are not to touch her."

"*Konechno net*," the man assured him with a bow of his head. Then he grabbed Abby by the collar, twisted it tightly, and marched her across the driveway to a massive door cut into the side of the stone house.

Nataliya waited for them both to disappear inside the villa, then said, "Everything still scheduled as planned?"

"Guests begin arriving later in afternoon," Sokolov assured her. "*Pizda* get here a couple hours later for cocktails. Always five o'clock somewhere."

As gentle and generous as Sokolov had been to Nataliya over the years, sometimes she wanted to shoot that fucking smile right off his self-satisfied Russian face. He didn't give a shit about the girl named Abby Evans, the degradation and depravity that lay ahead of her; a lifetime of drugs and sexual debasement, starting tomorrow night. This was not his concern, not

THE FALL OF VIVALDI • 275

in a free-market system where the flavor of the month would bring him a tidy sum and "stick it" to the western world. Particularly the Americans, since they had engineered the seizure of his real estate, the theft of his yacht, and the illegal appropriation of his financial assets. Assholes, every single one of them, including this fresh *kusok zadnitsy* who was becoming more trouble than she was worth.

On his mental spreadsheet, she was worth a great deal.

Nataliya could easily whisk Abby away from all this, get them both out there. She had more than enough money of her own, and no one had seized *her* property or bank accounts. She had three passports, and knew someone who would forge one for the girl. It was just a forty-minute drive to the airport, and she could talk a half dozen personnel there into letting them both board a plane out of here. She could find a new place to call home, start over again, get the girl back to Rome, no questions asked.

She could do all of those things, if she were so inclined. After all, the future really does belong to those who believe in the beauty of their dreams.

"Should be fun, Darling," she said instead, hooking her elbow into his and leaning her head on his shoulder.

This time Abby was put in physical restraints: serious restraints, beginning with a sturdy garment with long sleeves that wrapped her arms across her chest and bound them behind her back. All of it padded, so ligature marks and abrasions were kept to a minimum. Similarly, she was restrained to her bed, her head locked in an apparatus that would keep it immobile—at least as much as possible. Wrists and ankles in padded manacles that kept mobility to a minimum. An acrylic mouth guard with a hole in it had been fitted over her teeth, held in place by a fabric bandage that wouldn't leave behind any sticky goo or signs of chafing.

"Your face must be perfect," was how the Bitch Lady named Nataliya explained it later. "Bidding is expected to be brisk."

Bidding? Abby thought. *Bidding on what?* But there was no hiding the truth, no escaping the reality of what was happening, of what was *going to happen*. She felt like a cow standing in line to be slaughtered or, more apropos, awaiting a prize steer on a stud farm. The terror that coursed through her was beyond belief, the realization of everything these monsters were planning, bringing her to the very brink of hysteria.

Which was why they kept pumping the shit she assumed was poppy juice through the tube plugged into a port in her neck. She couldn't remove it because of the vice that was holding her head in place, couldn't free her hands or feet. Food and drink were out of the question, and any nutrients or liquids she might need were supplied via the same line.

Waste liquids emptied via a separate conduit to a bag at the foot of her bed.

All in all, she was screwed—no question about it.

Chapter 32

Logan knew Azzone and his wingman were planning to kill him; he just didn't know when that might be.

The heavy traffic and the overwhelming presence of polizia made them cautious. He suspected the Vatican pervert would want to question him about the whereabout of Alvize; specifically, how to contact him and how to find him. Alvize had warned him of this, explaining that Azzone was relentless and deliberate in pursuing his pathological obsessions, and violent at the drop of that blood-red hat.

That violence had come close to shattering Logan's jaw, and was responsible for the pulsing spasms shooting through his head.

He was equally convinced that when they got to wherever they were going, more torture and torment awaited him. His overactive imagination pictured all sorts of methodologies: fists, crowbars, baseball bats, jumper cables all came to mind. So did pliers, scalpels, and whatever mediaeval appliances might exist deep within the bowels of the Vatican. The gun that was digging into his neck would simply be the final act.

With every second that ticked by, Logan knew he was getting closer to the end.

Then he heard the gunshots—just a few at first, followed by the rapid fire of automatic weapons. Uzis and AK-47s and other military-grade rifles; short bursts here and there, followed by return volleys of similar duration.

What the hell was going on, and why did he think it had something to do with the two sonsofbitches in this goddamned car?

"Do you hear that?" Vinnie asked from the seat next to Aldo. "Sounds like gunfire."

"You think?" Aldo said, taking great care to maintain a modest distance between the Fiat and the Giulia a few car lengths ahead. "*Grado militare.*"

"Military? How can you tell?"

"Assault rifles. Army issue."

"We have assault rifles," Vinnie pointed out.

"Which we boosted from the Army," Aldo said. "Something big is going down."

"And not too far from here," Vinnie pointed out.

Aldo lifted his shoulder in a dispassionate shrug, said, "We're good where we are. No shooting here…not yet, at least. Hang tight…they're making another turn."

He spun the wheel, followed the Alfa Romeo down yet another street that was lined on either side with ancient stone walls, with the tops of trees waving in the wind above. There were only a few cars along here, which allowed the black Giulia to pick up speed.

"Think they know we're back here?" Vinnie asked him.

"I'm sure they've seen us, but no one in a car like this would tail a car like that. We keep going until they give us a reason to stop."

At that point the phone rang. It was Remy, calling instead of texting for an update.

"Still no intel on where we're going, but we have a visual on the target," Aldo reported.

"We just crossed under il Grande Raccordo Anulare," Remy said, referring to the E80 "Grand Ring" that—along with the A90—encircled just about all of Rome. "Heading north on Via Laurentina."

"Copy that," replied Vinnie, who binge-watched dubbed reruns of the American television series *24*. "We're headed your way. Will keep you posted on our progress."

Ninety seconds after Colonel Rossi issued his initial command, the directive had been transmitted up and down the full line of military command.

Evidence of this came when a live video feed of security forces positioned at Imperial Square near the Marconi Obelisk depicted all of them removing their caps. Those who were visible in the foreground appeared to be a little confused by what they'd heard in their earpieces, but they dutifully turned them inside-out and exposed the red lining before placing them back on their heads. Meanwhile, the impostore forces who had not received the encoded order kept moving along in the direction of the Nuvola, less than a thousand meters away.

Donald Poole had already turned President Mitchell's motorcade back toward his hotel. All twenty Detroit-built vehicles and local police on motorcycles made an abrupt right turn onto Viale Guido Baccelli before any of the vehicles got anywhere near Via Cristoforo Colombo and the fake soldiers. The Commander in Chief was not happy about missing the luncheon, where he was to deliver a grandiose speech about all the good that could be achieved through partnership among peaceful neighbors, and possibly improve his approval ratings; a moot point, really, since he was in his second term and was unable to run for a third.

In his headset, Poole heard the words of Generali Savio Fiorenza, in charge of the First Regiment Granatieri di Sardegna infantry division based in Rome. Not having the benefit of anything but guidebook Italian to work with, he had no idea of the exact words being said, but the grave tone of his voice indicated it was all business. A quick glance at Rossi, who also was tuned in to the coms system, confirmed his suspicions.

What happened over the next one hundred seconds was nothing short of breathtaking military coordination to the point of a Hollywood spectacular, all of it captured by the network of HD cameras positioned closest to the G20 summit. No tracking or dolly shots, no cranes or Steadicams, no POV—just clean video of what looked like hundreds of soldiers converging on the military checkpoints at the perimeter of the predetermined Red Zone. There they were met by an even greater number of Italian Army troops, along with strategically positioned tanks and armored assault vehicles, plus a few rocket launchers that had been deployed more for show than for actual combat activity.

As the bogeys advanced, Poole and Rossi and Mertens—everyone in the command center—stared at the monitors in silence as a standoff between the two sides ensued. It seemed the fake soldiers had been prepared for a battle within the summit grounds, or perhaps even in the Nuvola itself, where the leaders of the Deep State were to gather for their lunch. By the time anyone realized what was going on—that the Army had been infiltrated by *nazionalista* rebels—they would be inside the fencing and razor wire, advancing toward the grand ballroom.

At least, that had been the plan.

One of the impostores, an auto mechanic from Bologna with a wife and three children, fired first. It was just a single shot, one that was not recorded by any of the live cameras that fed the command screens. Later, a panel of investigators would subpoena a digital hard drive from a German news outfit that had been covering the arrival of the country's Chancellor, and had captured the shooting on video. The images would show that the fake soldata had aimed at a real soldier standing across the street at a distance of no more than twenty yards.

He pulled the trigger but missed. Several other soldiers from the First Regiment Granatieri di Sardegna infantry division responded with return fire, cutting the man down before he could squeeze off another round. That brought a salvo of shots from the bogeys, which encouraged more rounds from the troops in the red-lined caps. Several of the nazionalistas dropped to the pavement, and the disorganized confusion caused the attack to accelerate.

More gunshots erupted from both sides. Army soldiers sought cover behind anything they could find and unleashed their fury. The impostores had not yet appeared to grasp the visible difference between them and their opponents. They also were greatly outnumbered, as many of them had been deposited discreetly a good number of blocks away, and had yet to arrive on the scene. Those that had made it to the perimeter—several hundred strong, according to initial estimates—fired indiscriminately at anything in a uniform that moved. By doing so, they actually took down several of their own troops, killing two and leaving three others with serious but non-fatal wounds.

The highly trained Army guards steadfastly held their ground, taking aim at their attackers but firing only when necessary. The ViValDi forces to whom Bortolotti had promised violence and valor, and who had seemed so eager to fight the globalist swindlers and democratic elite, had not fully appreciated the realities of close-quarters combat. Not until their comrades in arms began to fall did they appear to reconsider their devotion to the cause, and attempt a hasty retreat. Those who didn't were summarily rounded up at gunpoint and forced to kneel on the sidewalk, restrained with zip cuffs while their guns were confiscated.

Five minutes after the first shot was fired, the melee was over. Preliminary casualties indicated twenty impostores were dead and another thirty wounded. One Army soldier had been killed, and another two injured. Dozens of would-be militants later were seen running through the streets, many of them still carrying their stolen weapons. Over the rest of the afternoon dozens were apprehended at various points around the city, including four who had attempted to rob a branch of Banca d'Italia in the name of ViValDi.

Renate Azzone had no way of knowing this as he whipped the Alfa Romeo into a space in the parking garage thirteen floors below Bortolotti's rented condo. As he cut the engine, he rested both hands on the wheel and took a deep breath, then slowly let it out.

"Now what?" asked Wilhelm Graf from the backseat.

"Now we get this *stronzo* upstairs and force him to talk."

"What about *il Duce*?"

"He'll be preoccupied with his revolution." Azzone glanced at Logan and said, "And this fucker's our first prisoner of war."

Upstairs, Bortolotti was peering through his military field glasses at the Nuvola in the distance. The high-powered lenses didn't quite bring the action close enough, and what he was hearing on the radio was chaotic and incomplete. Army soldiers had opened fire on other soldiers, and men were down. Some of them were bleeding, and many were not moving. It was a display of disorder and confusion, and there was a dearth of information coming from the scene.

From where he was standing on the balcony, il Duce could hear distant pops of gunfire. Through his Bluetooth earpiece he heard his commanders on the ground barking orders and yelling over each other as they assessed the pandemonium that was unfolding. Somehow, it appeared that the Italian Army had caught on to the presence of his fake troops trying to infiltrate their ranks, and was holding them off at the red zone perimeter.

The plan had always been for his nazionalistas to be dropped off in small numbers, and subtly join up as they progressed toward the Nuvola. They then were to arrive in a grand show of force and begin firing on those who stood in their way, thus overwhelming the G20 security forces and streaming inside the secure perimeter. It was inconceivable that any commander within the Italian Army would give the order to shoot his own troops, and by the time the ruse was discovered, Bortolotti's volunteers would be inside the building, taking hostages if possible, killing them if necessary. The more blood the better; strength in numbers.

Violentiam. Valeo. Diripio.

Then his phone rang. He'd been expecting word from his field general, Raphael Lavigne, who had talked his way through the roadblock at il Giardino della Cascate. He was closest to the action, and could give him the play-by-play of what was going on.

But it wasn't Lavigne; it was Renate Azzone.

"Where are you?" Bortolotti snapped at him.

"Downstairs, and coming up," Azzone replied. "We have a prisoner."

"Jesus fuck…now's not the time—"

"Remember, this was your idea. Twelfth floor?"

Bortolotti released a string of cuss words, mostly having to do with his mother, body parts, indecent activities. Then he said, "Hell, it's a war. Bring him up."

"Already on our way," Azzone told him, and ended the call.

The elevator was slow and rattled in its tracks as it traveled up the shaft. The ceiling light flickered, and the LED readout above the door only partially illuminated the number of each floor. Plus, it smelled of an electrical fire, an odor that was remarkably similar to old disc brakes on the verge of burning out, not something that instilled confidence in the three men riding in the car.

At the twelfth floor a bell dinged and the doors crawled open. Azzone stepped out into a hallway that smelled of marinara sauce, with a pungent undertone of garlic. He glanced both directions and said, "This way," indicating left.

Wilhelm Graf gave Logan a shove, and he stumbled out into the corridor. "*Bewegung!*" he barked in German, prodding him again—this time a bit rougher—with the barrel of the gun.

Logan did what he was told, trudging after Azzone with his head down like a prisoner on his way to the execution chamber. Which, he suspected, wasn't far from the truth.

He was a dead man walking.

Azzone eventually stopped in front of a door, blue with scuff marks and scratches. Instead of knocking, he produced a key from his pocket and inserted it in the lock, then gave it a push. It swung open, and all three of them quickly moved into a space that served as a foyer. It had walls the color of a creamy latte, marble floors and recessed lighting in the ceiling.

Logan could hear a man nearby, shouting and cursing in rapid-fire Italian that he couldn't hope to understand. The concerned look on Azzone's face suggested he was alarmed by the anger he was hearing, while the man named Graf jabbed the gun hard against his spine.

The implication: *Don't you fucking do a damned thing or you're dead.*

Chapter 33

"What in the name of Christ are you talking about?" Bortolotti raged as he stormed from the balcony into the living room, then back outside again. He held one of a half dozen burner phones in his hands, the speaker function turned on. "*Che cazzo eta succedendo?*"

"Our people met with unexpected resistance," explained Mateo Tufino, who'd had plenty of experience deflecting the man's wrath. "What I'm hearing is the security forces somehow knew we were there—"

"Who the fuck told them?" Il Duce barked. "If one of my generals is a traitor—"

"There's no evidence of that," Tufino interrupted him. "Meanwhile, there's an issue of what they do next."

"Next? What the fuck do you mean *next*? We fight on, that's what we do. Fatalities are to be expected in a revolution. Everyone in the movement was aware of the risks when they signed up, and we will fight to the finish."

"Signore?" Tufino said. "There's another problem you should be aware of—"

"Problem? What fucking sort of problem?"

"Well, sir…the men have abandoned their positions."

"*Ma che cazzo dici?*" Bortolotti yelled. Translation: What the fuck are you talking about?

Tufino inhaled a deep breath on his end and said, "Despite their complete loyalty to you and to the cause, these men are also husbands and fathers. Sons. They have lives and jobs and children and…well, signore, it appears a lot of them have gone home."

"*What*!? They just laid down their arms and *quit*?"

"Not exactly, sir. Many of them kept their guns."

This revelation precipitated another rapid-fire tirade that ended with, "Where the fuck are my generals—"

"That's the other half of the issue, signore," Tufino said. "What I'm hearing is that the miliary has gone into lock-down mode, searching for those responsible for today's…disruption."

"Disruption?" Bortolotti repeated. He was standing at the balcony railing, gazing in the direction of the Nuvola where by now he had expected to see thick plumes of smoke and blazing flames and a city under siege. Instead, there was nothing, except for a sky that seemed an even richer blue than usual, a few clouds loping along the eastern horizon.

"That's what they're calling it," Tufino told him.

"It's a fucking *rivoluzione*. The overthrow of the *Stato Profondo*, and a return of Italy—all of Europe—to the hands of the people." Not mentioning his true objective of the day, which was to arrest the current prime minister—if she managed to survive the onslaught—and give the boot to the Council of Ministers.

Bortolotti punched a finger to the screen and ended the call. He hurled the phone through the open glass slider into the living room, watched as it bounced off a leather couch and dropped to the floor. It was at that moment that he noticed Azzone and Graf standing in the foyer, a man with black tape over his mouth slumped between them.

"*Cristo Santo*, the last thing I need," he snapped.

"At your service, sir," the Deputy Director of the Vatican Governate said, clicking his heels together while snapping a tight salute.

The fuming neofascist shot Azzone a dark glare; to mock him was to put himself at great risk of bodily harm, even this man who was one step away from the Pope. Then his mind cleared a bit and he said, "I assume this is the prisoner you mentioned?"

"American, signore. A reporter, in fact. His speedy trial and execution will be a statement of justice to the treasonous spawn of the Deep State."

Bortolotti considered what his Vatican *collaboratore* was suggesting. A day that had started out so beautifully and been planned so perfectly had gone to shit, crushed by treachery and cowardice…and surrender. By now his pre-recorded message of self-determination, national solidarity, and patriotism would have been transmitted by cable and satellite around the globe, causing an upswell of support for his ultra-populist movement.

The entire world would be cheering him as the true leader of all of Italy.

"What crimes has this man committed?" he inquired, trying to mask the bitterness of his apparent defeat. Everything he'd pursued so diligently over the past few years had crashed and burned in a matter of minutes. Millions of dollars spent on uniforms and weapons and ammunition, and he still didn't have the drugs he needed to pay back Georgy Sokolov.

"He is a traitor to the people, a disseminator of lies and deceit," Azzone replied.

Logan tried to mumble something behind the tape, but his words went unheard.

Bortolotti seemed not to care about any of that, preoccupied by how his plans had soured so quickly. "What do you propose as a method of execution?" he asked, collecting his thoughts.

"Something that makes a statement," Azzone replied. "Quick double-tap, maybe a stiletto in the heart."

"Perhaps a long fall with a short rope," Wilhelm Graf, the German grandson of the Dachau Blockführer, suggested, nodding in the direction of the balcony.

Bortolotti appeared to consider all proposals, started to say something just as the door to the hallway burst open.

"No one moves," Aldo shouted as he and Vinnie stormed in, followed by his three cousins from Napoli, each of them brandishing a weapon. "Anyone even blinks an eye, they lose it."

Having been the last to come in from the hallway just moments before, Graf was closest to the door. He pivoted, swinging his Ruger up toward the intruders and, therefore, away from Logan's kidney; but Aldo had the drop on him, his finger reflexively tightening across the trigger. He released a single round that shattered the German's chin and scrambled his brain before exiting through a newly formed opening in the back of his head.

Graf literally was blown off his feet and into the living room, where he landed on his back with a thud.

"Anyone else care to dance?" Aldo shouted, drawing his gun from Azzone to Bortolotti.

Silence being the sleep that nourishes wisdom, neither said a word—or moved.

In the garage thirteen floors below, Capitano Segreto gave a quick nod to the other officers in the surveillance van. "*Merda*," he cursed, the device stuck in his ear serving both as a receiver and microphone. "Gunshots."

"Roger that," replied Tenente Julia Vece, who was seated beside him in the cramped quarters. "Team Two, deploy. I repeat: deploy."

Segreto and Vece swung open the twin rear doors of the vehicle and jumped out. Both were armed with an M4 carbine and a Beretta 92FS pistol, their official department-assigned weapon. Along with the other officers, they hustled across the concrete floor in a slight crouch, covering each other as they weaved through a maze of vehicles. Even though it was early afternoon on a weekday, many folks had opted to stay off the streets during the G20; otherwise, the garage would have been almost empty.

They met up with the other members of the assault team in the underground elevator foyer, and Segreto gave a brief oral summary of what would be anticipated over the next sixty seconds. "Target is upstairs, twelfth floor. Unknown number of persons with him. One shot fired. Assume everyone is armed and dangerous. Questions?"

Probably plenty, but none that were mentioned.

"All right…move out," the captain said. "Elevators are too small, so take the stairs. Go."

"This is how it's going to go down," Aldo continued: gun steady in his hand, four more similar weapons steady in four more hands. Altogether, there were five very anxious fingers across very sensitive triggers. "We have no interest in harming either of you, or why you have this man bound and taped. But he's coming with us."

He nodded his head to indicate he was referring to Logan.

"Like hell—" Azzone snarled. He'd managed to retreat a few steps into the living room, and was drawing his eyes from the blood pooling under Graf's body, back to the man who had shot him.

"Shut the fuck up," cousin Remy cursed, bringing his gun up with both hands, aiming it at the bridge of Azzone's nose. At a distance of less than three meters, it would be an easy shot. Then he flicked a glance to Logan and said, "*Dov'è l'orologio?*"

Logan mumbled something through the tape, but the words were unintelligible.

Aldo rolled his eyes, gripped the adhesive strip and yanked it off. Logan let out a sharp cry of pain, then shook his head. "Fuck—"

"*L'orologi,*" Aldo said again. "*Dov'è?*"

"I don't know what you're saying," Logan replied, shaking his head. "No Italian."

Aldo shot him a look of exasperation, then looked over at Remy and the cousins. "*Qualcuno di voi parla Inglese?*"

The question was met with a brief silence, then one of them raised his non-gun hand and said, "I speak a little." His name was Dante, and he was related to Remy on his mother's side.

"Ask him where the watch is," Aldo instructed him in Italian.

Dante nodded, and repeated the question in English.

"Jesus fucking Christ," Logan said. "What is it about this fucking watch?"

"What?"

"I don't have it," Logan confirmed. "The police showed up at my hotel this morning, demanded I turn it over. I told them the same thing."

Dante translated this as best he could. Aldo looked from him to Vinnie, then back at Logan. "If you're lying—"

"I'm not. Go ahead...search me."

This was something he really welcomed, but what else did he have to offer?

Dante translated, and Aldo shot Vinnie another look. "Do it," he ordered.

"You mean, search him? Like at the airport?"

"If he's got the watch, it won't be hard to find."

"*Scopami*," Vinnie cursed. He ran his hands through Logan's jacket pockets, then patted down his torso and his rear trouser pockets. "*Niente*," he said.

"Crotch," Aldo told him.

"*Sul serio?*"

Yes, Aldo was serious. But Vinnie's full pat-down turned up nothing.

"I'm telling you, I don't have it," Logan insisted.

There was no need for Dante to translate this time. Instead, Aldo looked at Vinnie and said, "Call your source."

Vinnie turned his back, as if that would give him a degree of privacy to talk. He started to punch in a number, when the door once more burst open, slamming against the wall behind it.

"On the floor...now," shouted an officer, who was gripping an M4 carbine, a half dozen armed personnel streaming in behind him.

Logan instinctively dropped to the floor and scrambled under a library table. Everyone else in the room—except for Wilhelm Graf, who was already dead—wheeled about and brought their guns up at the same time. For about two seconds there was a stalemate as everyone assessed the situation, the odds, the risks, the outcome.

Then Dante accidentally squeezed the pressure-sensitive trigger of his pistol, a Tanfoglio nine-millimeter semi-automatic with a seventeen-round capacity. In the moment he couldn't remember if he'd reloaded the thing after the last time he used it.

It didn't matter. He hit the floor hard, blown down by a gas-fired 5.56×45mm NATO round unleashed by Lieutenant Vece at very close range. Death was instant.

So was the return fire, from both sides—almost ludicrous when judged in the aftermath, a few handguns wielded by a small band of Camorra thugs against the serious firepower of a half dozen carabinieri with business on their minds. That business primarily being the arrest of Alessandro Bortolotti, who was standing motionless near the glass slider on the other side of the living room. He'd left his Beretta on a glass-topped table just inside the door, and he was at a loss how to get to it.

After Dante went down, Remy was the next to get hit—in the arm, a generous mercy shot since the gunman wielding the M4 easily could have obliterated his heart. The thug from Napoli spun as he dropped, unleashed a couple rounds in the direction of these armed troopers who had just burst in. Lead collided with Kevlar, knocking a few of the carabinieri back, but their body armor prevented any serious injury, except for one commando whose bicep was grazed by an errant slug.

The exchange of gunfire lasted only a few seconds, but seemed a lot longer. Smoke and plaster and drywall dust quickly filled the air, and a distinct odor of spent gunpower—burned nitroglycerin, sawdust, and graphite—hung in the air. So did the moans of Aldo and the other two cousins, who were suffering a range of injuries: holes in their bodies, shattered bones, ripped tendons, nicked arteries where blood was seeping out.

When the shooting ceased, Renate Azzone was pressed up against a wall in the living room, hands high in the air, indicating he wasn't carrying. One of Captain Segreto's men snapped a pair of cuffs on him and sat him roughly in a corner. Bortolotti was still out on the terrace, his eyes shifting from the carabinieri to his Beretta, his brain apparently calculating how long it might take for him to reach it, aim, and fire. It would have been a pointless exercise, since these marauders who had just infiltrated his apartment obviously were equipped with body armor, probably some sort of state-of-the-art fibers reinforced with bulletproof plates.

"*Chi cazzo credi di essere?*" Bortolotti barked at the storm troopers. Essentially: who the fuck do you think you are?

"Don't you move a muscle," Segreto said, in Italian.

Bortolotti unleashed a glob of spit at him, said, "Goddamned deep state *piedipatti.*" He again eyed the pistol on the table, just out of reach. "You have no right—"

"Hands in the air."

Bortolotti hesitated a second, then began to raise both arms in slow motion. "*Tu figlio di una puttana,*" he snarled. You son of a whore.

"Save your outrage and your insults for the judge," Tenente Vece said, standing slightly behind and to the right of Segreto. Instead of the M4, she had her Beretta trained dead-center on his heart. "You move, you're dead."

The ensuing standoff lasted a good five seconds, as Bortolotti seriously weighed risk against benefit. Should he surrender peacefully and go before an Italian court, a move that would bring him a sentence of life in prison? Or should he make a stand here on the twelfth floor and face almost-certain death? Either way, he'd become a martyr and folk hero, although neither scenario was particularly attractive from a personal point of view. The upside for the cause and his own infamy, however, could be tremendous.

He abruptly dropped to the floor, attempted some kind of a gymnastic move that resembled a somersault and managed to grab his gun. In the same long, continued move he sprang back to his feet, began squeezing off shots while yelling, "*Violentiam. Valeo. Diripio.*"

Tenente Vece was the only officer who fired a pistol. The rest of the assault squad—Segreto and the members of Teams Two and Three—used their M4s, the power of which kept blowing Bortolotti backwards. The force of dozens of rounds of 5.56×45mm ammo jolted his body as he lurched in reverse toward the balcony railing, shattering the tempered glass barricade into tiny fragments. He remained motionless for a moment as the gunfire ceased; then the law of gravity took over and he toppled over the edge and dropped out of sight.

A little more than two seconds later—thirty-two feet per second per second—a thud resounded from below, followed almost instantly by a car anti-theft alarm going off.

Chapter 34

Major Thompson had spent most of the afternoon in constant motion, riding alternate Metro lines end-to-end, changing cars and platforms at random intervals. Over time, the initial panic that had seized him when he'd read Phythian's note had shifted to resolve, and now he was weighing different scenarios by which he could silently approach his target, and be done with all this. Take the next train home to his chalet outside Montreux…or, better yet, board an airplane to some remote tropical archipelago and enjoy an extended vacation in the sun.

Professional arrogance convinced Thompson that, through his deliberate efforts to remain mobile, he'd managed to elude his killer. He'd seen no sign of Phythian since he'd left the hotel, and was growing increasingly confident that he'd lost him. The downside was that he had no clue where he might be, no leads to go on other than the encrypted dossier he'd received last night. It was a particularly comprehensive profile, detailing his history with the G3, offering insight into his incredible skillset. All of which was horseshit; no way was the asshole capable of half the things that were mentioned. The demonstration he'd witnessed twenty years ago at The Farm must have been a fluke, and not replicable under scientific conditions.

Which brought him back to his immediate challenge: before he could take any sort of action, he needed to find the motherfucker.

Phythian absorbed this entire thought process from just fifty yards across the Champs-Élysées. He didn't have the former British Army major in his line of sight, but he knew where the assassin was: standing on the sidewalk in front of the Porsche dealership, admiring the lime green 911 GT3 sitting in the center of the display floor. A small throng of admirers was gathered around the vehicle inside the showroom, fantasizing about touching their feet to the accelerator and shifting the PDK dual-clutch transmission. Thompson was familiar with the vehicle, five hundred two horsepower, three hundred forty-six-foot pounds of torque. It could zero-wheelspin launch to 30 miles per hour in one second.

Phythian sensed all of this as the disgraced major pushed one of the two double glass doors open and wandered inside, trying to appear like any other window shopper admiring the merchandise. The other people staring at the GT3 were mostly tourists, American and German and Italian accents giving them away. They admired the car's curves, fondled the soft leather as they slid in and out of the driver's seat. They ran their palms over the brushed aluminum trim, gripped the undersized wheel, reached down for the Alcantara shift knob, pretending they were doing two hundred kph on the Autobahn.

Eventually it was Thompson's turn to climb into the car, get a feel for how he fit behind the wheel. A half million dollars had just landed in his bank, and an equal amount would join it as soon as his current business here in Paris was finished. At that very second, however, he felt a vibration in his pocket, from the encrypted phone to which only one other person knew the number. *Fuck...now what?* he thought as he backed away from the vehicle.

"What?" he barked into the device as soon as he was back out on the sidewalk.

"Death, the great leveler. Not even the gods can defend a man, not even one they love, that day when fate takes hold and lays him out at last."

Jesus H. Christ: It was Phythian, quoting the fucking *Odyssey* again. "What the hell do you want?" he said, lowering his voice so no one in the showroom could hear his anger as he pushed his way back outside to the sidewalk. "Where are you?"

"The GT3 is a beautiful driving machine," Phythian replied, toying with him. "You can actually order those seats with matching green hand-stitching, you know."

Shit. The sonofabitch was here, somewhere, and could see what he was doing—*right now*, mingling with all the tourists and lovers and business people crowding the broad boulevard. Thompson was disciplined enough not to glance around and try to spot him; that would only betray the calm demeanor he was trying to maintain, and unmask the near-panic that had returned in an instant.

"It's not good form to stalk a man," he said.

"Wherever you go, there I am," Phythian replied. "But you already know that, if you read my dossier. They did send it, didn't they?"

"What do you want, *Rōnin*?" Putting undue emphasis on his given name, as if meant as an insult. "What kind of name is that, anyway?"

"It derives from the Japanese word for a samurai without a lord or master, and thus left unconstrained to kill at will," Phythian explained. "It's all there in my file, which you really should have studied. Now, let's get down to business."

Thompson shifted his eyes left to right, trying to spot his quarry without turning his head. There: the man across the street in a brown suede jacket, plaid cap perched on his head…could that be him?

"And what business might that be?" he asked. Wondering, *how the fuck did the bastard get access to this phone*?

"Please, Major…we both know you've been hired to kill me," Phythian answered. "And to answer your other question, the number I called came to me directly from your frontal lobe, where most of your cognition occurs."

Damn, the motherfucker was way more nimble than I thought.

"The rumors are true, aren't they?" Thompson inquired.

"You're stalling, but I'll play along. What rumors?"

"You dismantled the G3, didn't you? Took out everyone in the corner office."

"The least of my sins, believe me. But you are correct: the G3 no longer exists. At least not as a going concern. Of course, another opportunistic party was bound to come along at some point and take its place, hence the reason for your little junket here to Paris three days ago."

"What do you know about that?"

"I know you killed Gabrielle Lamoines. And now you're trying to kill me."

There was no point in denying what Phythian was saying. The *freaking psycho* had pulled every byte of this information right from his brain, and there was absolutely nothing he could do to stanch the flow, nothing he could do about much of anything, although he was loath to admit it at this point. As Aristotle supposedly said, hope is a waking dream.

"If you know all that, you also must know I'm not the only one looking for you," Thompson conceded.

"I'd expect nothing less," Phythian said, with a shrug Thompson couldn't see. "Five million dollars is a lot of bread, although I understand you're only being paid one. Seems to me your pimp is holding out on you."

This price differential clearly was news to Thompson, and he had no snappy rejoinder. "Like I asked a minute ago, what do you want?" he said instead.

Phythian sensed a thin wave of fear sweep through the former major's nervous system. "It's not so much what I want, as what you're going to do," he explained, then ended the call.

Thompson's first instinct was to throw the phone into the stream of traffic, but he didn't want to give Phythian the satisfaction of seeing his anger boil over. Plus, the device was his only line of communication with his employer, who would not understand why he'd destroyed it in a fit of rage.

Instead, he jammed it in his pocket and began wandering up the wide promenade alongside the Champs-Élysées, lined with a double row of elm trees on each side known as the *Grand Cours*. He'd been here before, many years ago, and recalled that it was particularly lovely during Christmastime, with hundreds of thousands of brilliant lights of all colors seeming to drip from the barren branches.

It was a particularly pleasant evening, and oddly he found himself no longer thinking about Phythian. There was no more panic, no obsession with how the former assassin—actually, it seemed, still very much active—had tracked him down and obtained his phone number. None of that seemed to matter now as the aroma of cheese and crepes and *café au lait* met his nose, and he began to feel a sense of nostalgia. Ennui mixed with a thread of sadness as he recalled that other time he'd walked along this beautiful boulevard in the City of Light, arm in arm with a beautiful young woman he had met while on leave from the army. He had fallen head over heels in love with her, but he feared she didn't feel the same for him—and that whatever their relationship might be, it would end on a sour note.

It had been early December, and her name was Chantelle. She was from Ghent, and was visiting Paris on a weekend holiday from university. They had shared a first kiss in front of a store—right there, he thought with a pang of sorrow—that now was a Sephora outlet, too many years ago to calculate, more than half a lifetime. The kiss had been brief; little more than just a peck, and lacking any real passion, at least on her part. He had wanted more, but knew better than to press any further. Instead, he had taken her hand and they had strolled along the sidewalk, dodging pedestrians either heading home from work or hustling to meet a friend for a drink, or perhaps dinner.

Now as then, he found himself wandering toward the Arc de Triomphe, where he had kissed her next. They had stood in line for a half hour before paying what seemed like an exorbitant fee to climb the stairs to the observation deck at the top. They both had been out of breath when they squeezed out through the passageway and took in the view that stretched all the way from the Eiffel Tower to the Sacré Coeur. Thompson had grabbed her right then, and she had not protested his impromptu smooch, which he'd been planning since the last one.

Now, he found himself inexplicably heading down the stairs to the passageway beneath the busy Place de Charles de Gaulle that encircled the monument. Perhaps it was just the nostalgic yearning for a time gone by, or a lingering sense of unfinished business all these years later. He had not seen or heard from the lovely Chantelle after that bittersweet weekend, and he often wondered what had become of her. Did she remain in Ghent? Was she someone's wife, perhaps a mother? Maybe she had a marriage that had grown stale and would welcome a call from an old friend after all these years…

Never once did he think his growing melancholy was part of a gentle nudge from Phythian, who was keeping his distance on the other side of the avenue. At that very moment he was tapping into a deep reservoir of emotions in Thompson's brain, guiding his actions as he now emerged from the pedestrian tunnel and joined a crowd of tourists milling about the circular plaza in the center of the Etoile.

The line to enter the towering limestone arch was shorter than last time, but the price of a ticket remained exorbitant. No matter: he was a millionaire many times over, and the tug of memory was growing stronger by the moment. He paid cash and joined the queue edging toward the stairway.

He climbed upwards one slow step at a time—two hundred eighty-four of them, he remembered—and again was nearly breathless by the time he reached the top. The sense of melancholy was greater now as he realized there would be no sudden kiss, no hand to hold. There would be no future with a beautiful Belgian girl to consider; just a darkness that continued to press on him, envelop him with an inconsolable feeling that life long ago had passed him by, and all that he had done from birth until now had been for nothing.

He stood there on the roof of the monument, gazed out at the city that extended to the horizon in all directions. He was drawn to the side that looked back down the Avenue des Champs-Élysées past Place de la Concorde and peered wistfully through the metallic blades of the suicide-prevention barrier—*was that here last time*?—to the Louvres in the distance. Aside from the magnificence of the mountains near his home in Switzerland, it was perhaps the loveliest view he had ever beheld—and, at just a little over five feet in height, the barricade didn't look that formidable.

In fact, it almost seemed to be challenging him.

Phythian didn't watch him jump. He knew it was coming, but turned away just moments before it happened in order to study a cinema marquee halfway down the block. The screams coming from the direction of the Arc de Triomphe told him all he needed to know.

"Fly, dotard fly…with thy wise dreams, and fables of the sky," he quoted once again, just as he had all those years ago at The Farm. Except this time, he kept the words between himself and the cool evening breeze.

He turned and casually headed around the Etoile to the far side of the monument; no need to look at the cause of the commotion. He kept his head down as he walked, in the event that one of several dozen cameras located around the monument might trigger a facial recognition algorithm that could place him at the scene of a tragic suicide: his old *modus operandi*, which could trigger questions he'd rather avoid.

His business here in Paris done, his thoughts turned to Utuliva. It was as far from the madding crowd as he could get and maintain whatever filament of normalcy he'd salvaged from a life that for too many years had been tied to death. It was an oasis of beauty and elegance that was a world away from the greed and human discord that was growing uglier at every turn.

His immediate destination was Neuilly-Porte Maillot, the same bus station that had been his port of entry in Paris not quite three days ago. It was a short stroll, and from there he would purchase a ticket to Paris Beauvais Aéroport, from which he could catch a flight that would have him off this continent and on another in five hours.

Twenty-four hours from now he would be nursing a glass of a local Tanzanian Syrah and watching the zebras and steenboks graze in his front yard.

The instant he felt his phone vibrate in his pocket he knew he was going to have to put those plans on hold.

"Beaudin," he said after glancing at the screen.

"Hope I didn't catch you in the middle of something," the locksmith replied from the cozy library above his shop in the capital city of a small country in the center of the Pyrenees.

"Just wrapped up that matter we discussed earlier. What's up?"

Beaudin hesitated, decided not to inquire about any details, thinking the less he knew, the better. "I just now received a phone call from a very reliable source," he said.

"And this source…why was he calling?"

"He's a she, and she owes me one."

"And—?" Phythian asked, impatience in his voice.

Beaudin took a moment to clear his throat, then said. "She knows who took out the contract on Mlle Lamoines."

"And she just called you up out of the blue and gave you this information?"

"I contacted her. She's in the position to know a great many things, where a great number of bodies are buried. She didn't have to dig very deep for this one."

"Are you going to tell me who it was?" Phythian inquired.

This time Beaudin gave a little cough before saying, "Georgy Sokolov."

Phythian recognized the name, and it brought the faintest of smiles to his face. Sokolov was one of the oligarchs who had not fared well when the west had lowered the boom on some of the Kremlin's closest comrades because of the Ukraine matter. Ironically, he also was the father of the arrogant young poacher who'd been about to bring down a magnificent African elephant two years ago in the Tanzanian National Park when he—Phythian—had fired a .50 BMG bullet through his spine. In a misguided attempt to seek revenge, Sokolov had sent an advance team to track down and identify his son's killer, while also dispatching a professional sniper to take him down in very much the same way as he had done to the Russian hunter.

Things had not gone well for her, or her two spotters.

"Your source is sure about this?"

"Yes, sir. She has sources of her own who owe *her*."

Information truly was the currency of the world. "Do we know why?" he asked.

"Something to do with Mlle Lamoines' investigation into Sokolov's finances, and his connection to a man named Alessandro Bortolotti."

Shit. Arnaud Clement had been right. Gabrielle had developed a fascination with the Italian far-right nationalist and the neo-fascist movement across Europe he was fomenting. She'd aired a segment about it on her show, which had resulted in death threats.

"You're certain of this?" he asked.

"I have every reason to believe her, *oui*. And there's something else you should know."

"What's that?"

"This Bortolotti…he allegedly tried to attack the G20 meeting in Rome a few hours ago. Things didn't go according to plan and…well, he was killed in an armed raid."

"Do we know where Sokolov is now?" Phythian asked. "Russia, I presume?"

"Actually, he's fallen out of favor with the Kremlin," Beaudin said. "And all of his known assets and real estate have been seized. But I'm told he has a place on Ibiza no one knows about, at least not until now."

"And you think he's there?"

"My source does."

"Good to know. Text me whatever you have. And Beaudin?"

"*Oui, monsieur?*"

"Did you ever look at what was on that SD card you found?"

"No, sir. Do you want me to do that now?"

"Absolutely not. Don't touch it, not until I give you further directions."

"Of course. Anything else?"

"*Oui*," Phythian told him. "*Merci beaucoup.*"

Phythian ended the call, then opened a travel app as he continued his stroll up the boulevard toward the shuttle bus station. He typed in "Paris to Ibiza—one-way" and hit "search," then waited until the program told him the next non-stop left PBA in a couple hours, and would land him on the island a little after ten.

He hit "select" and entered in the credit card info for Mason Graham from Malta that he'd pulled from Thompson's brain just a few hours ago, as he sat at the outdoor café sipping that ghastly sugar drink.

As Shakespeare once noted, *Make use of time, let not advantage slip*.

Part IV

Prestissimo

Chapter 35

Georgy Sokolov stood in the darkened doorway of the grand salon that opened out to the pool. He gazed at the crease of sky against sea in the distance, a contrast of black against black, disturbed only by the lights of a cruise ship flickering in the vast void beyond. In a few hours the sun would begin to outline the hill behind him, but for now it truly was the darkest before the dawn.

The massive room was obscured in shadow, all the lights having been extinguished hours ago. Yesterday had been long and tedious, beginning with the disappearance of the girl and the death of one of the guards—a fitting punishment for allowing a fourteen-year-old to outwit him and flee, less than a week after the last one had taken her own life. The fool had just about cost Sokolov his prize doll, whose reserve bid had just increased to a million-five.

Fortunately, the padre at the church had turned her over to Nataliya, and a generous donation in the name of Catedral la Santa Lucía des Cubells would cause him to forget the brief encounter.

Almost as troubling was the news that Alessandro Bortolotti's attempted revolution had been put down by a joint force of military and local security agencies. According to reporters on the scene, over a thousand nationalist revolutionaries had conspired to attack and kill as many G20 leaders as possible, and might have succeeded had it not been for a counter-intelligence operation that had infiltrated Il Duce's ultra-right-wing movement. News reports stated that a confidential informant had provided invaluable information of the plot, and the scheme had been quelled almost before it began. Hundreds of insurrectionists had been arrested, troops had been mobilized, the city was under curfew, and Bortolotti himself had plunged to his death.

Such irony, Sokolov thought: *the fall of ViValDi.*

It almost would have been comical, had he not secretly invested millions of dollars he couldn't afford into Bortolotti's jingoistic crusade of conspiracy and violence. Such sweet payback it would have been, watching the crooked globalists who had stripped him of his assets being tortured and killed in a mass execution witnessed by billions of people around the world.

Such a beautiful outcome, however, was not to be. The fates had manipulated destiny and concocted a different result, hence the increased importance of the coming auction, the scrappy American *shlyukha* in the basement being the ultimate payout.

"Mr. Sokolov."

The abrupt voice behind him caused him to wheel around, his hand reaching inside his robe for a gun that wasn't there. He'd left it upstairs when he'd retreated to bed earlier, and had failed to bring it with him when tonight's bout of insomnia hit. He spotted a figure standing in the doorway that led down a long hallway to the villa's luxurious guest wing, said, "*Kto ty?*" in Russian. Who are you?

A man emerged from the shadows, hands out to his side to demonstrate he was not a threat. "I apologize for startling you," he said in English, with an American accent. "I couldn't sleep. Jet lag from the flight over. Name's Thomas Knox, from Tulsa, Oklahoma."

"Mr. Knox…good to see you," Sokolov greeted him. Wary, wondering why the guy was up and exploring the house at such an early hour—or late, depending on one's nocturnal habits. "Please make yourself home. There's a particularly smooth eighteen-year-old Macallan in the library, if you'd like a nightcap."

"Eighteen years…old enough to know better," the man who called himself Knox replied.

"Aren't we all," the Russian replied, the glint in his eyes indicating understood the joke.

Knox chuckled, allowing an anxious second or two to pass before asking, "How did they miss this place, when they seized everything else of yours?"

It wasn't a question Sokolov was expecting, and for a brief moment he didn't recall inviting anyone from Tulsa to attend the auction—not online, and certainly not in person. This caused him to wonder, just for a fleeting second, if this visitor from America was more than he represented himself to be.

"Not mine," he said. "Belongs to friend of friend."

"It's good to have the right friends," Knox replied, with a nod. "And I apologize if I awakened you with my insomnia. Time to go to bed."

"Relax and enjoy. See you tomorrow by pool."

"I'm afraid I forgot to pack my swim trunks."

"Is optional," Sokolov told him with a wink. "Night-night."

Rōnin Phythian gripped the Russian's shoulder in a show of camaraderie, then turned and walked back outside to the expansive stone terrazzo.

He'd found the door wide open when he'd arrived a few hours ago, in search of a place to grab a little sleep after his nonstop flight from Paris. The cut-rate airline boasted no frills, but the flight attendant had managed to produce a split of passable Bordeaux that he'd made last from wheels-up to touchdown. He'd then mentally cajoled a cab driver to take him on what turned out to be a bumpy journey up to the villa, plenty of sharp curves and rocky outcroppings that caused the man behind the wheel to ride the brakes and curse a lot.

After being dropped off outside the locked gate, Phythian had worked his way around the eight-foot stone wall to the jagged rocks at the perimeter of the estate. After satisfying himself that there were no surveillance cameras or motion sensors, he slowly picked his way through scrub and cacti at the edge of the cliff. He had only the stars above and a few solar-powered patio lights to guide him, and his eyes easily adjusted to the darkness as he moved in near-silence. Eventually he'd come to the pool, where a few guests were still milling about, after-dinner drinks or glowing blunts in hand, enjoying the remnants of the night. Rather than wait them out, he simply elicited a mental push that gently induced them to retire early, and go to their rooms.

Once they were all gone and the house lights dimmed, he'd found a particularly comfortable chaise lounge that reminded him of the evenings he would sleep under the stars on his elevated deck, only the glow from the Milky Way above disrupting the darkness that stretched out as far as his eyes could take him. He'd already run a quick mental assessment of the villa: sixteen people on the premises, thirteen men and three women, including Sokolov and his lover, a former prostitute named Nataliya. This didn't include the two armed guards, assigned to protect a valuable asset that was stashed somewhere in the bowels of the building.

Initially, Phythian had come here for one reason only: to terminate the Russian oligarch who had put the hit out on Gabrielle Lamoines, but that was before he'd entered the grounds and realized something was not right about this place. After spending just five minutes inside the confines of the opulent residence, he was convinced that no one was here for virtuous purposes. All of them were possessed of black hearts and Cimmerian souls, except for one person—man or woman he couldn't yet determine—whose mind was so fogged by medications, that Phythian had no idea where he or she might be.

One thing was certain: nasty shit was about to go down in this den of inequity—something evil that superseded his mission to execute Sokolov, and he vowed to get to the core of it.

Abigail Evans sensed a shift in the air, much the way animals can feel the barometric pressure drop in advance of a storm, or maybe the infinitesimal slip of a fault line just before an earthquake.

The room was black as ebony, so she couldn't see a thing. Her wrists and ankles—just about everything—were bound to the rails of her bed, so she had nothing to touch. The juice that was dripping through the tube and into her neck kept pain at bay and her brain in a stupefied waltz that just swept her around and around in a dreamless state of paralysis.

Anesthetized as she was, she felt a cloying sense that things in this wretched place were about to change.

She'd seized upon a chance to escape from all this, and had come close…which, as her dad would say, counts only with horseshoes and hand grenades. She could hear the words now, his voice warm and attentive and rich, never condescending or mansplaining. Even when he'd found her making out with Jagger in the garage a week before they'd flown to Rome, and he'd said, "You're too young to be dating someone his age."

Abby wished she could flip a time switch and get a re-do. If she could reverse her life to three days ago, close her eyes and click her slippers together, she could be back in a black-and-white world that existed before she'd been tossed into this Technicolor nightmare.

That was not a possibility; the total deprivation of all her senses was sucking any fragment of resolve from her body, and the dispiriting realization of the future that lay ahead was causing her to lose all hope. Never before in her entire life had she felt so empty, so depressed to the point of sheer desolation and sorrow.

All she wanted was to just curl up and die.

Chapter 36

The last vehicle bearing guests arrived at the villa shortly before noon.

Phythian watched from the terrazzo as the black Range Rover pulled through the main gate and discharged a man and woman who both appeared in their fifties. He was dressed in jeans and a black sport coat over a gray T-shirt, she in a strapless floral dress cinched with a shiny white belt—leather sandals with dragonflies on them, and a broad-brimmed sun hat.

The mistress of the house—a woman whose name he'd determined was Nataliya—emerged through the front door to greet them, wearing painted-on jeans and a backless chainmail blouse with a deeply draped neckline. It looked cheap and sleazy, but she had a role to play, and her outfit oozed sexuality and desire.

He had seen her last night, on the periphery, playing hostess and exchanging pleasantries with the other visitors. This morning she had huddled several times with Sokolov, and they'd engaged in a harsh exchange of words. The dispute had to do with the seating chart for the dinner, and the event that was scheduled to follow. It was to be an auction of some sort, the centerpiece of which was someone the Russian referred to as *shlyukha*, but which Phythian knew meant whore—indicating the person being held captive deep within the estate was a woman.

To be more precise, a young girl.

The new arrivals were led inside to their guest suite, to make themselves comfortable. They had arrived at the perfect time—lunch was to be served in half an hour—and Nataliya invited them to come out to the pool terrace when they were all settled in. "Please, make sure your stay at Sol y Mar is as perfect as perfect could be," she told them.

Behind her pleasant demeanor, however, she was flustered—agitated, really, because Sokolov himself was agitated. It seemed several guests who had RSVP'd to participate in the auction later—one online, one in person—had pulled out, which had put him in a bad mood. One of them was a Japanese high-roller whom the Russian had been counting on to drive up the bidding, while the other no-show was a Swedish hacker named Sten Gustafsson-Jeglum. Unfortunately, he had been arrested that morning by Interpol agents at Orly Airport, and was being held on a variety of criminal charges that included sexual assault. It was an unexpected circumstance that had caused Phythian to crack the thinnest of smiles.

A few minutes later, Nataliya remerged from the villa with a set of windchimes in her hand. She hesitated a moment, then gently struck them with a thin bamboo wand. The gentle tinkling caused the guests mingling near the pool to glance her way, and she said, "Dearest friends, luncheon is served on the terrace. Please join us for a meal guaranteed to be an explosion of delicacies and delights."

Phythian was still wearing the clothes he'd dressed in yesterday morning: brown jacket over gray khakis and a button-down shirt with a blue and black pattern in it. Whatever else he'd brought with him from Utuliva to Cyprus to Paris he'd left behind in his tiny room in Pigalle. Jantine Hamel could do with them as she wanted, and he'd tucked two hundred-Euro notes in a place where she'd be sure to find them. All he had was what he had on his back and in his pockets, including his wallet and passport.

Now he knew how Jack Reacher felt.

People began to slowly move to the far side of the sprawling pool terrace, where five tables of four had been set up against a backdrop of whitewater crashing on the rocks below, and the deep blue Mediterranean that reached all the way out to the horizon. Throughout the morning he'd easily picked every brain in the place, a subtle exercise that provided him just enough knowledge to speak with the guests about metal commodities, international shipping tariffs, and the worsening drought in the Amazon basin. As he drifted with the others toward the luncheon tables, he drew the eyes of both Nataliya Moisie and Georgy Sokolov. Both were wondering the same thing: *who the fuck is this guy*? Gate crasher? Caterer? Neighbor? Interloper?

Neither of them figured on assassin, and Phythian quickly dissuaded them of any notion of impropriety by again introducing himself. "Good day to you both," he said, first to the Russian, and then to his girlfriend. "Again, I apologize for whatever surprise I might have caused last night."

"No worries, Mr. Knox," Sokolov greeted him, any lingering confusion about his identity fading as quickly as it had formed. "I trust the eighteen-year-old from Scotland was most comforting?"

"As they always are," Phythian replied with a chuckle. "And I thank you again for inviting me to join you at your humble abode."

"My pleasure. Make self at home."

"Anything you want, just ask," Nataliya added.

"How could I want any more than this?" Phythian asked, broadly sweeping his hand in a gesture that indicated everything as far as the eye could see, detecting just a hint of suspicion in her mind, one that dissipated with just another slight mental nudge.

"Are you finding your accommodations comfortable?" she asked him.

"Beyond superb," he assured her. "Your hospitality exceeds all expectations."

Sokolov made a grunting noise that Phythian took as a throaty Russian compliment. Then Nataliya took him by the elbow and said, "Come with me and I'll introduce you to the Cardosos," nodding at the man and woman who had gotten out of the black SUV earlier and now were coming outside to join the party.

"Of course," he replied. "It would be my pleasure."

Lunch begat siestas which, in turn, begat swim time, clothing optional. Cocktail hour followed shortly thereafter, a bright part of the day that the guests—mostly men but a few women—greeted with a costume change. Casual attire evolved to evening refinement, and even Phythian dressed for the hour, appearing in a dark gray sport coat and slacks, white shirt. All of it was courtesy of a guest who swore the two of them had met on a trip to Patagonia a few years back—so glad to see him again…what a coincidence…such a small world.

"Anything of mine is yours," he'd offered. "Please."

An open bar had been set up at the corner of the pool patio. Phythian would have enjoyed a glass of Armagnac, but settled on soda water with a twist of lemon. He needed to maintain mental clarity, and experience had taught him alcohol was not his friend when he was on the clock. A server in maroon skirt and white ruffled blouse, black choker collar, worked her way through the small crowd with a tray of caviar on toasted brioche, but he turned that down, as well.

In a different corner of the patio a quartet of young women—violin, viola, cello, and flute—was playing the *allegro non molto* beginning of *L'Inverno*, more commonly known as the winter concerto of Vivaldi's Four Seasons. The notion of snowflakes whirling in a gathering maelstrom seemed contrary to the warm sun that had baked the earth earlier, releasing an aroma of wild sage and olive leaves.

Phythian sensed the excitement building among the gathered guests. A total of sixteen, and he knew all there was to know about them: their businesses and net worth, their spouses and lovers, their pieds-à-terre in London and chateaus on the Cote d'Azur. Hard to keep them all straight, but he doubted that would make much difference as the evening evolved into night, and a dinner of roasted suckling lamb with arroz marinera eventually segued into cigars and after dinner drinks.

Then it pivoted to the main event.

In all the years Nataliya had spent with Sokolov, she could not remember a single occasion that had been so rattling and exasperating as the last seven days.

The entire week had been hell on earth, ever since the young girl from Copenhagen had been found dead on the rocks beneath the horizon pool, where she had flung herself after inexplicably managing to escape from the cabana in which she'd been held captive. Her name was Emma Sørensen, and she'd come to the villa by way of Barcelona, where she had been scooped up from the crowd that was gathered in front of Gaudi's *Sagrada de Familia*. She had been the intended centerpiece of tonight's auction, but her death had caused Nataliya to improvise, one of many talents she'd acquired over the years.

Poor Emma's disappearance would remain a mystery forever.

No matter: that was then, and right now she had a girl just shy of fifteen to prep for her high-end debut, a girl who was heavily medicated, in dire need of a bath, and whose face would require at least an hour of serious painting in order to prepare her for her red carpet entrance.

"Go...leave us in peace," Nataliya told the guard seated on a chair outside her room. "On order of the *tsar* himself." Sokolov was known by many names, a good number of them not the least bit flattering, but he preferred the one that hinted at the old order of power and influence within the Russian hierarchy.

"Gladly," the sentry said as he gave up his post. "Be careful in there. She's a wild one."

"You'd better not have touched her—"

"And risk my *yaichki* for a drugged-out piece of ass? Fuck that."

Nataliya waited a moment for him to walk to the end of the subterranean hallway, then pressed her thumb to the touch screen embedded in the wall to the side of the door. A second later a red light turned to green and the lock clicked, popping the steel slab open a fraction of an inch. She flicked the light on, bathing the interior in a harsh white glow, then slipped inside and tugged it closed behind her.

She made a point of not looking at the bloody stain where the guard had died as she entered. Instead, she let her eyes fall on the withered waif lying in the bed positioned against the far wall. Abby looked so small, so frail compared to the girl she had dragged out of the church yesterday. Her lips seemed wilted and colorless, and her skin resembled uncooked pizza dough. Her eyes were open, but there was no indication of life in them. One pupil looked larger than the other, and she barely blinked. Not a nerve in her face twitched, and she made a dry, wheezing sound with every breath she exhaled.

This was not the visage of a sensual nymph who would fetch the hefty opening bid Georgy Sokolov was expecting two hours from now.

Nataliya had her work cut out for her, beginning with a drip of epinephrine directly into Abby's IV line. Barring any side effects—of which there were many—the girl should emerge from her opioid stupor in a manner of seconds, and the vial of cocaine she had in her pocket was enough to keep her mood elevated for the rest of the evening.

For now, however, it was best to keep her subdued. It would be easier to apply her make-up that way, then clothe her in the hooker outfit she'd ordered just for this special occasion: a shimmery burgundy wrap dress, backless with spaghetti straps and an inviting slit all the way up her thigh. Decidedly daring and sensual, pushing right up to the edge of erotic but not quite slipping over the line of obscenity. Everything about tonight was designed to have the five dozen participants—both here at Sol y Mar and around the world—bidding in the millions to be the first to take her to bed. Then she would be passed on to the next-highest bidder, and then the next, and the next. All the way down the line.

Chapter 37

"Rules are simple," Sokolov announced seventy minutes later, standing on a podium that had been erected in a corner of the grand salon.

He was speaking to a closed loop of sixty invited guests, sixteen of them seated in chairs in front of him, numbered paddles in one hand and an after-dinner drink in the other. Smoking was not allowed inside, so those who preferred cigars or pipes had been encouraged to partake earlier on the terrazzo. The forty-four off-site players were displayed on an eighty-inch screen set off to the right of the stage. Each of them was patched in from their secure location on all six populated continents via an encrypted dark web router. A total of fifty-four men, six women; after all, this was an equal opportunity event, no questions asked and no judgment rendered.

Sokolov enjoyed a sip of Absinthe, which mixed marvelously well with the lines of blow he'd done just before coming up on the dais. Dinner had ended well over an hour ago, and the last of the caterers and kitchen help had long since departed, the same with the string quartet.

"Bidding begins at two million," he continued, his eyes fixed on the camera in the aisle between the two sections of chairs, playing to the audience at home. "Euros, not dollars. Each of you is allocated three bids: opening offer, one subsequent counter, and then final price—after which you will be locked out of competition. This helps move auction along by eliminating small, incremental bidding and—frankly—identifying those who have greatest interest and incentive. Questions so far?"

It appeared there weren't any, not from anyone in the audience, nor in the grid pattern on the eighty-inch screen at the front of the room.

"Okay...we continue. Winner will receive princess tonight, if you are here. Or within twenty-four hours, if you bid online. She will fly to you by private jet, expenses included in price. She is yours for one full day and night, then back on jet for transport to runner-up. Another day and night, then jet to third place. Until last bidder is done."

At that point a man in the front row raised his auction paddle high in the air.

Sokolov leveled a glare at him and said, "Kasim, you have question?"

"Can we bid for keeps?" he asked.

"I don't know what 'for keeps' means. Please explain."

"Can I pay a premium to keep her to myself?"

"Is contrary to spirit of game," Sokolov replied, shaking his head.

"Then what becomes of princess once the *game* is over?"

"I have private buyer for seasoned *shlyukha*." The Saudi named Kasim looked confused by the Russian colloquialism, so Sokolov added, "Look it up later."

"When do we get to see her?" inquired a man on the video grid, third from the left in the second row.

"As soon as we are finished with rules," Sokolov assured him. "Once you have made your final bid, you will leave room. Or, if bidding online, feed will be cut. That way you not know outcome after you make last offer. You will be notified of your place in line, and approximate date private jet shall deliver princess."

"How can we be guaranteed she is untouched, as you have promised?" This question came from an industrialist from Brazil, who had made his fortune in copper.

"A common question, and those experienced in female physiology will know for certain," the Russian explained. "If you are top bidder, that is. After that, is of no consequence. But so you know, licensed gynecologist has performed examination, and has certified inspection."

Nataliya was neither a gynecologist nor licensed in anything but driving, but no one playing tonight's game need ever know that. Despite their host's enumeration of the rules, there actually were very few of them. The auction was an obscene display of lubricious debauchery, a depraved violation of the flesh that to all those participating—both at the villa and playing at home—made it that much more tempting. It was assumed by everyone in the room that the girl they were about to vie for was not here of her own free will, and one participant—the founder of one of the world's largest pharmaceutical firms bidding from his penthouse in Rome—might actually recognize her from local newscasts.

While this was not the first of Sokolov's deranged events, Phythian—sitting near the wall and nursing his fourth soda water of the evening—was damned sure going to make it the last.

Crown Princess Abigail, as Sokolov introduced her, was carried in on a gold litter draped with silk and festooned with brightly colored jewels. She actually wore a cubic zirconia tiara on her head, a last-minute afterthought that came from Etsy. She was seated on a large, fluffy pillow, the wrap dress clinging to every inch of her body the way Nataliya imagined it when she'd ordered it.

She was drugged to the max, the coke giving her an energy rush that enhanced the smoothness of the oxy that lingered in her system. The drip of synthetic adrenaline had dissipated a while ago, but she likely would remain docile long after the winning bidder made his—or her—final offer. After that, things were known to get dicey, but the auction's participants were well aware there might be mood swings or conflicts of the will. Displays of resistance were not uncommon, and had become a source of enjoyment for those in attendance.

Abigail Evans really did look lovely. The dress and pearl earrings and mascara, just a little rouge and a touch of lipstick, made her appear both younger and older at the same time—wizened to the world, yet innocent at heart. Young curves, exposed thigh and bosom: the awakening of a young woman's innocence made her appear to be Professor Humbert's ideal Lolita, in the flesh.

Sokolov stood to the side of the podium while his players assessed, ogled, and leered. He wanted to give them ample time to assess her natural sensuality, imagine the scent of her skin as she lay with them, and anticipate the sexual pleasure that awaited each potential suitor at the end of tonight's game, enjoying this young specimen of desire in turn, one by one.

It was all Phythian could do to just sit there impassively and let it play out.

"The first round of bidding will begin in five minutes," Sokolov told the live audience and those watching at home. "And just a reminder: if any of you find that our beautiful princess tonight is not to your satisfaction, you may leave now. No questions asked, no insult taken. And your deposit will be returned to your bank account within twenty-four hours. Anyone?"

No one in the room moved, but after a couple seconds three of the faces on the digital screen blinked out.

"All right, then," Sokolov continued. "We're down from sixty to fifty-seven, and now we know where rubber meets road."

He should have been in a celebratory mood, knowing that another of his infamous private auctions was about to commence. Instead, he felt a little melancholic, and more than a bit depressed. The feeling had begun with the onset of a headache that felt as if it were gripping the sides of his skull, somewhat like an old medieval torture device gently tightening around a prisoner's head. Was it something he'd eaten at dinner, maybe the wild mushrooms in the sauce that accompanied the lamb? Or perhaps the Chateau Margaux he'd had decanted from a bottle in his private collection?

Whatever it was, a thin wave of nausea began to undulate in his stomach, reaching well down into his intestinal tract. Cramps and the uncomfortable sensation of gas began to set in. The last thing he needed as he played auctioneer in front of all these wealthy scions of perversion was to be hit with a bout of explosive diarrhea.

He closed his eyes a moment as he tried to ride through one particularly sharp stab of pain. When he opened them, he found himself staring at Thomas Knox in the second row, who was the only person in the room other than himself not leering at the porcelain doll seated on the stage. In fact, the car dealer from *fucking America* was staring straight at him, with the slightest of smiles on his face. It reminded him of the Mona Lisa, which he'd once waited over an hour in line to see at the Louvre. All that hysteria over a small painting that really wasn't all that remarkable, although for a moment it did cause him to consider how he might go about adding it to his private collection.

"I'll be back in a few minutes," he excused himself. "Then we start."

He stepped off the stage and slipped out a door into a long hallway, at the end of which was a rest room that had been designated for the exclusive use of guests. Under normal circumstances he might have hustled upstairs to use the lavatory in his private suite, but the urgency he was starting to feel was neither normal, nor one that hustling a long distance would assuage. He only hoped it wasn't already in use, as time was of the essence.

Phythian was standing outside the door waiting when Sokolov emerged a couple minutes later.

"There's another facility next to library, if you need," the Russian told him.

Phythian waved off his advice and said, "That's not why I'm here."

The Russian narrowed his eyes and stared at him a second. "You're not really Thomas Knox, are you?" he asked.

"Only when I need to be."

"Then what the fuck you doing in my house?" He glanced around for one of the two guards who had carried his princess up onto the stage, but neither was to be found.

"Forget Ramos and Ivan," Phythian said. "They're not here."

Sokolov instinctively reached inside his jacket for the Glock he usually kept tucked into a shoulder holster, but came up empty. "*Kakogo khrena*—?" What the fuck?

"You stashed it in the waste bin on your way out just now," Phythian reminded him. "Or perhaps you don't remember."

He did, and a sudden electro-chemical reaction in his brain—errant sparks jumping across synapses—caused a tangle of confusion and panic. He tried to keep it all in check as he said, "Who are you, really? And what do you want?"

There was no need for Phythian to answer verbally, as it would have been just as easy to mentally push the answer into his brain and bypass the stilted language barrier. The Russian wanted a real answer, however, so he offered one.

"I'm the man who killed your son," he said.

"You...*what*? No fucking way. I had that *podonok* murdered—"

"Wrong. You hired a sniper to shoot me, a woman named Diana Petrie. She failed."

A flicker of rage flashed in Sokolov's eyes, and he said, "What you know of this?"

"What I know is, your son was in a place he shouldn't have been, doing something he shouldn't have been doing." Phythian glanced over his shoulder in the direction of the auction room. "Looks like it runs in the family."

"You Goddamned sonofabitch—"

He took a swing at Phythian, who knew the fist was coming well beforehand and easily sidestepped it. The force of Sokolov's follow-through was enough to throw him off balance, and he lost his footing. He thrust a hand against the wall as he stumbled, then righted himself and spun around to face his adversary.

"You don't want to do this, Sokolov," Phythian said.

Odd thing was, the Russian really didn't. He didn't want to fight, definitely didn't want the pounding migraine that seemed to be growing worse by the minute, and definitely didn't want the sharp gnawing in his gut that felt as if it were full of piranha that hadn't eaten in a month. Still, he said, "You killed my boy—"

"He was there to shoot an elephant," Phythian replied. "All I did was level the playing field a bit."

If the truth stung, Sokolov didn't show it. He'd forked over a hefty deposit for this man to be taken off the board, but the sniper had disappeared, along with her two spotters. He'd hoped they were laying low out of an abundance of caution, keeping a low profile to minimize any international blowback. Even his man in the field—Galkin—had failed to find a single trace of them.

"She was good woman," he said. "And great shot. How did she miss?"

"She didn't know who she was up against."

Sokolov let out a snort, then flashed back to when he'd identified his son's body in the morgue, eight days after his murder. The high-velocity bullet had pulverized his spine and caused considerable damage to the organs surrounding it: horrific through-and-through damage that he would never be able to un-see. "She was a good shot," he said. "One of the best."

"I had home field advantage," Phythian replied. "But we're wasting our time. The bidding is set to begin in just a moment."

A wave a dizziness compounded the nausea and the headache. Sokolov swallowed hard, then said, "Why are you here? Really?"

"You already know the answer to that, Sokolov."

"You think you're going to kill me in my own home? For what reason?"

"Gabrielle Lamoines," Phythian reminded him, squeezing the Russian's brain just a bit tighter, causing it to feel as if the skull might fracture at any second. "Tell me why."

"She had information," Sokolov said, pressing his eyes closed because of the mounting torment. "Was going to leak on television."

"Information about what?"

"What you think? Assets, houses, stuff those fucking bastards couldn't find."

"And your involvement with Bortolotti," Phythian pointed out. "That didn't turn out so well, did it?"

Sokolov was in such agony he thought he might pass out. It would be a welcome development, since that way he might escape the pain. "*Please...*I must go. Head is killing me."

"Perhaps a dip in the pool might help," Phythian suggested, gently easing the notion into his brain, until it took form as a thought of his own.

"*Da, da*...anything to make it go away."

Phythian offered him an arm under his shoulder, supported him as they labored down the hallway, then hung a right into the kitchen. Just hours earlier the place had been bustling with some of the best chefs on the island, but now it was dark and quiet. A thin aroma of broiling lamb remained, mixed with the *flaó* that had been served at dessert—still Sokolov's favorite, but he seemed not to notice now as he struggled past the still-warm eight-burner stove, leaning his weight against the man who had murdered his son in cold blood.

A doorway at the far end of the corridor led into the dining room, and beyond that was a sectioned glass wall, whose panels had been slid into pockets at either side. The effect was a massive open-air, indoor-outdoor space that extended out to the pool terrace, with the vast sea beyond. The last hint of the sun had slipped below the horizon, leaving just a ruby red glow at the edge of the world.

"The pool...quick," Sokolov said, almost begging now.

"Deep end," Phythian agreed, as he released his support of the Russian. "Full immersion works best."

"*Da*. Will ease pain."

"Release your breath and meditate. Stay under at least a minute. Maybe two."

Sokolov seemed to consider the suggestion, so Phythian pushed the concept just a little harder. "Agree," he finally said. "Is best remedy."

Not giving it a second thought, he stepped off the stone apron and slipped into the water without causing hardly a ripple. He dropped like a stone to the bottom, where he remained inert and upright while Phythian counted off the passing seconds one by one, at the same time mentally pushing him to relax and inhale a deep breath, let the water replace the air in his lungs. He watched the bubbles rise to the surface, initially coming in a rush of big globules that eventually tapered off to just a fine spritz.

At ninety-six seconds Sokolov's heart registered its last beat—a feeble little contraction—and a single, final spark of life flickered in his brain.

Then his body shut down: no cognition, no brain stem function. There was no heartbeat at all, just a fully clothed body floating in nine feet of water, his limp arms stretched out on the surface of the water at his side. The sonofabitch was dead.

Phythian returned the way they'd come, back through the dining room and kitchen to the hall. There he popped into the guest bathroom—very briefly, because Sokolov actually *had* endured a serious bowel attack—and retrieved the Glock from the waste bin. He checked the magazine: sixteen rounds, plus one in the chamber ready to go. He hoped he wouldn't need it, but armed guards were on the premises, and he knew the slutty babe named Nataliya also packed a tiny gun in her purse. Six of the evening's guests had shown up with arms of various sizes and styles, all of which had been collected with the promise that they'd be returned upon their departure. There also was a safe in the master suite upstairs that held a half dozen firearms, including a gas-operated AK-47.

That meant a lot of firepower.

A more immediate concern, however, was the auction that was late getting underway. He sensed the players growing restless, which could pose a problem when they found out their host was dead—and that no young girl from San Francisco would be going home to the highest bidder. There would be no auction tonight, not ever again. The participants online could simply click off their cameras and crawl back under their rocks, but the sixteen leering men and women in the grand salon at the end of the hall could prove to be tricky.

Phythian had maybe two minutes to carry out the *ad hoc* plan he'd devised earlier that afternoon, while everyone else was either napping or otherwise preoccupied. He took out his cellphone and called Martin Beaudin in Andorra, three hundred miles directly to the north. He'd already alerted him earlier that he might need his services, and to remain on standby for further instructions.

"Sokolov's down," he said, skipping the unnecessary chatter. "Ready to go?"

"Whenever you are," Beaudin assured him.

"We won't have much time."

"Don't need much. Just let me know when to flip the switch."

"Stand by."

Phythian ended the call, then made his way to the doorway of the salon.

There was some low chatter going on, murmurings about where Sokolov might be, what was taking so long? He slipped inside, spotted Nataliya standing in the shadows at the back of the room. As he circled around the perimeter toward her, she warily followed his every movement as he approached.

"Is everything okay, Mr. Knox?" she asked as he edged up beside her. She checked her watch, seemingly irritated that Georgy hadn't yet started the bidding.

"I've changed my mind," Phythian said. "I wish to bow out."

"The cut-off was eight o'clock," Nataliya said. "It's ten past."

"Yet the auction hasn't begun, and thus I wish to take my leave."

The last thing Nataliya needed was another setback, on top of the fact that she couldn't find Georgy anywhere. Mr. Knox from Oklahoma was right: the auction was late getting started, and he was definitely within his rights to demand that she return his deposit. All potential bidders were required to ante up five million dollars when tendering their RSVPs, with the understanding that all funds would be deposited in an independent escrow account. Any balance not spent on that evening's prize would be transferred back to the player's personal account by noon the following day.

"It's common for participants to get cold feet," she said. "Perhaps a glass of Scotch might help change your mind. Or something a little more potent—"

"Just my deposit," Phythian said. "Unless that presents a financial problem for you."

She crossed her arms—no, it definitely was not a problem—and said, "It really is against the rules, but you're right. The activities of the evening do seem to be starting later that anticipated, and I can give you a rain check. Good for any future event."

"Full cancellation, and money back," the man she knew as Knox insisted.

Nataliya usually could employ all sorts of body language to change a participant's mind, and one time she'd even engaged in quick oral sex to keep a player in the game. Tonight, however, she was too preoccupied with Georgy's whereabouts, and the car dealer from America was being unusually insistent. She hated to lose another participant from the bidding pool, but she had neither the time nor patience to negotiate with him... nor would she be able to anyway.

"Very well," she said. "You can expect your funds to be transferred to your bank from ours by noon tomorrow."

"And what bank is that?" Phythian inquired.

"A private one," she replied with a tight smile. "The deposit will be from an account that ends in six-four-four-seven."

She was referring to a financial institution in Latvia, where just a remnant of Sokolov's vast holdings had thus far eluded western sanctions. He'd asked the question only to unlock the information from her brain, which he then would provide to Martin Beaudin.

"Much obliged, and I thank you," he said. "And no worries about transportation; I'll call my car service to take me to the airport."

"As you wish," she said in that snipped voice of hers.

Phythian nodded his head in an informal bow, then made his exit the same way he'd arrived. As soon as he was back outside the salon he hit redial, got Beaudin on the first ring.

"Six-four-four-seven, AEF International in Riga," he said.

"Should be more than enough."

"Just get in and out as quick as you can," Phythian replied. "Shit's about to fly far and wide here."

"Shouldn't take me more than thirty seconds to get in…wait, I see it right there. You said six-four-four-seven, right?"

"Correct," Phythian confirmed, impatience in his voice. In all his years in the employ of the G3 he'd always worked alone: get in, set up the kill, make a smooth exit. He wasn't accustomed to dealing with so many moving parts, and it made him nervous. "How long?"

"Transferring now," Beaudin assured him. "It's not like I'm moving massive files, just shifting bits of data from one IP address to another. And…there it is. All done."

"All two-hundred eighty million?"

"That's what it looks like."

"Do you have access to the other participants' accounts, too?" Phythian asked.

"That'll take a little longer, but no one will be looking for it," Beaudin said. "Just get out of there before the apocalypse hits."

At that moment, a shrill scream from outside on the pool terrace split the night. "I think the first horseman just rode in," Phythian said into the phone. "Gotta move."

The scream originated from deep within the lungs of Nataliya Moisei, who had wandered out onto the patio in search of Georgy. The guests were growing increasingly anxious, and she was genuinely worried about him. As much as she despised him for all he'd done to her, he'd given her a life: a villa on Ibiza, baubles and clothes and expensive champagne, and a private jet that would take her anywhere in the world. She got relatively sufficient sex, even if it was rough at times, plus all the deadly sins she could handle.

All of it was because she'd been the prize of his very first auction, and he'd hung on to her after all the bids had been fulfilled.

Despite all that—maybe because of it—if anything were to happen to him, she didn't know what she would do. Where would she turn next? How would she cope that day, or the next, or the next?

Yet here he was, floating in his horizon pool, the soggy tails of his sport coat spread out like the wings of a manta ray gently undulating in the water. His form was illuminated from below by an LED light that slowly changed from blue to green to red to violet.

She screamed again, then dropped to her knees and buried her face in her hands.

No time to waste, as the shrieking out on the patio caused the bidders in the salon to scramble out of their chairs in a near-stampede to take a look. Then there would be even more screams, and plenty of shouting and cursing, too. Phythian couldn't have concocted a better distraction but, then again, he was well-schooled in how the human mind worked.

Once the auction room emptied out, the only person who hadn't moved was Abigail Evans. She remained cuffed to the bejeweled litter, eyes wide with terror, her mind just beginning to return from the land of the lost, dwelling on the fringe of hysteria, which could make the next part of his job even more difficult.

Oddly, the eighty-inch television monitor in the corner of the room still displayed the faces of the forty-two bidders who were participating from around the world. Each of them appeared confused about what was going on, since all that was visible on their computers—or whatever device they were using to tie in to the evening's event—was Sokolov's Crown Princess. No explanation of what was transpiring off-camera, no audio at all.

Phythian entered the room from the rear and flicked off the power to the lone camera. His reason for cutting the feed was two-fold: so none of these online participants could see what he was about to do, and so the video files would not reveal his presence in the room. Local, national, and global authorities would be poring over every frame for days, and it was critical that his face not show up in a single one.

It was the same reason he'd worn gloves all afternoon, and why he'd wiped his glass every time he took a sip, and pocketed the flatware he'd used for lunch and dinner. There would be no DNA, no trace evidence to worry about.

The clock was ticking. Within moments the initial shock would wear off and the police would be called. People probably were already dialing one-one-two, the Ibiza version of nine-one-one. No problem there: the sudden arrival of cars with flashing lights would cause people to panic, and chaos would ensue. The closest village was thirty minutes away, which worked in Phythian's favor, but he still needed to be as far from the villa as he could get...and so did Abby Evans.

"No," she yelped as Phythian jumped up on the stage. "Get away."

"I'm here to help you," he told her in the most encouraging vice he could muster. "I know who you are."

"Just leave me alone—"

"You're Abigail, from San Francisco," he assured her, information he'd pulled from her as she'd been ceremoniously carried into the room, despite the heavy fog that had folded in on her brain.

His words seemed to calm her, a bit. "How did you get here?" she asked.

"Long story. Come with me. I'm going to get you out of here."

The terror in her eyes didn't let up, and for a moment he was afraid she might let out a blood-curdling scream. Then Phythian's mental snare reeled her in, and the convulsions of fear seemed to ease.

"Where are you taking me?" she asked.

"Rome, with your parents. But we have to go now."

"But my cuffs—" She emphasized her plight by twisting her wrists and ankles, all of which were still locked by gold-plated restraints to the litter.

"No problem," Phythian assured her. He dug into a pocket, pulled out the ring of keys he'd lifted from Sokolov's pocket not ten minutes ago, when he'd helped him weave down the hallway toward the pool.

Unlocking all her shackles took another thirty precious seconds. As expected, she was weakened from the sensory deprivation and the IV fluids and the sheer terror, but at least she could stand on two feet.

"Are you okay to walk?" he asked her.

"I'll run a marathon if I have to," Abby replied.

Again, while others had been napping or bathing or copulating earlier in the afternoon, Phythian had been mentally mapping the house. From his very first assignment with the G3, he'd made a point of memorizing the layout of any building within which he might be called upon to operate. That way he left nothing to chance, particularly his means of egress when the job was done.

He'd counted fifty-two steps from the podium, down the hall, through the billiard room, to the side door that opened out into the cobbled driveway. The blue SUV was parked with its keys still in the ignition—something he'd gleaned from Nataliya, who had left them there under the mistaken impression that no one would dare steal it.

The first forty steps passed peacefully. Phythian could still hear the wails and sobs out by the pool, but no one had any reason to come looking for them.

He and Abby paused just inside the exterior door, and he put a hand to her lips. "There's a car right outside," he told her, his voice just a decibel above a whisper.

"A Jaguar," she replied.

"That's right. We're going to walk toward it as if nothing is wrong. If we see anyone, just get in and let me deal with it."

She nodded, and he turned the door handle, gave it a gentle push. A second later they were outside, about ten yards from the vehicle. One of the guards who earlier had carried Abby's ceremonial litter was leaning against the fender, apparently unconcerned about the commotion coming from the other side of the house. He was certainly not worried enough to lay down the smoldering joint that was dangling from one hand, or the black polymer semi-automatic pistol he held in the other.

"Who the fuck are you?" he said, quickly drawing the gun up and aiming it directly at Phythian's face.

Chapter 38

"I'm Thomas Knox," Phythian introduced himself. "Taking my angel for the ride of her life."

"What?" the confused guard said. "Auction's over already?"

"It was over almost before it started. My opening bid blew everyone out of the water."

It was a passable lie, but the sentry—named Ramos—didn't need any further convincing. He wondered how much this old fart had paid to deflower the young filly in the burgundy dress and diamond tiara pinned to her hair. How nice it must be to be rich and idle.

"Ten million-five," Phythian said, answering the question that had not been asked. "And while it's none of my business, you may want to check out what's up with all the screaming."

"Not my concern," the guard replied. "I'm off duty."

"I heard someone mention an accident at the pool. Hope one of the guests didn't go and drown."

"Oh, fuck." Ramos took another puff, then pushed his ass off the fender. The power of persuasion could be compelling, especially when it came from Phythian. "Guess I'd better go check it out."

"Good idea," Phythian assured him. "Leave the gun."

The sentry named Ramos actually had no choice in the matter, just did what this rich bastard from America said and took off at a trot. As soon as he disappeared around the corner of the villa, Phythian said to Abby, "Get in the car."

She didn't need to be told twice. She dragged herself around to the other side and managed to get the door open, then hoisted herself up into the seat. He grabbed the pistol that the guard had left on the hood, then slipped in behind the wheel.

"Buckle up," he told her.

Abby did, at the same instant Phythian keyed the engine to life. He shifted into drive and pulled forward, just as Nataliya marched around the corner of the building, steadying a gun in both hands.

"On the floor," Phythian said to Abby. "And stay there."

She did as she was told, and he tapped his foot to the gas. Nataliya was mouthing something that looked like *don't fucking move*, but it was a little late for that. He pushed his foot harder on the pedal just as she unleashed a trio of shots, resulting in a triangle of neatly placed holes that spider-webbed the windshield. It sagged in its frame but remained intact, at least for another second or two. Then the accelerating Jaguar plowed into the bitch lady from Romania, hurling her up onto the hood and smashing her face into the glass, causing it to rupture into a galaxy of stars.

Phythian hung a sharp left through the courtyard as Nataliya tumbled to the pavers. The gate was closed, and he had no way of knowing how it opened. Was it automatic, or did it have to be done manually? He found a remote control clipped to the sun visor, and when he pressed a button the iron fencing began to roll to the side.

By now a few of the evening's guests had wandered around the corner of the villa into the courtyard, saw the bloody mass where their hostess lay crumpled on the warn cobbles. Phythian caught a couple of them in the rearview mirror rushing toward the Jaguar, led by the guard named Ramos.

"Stay down," he told Abby. "This is going to be close."

He waited just inches from the gate, engine idling, until it had opened just enough for the SUV to edge through. Then he punched his foot all the way to the floor and the vehicle shot through the gap, scraping the stone wall and causing the sideview mirror to snap off. The Jag fishtailed a moment on some loose gravel as the wheels gained traction, and then it was gone.

As soon as they were clear of the villa, Phythian was back on the phone with Martin Beaudin.

"Status report?" the locksmith in Andorra inquired, getting right to it.

"Out of the lion's den. I need you to do a few things for me."

"Whatever you want."

"Find me a hospital in Ibiza. Text the address to me, along with the number for the Ibiza police. Rome, too. I may be out of range for a bit, so I'll let you know when I receive them."

"Doing it now. And Mr. Phythian? The bank transfers are confirmed."

Phythian knew Beaudin was referring to the numbered accounts of each of the evening's sixty original bidders, each of whom had fronted a five-million-dollar refundable to participate. Their financial loss actually was a small forfeiture, considering they were sexual predators who really needed to be eliminated from the world's gene pool—something Phythian would have strongly considered acting upon in the past.

But that was *before*. Before his life at Utuliva, which had introduced an Eden of peace and tranquility, and had shifted his perspective on death and dying as he watched hyenas and leopards chase down zebras and wildebeests on the vast plain that stretched out as far as the sky allowed. On the Serengeti, hunting was a matter of necessity rather than sport, and he took it upon himself to kill only when he believed it to be absolutely essential. If there was some hypocrisy in the yin and yang of his life, he suspected it would sort itself out within the natural order of the universe, if and when the time arrived.

"Good work," he said into the phone. "Get those numbers to me ASAP."

The road from Es Cubells to Ibiza Town was a paved two-lane highway.

At that hour of the night it was mostly free from traffic, and Phythian covered the twenty-minute trip in just under fifteen. He wasn't concerned about being pulled over by the local police; traffic stops had become a non-issue the day he walked out of The Farm. The lack of a windshield made the trip a little rough, a constant torrent of wind pouring into the SUV, but time was of the essence. Several emergency vehicles raced by in the opposite direction, blue roof bars flashing, a pair of ambulances trailing close behind. Definitely not soon enough to do Georgy Sokolov much good nor, in all likelihood, Nataliya Moisei.

Once he sensed he and Abby were in the clear, he said to her, "Tell me what happened in Rome."

"How do you know about that?"

"It's all over the news," he said, dodging the truth. "Your parents are worried sick about you."

She sniffed, then wiped her nose with her arm. "They're going to be so mad at me—"

"They'll be thrilled just to see you. You know they love you, right?"

Abby nodded, sniffed again. She had no way of knowing that he was rifling through her thoughts and memories, and already knew the answers to his rhetorical questions. "We were at the Trevi Fountain, and I wandered off to take a selfie," she eventually told him. "Someone came up behind me and stuck me with something, and the next thing I knew I was in some filthy, creepy room."

"Did they hurt you?" Phythian asked. He could tell she was embarrassed by the question, so he added, "You don't need to tell me. Not if you don't want to. But I'm taking you to a hospital so a doctor can take a look at you."

"I really just want to go home—"

"And you will," he assured her. "The police are going to take care of that. And the hospital is the best place for you to be until they come to get you."

"Why can't we just go to the airport?"

"You don't have a passport. And as for me...well, it's kind of complicated."

She nodded at what he was telling her, but he sensed she really didn't want to go through a full medical exam.

"Don't worry about any of that," he said. "The doctors and nurses will be very gentle. Everything's going to be fine."

"How did you know what I was thinking—?"

"It's what I'd be thinking, if I were you."

Another nod, and more silence.

"There is one thing you should know," he told her as he swerved around a rock that had rolled into the roadway. "You've become rather famous since you disappeared. Reporters are going to be everywhere you go."

"Last thing I need," she said, almost to herself.

The hand-off at the hospital went smoothly. Abby was nervous but realized—for reasons she accepted but didn't quite understand—that Phythian couldn't accompany her inside to the emergency room. No matter; he had saved her life and she didn't give a *fig* what his rationale might be. All she knew was his name was Thomas Knox, and he owned a chain of used car dealerships based in the state of Oklahoma.

As soon as he edged the blue Jaguar out of the emergency pull-through, he called the number Beaudin had given him for the local police.

The dispatcher who answered was fluent in three languages, English being one of them. He quickly filled her in on what was going on, explained that the girl who'd been kidnapped in Rome was here on the island, at the hospital on Carrer de Corona. No, he was not about to give her his name, but she could call the ER to confirm, if she felt the need. She didn't, but agreed to send a couple of officers immediately to check it out.

His next and final call went to carabinieri headquarters in Rome; same story, same initial doubts, same request for his name, same denial. Phythian told the wary voice the same thing he'd said to the police in Ibiza: contact the hospital for details.

When he was done, he turned off the burner and tossed it out the window into a dry culvert. Ten minutes later he ditched the Jag in the short-terming lot at the Ibiza International Airport, figured it was only a matter of time before someone spotted the missing windshield and called the airport police. In the glove box he found a silk scarf that probably belonged to Nataliya, and used it to wipe down the wheel, door handle, shift lever, remote control. It was critical that he sanitize everything he might have touched from the moment he'd climbed into it back at the villa, except for the fragments of glass that remained scattered throughout the interior.

He kept his head down as he followed the signs toward check-in, with only his passport and wallet in his pocket. A non-stop to Athens was leaving just after midnight, one that would have him on the ground three hours after that, with plenty of time to make his connection to Nairobi first thing in the morning.

The ticket agent had one first-class seat available. At first, she balked at accepting cash for the flight, but suddenly felt a twinge of a headache coming on, and was desperate to find some ibuprofen before it turned into migraine. If he wanted to pay the fare in paper Euros, fine with her.

Thirty minutes later he was in his seat. The flight attendant edged her way up the aisle and handed him an Armagnac he hadn't verbally requested, and inquired whether there was anything else she might be able to procure for him. Nothing at the moment, he'd replied, as he let his mind drift to Paris, wondered for a moment whether the police had identified Major Thompson's body.

Eventually his thoughts turned to Africa, as they often did when he was far from home. He closed his eyes, mentally pictured himself relaxed in his lone chair on the wood deck, glass of wine in hand as the giraffes nosed through the tops of the acacia trees just yards away. He imagined the herd of gazelles he'd spent an hour watching just the other afternoon, grazing not too far off in the distance. And the elephants: what magnificent, imposing creatures they were as they lumbered through the brush, their trunks swaying like metronomes keeping time with life on the Serengeti, their large eyes meeting his in a fleeting exchange of mutually recognized benevolence.

All of them ever wary of predators, lurking in the tall grass, waiting to attack.

How well he knew the feeling.

Part V

Coda

Chapter 39

"They've agreed to return your passport?"

That was Raleigh Durham, as her index finger danced the light fantastic down Carter Logan's chest. Her eyes drifted to the clock radio on the nightstand; she had a plane to catch, but her suitcase was already packed and she didn't seem overly worried about grabbing a cab to the airport.

"Yup," he replied, not wanting to break the mood with more words. The phone call a minute ago from General Lionetti of the Guardia di Finanza had already done that, and he was hoping to recapture the lustful bliss he'd been feeling before the device had chirped. "All I need to do is go in and sign a few papers, and then I'm free to fly home."

"What about that damned watch? They still think you stole it?"

Logan rolled his eyes at the mere mention of the thing. "They finally found it, half a mile up the street from where the guy died. Car ran over it, so they couldn't track it."

"All that for nothing," she said.

"I'd hardly call this nothing," he whispered as he pulled her on top of him.

Later, he watched her as she slipped a light rain coat over her travelling clothes. The skies above Rome were gray and gloomy, and a light drizzle was falling on the street down below her window.

"I can't get over how close you came to being killed," she said as she checked her hair in the bathroom mirror. "I don't know what I would have done."

"Me, neither," he replied, downplaying his close call, even though the shoot-out in Bortolotti's apartment was still with him twenty-four/seven. The gunshots and bullets and blood and brains and dead people lying about once the shootout had ended was a vision he would never be able to un-see, although Raleigh's magic fingers and other *modos operandi* certainly had helped distract him.

"Such a man," she snickered. "And I mean it: I don't know what I would have done if I'd had to report on the death of my...well, my absolute best friend."

"I've been promoted to *absolute*?" Logan asked her.

"A long time ago."

"Thanks for telling me," he said.

"Need to know basis," Raleigh replied as she zipped up her paisley backpack. "By the way, how'd you get your knuckles all bloody?"

"Termini," he replied.

"The metro station?"

"I ran into someone who owed me, and I...well, I collected," Logan explained with a casual shrug, not wanting to get into the details about the ticket scammer who'd ripped him off for fifty Euros the day he'd arrived in Rome.

"I don't think I want to know," Raleigh said as she pulled out the collapsible handle of her rollaboard. "And I hate to break the spell, but I really do have to go. My carriage awaits."

"Do you mind if I don't get up?"

"Done and done," she said with a chuckle. "But no, you can stay there as long as you want. At least until check-out."

"Much appreciated. See you back in DC."

"Any idea when that will be?"

"As soon as I can book a flight. Meantime I've got a story to write. Several of them, in fact."

She opened the door that led to the hallway, then turned back. "Well, break a leg. And keep an eye open for stray bullets."

"It's the ones that find their mark that I'm worried about," he told her. "Love you."

"Love you, too," she replied.

She was out the door before either of them realized what they'd both just said.

Chapter 40

TEEN KIDNAPPED AT TREVI FOUNTAIN
SAFELY RETURNED TO PARENTS

ROME – June 11 [*Associated Press*]: Abigail Evans, the 14-year-old teenager from San Francisco who was abducted at the famed Trevi Fountain five days ago, has been returned to her parents.

Police on Ibiza, part of the Balearic archipelago and a province of Spain, said Miss Evans was found at a local hospital after an unidentified male dropped her off at the emergency room. The young woman apparently had been held captive at an oceanfront villa on the west coast of the island, where her kidnappers had transported her after seizing her at the popular Roman tourist attraction. An anonymous tipster alerted the police to let them know where she could be found, and then disappeared.

Authorities are reviewing airline and cruise ship manifests, and inspecting surveillance video, to determine the individual's identity.

Ms. Evans told police she had been taking a photograph of herself at the fountain when she felt a sharp prick in her neck, and almost instantly blacked out. She awoke sometime later in an apartment, from which she was transported to an airport outside Rome and placed on a private aircraft. She said she had no idea where she had been taken until nurses at the hospital told her she was in Ibiza.

A spokesperson from Interpol said in a statement that Ms. Evans' kidnapping is believed to be one of many conducted by a sex trafficking ring headed by Georgy Sokolov, a Russian Oligarch who had been targeted by heavy sanctions levied after his country's invasion of Ukraine in 2022. He and an associate, Romanian-born Nataliya Moisei, were both found dead at the oceanfront villa from which the young woman was rescued. Investigators say they discovered evidence indicating that a human auction had been in progress when Ms. Evans and her rescuer escaped in a car registered to Gazoyl Global'nyy Ltd., a Belarussian oil and gas company that is listed as the owner of the Ibiza property.

Investigators said they seized digital files identifying all participants in the auction, and will be conducting a thorough investigation into their involvement in the proceedings, as well as their relationship to Miss Evans' abductors.

Daniel and Beverly Evans, the young woman's parents, said through their attorney that their daughter is in good medical condition and is resting comfortably. The attorney did not indicate when they will be returning to the United States, and asked for the media to respect their privacy.

Ibiza, a UNESCO World Heritage Site, is well-known for its nightlife and dance club scene...

EU ANNOUNCES INVESTIGATION INTO PLANNED G20 ATTACK

ROME – June 12 [*La Nazione de Italia*]: The European Union is spearheading an international investigation into the thwarted attack on world leaders who participated in the G20 summit in Rome last week.

Rebeka Cernak, president of the EU and a potential target of the attempted strike against democracy, announced the move at a press conference at the Commission's headquarters in Brussels. "After last week's attack on human rights and the rule of law, the European Union remains fully committed to representative democracy throughout the continent, transparency and accountability of all democratic institutions, and inclusiveness of the democratic process. The actions of a few rogue actors to force an illegitimate, far-right agenda on the people of Europe will not stand, and we pledge to use every legal means necessary to bring all of those responsible to justice."

Ms. Cernak noted that Alessandro Bortolotti, the *de facto* head of the nationalist group responsible for the thwarted attack, was killed during an armed raid of his rented home in a neighborhood south of Rome. Nicknamed Il Duce by followers throughout the continent and as far away as Indonesia and Chile, Bortolotti had stoked anti-immigrant and pro-nationalist sentiment among his loyal followers for years. Despite Italy's recent election of a neofascist premiere, the twice-defeated candidate for the Italian parliament called for violence and destruction as a means of defeating the *status quo*. The three keywords of his platform – v*iolentiam, valeo, diripio* – became the call to arms of the group's steadfast adherents, who shortened the rallying cry to "ViValDi."

Rumors that a government source may have been working inside Bortolotti's organization have been neither confirmed nor denied.

Virtually every member nation of the EU is using its police and financial resources to track down and prosecute those directly involved in the insurrection, as well as those who planned it.

Authorities Say Three Deaths In Paris Are Linked

PARIS – June 13 [*France 365*]: Paris police say three deaths in the city this past week are connected, even though they're not yet sure if all of them are homicides or, if they are, whether the same suspect was responsible for all of them.

Speaking at a news conference earlier today, Deputy Chief Inspector Francois Fourgét said the execution-style shooting of popular television reporter Gabrielle Lamoines, whose body was found in her St. Germaine flat, was definitely related to the deaths of a Polish national named Xenon Gorsky, and an as-yet unidentified man who died at the Arc d' Triomphe one week ago. "Evidence definitely suggests a relationship of some sort existed between the victims in all three incidents, but it's still too early to determine the circumstances behind their connection and whether—or even how—it played a role in their deaths," he said.

The remains of Mr. Gorsky were found on the pedestrian walkway beneath the Pont des Arts. He had been shot once in the head, and there were signs that he had been tortured prior to his death. The third body was that of a man whom witnesses said climbed over the suicide barrier at the top of the Arc d' Triomphe and leaped to his death. No identification was found on his body, and Fourgét said he could not confirm the identity of the victim at this time.

He also did not specify why police believe both of those deaths are linked to that of Mlle Lamoines...

HUMAN TRAFFICKING VICTIM REVEALS YEARS OF ABUSE INSIDE VATICAN

By Carter Logan

ROME – June 14: Eight years ago, Cardinal Allessio Giudice was walking along Via Gregorio VII from his residence inside the Vatican to a dentist appointment several blocks away. He had lost a crown from a tooth the night before, and was in a hurry to get it replaced so he could return to his office. He stopped at the corner of Via Cardinale Tripepi to wait for the light to change when, as witnesses later said, he abruptly stepped off the curb and into the path of an oncoming truck.

The Cardinal—a close colleague and confidant of the Pope, and considered to be on the short list of eventual successors—was killed instantly.

What no one realized at the time was that Mr. Giudice—known among his brethren as Quello Feroce, or "the Fierce One"—left behind a sordid secret, one that involved the kidnapping and human trafficking of children in and around the city of Rome.

One of his victims was a teenage boy who was snatched from the plaza in front of the Trevi Fountain and subsequently "groomed" by a series of handlers before being gifted to the high-ranking church official. During a lengthy and expansive interview last week, this courageous young man revealed the grim details surrounding his ordeal. Speaking under the condition of anonymity—he chose to be referred to as Leandro in this article—he recounted the torment and indignity he went through, and the pain and anguish he endured...

...Following Giudice's death he said he was "passed on" to the Cardinal's protégé, Renate Azzone, who was on a political fast track within the Vatican City State. Leandro said he had hoped at the time that he would fare better under this new "tutelage," but the horrors he underwent were far more heinous than anything he'd experienced before....

MAN KIDNAPPED TEN YEARS AGO REUNITED WITH PARENTS

ROME – June 16 [*La Nazione de Italia*]: A man in his early twenties who was kidnapped in Rome nearly ten years ago had a tearful reunion with his parents over this past weekend.

The man, whom this news outlet is identifying as Leandro to protect his privacy, was drugged and abducted from the piazza around la Fontana di Trevi while in Rome with his father, who was on a business trip. Local polizia and carabinieri mounted a massive search for the boy at the time but, despite numerous tips, they were never able to locate him or his captors. It was speculated that he'd been taken and held by human traffickers who reportedly were working in the city, but no arrests were ever made.

Leandro's disappearance is remarkably similar to that of American teenager Abigail Evans, who was kidnapped in the vicinity of the famed fountain ten days ago. She had been flown to the island of Ibiza, where authorities believe she about to be auctioned off to wealthy customers from around the world.

He told investigators with la Guardia di Finanza that he'd been held captive in a private residential wing in the Vatican, and managed to escape after causing a distraction. The man suspected of holding him against his will is Renate Azzone, the Deputy Secretary General of the Governate for Vatican City State, who was brought in for questioning following last week's thwarted attack on world leaders attending the G20 Summit.

As an official of a foreign nation, however, Azzone is protected by diplomatic immunity when traveling outside the city-state, and therefore no formal charges have been filed. Sources tell *La Nazione* that he is maintaining his innocence in both matters, and has not been seen since police were forced to release him from custody. It is thought that he has secluded himself within the Vatican, but officials there are not commenting.

The Italian government has formally petitioned the Pope to terminate Azzone's employment and thus make him available for prosecution, but His Holiness thus far has remained silent on the issue.

WANTED EX-VATICAN OFFICIAL DIES
IN FALL FROM SINGAPORE SKYSCRAPER

SINGAPORE – October 20 [*USA Today*]: A former official of the Vatican City State died Sunday after plunging from the 52nd floor of the Marina Bay Towers in Singapore.

Renate Azzone, former Deputy Secretary General of the Governate for Vatican City State, disappeared last July after the Pope stripped him of his official duties and expelled him from the small country. Italian police and investigators from Interpol launched a global search for him, acting on tips from numerous countries around the world. He was wanted in connection with his alleged participation in an aborted attack at the G20 Summit in Rome, as well as the kidnapping and sexual abuse of a minor.

Several witnesses said they saw Azzone speaking with a man in his late fifties or early sixties not long before he somehow scaled the glass suicide barrier and plunged to his death from the top floor of the landmark building...

Chapter 41

The flight home from Singapore took almost two full days, with layovers in Bangkok and Dubai. The mission had been particularly sensitive, a pop-up gig after Martin Beaudin had tracked the former Vatican official from Rome to Cairo to Mumbai, and finally to a safe house in a suburb outside the southern Malaysian city of Johor Bahru. From there it was just a quick trip across the narrow strait, as he followed his target to the top floor of the city's architectural marvel.

Once Phythian had landed back in Nairobi, he faced a four-hour bus ride to Namanga, a dreary and desolate customs check-point on the border of Kenya and Tanzania. He paid sixty US dollars for a room with a private bath at a hotel that was painted the color of curry with cayenne trim, and which held the rich aroma of an Eritrean restaurant that adjoined it to the rear. A never-ceasing rumble of massive trucks at the vehicle crossing two blocks over generated a steady vibration while he took a cold shower, then put on the light cotton shirt and trousers he'd purchased earlier in a shop in the airport terminal. A wide-brimmed hat covered his head and kept his face deep in shadow, as he was forced to do whenever he was in range of surveillance cameras and police officers were close by. Fortunately, the latter tended not to be much a threat in this town, where authorities were focused primarily on smuggling and poaching, but closed-circuit lenses were just about anywhere. It was no use taking a chance, especially here in this lonely corner of Africa, when he was so close to home.

He had to go out to the street and walk next door to enter the dining room. No one appeared to be watching him, no cars with suspicious men lurking behind grimy windows, tracking his moves. There was no point sighing a breath of relief, however, since one slip-up, one AI algorithm could have a legion of agents here within hours.

Phythian ordered a meal of *alicha*—a spicy dish of potatoes, carrots, cabbage—and a plate of lentil *sambusa*. A bottle of South African cabernet arrived, too, something that involved a mental nudge with the proprietor since this was a Muslim country, and intoxicants were not officially permitted. None of the other tables in the place was occupied, but it was still early in the afternoon. By evening a sizable crowd would have gathered, and much food and drink would be consumed.

In the morning he would find a trucker willing to take him across the border and drive him as far as Arusha, perhaps even on to Terrat. The round-trip journey had tired him, and all he wished for was the peace and tranquility of Utuliva, the serenity of its surrounding wonders, and the absolute silence of time.

For now, though, he was content with sipping his wine, and enjoying a lack of concern with the problems and challenges of the outside world.

Then his cellphone rang: Martin Beaudin, calling from Andorra. Who else could it be, since no one else had this number?

"I trust you're safely home?" the Frenchman said when Phythian answered, painfully aware that it was prudent not to ever ask him where he was, where he'd been, or might be headed.

"Close enough. What's the status report?"

"The two foundations have been established, as you requested. Anonymous benefactors for each, no way to track the funds. One hundred million donated to establish the Gabrielle Lamoines Department of Journalism at the Université Paris Cité, with Arnaud Clément as trustee. Likewise, a sum in the same amount will endow the new School of Journalism at the University of Iceland, in remembrance of Katya Leiffson. Her parents and her former fiancé, Carter Logan, will be co-executors."

"When do these become finalized?" Phythian asked.

"Chancellors and lawyers at both schools have to sign off on it, but neither is expected to turn down a bequest of that size. I'd say a week or two."

"Good. Shoot me a text when both deals are complete. And set up an offshore account in the Caymans for our friend, Mr. Logan. Five million should do it, but don't let him know."

"Consider it done," Beaudin said.

"And that SD card you found in Gabrielle Lamoines room...do you still have it?"

"Haven't touched it since I secured it in the safe downstairs."

"Good. I want you to send it to Carter Logan, no return address."

"Sir?" the locksmith from Andorra asked. He knew better than to second-guess his boss, but he also knew the contents on that chip could be worth billions of dollars.

"Whatever's on that thing, I'm sure our reporter friend will make good use of it," Phythian said.

"I'll take care of it, first thing," Beaudin assured him, a noticeable hitch in his voice.

"Is there something else?"

"Not that I can think of, no—"

But there was, and Phythian of course knew what it was. "Oh…I almost forgot," he continued, so the cautious Frenchman wouldn't have to humble himself by asking. "Make sure you give yourself the usual bonus plus fifty percent for your effort in all this."

"Certainly, sir. *Merci beaucoup*. Oh, and Mr. Phythian—"

"Yes, Beaudin?"

"Uh…never mind. That is all."

"Good-bye, then," Phythian said as he ended the call, knowing that his compadre was curious about the details of his recent business in Singapore, but knew better than to inquire.

After ending the call, he settled into his chair, wiped a bead of moisture from his brow. October was just the beginning of the wet period in this corner of the world, and the annual rains were set to start in just a few weeks. It was good to be back home again, or close to it, with this year's *hunting season* behind him. That's how he viewed the months from June until now, when endless safaris delivered throngs of tourists to a Serengeti that was teeming with wildlife, while he decamped to other parts of the world to do what needed to be done. Like the business this summer in Cyprus and Paris and Ibiza and Dubai and Tokyo and, most recently, Singapore.

Phythian thought for a moment about Paris, still feeling a touch of melancholy for how that leg of his travels had turned out. He had not wanted, nor expected, Gabrielle Lamoines to die, and for that he had added yet another layer of remorse to his life. No amount of anguish, no degree of grief could bring her back, or allow him to shed the regret and contrition he felt.

Just as he lifted his wine glass to take another sip, the front door opened and a man stepped inside. The newcomer glanced around the near-empty restaurant, spotted Phythian sitting at a corner table, his back to the wall. Russians had a certain bearing anywhere in the world, and this one was no different. He was bald, with a bulbous nose that carried the red tinge of vodka, maybe fifty, with a dark brow and a round face. He was dressed in jeans and a T-shirt with the logo of a nineties rock band on it, appearing as a friendly stranger in an equally strange foreign outpost, perhaps a weary trucker in search of a good meal and, perhaps, friendly conversation.

Phythian watched and waited as the man slowly wandered over to his table, his attempt to appear genial and affable betrayed by a mental thread that betrayed his former life as a former FSB agent. The fact that his mind kept going to the HK VP9 tucked into his waistband didn't help his cause, easy pickings from a brain that was dehydrated and badly in need of alcohol. Which, despite the local beliefs and customs, could be found in Namanga if one knew where to look.

"Good afternoon, sir," the stranger said as he extended his hand. "Leonard MacLean, from Edinburgh. Is good to see a friendly face in such a Godforsaken corner of world."

The attempt at a Scottish accent was almost comical, burdened as it was with a flat Russian intonation and an almost subconscious avoidance of excess vowels.

In fact, the man's real name was Nikolai Galkin. Phythian had first encountered it two summers ago, when he'd hitched a ride with a pair of Australian facilitators who were tracking a white man who recently had killed the son of a Russian oligarch in the Tanzania National Park. The two men had come to assist a professional sniper with his execution, but both had met with some unexpected resistance.

Neither of them had been seen since.

The last time the name Galkin had come up was last June, just before Georgy Sokolov had taken a deep plunge into the pool of his villa on the island of Ibiza.

"I'm at the end of a long journey, and I'm far too weary for subterfuge," Phythian told him. "And too tired to be anything but blunt."

"Excuse me?" Galkin inquired, doing a genuine double-take.

"When was the last time you spoke with your Russky employer?"

"I'm sure I don't know what you're talking about—"

"Yes, you do, but I'll be as straightforward as I can. Sokolov is dead.

And you will be, too, if you don't get out of here while I'm still of a mind to let you go."

"Who the fuck do you think you are—?"

"The man you came to kill. You *are* here to avenge the death of that idiot Russian named Vasily, right?"

"How you know about that?" Galkin asked, finally dropping the Scottish pretense.

"I shot him when he was hunting elephants," Phythian interrupted him. "Used a McMillan Tac-50 long-range anti-personnel rifle, got him through and through."

"*Ty ublyudok—*"

Phythian made a show of exasperation, rolling his eyes out of tedium. "Spare me the outrage, Galkin. I told you: I have no patience for your games, and I'd like to enjoy my wine in peace. And don't even think of reaching for the gun nestled in the crack of your ass."

The Russian thug went for it anyway, bringing it up and aiming it at this stranger who knew a helluva lot more about him than he should have. Who he was, why he was there, what he was hired to do?

Odd thing was, while Galkin's finger was firmly touching the trigger, he couldn't muster the pressure needed to fire a shot.

"Take your problems outside," Phythian directed him, both mentally and verbally.

"Do *what*?"

"Get out of here. Take your gun. And remember, I gave you a chance."

"What you're giving me is a fucking headache," Galkin managed to say.

"It happens from time to time," Phythian replied. "And this is the last time I'll warn you: get your ass out of here."

All the bounty hunter could focus on, however, was the hammering that was starting to pound out a bass riff inside his skull. It had started as just a gentle squeeze, one that seemed to grow tighter the longer he stood there. He lowered the gun and blinked a few times, as if trying to shake himself out of a trance. Then he made a quick pivot and, without saying another word, walked out the same door he had come through just three minutes before. Phythian studied the confused and agonized Russian through the grimy window a moment, watched as he lurched out into the baking sun and hesitated. He remained there a moment, as if deciding which direction to turn, then turned left and disappeared up the street.

The sound of the gunshot came a good ten seconds later—a single round that seemed right at home in this dusty town at the edge of the Serengeti, where all of time was relative and life counted out its cadence in this, the oldest womb of human life on the planet.

Phythian took another sip of cabernet—nothing particularly remarkable about it, other than there happened to be a bottle of it here in Namanga—and let out the deep breath he'd found he was holding in his lungs. Thinking about the long road he still had ahead of him—not just physically, as he made the journey home to Utuliva, but also as a metaphor of the long and winding path his life had traveled thus far, and still stretched out before him. The fine edge of the horizon beckoning him with the promise of resolution that marked the end for all living things.

Outside he heard someone scream, but he had no urge to go and look. The wine had opened up a bit, with the taste of black currants and plums, and earthy notes of what someone might think of as burned oak. He took another long sip, allowed his thoughts to stray until they momentarily settled on a random line widely attributed to the late rocker Jim Morrison—a young man whose life had been cut short when a bright future still lay ahead of him, and who now was buried alone in a cemetery in Paris just a few miles from where Gabrielle Lamoines had taken her last breath.

It was a line he'd sensed dart through Major Thompson's mind while riding the metro that afternoon last summer in Paris, just a few hours before he'd made his tragic leap from the Arc de Triomphe:

No one here gets out alive.

Author's Notes

As noted in my first Rōnin Phythian novel, *Greenwich Mean Time*, Project MINDGAZE is a fictitious intelligence program based on the Stargate Project, the official code name for a very real clandestine U.S. military research project founded almost 50 years ago under deep cover of the Defense Intelligence Agency and SRI International.

Also as previously noted, Rōnin Phythian is a fictional character whose first name derives from the Japanese term for drifter or wanderer, essentially a samurai without a master.

Much of the G20 security and communications protocols referred to are based on actual systems put in place for the most recent global meeting held in Rome in October 2021. ICASP—aka Integrated Communications And Security Protocol—is patterned after TETRA, the acronym for TErrestrial Trunked RAdio, a proprietary communications program that connected all international security forces at that 2021 leadership summit.

The red lining of Italian Army caps featured in Part IV is a literary device based on unverified fact. During my research phase I found one source that suggested this was, indeed, an official feature of the official headgear, but I was unable to find a second source to corroborate this fact. Not to worry; I took literary license and ran with the idea anyway.

The TruthCorps mentioned in this book is entirely fictional, and has no relationship with an ecclesiastic missionary program, or any other group bearing the same name.

Maison de Quantum is an actual chateau located in the village of Ajou in the Normandy region of France. Dating back to 1350 and previously owned by my brother and sister-in-law, it is now run as a bed and breakfast. Check out Chateau de Saint Aubin sur Risle if you're interested in staying there; it appears the rates are rather reasonable.

The Dali Universal Tarot deck was originally commissioned by Albert Broccoli for the 1973 James Bond film *Live and Let Die*, but the artist's proposed fee reportedly was so large that it was not used in the film. Dali's depiction of The Magician in this exclusive deck actually is a self-portrait.

Sometimes the words of notable historical figures are more memorable than my own, and I've worked them in throughout the pages of this book. Whenever feasible, I have quoted the source as part of the story, but on occasion that's impractical without adding footnotes, or making the text sound like an academic paper. To give credit where it is due, here are the origins of a few phrases or aphorisms I did not directly cite:

- *Caution being one thing and courage yet another* – adapted from Martin Luther King, Jr.
- *The sword of justice has no scabbard* – Antoine de Rivarol, Royalist French writer and translator
- *It is better to die for the truth than to live for a lie* – Bavarian writer/educator Christoph von Schmid
- *The future really does belong to those who believe in the beauty of their dreams* – adapted from a quote by Eleanor Roosevelt
- *Silence being the sleep that nourishes wisdom* – Sir Francis Bacon

During the creation of any novel there are always a number of people to recognize for their invaluable input. First up is Tom Hamil, my third-grade teacher at River School in Carmel, California who not only was an award-winning author and illustrator of numerous books, but a remarkable contemporary artist. Without his inspiration during my Wonder Years, I probably would have chosen a more lucrative—but nowhere near as fulfilling—career. I learned of his passing at age 94 as I was finishing the last draft of this novel, and this book is dedicated to him.

Many thanks also to Dr. David Kertzer, my undergraduate adviser at Bowdoin College and the Pulitzer Prize-winning author of the book *The Pope And Mussolini: The Secret History Of Pius XI And The Rise Of Fascism In Europe*. No one has a better grasp of the subject than he, and his research and analysis was invaluable while I was building the Allesandro Bortolotti character, as well as describing the burgeoning nationalist movement that's spreading across Europe. Whatever I depicted correctly in this discussion was because of his expertise; likewise, anything I got wrong is totally on me.

My mother instilled in me a love of classical music and, particularly, my favorite composer: the red-haired virtuoso from Venice, Antonio Vivaldi. While ordained as a priest in the Catholic church, he chose instead to follow his life's passion and created hundreds of musical works—several of which are mentioned in these pages. He perhaps is best known for his collection of concertos popularly identified as *The Four Seasons* (*Le Quattro Stagioni*), each of which gives musical expression to a season of the year. Including, quite appropriately for the title of this book, Fall.

As always, I'd like to offer a shout-out to all the folks at Epicenter Press/ Coffeetown Press in Seatle, particularly Phil Garrett and Jennifer McCord for all their support along the way.

I particularly wish to thank my marvelous friend, confidant, and agent Kimberley Cameron, for her continued optimism and diligence in finding good homes for my books.

Thank you, too, to my beta readers (you know who you are) who provided me with encouragement as well as much-needed criticism during the final stages of editing and polishing.

Last, but by no means least, I offer heartfelt hugs and kisses to my wonderful wife Diana, whose unyielding encouragement, assurance, and constructive criticism have kept me plugging away all these years. Bold and dashing, always.

About the Author

Reed Bunzel is the author of a half dozen crime novels and thrillers, as well as several nonfiction books. He also is the author of *BunzelGram*, a weekly newsletter that focuses on mysteries and thrillers both in print and on the screen.

A former media industry executive, Bunzel was editor-in-chief for United News and Media's San Francisco publishing operations, overseeing the weekly publication of *The Gavin Report* and *Gavin.com*.

Earlier in his career he was editor-in-chief of Streamline Publishing's *Radio Ink* and *Streaming* magazines, as well as an editor at *Radio & Records* and *Broadcasting* magazine. Additionally, he served in an executive capacity at both the National Association of Broadcasters and the Radio Advertising Bureau.

A graduate of Bowdoin College in Brunswick, Maine, Bunzel holds a Bachelor of Science degree in Anthropology, *cum laude*. A native of the San Francisco Bay Area, he resides with his wife Diana in Charleston, South Carolina.